F A C T O R I N G
H U M A N I T Y

Novels by Robert J. Sawyer

Golden Fleece
Far-Seer
Fossil Hunter
Foreigner
End of an Era
The Terminal Experiment
Starplex
Frameshift
Illegal Alien
Factoring Humanity

Factoring

H U M A N I T Y

Robert J. Sawyer

TOR®

A   TOM   DOHERTY
ASSOCIATES   BOOK

New York

FACTORING HUMANITY

Copyright © 1998 by Robert J. Sawyer

Edited by David G. Hartwell
Interior art by Larry Stewart

A Tor Book
Published by Tom Doherty Associates, Inc.
175 Fifth Avenue
New York, NY 10010

Tor Books on the World Wide Web:
http://www.tor.com

Tor® is a registered trademark of Tom Doherty Associates, Inc.

Design by Susan Hood

Library of Congress Cataloging-in-Publication Data

Sawyer, Robert J.
       Factoring humanity / Robert J. Sawyer — 1st ed.
            p.   cm.
       "A Tom Doherty Associates book."
       ISBN 0-312-86458-2 (acid-free paper)
       I. Title.
PR9199.3.S2533F3   1998
813'.54—dc21   98-14527
                                               CIP

First Edition: June 1998

Printed in the United States of America

0 9 8 7 6 5 4 3 2 1

FOR ASBED BEDROSSIAN

…who has lived far away from Toronto now for ten times longer than the two years he spent here—and is still one of my best friends. Thank goodness for E-mail!

Acknowledgments

Sincere thanks to my agent, Ralph Vicinanza, and his associate Christopher Lotts; my editor at Tor, David G. Hartwell; Joy Chamberlain and Jane Johnson of HarperCollins UK; Rudy Rucker; Tad Dembinski; Tom Doherty, Andy LeCount, Jim Minz, and Linda Quinton of Tor; and Robert Howard and Suzanne Hallsworth of H. B. Fenn.

Special thanks to Ottawa artist Larry Stewart, who graciously provided the line drawings.

Many thanks to those who read and commented on all or part of the manuscript: Ted Bleaney, Linda C. Carson, Merle Casci, David Livingstone Clink, Martin Crumpton, James Alan Gardner, Terence M. Green, Tom McGee, Howard Miller, Ariel Reich, Alan B. Sawyer, Edo van Belkom, and especially to my lovely wife, Carolyn Clink.

What is mind? No matter.
What is matter? Never mind.

—Thomas Hewitt Key
(1799–1875)
British classicist

The messages from space had been arriving for almost ten years now. Reception of a new page of data began every thirty hours and fifty-one minutes—an interval presumed to be the length of the day on the Senders' homeworld. To date, 2,841 messages had been collected.

Earth had never replied to any of the transmissions. The Declaration of Principles Concerning Activities Following the Detection of Extraterrestrial Intelligence, *adopted by the International Astronomical Union in 1989, stated: "No response to a signal or other evidence of extraterrestrial intelligence should be sent until appropriate international consultations have taken place." With a hundred and fifty-seven countries comprising the United Nations, that process was still going on.*

There was no doubt about the direction the signals were coming from: right ascension 14 degrees, 39 minutes, 36 seconds; declination minus 60 degrees, 50.0 minutes. And parallactic studies revealed the distance: 1.34 parsecs from Earth. The aliens sending the messages apparently lived on a planet orbiting the star Alpha Centauri A, the nearest bright star to our sun.

The first eleven pages of data had been easily deciphered: they were simple graphical representations of mathematical and physical principles, plus the chemical formulas for two seemingly benign substances.

But although the messages were public knowledge, no one anywhere had been able to make sense of the subsequent decoded images . . .

1

HEATHER DAVIS TOOK A SIP OF HER COFFEE and looked at the brass clock on the mantelpiece. Her nineteen-year-old daughter Rebecca had said she'd be here by 8:00 P.M., and it was already eight-twenty.

Surely Becky knew how awkward this was. She had said she'd wanted a meeting with her parents—both of them, simultaneously. That Heather Davis and Kyle Graves had been separated for almost a year now didn't enter into the equation. They could have met at a restaurant, but no, Heather had volunteered the house—the one in which she and Kyle had raised Becky and her older sister Mary, the one Kyle had moved out of last August. Now, though, with the silence between her and Kyle having stretched on for yet another minute, she was regretting that spontaneous offer.

Although Heather hadn't seen Becky for almost four months, she had a hunch about what Becky wanted to say. When they spoke over the phone, Becky often talked about her boyfriend Zack. No doubt she was about to announce an engagement.

Of course, Heather wished her daughter would wait a few more years. But then again, it wasn't as if she was going to university. Becky worked in a clothing store on Spadina. Both

Heather and Kyle taught at the University of Toronto—she in psychology, he in computer science. It pained them that Becky wasn't pursuing higher education. In fact, under the Faculty Association agreement, their children were entitled to free tuition at U of T. At least Mary had taken advantage of that for one year before . . .

No.

No, this was a time of celebration. Becky was getting married! That was what mattered today.

She wondered how Zack had proposed—or whether it had been Becky who had popped the question. Heather remembered vividly what Kyle had said to her when he'd proposed, twenty-one years ago, back in 1996. He'd taken her hand, held it tightly, and said, "I love you, and I want to spend the rest of my life getting to know you."

Heather was sitting in an overstuffed easy chair; Kyle was sitting on the matching couch. He'd brought his datapad with him and was reading something on it. Knowing Kyle, it was probably a spy novel; the one good thing for him about the rise of Iran to superpower status had been the revitalization of the espionage thriller.

On the beige wall behind Kyle was a framed photoprint that belonged to Heather. It was made up of an apparently random pattern of tiny black-and-white squares—a representation of one of the alien radio messages.

Becky had moved out nine months ago, shortly after she'd finished high school. Heather had hoped Becky might stay at home a while—the only other person in the big, empty suburban house now that Mary and Kyle were gone.

At first, Becky came by the house frequently—and according to Kyle, she had seen her father often enough, too. But soon the gaps between visits grew longer and longer—and then she stopped coming altogether.

Kyle apparently had become aware that Heather was looking

at him. He lifted his eyes from the datapad and managed a wan smile. "Don't worry, hon. I'm sure she'll be here."

Hon. They hadn't lived together as husband and wife for eleven months, but the automatic endearments of two decades die hard.

Finally, at a little past eight-thirty, the doorbell rang. Heather and Kyle exchanged glances. Becky's thumbprint still operated the lock, of course—as, for that matter, did Kyle's. No one else could possibly be dropping by this late; it had to be Becky. Heather sighed. That Becky didn't simply let herself in underscored Heather's fears: her daughter no longer considered this house to be her home.

Heather got up and crossed the living room. She was wearing a dress—hardly her normal at-home attire, but she'd wanted to show Becky that her coming by was a special occasion. And as Heather passed the mirror in the front hall and caught sight of the blue floral print of the dress, she realized that she, too, was acting as Becky was, treating her daughter's arrival as a visit from someone for whom airs had to be put on.

Heather completed the journey to the door, touched her hands to her dark hair to make sure it was still properly positioned, then turned the knob.

Becky stood on the step. She had a narrow face, high cheekbones, brown eyes, and brunette hair that brushed her shoulders. Beside her was her boyfriend Zack, all gangly limbs and scraggly blond hair.

"Hello, darling," said Heather to her daughter, and then, smiling at the young man, whom she hardly knew: "Hello, Zack."

Becky stepped inside. Heather thought perhaps her daughter would stop long enough to kiss her, but she didn't. Zack followed Becky into the hall, and the three of them made their way up into the living room, where Kyle was still sitting on the couch.

"Hi, Pumpkin," said Kyle, looking up. "Hi, Zack."

His daughter didn't even glance at him. Her hand found Zack's, and they intertwined fingers.

Heather sat down in the easy chair and motioned for Becky and Zack to sit as well. There wasn't enough room on the couch next to Kyle for both of them. Becky found another chair, and Zack stood behind her, a hand on her left shoulder.

"It's so good to see you, dear," said Heather. She opened her mouth again, realized that what was about to come out was a comment on how long it had been, and closed it before the words got free.

Becky turned to look at Zack. Her lower lip was trembling.

"What's wrong, dear?" asked Heather, shocked. If not an engagement announcement, then what? Could Becky be ill? In trouble with the police? She saw Kyle lean slightly forward; he, too, was detecting his daughter's anxiety.

"Go ahead," said Zack to Becky; he whispered it, but the room was quiet enough that Heather could make it out.

Becky was silent for a few moments longer. She closed her eyes, then re-opened them. "Why?" she said, her voice quavering.

"Why what, dear?" said Heather.

"Not you," said Becky. Her gaze fell for an instant on her father, then it dropped to the floor. *"Him."*

"Why what?" asked Kyle, sounding as confused as Heather felt.

The clock on the mantelpiece chimed; it did that every quarter-hour.

"Why," said Becky, raising her eyes again to look at her father, "did you . . ."

"Say it," whispered Zack, forcefully.

Becky swallowed, then blurted it all out. "Why did you abuse me?"

Kyle slumped against the couch. The datapad, which had

been resting on the couch's arm, fell to the hardwood floor with a clattering sound. Kyle's mouth hung open. He looked at his wife.

Heather's heart was racing. She felt nauseous.

Kyle closed his mouth, then opened it again. "Pumpkin, I never—"

"Don't deny it," said Becky. Her voice was quaking with fury; now that the accusation was out, a dam had apparently burst. "Don't you dare deny it."

"But, Pumpkin—"

"And don't call me that. My name is Rebecca."

Kyle spread his arms. "I'm sorry, Rebecca. I didn't know it bothered you, my calling you that."

"Damn you," she said. "How could you do that to me?"

"I never—"

"Don't lie! For God's sake, at least have the guts to admit it."

"But I never—Rebecca, you're my daughter. I'd never hurt you."

"You did hurt me. You *ruined* me. Me, and Mary."

Heather rose to her feet. "Becky—"

"And *you!*" shouted Becky. "You knew what he was doing to us and you didn't do anything to stop him."

"Don't yell at your mother," said Kyle, his voice sharp. "Becky, I never touched you or Mary—you *know* that."

Zack spoke in a normal volume for the first time. "I knew he'd deny it."

Kyle snapped at the young man. "Damn you—you keep out of this."

"Don't raise your voice at him," said Becky to Kyle.

Kyle fought to be calm. "This is a family matter," he said. "We don't need him here."

Heather looked at her husband, then at her daughter. "Becky," Heather said, fighting to keep her own voice under control, "I swear to you—"

"Don't you deny it, too," Becky said.

Heather took a deep breath, then let it out slowly. "Tell me," she said. "Tell me what you think happened."

There was silence for a long time as Becky apparently composed her thoughts. "You *know* what happened," she said at last, the accusatory tone still in her voice. "He'd slip out of your room after midnight and come to mine or Mary's."

"Becky," said Kyle, "I never—"

Becky looked at her mother, but then closed her eyes. "He'd come into my room, have me remove my top, f-fondle my breasts, and then—" She choked off, opened her eyes and looked again at Heather. "You must have known," she said. "You must have seen him leaving, seen him come back." A pause as she took a shuddering breath. "You must have smelled the sweat on him—smelled *me* on him."

Heather was shaking her head. "Becky, please."

"None of that ever happened," said Kyle.

"There's no point staying if he's going to deny it," said Zack.

Becky nodded and reached into her purse. She pulled out a tissue and wiped her eyes, then got to her feet and began walking away. Zack followed her, and so did Heather. Kyle rose as well, but in a matter of moments, Becky and Zack were down the stairs and at the front door.

"Pump—Becky, please," said Kyle, catching up with them. "I'd never hurt you."

Becky turned around. Her eyes were red, her face flushed. "I hate you," she said, and then she and Zack scurried out the door into the night.

Kyle looked at Heather. "Heather, I swear I never touched her."

Heather didn't know what to say. She headed back up to the living room, holding the banister for balance. Kyle followed. Heather took a chair, but Kyle went to the liquor cabinet and poured himself some Scotch. He drained it in a gulp and stood leaning against the wall.

"It's that boyfriend of hers," said Kyle. "He put her up to this. They'll be filing a lawsuit, betcha anything—can't wait for the inheritance."

"Kyle, please," said Heather. "It's your daughter you're talking about."

"And it's her father *she's* talking about. I'd never do anything like that. Heather, you *know* that."

Heather stared at him.

"Heather," said Kyle, a note of pleading in his voice now, "you must know it's not true."

Something had kept Rebecca away for almost a year. And something before that had—

She hated to think about it, and yet it came to mind every day. Every hour . . .

Something had driven Mary to suicide.

"Heather!"

"I'm sorry." She swallowed, then after a moment, nodded. "I'm sorry. I know you couldn't do anything like that." But her voice sounded flat, even to her.

"Of course not."

"It's just that . . ."

"What?" snapped Kyle.

"It's—no, nothing."

"What?"

"Well, you did have a habit of getting up, of leaving our room in the middle of the night."

"I can't believe you're saying that," said Kyle. "I can't fucking believe it."

"It's true. Two, three nights a week sometimes."

"I have trouble sleeping—you *know* that. I get up and go watch some TV, or maybe do some work on my computer.

Christ, I *still* do that, and I live alone now. I did it last night."

Heather said nothing.

"I couldn't sleep. If I'm still awake an hour after I go to bed, I get up—you *know* that. No bloody point just lying there. Last night I got up and watched—Christ, what was it? I watched *The Six Million Dollar Man* on Channel 3. It was the one with William Shatner as the guy who could communicate with dolphins. You call the TV station—they'll tell you that's the one that was on. And then I sent some e-mail to Jake Montgomery. We can go to my apartment right now—*right now*—and look at my outbox; you'll see the time stamp on it. Then I came back to bed around one twenty-five, one-thirty, something like that."

"Nobody accused you of doing anything wrong last night."

"But that's the kind of thing I do *every* night I get up. Sometimes I watch *The Six Million Dollar Man,* sometimes *The John Pellatt Show.* And I look at The Weather Channel, see what it's going to be like tomorrow. They said it was going to rain today, but it didn't."

Oh, yes, it did, thought Heather. It came down in fucking buckets.

2

THE UNIVERSITY OF TORONTO—THE SELF-styled Harvard of the North—was established in 1827. Some fifty thousand full-time students were enrolled there. The main campus was downtown, not surprisingly anchored at the intersection of University Avenue and College Street. But although there was a traditional central campus, U of T also spilled out into the city proper, lining St. George Street and several other roads with a hodgepodge of nineteenth-, twentieth-, and early twenty-first-century architecture.

The university's most distinctive landmark was the Robarts Library—often called "Fort Book" by students—a massive, complex concrete structure. Kyle Graves had lived in Toronto all of his forty-five years. Still, it was only recently that he'd seen an architect's model of the campus and realized that the library was shaped like a concrete peacock, with the hooded Thomas Fisher rare-books tower rising up as a beaked neck in front and two vast wings spreading out behind.

Unfortunately, there was no place on campus where you could look down on Robarts to appreciate the design. U of T did have three associated theological colleges—Emmanuel, affiliated with the United Church of Canada; the Presbyterian

Knox; and the Anglican Wycliffe. Perhaps the peacock was meant to be seen only by God or visitors from space: sort of a Canadian Plains of Nazca.

Kyle and Heather had separated shortly after Mary's suicide; it had been too much for both of them, and their frustration over not understanding what had happened had spilled out in all sorts of ways. The apartment Kyle lived in now was a short walk from Downsview subway station in suburban Toronto. He'd taken the subway down to St. George station this morning and was now walking the short distance south to Dennis Mullin Hall, which was located at 91 St. George Street, directly across the road from the Robarts Library.

He passed the Bata Shoe Museum—the world's largest museum devoted to footwear, housed in another miracle of twentieth-century design: a building that looked like a slightly squashed shoebox. One of these days he'd actually go inside. In the distance, down at the lakeshore, he could see the CN Tower—no longer the world's tallest freestanding structure, but still one of its most elegant.

After about two minutes, Kyle reached Mullin Hall, the new four-story circular building that housed the Artificial Intelligence and Advanced Computing Department. Kyle entered through the main sliding-glass doors. His lab was on the third floor, but he took the stairs instead of the waiting elevator. Ever since his heart attack, four years ago, he'd made a point of getting little bits of exercise whenever he could. He remembered when he used to huff and puff after just two flights of stairs, but today he emerged without breathing hard at all. He headed down the corridor, the open atrium on his left, until he reached his lab. He pressed his thumb against the scanning plate, and the door slid open.

"Good morning, Dr. Graves," said a rough male voice as he entered the lab.

"Good morning, Cheetah."

"I have a new joke for you, Dr. Graves."

Kyle took off his hat and hung it on the old wooden coat rack—universities never threw anything out; this one must have dated back to the 1950s. He started the coffeemaker, then took a seat in front of a computer console, its front panel banked at forty-five degrees. In the center of the panel were two small lenses that tracked in unison like eyes.

"There's this French physicist, see," said Cheetah's voice, coming from a speaker grille below the mechanical eyes. "This guy's working at CERN and he's devised an experiment to test a new theory. He starts up the particle accelerator and waits for the results of the collision he's arranged. When the experiment is over, he rushes out of the control room into the corridor, holding a printout showing the trails of the resulting particles. There, he runs into another scientist. And the other scientist says to him, 'Jacques,' he says, 'did you get the two particles you were expecting?' And Jacques points first to one particle trail and then to the other and exclaims: '*Mais oui!* Higgs boson! Quark!' "

Kyle stared at the pair of lenses.

Cheetah repeated the punch line: "*Mais oui!* Higgs boson! Quark!"

"I don't get it," said Kyle.

"A Higgs boson is a particle with zero charge and no intrinsic spin; a quark is a fundamental constituent of protons and neutrons."

"I know what they are, for Pete's sake. But I don't see why the joke is funny."

"It's a pun. *Mais oui!*—that's French for 'but yes!'—*Mais oui!* Higgs boson! Quark!" Cheetah paused for a beat. "Mary Higgins Clark." Another pause. "She's a famous mystery writer."

Kyle sighed. "Cheetah, that's too elaborate. For a pun to work, the listener has to get it in a flash. It's no good if you have to explain it."

Cheetah was quiet for a moment. "Oh," he said at last. "I've disappointed you again, haven't I?"

"I wouldn't say that," said Kyle. "Not exactly."

Cheetah was an APE—a computer simulation designed to Approximate Psychological Experiences; he aped humanity. Kyle had long been a proponent of the strong-artificial-intelligence principle: the brain was nothing more than an organic computer, and the mind was simply the software running on that computer. When he'd first taken this stance publicly, in the late 1990s, it had seemed reasonable. Computing capabilities were doubling every eighteen months; soon enough, there would be computers with greater storage capacity and more interconnections than the human brain had. Surely once that point was reached, the human mind could be duplicated on a computer.

The only trouble was that that point *had* by now been attained. Indeed, most estimates said that computers had exceeded the human brain in information-processing capability and degree of complexity four or five years previously.

And still Cheetah couldn't distinguish a funny joke from a lousy one.

"If I don't disappoint you," said Cheetah's voice, "then what's wrong?"

Kyle looked around his lab; its inner and outer walls were curved following the contours of Mullin Hall, but there were no windows; the ceiling was high, and covered with lighting panels behind metal grids. "Nothing."

"Don't kid a kidder," said Cheetah. "You spent months teaching me to recognize faces, no matter what their expression. I'm still not very good at it, but I can tell who you are at a glance—and I know how to read your moods. You're upset over something."

Kyle pursed his lips, considering whether he wanted to answer. Everything Cheetah did was by dint of sheer computational power; Kyle certainly felt no obligation to reply.

And yet—

And yet no one else had come into the lab so far today. Kyle hadn't been able to sleep at all last night after he'd left the house—he still thought of it as "the house," not "Heather's house"—and he'd come in early. Everything was silent, except for the hum from equipment and the overhead fluorescent lights, and Cheetah's utterings in his deep and rather nasal voice. Kyle would have to adjust the vocal routine at some point; the attempt to give Cheetah natural-sounding respiratory asperity had resulted in an irritating mimicry of real speech. As with so much about the APE, the differences between it and real humans were all the more obvious for the earnestness of the attempt.

No, he certainly didn't have to reply to Cheetah.

But maybe he *wanted* to reply. After all, who else could he discuss the matter with?

"Initiate privacy locking," said Kyle. "You are not to relay the following conversation to anyone, or make any inquiries pursuant to it. Understood?"

"Yes," said Cheetah. The final "s" was protracted, thanks to the vocoder problem. There was silence between them. Finally, Cheetah prodded Kyle. "What was it you wished to discuss?"

Where to begin? Christ, he wasn't even sure why he was doing this. But he couldn't talk about it with anyone else—he couldn't risk gossip getting around. He remembered what happened to Stone Bentley, over in Anthropology: accused by a female student of sexual harassment five years ago; fully exonerated by a tribunal; even the student eventually recanted the accusation. And still he'd been passed over for the associate deanship, and to this day, Kyle overheard the occasional whispered remark from other faculty members or students. No, he would not subject himself to that.

"It's nothing, really," said Kyle. He shuffled across the room and poured himself a cup of the now-ready coffee.

"No, please," said Cheetah. "Tell me."

Kyle managed a wan smile. He knew Cheetah wasn't really curious. He himself had programmed the algorithm that aped curiosity: when a person appears to be reluctant to go on, become insistent.

Still, he *did* need to talk to someone about it. He had enough trouble sleeping without this weighing on him.

"My daughter is mad at me."

"Rebecca," supplied Cheetah. Another algorithm; imply intimacy to increase openness.

"Rebecca, yes. She says—she says . . ." He trailed off.

"What?" The nasal twang made Cheetah's voice sound all the more solicitous.

"She says I molested her."

"In what way?"

Kyle exhaled noisily. No real human would have to ask that question. Christ, this was stupid . . .

"In what way?" asked Cheetah again, no doubt after his clock indicated it was time to prod once more.

"Sexually," said Kyle softly.

The microphone on Cheetah's console was very sensitive; doubtless he heard. Still, he was quiet for a time—a programmed affectation. "Oh," he said at last.

Kyle could see lights winking on the console; Cheetah was accessing the World Wide Web, quickly researching this topic.

"You're not to tell anyone," said Kyle sharply.

"I understand," said Cheetah. "Did you do what you are accused of?"

Kyle felt anger growing within him. "Of course not."

"Can you prove that?"

"What the fuck kind of question is that?"

"A salient one," said Cheetah. "I assume Rebecca has no actual evidence of your guilt."

"Of course not."

"And one presumes you have no evidence of your innocence."

"Well, no."

"Then it is her word against yours."

"A man is innocent until he's proven guilty," said Kyle.

Cheetah's console played the first four notes from Beethoven's Fifth Symphony. No one had bothered to program realistic laughter yet—Cheetah's malfunctioning sense of humor hardly required it—and the music served as a placeholder. "I'm supposed to be the naïve one, Dr. Graves. If you are not guilty, why would she make the accusation?"

Kyle had no answer for that.

Cheetah waited his programmed time, then tried again. "If you are not guilty, why—"

"Shut up," said Kyle.

3

HEATHER WASN'T TEACHING ANY COURSES
during the summer session, thank God. She'd tossed and
turned all night after Becky's visit and hadn't managed to get
out of bed until 11:00 A.M.

How do you go on from something like this, she wondered.

Mary had died sixteen months ago.

No, thought Heather. No—face it head-on. Mary had committed suicide sixteen months ago. They'd never known why.
Becky had been living at home back then; it had been she who
had found her sister's body.

How do you go on?

What do you do next?

The year Becky was born, Bill Cosby had lost his son Ennis.
Heather, with a newborn sucking at her breast, and a two-year-
old bundle of energy racing around the house, had been moved
to write a note to Cosby, in care of CBS, expressing sympathy.
As a mother, she knew nothing could be more devastating than
the loss of a child. Tens of thousands wrote such notes, of
course. Cosby—or his staff, at any rate—had replied, thanking
her for the concern.

Somehow, Bill Cosby had gone on.

At the same time, another father was in the news every night: Fred Goldman, father of Ron Goldman, the man killed alongside Nicole Brown Simpson. Fred was furious with O.J. Simpson, the person he was convinced had slaughtered his boy. Fred's anger was palpable, exploding from the TV set. The Goldman family published a book, *His Name Is Ron*. Heather had even gone to meet them when they'd autographed copies at the Chapters superstore down by the university. She knew, of course, that the book would be remaindered a few months later, like all the other flotsam tied into the Simpson trial, but she bought a copy anyway, getting Fred to sign it—showing her support, one parent to another.

Somehow, Fred Goldman had gone on.

When Mary had killed herself, Heather had looked to see if the Goldman book was still among their collection. It was indeed, standing on a living-room shelf, next to Margaret Atwood's *Alias Grace,* another hardcover Heather had broken the budget for at about the same time. Heather had taken down the Goldman book and opened it. There were pictures of Fred in it, but all of them were happy, family shots—not the face she remembered, the one seething with fury, all of it directed at Simpson.

When your child takes his or her own life, where do you direct the anger? At whom do you aim it?

The answer is no one. You internalize it—and it eats you up from the inside, bit by bit, day by day.

And the answer is everyone. You lash out, at your husband, your other child, your coworkers.

Oh, yes. You go on. But you're never the same.

But now—

Now, if Becky was right—

If Becky was right, there *was* someone to aim the anger at.

Kyle. Becky's father; Heather's estranged husband.

As she walked south along St. George Street, she thought

about that framed alien radio message on their living-room wall. Heather was a psychologist; she'd spent the last decade trying to decipher the alien messages, trying to plumb the alien mind. She knew that particular message better than anyone else on the planet did—she'd published two papers about it—and yet she still had no idea what it really said; she didn't really know it at all.

Heather had known Kyle for almost a quarter of a century.

But did she really know *him* at all?

She tried to clear her mind, tried to set aside the shock of the night before.

The sun was bright that afternoon. She squinted against it and wondered again about the aliens who were sending the messages. If nothing else, sunlight like this was something humans shared with the Centaurs—no one knew what the aliens looked like, of course, but political cartoonists had taken to drawing them like their namesakes from Greek mythology. Alpha Centauri A was almost an exact twin for Earth's sun: both were spectral-class G2V, both had a temperature of 5800 Kelvin—so both shone down on their planets with the same yellow-white light. Yes, cooler, smaller Alpha Centauri B might add an orange hue when it, too, was visible in the sky—but there would be times when only A would be up—and at those times, the Centaurs and the humans would have looked out on identically illuminated landscapes.

She continued on down the street, heading to her office.

We go on, she thought. We go on.

The next morning—Saturday, July 22—Kyle rode the subway four stops past his usual destination of St. George station, all the way to Osgoode.

Becky's boyfriend Zack Malkus worked as a clerk at a bookshop on Queen Street West. That much Kyle remembered from what little Becky had said to him over the past year. Which bookshop Kyle didn't know—but there weren't many left. During his high-school years, Kyle had often ventured down to Queen on a Saturday afternoon, looking for new science fiction at Bakka, new comics at The Silver Snail, and out-of-print works at the dozen or so used bookstores that had lined the street back then.

But independent bookstores had been having a hard time. Most had either relocated to less-trendy areas, where the rent was more modest, or had simply gone out of business. These days, Queen Street West was home mostly to trendy cafés and bistros, although the rococo headquarters of one of Canada's broadcasting empires was located near the subway exit at University Avenue. There couldn't be more than three or four bookstores left, so Kyle decided to simply try them all.

He began with venerable Pages, on the north side. He looked around—unlike Becky, Zack *was* in university, so he presumably probably did work on weekends, rather than during the week. But there was no sign of Zack's blond, rangy form. Still, Kyle went up to the cashier, a stunning East Indian woman with eight earrings. "Hello," he said.

She smiled at him.

"Does Zack Malkus work here?"

"We've got a Zack Barboni," she said.

Kyle felt his eyes widening slightly. When he'd been a kid, everyone had had normal names—David, Robert, John, Peter. The only Zack he'd ever heard of was the bumbling Zachary Smith on the old TV series *Lost in Space*. Now it seemed that every kid he ran into was a Zack or an Odin or a Wing.

"No, that's not him," said Kyle. "Thanks anyway."

He continued west. Panhandlers hit him up for donations along the way; there'd been a time in his youth when panhandlers were so rare in Toronto that he could never bring himself to say no. But they'd become plentiful in downtown, although they always solicited with studied Canadian politeness. Kyle had perfected the straight-ahead Torontonian gaze: jaw set, never meeting the eyes of a beggar, but still making his head swing through a tiny arc of "no" to each request; it would be rude, after all, to completely ignore someone who was talking to you.

Toronto the Good, he thought, recalling an old advertising slogan. Although the beggars today were a mixed group, many were Native Canadians—what Kyle's father still called "Indians." In fact, Kyle couldn't remember the last time he'd seen a Native Canadian anywhere except begging on a street corner, although there were doubtless still many on reservations someplace. Several years ago, he'd had a couple of Natives in one of his classes, sent there on a now-defunct government program, but he couldn't think of a single U of T faculty member—even, ironically, in Native Studies—who was a Canadian aborigine.

Kyle continued on until he came to Bakka. The store had started on Queen West in 1972, had moved away a quarter-century later, and now was back, not far from its original location. Kyle felt sure he'd have remembered—and that Becky would have mentioned it—if Zack worked there. Still . . .

Painted on the shop's plate-glass front window was the derivation of the store's name:

Bakka: noun, myth.; in Fremen legend the weeper who mourns for all mankind.

Bakka must be working overtime these days, thought Kyle.

He entered the store and spoke to the bearded, elfin man behind the counter. But no Zack Malkus worked there, either.

Kyle continued to search. He was wearing a Tilley safari shirt and blue jeans—not much different from what he wore while teaching.

The next store was about a block farther along, on the south side of the street. Kyle waited for a red-and-white streetcar—

recently converted to maglev travel—to hum quietly past, then made his way across.

This store was much more upscale than Bakka; someone had recently put a lot of money into renovating the old brownstone building that housed it, and the stone facade had been sand-blasted clean; most people drove skimmers these days, but many of the buildings still carried the grime of decades of automobile exhaust.

A chime sounded as Kyle entered. A dozen or so patrons were in the shop. Perhaps in response to the chime, a clerk appeared from behind a dark wooden bookcase.

It was Zack.

"Mis—Mister Graves," he said.

"Hello, Zack."

"What are *you* doing here?" He said it with venom, as if any reference to Kyle was distasteful.

"I need to talk to you."

Dismissively: "I'm working."

"I can see that. When's your break?"

"Not until noon."

Kyle did not look at his watch. "I'll wait."

"But—"

"I have to talk to you, Zack. You owe me that much."

The boy pursed his lips, thinking. Then he nodded.

Kyle did wait. Normally, he liked browsing in bookshops—especially the kind with real paper volumes—but he was too nervous to concentrate today. He spent some time looking at an old copy of *Colombo's Canadian Quotations,* reading what people had said about family life. Colombo contended that the most famous Canadian quotation of all was McLuhan's "The medium is the message." That was likely true, but one that was uttered more frequently, even if it wasn't uniquely Canadian, was "My children hate me."

There was still some time to kill. Kyle left the store. Next door was a poster shop. He went in and looked around; it was decorated all in chrome and black enamel. There were lots of Robert Bateman wildlife paintings. Some Group of Seven stuff. A series of prints by Jean-Pierre Normand. Photo portraits of current pop-music stars. Old movie posters—from *Citizen Kane* to *The Fall of the Jedi*. Hundreds of holoposters of landscapes and spacescapes and seascapes.

And Dali—Kyle had always liked Dali. There was "Persistence of Memory"—the one with the melting watches. And "The Sacrament of the Last Supper." And—

Say, that one would be great for his students. "Christus Hypercubus." It had been years since he'd seen it anywhere, and it sure would liven up the lab.

He'd doubtless take some flak for hanging a picture with religious overtones, but what the heck. Kyle found the slot that had rolled-up copies of the poster in it and took one up to the cashier, a small Eastern European man.

"Thirty-five ninety-five," said the clerk. "Plus plus plus." Plus PST, GST, and NST—Canadians were the most taxed people in the world.

Kyle handed over his SmartCash card. The clerk placed it in the reader, and the total was deleted from the chip on the card. The clerk then wrapped a small bag around the poster tube and handed it to Kyle.

Kyle headed back to the bookstore. A few minutes later, Zack's break came.

"Is there somewhere we can talk?" asked Kyle.

Zack looked as though he was still very reluctant, but after a moment he said, "The office?" Kyle nodded, and Zack led him into the back room, which seemed to be more a storage facility than anything that might justly be termed an office. Zack closed the door behind them. Rickety bookcases and two beat-up wooden desks filled the space. No money had been spent upgrading this part of the store; outward appearances were everything.

Zack offered Kyle the single chair, but Kyle shook his head. Zack sat down. Kyle leaned against a bookcase, which shifted slightly. He backed off, not wanting it to come toppling down on him; he'd had enough of that lately.

"Zack, I love Becky," said Kyle.

"No one," said Zack firmly, "who loved her could do what you did." He hesitated for a moment, as if wondering whether to push his luck. But then, with the righteousness of the young, he added, "You sick bastard."

Kyle felt like hauling back and hitting the kid. "I didn't do anything. I'd never hurt her."

"You *did* hurt her. She can't . . ."

"What?"

"Nothing."

But Kyle had learned a lesson or two from Cheetah. "Tell me."

Zack seemed to consider, then, finally, he just blurted it out. "She can't even have sex anymore."

Kyle felt his heart jump. Of course Becky was sexually active; she was nineteen, for Pete's sake. Still, although he'd suspected it, he didn't like hearing about it.

"I never touched her inappropriately. Never."

"She wouldn't like me talking to you."

"Damn it, Zack, my family is being torn apart. I need your help."

Sneering now: "That's not what you said Thursday night. You said it was a family matter. You said I had no place there."

"Becky won't talk to me. I need you to intercede."

"What? Tell her that you didn't do it? She *knows* you did it."

"I can *prove* that I didn't do it. That's why I came here. I want you to agree to come by the university."

Zack, who was wearing a Ryerson T-shirt, bristled; Kyle

knew that those who attended Toronto's other two universities hated the way U of T types always referred to it as *the* university. "Why?" asked Zack.

"They teach forensics at U of T," said Kyle. "We've got a polygraph lab, and I know a guy who works there. He's been an expert witness in hundreds of cases. I want you to come to that lab, and I'll have myself hooked up to a lie detector. I'll let you ask me any questions you want about this topic, and you'll see that I'm telling the truth. I didn't hurt Becky—I couldn't hurt her. You'll *see* that that's true."

"You could get your friend to rig the test."

"We can have the test done somewhere else, then. You name the lab; I'll pay for it. Then, once you know the truth, maybe you can help me get through to Becky."

"A pathological liar can beat a lie detector."

Kyle's face went flush. He surged forward, grabbed the boy's shirtfront. But then he backed off, spreading his arms, palms face out. "Sorry," he said. "Sorry." He fought to calm down. "I tell you, I'm innocent. Why won't you let me prove it?"

Zack's face was flush now; adrenaline must have surged through him when he thought Kyle was going to rough him up. "I don't need you to take a test," he said, his voice ragged. "Becky told me what you did. She's never lied to me."

Of course she has, thought Kyle. People lie to other people all the time. "I didn't do this," he said again.

Zack shook his head. "You don't know the kinds of problems Becky had. She's getting better now, though. She cried for hours after we left your place on Thursday, but she's a lot better."

"But, Zack, you *know* that Becky and I have lived apart for almost a year now. If I'd really been doing something wrong, surely she would have left earlier, or at least have said something as soon as she got out of the house. Why on earth—"

"You think this is easy to talk about? Her therapist says—"

"Therapist?" Kyle felt as if he'd been struck. His own daughter was in therapy. Why the fuck didn't he know this? "What the hell was she in therapy for?"

Zack made a face indicating the answer was obvious.

"What's the therapist's name? If I can't convince you, maybe I can convince him."

"I . . . don't know."

"You're lying."

But the accusation just made Zack more determined. "I'm not. I don't know."

"How did she find this therapist?"

Zack shrugged a little. "It was the same one her older sister had used."

"Mary?" Kyle staggered backward, bumping into the other wooden desk. There was a half-eaten donut sitting on a napkin on its corner; it fell to the floor, crumbling in two. "Mary was in therapy, too?"

"Of course she was. Who can blame her, after what you did to her?"

"I didn't do *anything* to Mary. And I didn't do anything to Becky, either."

"Now who's lying?" said Zack.

"*I'm not*—" He paused, trying to get his voice under control. "Damn it, Zack. God fucking damn it. You *are* in this with her. The two of you are going to file a lawsuit, aren't you?"

"Becky doesn't want your money," Zack said. "She just wants peace; she just wants closure."

"*Closure?* What the fuck kind of word is that? Is that what her therapist told her this was all about? Fucking *closure?*"

Zack stood up. "Mr. Graves, go home. And for God's sake, get to a therapist yourself."

Kyle stormed out of the office, through the retail area, and out into the hellish heat of the summer day.

4

KYLE REMEMBERED THE DAY HE'D LEARNED
that Heather was pregnant with their first child, Mary.

It had come as a complete shock. They'd been living together
for about a year, sharing an apartment in St. Jamestown with a
few hundred cockroaches. Kyle was in the second year of his
master's in computer science; Heather was just starting her
master's in psychology. They were in love—no doubt—and had
talked about building a life together. But Kyle and Heather both
knew they should each go somewhere other than U of T for
their doctorates. Not that U of T wasn't a fine place for grad
school; indeed, if it really did have any claim to that "Harvard
of the North" label, it was because of its graduate studies. But
having all three degrees from the same institution would be an
automatic red flag in future job interviews.

Then, suddenly, Heather was pregnant.

And they'd had tough decisions to make.

They'd talked about abortion. Although they did eventually
want children, this was without doubt an unplanned pregnancy.

But . . .

But, hell, when *would* be the right time?

Not while they were finishing their masters' degrees, of course.

And certainly not while doing their doctorates.

And, well, the starting salaries for associate professors were abysmal—Heather had already decided that an academic life was what she wanted, and Kyle, who didn't enjoy stressful situations, was leaning toward that as well, rather than the high-pressure world of commercial computing.

And then of course they wouldn't really be secure until at least one of them had tenure.

And by then—

By then, more than a decade would have slipped by, and Heather would be into the high-risk age for pregnancy.

Choices.

Turning points.

It could go one way or the other.

At last they'd opted to have the child; countless student couples had done the same over the years. It would be difficult—a stretch financially, an additional demand on their already over-taxed time.

But it would be worth it. Surely it would be worth it.

Kyle remembered vividly the class he'd been in the day Heather had told him she was pregnant. It had seemed so appropriate, somehow.

"Suppose," Professor Papineau had said to the dozen students in the seminar that had seemed to start out a long way from computer science, "that you live just north of Queen's Park and you work just south of it. Further suppose that you walk to work each day. You're faced with a choice every morning. You can't walk down the center line, since the Parliament Buildings get in the way. Of course, I'm sure there've been times when many of us have wanted to plow through the Legislature in a tank . . . but I digress."

Laughter from the students. Papineau had been a wonderful

prof; Kyle had gone to his retirement dinner fifteen years later, but hadn't seen him since.

"No," said Papineau, once the chuckling had stopped, "you have to go *around* the buildings—either to the east, or to the west. Each way is pretty much the same distance; you leave home at the same time and you arrive at work at the same time regardless of which route you choose. So, which route *do* you choose? You, there—Kyle. Which way would you go?"

Kyle had his beard even back then. As today, it was red, even though his hair was black. But in those days he'd kept it scruffy, unkempt—never trimming it, never shaving his neck beneath. He cringed now to think about it. "Down the west," he said, shrugging to convey that it was a purely arbitrary selection.

"A fine choice," said Papineau. "But it's not the only choice. And in the many-worlds interpretation of quantum mechanics, we believe that any time a choice can be made one way, the alternative choice is also made—but in a parallel universe. If Kyle did indeed come down the west side in this universe, there would also exist a parallel universe in which he came down the east side."

"But surely that's just a metaphor," said Glenda, a student Kyle sometimes thought he might have pursued had he not already met Heather. "Surely there's really only one universe, no?"

"Or," said D'Annunzio, a biker type who always seemed out of place in class, "even if another universe does exist, there's no way to prove it, so it's not a falsifiable hypothesis, and therefore not real science."

Papineau grinned broadly. "You know," he said, "if this were a nightclub performance, people would accuse me of having planted the two of you in the audience. Let's look at that question: is there any direct evidence that multiple universes might exist? Roopshand, will you get the lights, please?"

A student in the back stood up and turned off the lights.

Papineau moved next to a slide projector sitting on a metal cart; he turned it on. A diagram appeared on the screen.

"This picture shows some experimental apparatus," said Papineau. "At the top, we have a lightbulb. In the middle there's a bar representing a horizontal wall as seen from above. You see those two breaks in the bar? Those are two vertical slits that go right through the wall—one on the left and one on the right." He used a small telescoping pointer to indicate these. "And at the bottom we have a horizontal line representing a sheet of photographic film seen edge-on from above. The wall in the middle is like Queen's Park, and the two slits are like the two possible paths around the Parliament Buildings—one on the east and one on the west." He paused while the students digested this. "Now, what happens when we turn on the lightbulb?"

He pushed a key; the carousel clicked around and a new slide came on. The photographic film at the bottom showed a zebra pattern of light and dark lines.

"You all know what that is from high-school physics, right? It's an interference pattern. Light from the bulb, traveling like a wave, passes through the two slits—which behave now like two separate light sources, each with waves of light emanating from it. Well, when the two sets of waves crash against the photographic plate, some of the waves cancel out, leaving dark areas, and others reinforce each other, making the bright bands."

Some students nodded.

"But you also know from high-school physics that light doesn't always behave like a wave—sometimes it behaves like a particle, too. And, of course, we call particles of light 'photons.' Now, what happens if we turn down the power going to the lightbulb? What happens when the power is turned down so low that photons are coming out of the lightbulb one at a time? Anyone?"

A redheaded woman held up a hand.

"Yes, Tina?" said Papineau.

"Well, if only one photon is going through, then it should make one little spot of light on the photographic film—assuming it finds its way through one of the slits."

Papineau smiled. "That's what you'd expect, yes. But even when photons are released one at a time, you *still* get the light and dark bands. You still get interference patterns."

"But how can you get interference if there's only one particle passing through at a time?" asked Kyle. "I mean, what's the particle interfering *with*?"

Papineau raised his index finger. "That *is* the question! And there are two possible answers. The one that's simply weird is that in transit between the lightbulb and the film, the single photon breaks up into a series of waves, some of which go through one slit and some through the other, forming the interference pattern.

"But the other answer—the really interesting answer—is that the photon never breaks up, but rather remains a discrete particle, and as such, it has no choice but to go through only one of the two possible slits—*in this universe*. But just as you, Kyle, could have taken either route around Queen's Park, so the photon could have taken the path through either slit—*and in a parallel universe, it took the other path*."

"But how come we see the interference pattern?" asked D'Annunzio, chewing gum as he spoke. "I mean, if we stood south of the Parliament Buildings, we'd never see two versions of Graves, one coming around the east side and one around the west."

"Excellent question!" crowed Papineau. "The answer is that the two-slit experiment is a very special example of parallel universes. The original single universe splits into two universes once the photon encounters the slits, but the two universes exist separately only so long as the photon is traveling. Since it makes no difference now *or ever* which path the photon actually took, the universes collapse back together into a single universe. The only evidence that the two universes ever existed is the interference pattern left behind on the film."

"But what if it *does* make a difference which slit was chosen?" asked Roopshand from the back.

"In any experiment you can devise in which the choice of slit actually matters—indeed, in any experiment in which you can detect which slit the photon went through—you don't get the interference pattern. If it matters at all, the universes never stitch back together into one; they continue on as two separate universes."

It had been a heady class—as all of Papineau's were. And it had also been a metaphor that Kyle carried with him throughout his life: choices, branching paths.

Back then, back in 1996, even though he and Heather were still students, he knew which choice he wanted. He wanted to live in the universe in which they *did* have a baby.

And so that November, their first child, Mary Lorraine Graves, was born.

5

KYLE WAS WALKING ALONG WILLCOCKS Street, heading from New College back toward Mullin Hall, but he was accosted before he could cross St. George.

"Sir—excuse me. Sir, pardon me! Yes, you. Dale Wong, City-TV. We'd like to ask you a question."

"A streeter?" said Kyle, the word coming to him from somewhere.

The young man with the camcorder was amused. "Exactly, sir. A streeter. Here's our question. Today is the tenth anniversary of the receipt of the first radio message from Alpha Centauri."

"Is it really?"

"Yes, sir. How has it affected you this past decade, knowing that there's intelligent life elsewhere in the universe?"

Kyle frowned, thinking. "Well, that's a good question. It's certainly interesting—my wife actually works on trying to decode the alien radio messages."

"But how has it changed *you*—changed your outlook?"

"Well, I suppose it gives me a little perspective on things. You know—all our problems don't amount to much, compared to the limitless universe." The words rang false as they came out. Kyle paused—long enough, he knew, that the man wouldn't be able to use the video clip without editing. "No, no, that's not it. You want the truth? It hasn't changed a damn thing. No matter how big the universe gets, we're always looking inside."

"Thank you, sir. Thank— Ma'am! Ma'am! A moment of your time, please!"

Kyle continued to walk. He hadn't really thought about it before, but his current research project clearly had had its genesis back in the spring of 1996, the same day he'd learned that Heather was pregnant.

"So," Professor Papineau had said, "the interference patterns that result when a single photon passes through two slits might be proof of the existence of multiple universes. But what, you may ask, does this have to do with computing?" He beamed at his seminar students.

"Well, remember our example of Kyle coming to work. In one universe, he walks around the east side of Queen's Park; in the other, he walks around the west side. Now, Kyle, suppose your boss had asked you to solve two problems before you came into work, and—having never overcome your student ways—you've left them both to the last moment. There's time to puzzle out the answer to just one of them in your head as you walk to work. Let's say that if you went down the west side, you'd spend your time solving problem A, and if you went down the east side, you'd spend your time solving problem B. Is there any way without slowing down or taking the journey around the Parliament Buildings twice that by the time you got to work, you'd have the answers to both problems?"

Kyle was sure he'd had a blank expression.

"Anyone?" asked Papineau, bushy eyebrows raised.

"I'm surprised you think Graves would come up with even one answer," said D'Annunzio.

Snickers from several students. Papineau smiled.

"Well, there *is* a way," said the professor. "You know the old saying, 'Two heads are better than one'? Well, if our Kyle—the one from this universe who went down the west side and who solved problem A—could join back up with the other Kyle—the one from the parallel universe who went down the east side and solved problem B—then he'd have both answers."

A hand went up.

"Glenda?"

"But when talking about the photon and the slits, you said the only way the two universes could rejoin is if there was no way to tell which slit the photon had taken in each universe."

"Exactly. But if we could devise a method by which it made no difference whatsoever which way Kyle went in this universe—indeed, a method by which Kyle himself didn't know which way he had gone, and no one saw him during his journey—then, at the end of it all, the two universes might stitch back together. But in the rejoined universe, Kyle would know the answer to both problems, even though he'd really only had time to solve one of them."

Papineau grinned at the class.

"Welcome," he said, "to the world of quantum computing." He paused. "Of course, there were really more than two possible universes for Kyle—he could have stayed home, he could have driven to work, he could have taken a cab. Likewise, it's possible to envision the lightbulb experiment with dozens or even hundreds of slits. Well, suppose each of the photons coming off the lightbulb represented a single bit of information. Remember, all computing is done with glorified abacuses; we actually move things around in order to compute, whether it's pebbles or atoms or electrons or photons. But if each of those things could simultaneously be in multiple places at once, across parallel universes, extraordinarily complex computing problems could be solved very, very quickly.

"Consider, for instance, the factoring of numbers. How do

we do that? Essentially by trial and error, although there are a few tricks that help. If we want to determine the factors of eight, we start dividing numbers into it. We know that one goes evenly into eight—it goes evenly into every whole number. What about two? Yes, it's a factor: it goes in four times. Three? No—it doesn't go in evenly. Four? Yes, it goes in twice. That's how we do it: by brute-force computing, testing every possible factor in turn. But as numbers get bigger, the number of factors they have get bigger. Earlier this year, a network of sixteen hundred computers succeeded in finding all the factors of a 129-digit number—the largest number ever factored. The process took *eight* months.

"But imagine a quantum computer—one that was in touch with all the possible alternative computers in parallel universes. And imagine a program that factors large numbers by working on all the possible solutions *simultaneously.* Peter Shor, a mathematician at AT&T Bell Laboratories, has worked out a program to do just that; it would try every possible factor of the big number simultaneously by testing just one possible factor in each of many parallel universes. The program outputs its results as interference patterns, sent to a piece of photographic film. Shor's algorithm would cause those numbers that aren't factors to cancel out in the interference pattern, leaving darkness. The patterns of light and dark would form a sort of barcode that could be read to indicate which numbers actually are factors of the big number you started with. And since the calculations are performed across parallel universes, in the time it takes for our universe to test any one number, all the other numbers are tested as well, and we have the result. So long as it makes no difference which number our own computer calculated, the result should be achieved almost instantaneously; what normal computers took eight months to do, quantum computers could do in a matter of seconds."

"But there's no such thing as a quantum computer," said Kyle.

Papineau nodded at him. "That's right, at least not yet. But someday someone is going to build a quantum computer. And then we'll know for sure."

6

KYLE AND HEATHER HAD DINNER TOGETHER every Monday night.

They'd been separated for a year now. It had never been intended to be permanent—and they'd never mentioned the D-word. They'd just needed some time, they both felt, to come to terms with Mary's death. They'd both been on edge, sniping at each other, little things that shouldn't have mattered at all escalating into huge fights, unable to console each other, unable to comprehend why it had happened.

They'd never missed a Monday dinner together, and although tensions were high since Becky's visit four days ago, Kyle assumed that Heather would show up at their usual restaurant, a Swiss Chalet franchise a few blocks from their house.

Kyle stood outside, enjoying the warm evening breeze. He couldn't bring himself to go in yet; Heather's car wasn't in the lot, and if she didn't show, the embarrassment would be too much.

At about 6:40—ten minutes late—Heather's powder-blue skimmer floated into the lot.

Still, things were different. For an entire year now, they'd greeted each other on Monday nights with a quick kiss, but this time—this time they both hesitated. They entered the restaurant, Kyle holding the door for Heather.

The server tried to seat them beside another couple, even though there was no one else in the place. Kyle hated that at the best of times, and this evening he did protest. "We'll sit over there," he said, pointing to a distant corner.

The server acquiesced, and they were escorted to a booth at the back. Kyle ordered red wine; Heather asked for a glass of the house white.

"I was beginning to think you weren't coming," said Kyle.

Heather nodded, but her face was impassive. The lamp hanging above their table made her normally pleasant features look severe. "I'm sorry I was late."

There was silence for a time.

"I don't know what we're going to do about this," said Kyle.

Heather looked away. "Me neither."

"I swear to you—"

"Please," said Heather, cutting him off. "Please."

Kyle nodded slowly. He was quiet for a moment longer, then: "I went to see Zack on Saturday."

Heather looked apprehensive. "And?"

"And nothing. I didn't get into a fight with him, I mean. We talked a bit. I wanted him to agree to come to the forensics lab at the university. I was going to take a lie-detector test, prove that I didn't do it."

"And?" said Heather again.

"He refused." Kyle lowered his eyes, looking at the paperite place mat with the current month's chicken promotion illustrated on it. He looked up again and sought Heather's eyes. "I could do the same thing for you," he said. "I could prove my innocence."

Heather opened her mouth, but immediately closed it.

It was a turning point, a crux. Kyle knew it, and he was sure

Heather knew it, too. The future depended on what would happen next.

She had to be thinking it all through . . .

If he was innocent—

If he was innocent, she must know he'd never be able to forgive her for demanding proof, for her lack of faith. If he was innocent, then surely their marriage *should* survive this crisis. They'd both thought they would get back together again, sooner or later. If not by the beginning of the coming school year, surely by its end.

If he was innocent, the marriage should survive, but if Heather had doubt, and admitted it, admitted the possibility, would he ever be able to hold her again, to love her again? When he'd needed her most, had she believed in him?

"No," she said, closing her eyes. "No, that won't be necessary." She looked at him. "I know you didn't do anything." Kyle kept his expression neutral; he knew she must be searching his face for any sign that he thought the words might be insincere.

"Thank you," he said softly.

The server returned with their drinks. They ordered: a grilled chicken breast and plain baked potato for Kyle; the quarter barbecue chicken dinner with fries for Heather.

"Did anything else happen with Zack?" asked Heather.

Kyle took a sip of his wine. "He told me that Becky is in therapy."

Heather nodded. "Yes."

"You knew that?"

"She started seeing someone after Mary died."

"It was the same therapist Mary had been going to," said Kyle. "Zack told me that."

"*Mary* was in therapy, too? Good God, I didn't know that."

"I was shocked, too," said Kyle.

"You'd think she'd have told me."

"Or me," said Kyle, forcefully.

"Of course," said Heather. "Of course." She paused. "I wonder if it had anything to do with Rachel?"

"Who?"

"Rachel Cohen. Remember? Mary's friend—she died of leukemia when Mary was eighteen."

"Oh, yes. Poor girl."

"Mary had been quite distraught about that. Maybe she started seeing a therapist over it—a little grief counseling, you know?"

"Why wouldn't she have come to you?" asked Kyle.

"Well, I'm hardly a clinician. Besides, no girl wants her mother for a therapist—and I suspect she wouldn't have wanted anyone I might have recommended, either."

"So how would Mary find a therapist?" asked Kyle.

"I don't know," said Heather. "Maybe Dr. Redmond recommended somebody." Lloyd Redmond had been Kyle's physician, and later, the whole family's physician, for nearly thirty years. "I'll call him in the morning and see what I can find out."

Their meals arrived. They ate mostly in silence, and afterward went to their separate homes.

The phone rang in Kyle's lab at 10:30 Tuesday morning. A couple of grad students were present, working quietly inside Cheetah's console; the console's faceplate, including Cheetah's eyes, had been removed and was leaning now against the curving outer wall.

The Caller ID showed it was Heather, calling from her office in Sidney Smith Hall on the west side of St. George Street, a block farther south.

"I was right," said Heather. "Dr. Redmond *did* recommend a therapist to Mary several months before she died."

"What's the therapist's name?

"Lydia Gurdjieff." She spelled the unusual last name.

"Ever heard of her?"

"No. I've checked the online directory for the OPA; she's not listed."

"I'm going to go see her," said Kyle.

"No," said Heather. "I think I should go—alone."

Kyle opened his mouth to object, but then realized his wife was right. Not only was he the enemy in this therapist's eyes, but Heather, not Kyle, was the trained psychologist.

"When?" he asked.

"Today, if possible."

"Thanks," said Kyle.

Heather might have shrugged or nodded, or even smiled encouragingly; there was no way for Kyle to tell. Sometimes he wished video phones *had* taken off.

"Hello, Ms. Gurdjieff," said Heather, walking into the therapist's consulting room. The walls were covered with blue wallpaper but it was curling a bit at the seams, revealing the painted surface beneath. "Thank you for seeing me."

"My pleasure, Ms. Davis—or may I call you Heather?"

Heather wasn't taking any special pains to disguise her identity; she used her own last name, but Rebecca and Mary had shared Kyle's last name. There was no reason to think this Gurdjieff person would make the connection. "Heather is fine."

"Well, Heather, we don't often have a cancellation, but I guess today is your lucky day. Please, have a seat, or use the couch if you prefer."

Heather considered for a moment, then, with a little shrug, lay down on the couch. Even with all her training in psychology, she'd never actually lain on a therapist's couch before and it seemed an experience not to be missed.

"I'm not sure why I'm here," Heather said. "I haven't been

sleeping well." She looked beyond the therapist to the walls; there were framed diplomas on them. The highest degree seemed to be a master's.

"That's surprisingly common," said Gurdjieff. Her voice was warm and pleasant, with perhaps a trace of a Newfoundland accent.

"I also don't have much of an appetite," said Heather.

Gurdjieff nodded and took a datapad off her desk. She started writing on it with a stylus. "And you think there's a psychological cause for this?"

"At first I thought it was some kind of flu," said Heather, "but it's been going on for months."

Gurdjieff made another note on her pad. She was putting too much pressure on the stylus; it made a slight chalk-on-blackboard screech against the glass plate.

"You're married, aren't you?"

Heather nodded; she still wore a plain wedding band.

"Children?"

"Two boys," said Heather, although she regretted it at once. She probably should have included at least one daughter. "Sixteen and nineteen."

"And they're not the source of the problem?"

"I don't think so."

"Are your parents still alive?"

Heather saw no reason not to answer that truthfully. "No."

"I'm sorry."

Heather tilted her head, accepting the comment.

They talked for another half hour, the therapist's questions seemingly innocuous.

And then she said it: "A classic case, really."

"What?" asked Heather.

"Incest survivor."

"*What?*"

"Oh, you don't consciously remember it—that's not at all unusual. But everything you've said suggests that's what happened."

Heather tried to keep her tone flat. "That's ridiculous."

"Denial is natural," said Gurdjieff. "I don't expect you to come to terms with it right away."

"But I wasn't abused."

"Your father is dead, you said?"

"Yes."

"Did you cry at his funeral?"

That struck a little too close to home. "No," Heather said softly.

"It was him, wasn't it?"

"It was nobody."

"You didn't have a much-older brother, did you? Or a grandfather who visited a lot? Maybe an uncle you were often alone with?"

"No."

"Then it was probably your father."

Heather tried to make her voice sound firm. "He couldn't possibly have done anything like that."

Gurdjieff smiled sadly. "That's what everyone thinks at first. But you're suffering from what we call post-traumatic stress disorder. It's the same thing that happened to those vets from the Gulf and Colombian Wars, only instead of reliving the memories, you're repressing them." Gurdjieff touched Heather's hand. "Look, it's nothing to be ashamed of—you have to remember that. It's nothing you did. It's not your fault."

Heather was quiet.

Gurdjieff lowered her voice. "It's more common than you think," she said. "It happened to me, too."

"Really?"

The therapist nodded. "From when I was six or so until when I was fourteen. Not every night, but often."

"That's—that's terrible. I'm so sorry for you."

Gurdjieff held up her left hand. "Don't feel sorry for me—or for yourself. We have to take strength from this."

"What did you do?"

"It's too bad your father is dead; you can't confront him. That's the best thing, you know: confronting your abuser. It's enormously empowering. It's not for everyone, of course. Some women are afraid to do it, afraid that they will end up being disinherited, or cut off from the rest of their family. But when it works, it's terrific."

"Oh?" said Heather. "You've had other patients go through this?"

"Many."

Heather wasn't sure how hard to push it. "Anyone recently?"

"Well, I can't really talk about other patients . . ."

"Of course not. Of course not. Just in general terms, I mean. What happens? An average case."

"Well, one of my patients did confront her abuser just last week."

Heather felt her heart begin to race. She tried to be very careful. "Did it help him?"

"Her, actually. Yes."

"In what way? I mean, is she free of whatever was bothering her?"

"Yes."

"How do you know? I mean, how can you tell it made a difference?"

"Well, this woman—I guess it won't hurt to tell you she had an eating disorder. That's common in cases like this; the other common symptom is trouble sleeping, like what you're having. Anyway, she was bulimic—but she hasn't had to purge since then. See, what she really wanted to purge, what she really wanted to get out of her system, is out now."

"But I don't think I was abused. Was she like me, unsure?"

"At first, yes. It was only later that it all came out. It'll come out for you, too. We'll find the truth and we'll face it together."

"I don't know. I don't think this happened. And—and—I mean, come on. Incest—sexual abuse. That's the stuff of tabloids, no? I mean, it's practically a cliché."

"You're so wrong, it's staggering," said Gurdjieff sharply. "And it's not just you—it's society in general. You know, in the nineteen-eighties, when we really started talking about sexual abuse and incest, the topic did get a great deal of exposure. And for people like me—people who had been abused—it was a breath of fresh air. We weren't a dirty little secret anymore; the horrible things that had been done to us were out in the open, and we finally understood that it wasn't our fault. But it's an unpleasant truth, and people like you—people who saw their neighbors and their fathers and their churches in a whole new light—were uncomfortable with it. You liked it better when it was hidden away, something you didn't have to deal with. You want to force it into the background, marginalize it, remove it from the agenda, prevent it from being discussed."

Heather thought about this. Incest, pedophilia, child abuse— they were all things that might naturally come up in psychology classes. But how often did she mention them? A passing reference here, a brief aside there—and then moving on quickly, before it got too unpleasant, to Maslow's drive for self-actualization, to Adler's introverts and extroverts, to Skinner's operant conditioning. "Perhaps," she said.

"Maybe you're right," said Gurdjieff, apparently willing to concede a little if Heather was also willing to do so. "Maybe nothing did happen in your past—but why don't we find out for sure?"

"But I don't remember any abuse."

"Surely you have some anger toward your father?"

Heather felt it hitting home again. "Of course. But there's no way he could have done anything to me."

"It's natural that you don't remember it," said Gurdjieff. "Almost no one does. But it's there, hidden beneath the surface. Re-pressed." She paused again. "You know, my own memories *weren't* repressed—for whatever reason, they weren't. But my sister Daphne—she's two years younger than me—hers *were* repressed. I tried to talk about this with her a dozen times, and she said I was nuts—and then one day, out of the blue, when we were both in our twenties, she phoned me. It had come back to her—at last the memories, which she'd suppressed for fifteen years, had come back. We confronted our father together." A pause. "As I said, it's too bad you can't confront your father. But you *will* need to deal with this, to get it out into the open. Eulogies are one way."

"Eulogies?"

"You write out what you would have said to your father had you confronted him while he was still alive. Then you present it at his graveside." Gurdjieff held up a hand, as if she realized how macabre this sounded. "Don't worry—we'd do it during the daytime. It's a wonderful way to bring closure."

"I'm not sure," said Heather. "I'm not sure about any of this."

"Of course you're not. That's perfectly normal. But, trust me, I've seen lots of cases like yours. Most women have been abused, you know."

Heather had seen studies suggesting as much—but to get the "most" conclusion, they included everything down to having to kiss a disliked relative on the cheek and schoolyard tussles with little boys.

Gurdjieff looked up above Heather. Heather rolled her head and saw that there was a large wall clock mounted behind her. "Look," said Gurdjieff, "we're almost out of time. But we've made a really good start. I think we can lick this thing together, Heather, if you're willing to work with me."

7

Heather called Kyle and asked him to come by the house.

When he arrived—about 8:00 P.M., after they'd both eaten separately—he took a seat on the couch, and Heather sat down in the easy chair opposite him. She took a deep breath, wondering how to begin, then just dived in. "I think this may be a case of false-memory syndrome."

"Ah," said Kyle, sounding sage. "The coveted FMS."

Heather knew her husband too well. "You don't have the slightest idea of what I'm talking about, do you?"

"Well, no."

"Do you know what repressed memories are—in theory, that is?"

"Oh, repressed memories. Sure, sure, I've heard something about that. There've been some court cases, right?"

Heather nodded. "The first one was ages ago, back in—oh, what was it now? Nineteen eighty-nine or so. A woman named . . . let me think. I taught this once before; it'll come back. A woman named Eileen Franklin, who was twenty-eight or twenty-nine, claimed to suddenly remember having seen the rape and murder of her best friend twenty years previously. Now, the rape-murder was an established fact; the body had been found shortly after the crime was committed. But the shocking thing wasn't just that Eileen suddenly remembered seeing the crime being committed, but she also suddenly remembered who had done it: her own father."

Kyle frowned. "What happened to the father?"

Heather looked at him. "He was convicted. It was later overturned, though—but on a technicality."

"Was there corroborating evidence, or did the original conviction rest solely on the daughter's testimony?"

Heather shrugged a little. "Depends how you look at it. Eileen seemed to be aware of things about the crime that weren't generally known. That was taken as evidence of her father's guilt. But upon investigation, it was shown that most of the supposedly telling details had indeed been reported in the press around the time the little girl had been killed. Of course, Eileen wasn't reading newspapers when she was eight or nine, but she could have looked them up later at a library." Heather chewed her lower lip, remembering. "But you know, now that I think about it, some of the details she reported *were* in the newspaper accounts—but were wrong in those accounts."

Kyle sounded confused. "What?"

"She remembered—or claimed to remember—things that turned out to be untrue. For instance, the little girl who was killed was wearing two rings, a silver one and a gold one. Only the gold one had a stone in it, but one of the newspapers reported that the stone was in the *silver* ring—and that's exactly what Eileen said when she told the police about the crime." Heather held up a hand. "Of course that's a trivial detail, and anyone remembering anything that long ago is likely to mix up some facts."

"But you didn't just say repressed memories. You mentioned *false* memories."

"Well, it's either one or the other, and that's the problem. In fact, it's been a bone of contention in psychology for decades now—the question of whether the memory of something traumatic can be repressed. Repression itself is an old concept. It's the basis for psychoanalysis, after all: you force the repressed thought into the light of day, and whatever neuroses you've got should clear up. But millions of people who've had traumatic experiences say the problem is the opposite: they *never* forget what's happened. They all say things like 'Not a day goes by when I don't think about my car blowing up,' or 'I have constant nightmares about Colombia.' " Heather lowered her eyes. "Certainly I've never forgotten—and never will forget— the sight of Mary lying dead in the bathroom."

Kyle nodded slowly. His voice was soft. "Me neither."

Heather took a moment to compose herself. "But those things—a war, a car exploding, even a child dying—they are common enough occurrences. They're not unthinkable; indeed, there's not a parent alive who doesn't fret about something happening to one of their children. But what if something occurs that is *so* unexpected, so out of the ordinary, so shocking that the mind just can't deal with it? Like a little girl seeing her daddy rape and murder her best friend? How does the mind react then? Maybe it *does* wall it off; there certainly are some psychiatrists and no end of putative incest survivors who believe that. But . . ."

Kyle raised his eyebrows. "But what?"

"But there are many psychologists who believe that that simply can't happen—that there's no mechanism for repression, and so when traumatic memories suddenly appear years or decades after the supposed event, they *have* to be false memories. We've been debating this in psychology for a quarter-century or more now, without ever coming up with a solid answer."

Kyle took a deep breath, then let it out slowly. "So what does it come down to? Humans can either shut out memories of traumatic events that really did happen—or we can have vivid memories of things that never occurred?"

Heather nodded. "I know; neither is an appealing idea. No matter which one you accept—and, of course, there's a chance that both happen at different times—it means that our memories, and our sense of who we are and where we came from, are much more fallible than we'd like to believe."

"Well, I know for a fact that Becky's memories are bogus. But what I don't understand is where such memories could come from?"

"The most common theory is that they're implanted."

"Implanted?" He said it as if he'd never heard the word before.

Heather nodded. "In therapy. I've seen the basic principle demonstrated myself, with children. You have a child visit you every day for a week. On the first day, you ask him how things went at the hospital after he cut his finger. He says, 'I never went to the hospital.' And that's true, he didn't. But you ask him again tomorrow, and the next day, and the next day. And by the end of the week, the child is convinced that he *did* go to the hospital. He'll be able to tell you a detailed, consistent story about his trip there—and he'll really believe it happened."

"Kind of like Biff Loman."

"Who?"

"*Death of a Salesman.* Biff wasn't a young kid, but as he says to his father, 'You blew me so full of hot air, I could never stand taking orders from anybody.' He really came to be convinced by his father that he'd had a much better job in a company than the lowly position he'd actually held."

"Well, that can happen. Memories can be implanted, even just through suggestion and constant repetition. And if a therapist augments that with hypnosis, really unshakable false memories can be created."

"But why on earth would a therapist do that?"

Heather looked grim. "To quote an old Psych Department joke, there are many routes to mental health, but none so lucrative as Freudian analysis."

Kyle frowned. He was quiet for several seconds, apparently contemplating whether to ask another question. And at last he did. "I'm not trying to be argumentative here, but your endorsement of my innocence has been less than ringing. Why do you think Becky's memories might be false?"

"Because her therapist suggested that my father might have molested *me.*"

"Oh," said Kyle. And then, *"Oh."*

8

AFTER KYLE HAD GONE HOME, HEATHER SAT in the darkened living room, thinking. It was past time she went to bed—she had a 9:00 A.M. meeting tomorrow.

Damn, maybe Kyle's insomnia was contagious. She was bone-tired but too nervous to sleep.

She'd said something—words tumbling out without thinking—to Kyle, and now she was trying to decide if she'd really believed it.

But those things—a war, a car exploding, even a child dying—they are common enough occurrences. They're not unthinkable; indeed, there's not a parent alive who doesn't fret about something happening to one of their children.

But it wasn't an undefined "something" that had happened to Mary. No, Mary had taken her own life, slitting her wrists. Heather hadn't been expecting that, or even fearing it. It had been as shocking to her as . . . as . . . well, as what Eileen Franklin had supposedly seen, the rape and murder of her childhood friend by her own father.

But Heather hadn't walled off the memories of what had happened to Mary.

Because . . .

Because, perhaps, suicide was *not* unthinkable to her.

Not, of course, that Heather had ever contemplated taking her own life—not seriously, anyway.

No, no, that wasn't it. But suicide *had* touched her life once before in the past.

She did not often think of it.

In fact, she hadn't thought of it in years.

Had the memories been repressed? Had recent stress brought them to light?

No. Surely not. Surely she could have recalled it all at any time and had just been choosing not to.

It had been so long ago, and she had been so young. Young and foolish.

Heather had been eighteen, fresh out of high school, leaving the small town of Vegreville, Alberta, for the first time, coming halfway across the continent to giant, cosmopolitan Toronto. She'd tried so many new things that wild first year. And she'd taken an introductory astronomy course—she'd always loved the stars, crystal points above the flat prairie sky.

Heather had fallen head over heels in love with the teaching assistant, Josh Huneker. Josh was six years older, a grad student, thin, with delicate, surgeon-like hands, soulful pale-blue eyes, and the gentlest, kindest demeanor of anyone she'd ever met.

Of course, it hadn't been love—not really. But it felt something like it at the time. She'd so wanted to be loved, to be with a man, to experiment, to experience.

Josh had seemed . . . not indifferent, but ambivalent perhaps, to Heather's obvious attention. They'd met at the beginning of the academic year in September; by Canadian Thanksgiving, five weeks later, they were lovers.

And it was everything she could have hoped for. Josh was sensitive and gentle and caring, and afterward, he would talk with her for hours—about humanity, about ecology, about whales, about rain forests, and about the future.

They'd dated off and on for much of that academic year. No commitment, though—Josh didn't seem to want one, and, truth be told, Heather didn't either. She'd been looking to broaden her experience, not to settle down.

In February, Josh had had to go away. The National Research Council of Canada operated a forty-six-meter radio telescope at Lake Traverse in Algonquin Park, a huge area of untamed forest and Precambrian shield in northern Ontario. Josh was slated to spend a week there, helping monitor the equipment.

And he'd gone. But the other astronomer who was there with him had gotten sick: appendicitis. An air ambulance had taken him from the telescope building to a hospital in Huntsville.

Josh had stayed on, but then snowstorms had prevented anyone from coming up to join him. He'd been alone with the giant telescope for a week, snowed in.

It shouldn't have been any problem; there'd been food and water enough for two for the entire duration of the planned stay. But when the roads finally were cleared and someone could get up to the observatory from Toronto, they found Josh dead.

He had killed himself.

Heather had had no special status; the police never notified her directly. She'd first learned about it from an article in *The Toronto Star.*

They said he'd killed himself over quarrels with his lover.

Heather had known that Josh had a roommate. She'd met Barry—a philosophy student with a closely cropped beard—several times.

But she hadn't realized just how close Josh and Barry had been, or how much of a—well, if not a pawn, certainly a complicating factor in their troubled relationship she'd been.

No, she didn't often think of that.

But no doubt it had had an impact. Perhaps she was less surprised than most mothers would be when her own daughter had turned out to have hidden demons and undisclosed issues—when her own daughter had taken her life.

And if it hadn't been a great, unthinkable shock, then she couldn't have repressed the memories of Mary's death . . . regardless of how much she wanted to.

Kilometers away, Kyle lay in bed in his one-bedroom apartment, also trying to get to sleep.

False memories.

Or repressed memories.

Was there anything in his life that had been so traumatic, so painful, that if he could, he would have shut out its memory?

Of course there was.

Becky's accusation.

Mary's suicide.

The two worst things that had ever happened to him.

Yes, if repression were possible, surely he'd repress those.

Unless—unless, as Heather said, even they weren't sufficiently unthinkable to trigger the suppression mechanism.

He racked his brain, trying to recall other examples of things he might have suppressed. He was conscious of what an impossible task that was: trying to remember things that he wouldn't allow himself to remember.

But then it hit him—something from his childhood. Something he'd never conceived of. Something that had cost him his faith in God.

Kyle had been brought up in Canada's United Church, an easygoing Protestant denomination. But he'd drifted away from it over the years and today was seen in a hall of worship only when weddings or funerals required it. Oh, in moments of quiet reflection, he thought there might be some sort of Creator, but ever since that day when he was fifteen, he had been unable to believe in the benevolent God his church had preached.

Kyle's parents were out for the evening, and he had decided to stay up as long as he could. He didn't get to play with the remote when his father was home, but now he was flipping channels madly, hoping for something titillating on late-night TV. Still, when he came across a nature documentary, he paused. You never knew when some topless African woman was going to wander into the scene.

He saw a female lion stalking a herd of zebras beside a water hole. The lion's tawny hide was almost invisible in the tall yellow grasses. There were hundreds of zebras, but she was interested only in the animals at the margin. The narrator spoke in hushed tones, like the commentator on his dad's golf shows, as if words added long after the footage was shot could somehow disturb the unfolding of the scene. "The lioness looks for a straggler," he said. "She wants to pick out a weak member of the herd."

Kyle sat up; this was much more vivid than the ancient, grainy *Wild Kingdom* episodes he'd seen before.

The lion continued to stalk. The background noises consisted of zebra hooves falling on baked earth, the rustling of grass, the calls of birds, and the droning of insects. The shadows were short, hugging the animals' legs like shy toddlers clutching their parents.

Suddenly the lion surged forward, legs pumping, mouth hanging wide open. She leaped onto a zebra's haunch, biting deeply into it. The other zebras began to gallop away, clouds of dust rising in their wake, the footfalls like thunder. Birds wheeled into flight, squawking loudly.

The attacked animal now had stripes of red running between its black and white ones. It fell to its knees, propelled down by the impact of the lion. The blood mixed with the parched soil, forming a maroon-colored mud. The lion was hungry, or at least thirsty, and it bit deeply into the zebra's flesh again, scooping out a wet mound of muscle and connective tissue. All the while, the zebra's head continued to move and its eyelids beat up and down.

The poor thing was alive, thought Kyle. It's bleeding all over the savannah, it's about to be eaten, and it's still alive.

A zebra. Genus *Equus*, they'd said in science class. Just like a horse.

Kyle had done some riding at summer camp. He knew how intelligent horses were, how sensitive they were, how *feeling* they were. A zebra couldn't be that different. The animal had to be in agony, had to be panicked, had to be terrified.

And it hit him. Fifteen years old, it hit him like a ton of bricks.

It wasn't just this zebra, of course. It was almost all zebras— and Thomson's gazelles and wildebeests and giraffes.

And it wasn't just Africa.

It was almost all prey animals anywhere in the world.

Animals didn't die of old age. They didn't quietly expire after long, pleasant lives. They didn't pass on unaided.

No.

They were torn apart, often limb from limb, hemorrhaging severely, usually still conscious, still aware, still sensing.

Death was a horrible, vicious act, almost without exception.

Kyle's grandfather had passed away the year before. Kyle had never really thought about getting old himself, but suddenly the litany of terms he'd heard his parents bat about during Granddad's illness came back to him.

Heart disease.

Osteoporosis.

Prostate cancer.

Cataracts.

Senility.

Throughout all of history, most people had died horrible deaths, too. Humans had generally not lived long enough to experience old age; evolution, which, as he'd learned in school, had fine-tuned so much of human physiology, had simply had no opportunity to address these problems because almost no one in previous generations had lived long enough to experience them.

The zebra gutted by the lion.

The rat swallowed whole by the snake.

The paralyzed insect that felt itself being eaten alive from within by implanted larvae.

All of them surely aware of what was happening to them.

All of them tortured.

No quick deaths.

No *merciful* deaths.

Kyle had put down the remote after that, his interest in catching a glimpse of naked breasts gone. He'd gone to bed, but had lain awake for hours.

From that night on, whenever he tried to think of God, he found himself thinking instead of the zebra, its blood staining the water hole.

And to this day, try as he might, he'd been unable to repress that memory.

Heather still wasn't able to sleep. She got up off the couch, went to the closet in the bedroom and found some old photo albums; for the last ten years or so, she'd taken only filmless electronic photos, but all of her early memories were stored as prints.

She sat back down on the couch, one leg tucked up underneath her. She opened one of the albums, spread it on her lap.

The pictures were from fifteen or so years ago—the turn of the century. The old house on Merton. God, how she missed that place.

She flipped a page. The photos were under acetate, held in place by a slight adhesive on the backing sheets.

Becky's fifth birthday party—the last one they'd had in the Merton house. Balloons clinging to the wall with static electricity. Becky's friends Jasmine and Brandi—such sophisticated names for such little girls!—playing pin the tail on the donkey.

Of course, that was the party that Heather's sister, Doreen, had failed to show up at—Becky was crushed that her aunt hadn't made it. Heather was still angry about that; she'd bent over backward making a fuss for Doreen's children's birthdays, baking cakes, picking out gifts, and more. But Doreen had been too busy, begging off because some better offer had come along . . .

She turned the page again and—

Well, fancy that.

More pictures from the party.

And there was Doreen. She had shown up after all.

Heather peeled up the acetate sheet; it made a sucking sound as it pulled away from the adhesive backing. She then removed the print and read the caption she'd written on the back: "Becky's 5th B-Day." And just in case there was any doubt, there was the date printed by the photofinisher, two days after Rebecca's actual birthday.

She'd been mad at Doreen for a decade and a half over this. Doreen must have originally said she wasn't coming, but had actually shown up at the last minute. Heather had remembered the first part, but had completely forgotten the second.

But there was the photograph: Doreen crouching down next to Becky.

Photos didn't lie.

Heather exhaled.

Memory *was* an imperfect process. Of course, the photos reminded her of things. But they were also telling her things she'd never known, or had completely forgotten.

And yet, how many rolls of film had she ever shot? Maybe a couple of hundred—meaning that scattered about in photo albums and shoeboxes, there were a few thousand still frames from her life. Of course there were some home videos, too, and the electronic snapshots she'd saved to disk.

And there were diaries, and copies of old correspondence.

And little mementos and souvenirs that brought to mind events long past.

But that was it. The rest was stored nowhere else but in her fallible brain.

She closed the album. The word "Memories" was stamped in gold foil on its beige vinyl cover, but the gold was flaking off.

She looked across the room, down the hallway.

Her computer was down there; when he'd still lived here, Kyle's had been in the basement.

They had practiced safe computing. Every morning when she went to work, she had a memory wafer in her purse containing the previous night's backup of Kyle's optical drive; the drive itself was almost crash-proof, but off-site storage was the only real insurance against loss due to fire or theft. Kyle, likewise, had always taken a memory wafer to his lab with Heather's backup on it.

But what of real value was on their home computers? Financial records, all of which could be reconstructed with some effort. Correspondence, most of it utterly ephemeral. Student grades and other work-related stuff, which all could be redone, if need be.

But for the most important events of their lives, there were no backups, no archives.

Her gaze fell on the stereo cabinet. On top of it sat some framed photographs—of herself, of Kyle, of Becky, and yes, of Mary.

What had really gone on?

If only there were an archive of our memories—some infallible record of everything that had ever happened.

Irrefutable proof, one way or the other.

She closed her eyes.

If only.

9

KYLE HAD A HUGE DEMONSTRATION COMING up; it was vitally important to the continued funding of his research project. He should have been worring about that—but he wasn't. Instead, as always these days, he was preoccupied with Becky's accusation.

So far, besides Heather and Zack, he'd spoken about it with no one except Cheetah. The only person he'd confided in wasn't a person at all; he might as well have unburdened himself to Mr. Coffee.

Kyle needed to talk this over with somebody *really* human. He thought long and hard about whom he could confide in. No one in the Computer Science Department would do; he wanted to leave that pristine, except for his locked talks with Cheetah. In the months ahead, his lab might be the only haven he would know.

Mullin Hall was right next door to the Newman Centre, which housed the Roman Catholic Chaplaincy at U of T. Kyle thought briefly about speaking to the chaplain, but that wouldn't do, either. The pattern was completely different, but a cassock was black and white. Just like a zebra's hide.

And then it hit him.

The perfect person.

Kyle didn't know him well, but they'd served on three or four committees together over the years, and they'd eaten lunch together, or at least as part of the same group, in the Faculty Club from time to time.

Kyle picked up his office phone and spoke the name he wanted. "Internal directory: Bentley, Stone."

The phone bleeped, then a reedy voice came on. "Hello?"

"Stone? It's Kyle Graves."

"Who? Oh—Kyle, sure. Hi."

"Stone, I wonder if you might be free for drinks tonight."

"Uh, okay. Sure. The Faculty Club?"

"No, no. Somewhere off campus."

"How about The Water Hole, on College Street?" said Stone. "Know it?"

"I've walked past it before."

"You'll be coming from Mullin?"

"That's right."

"Stop by my office at five. Persaud Hall, Room Two Twenty-two—just like the old TV show. It's on the way."

"I'll be there."

Kyle clicked off, wondering what exactly he'd say to Stone.

Heather entered her office at U of T. It wasn't huge, but at least universities had never adopted cubicles for their academics. Normally, she shared the office with Omar Amir—another associate prof—but he spent all of July and August at his family's cottage in the Kawarthas. So, for the summer at least, she had total privacy in which to think and work. Indeed, although some of the newer offices had frosted-glass panes running floor-to-ceiling next to their thin doors, Heather and Omar's office was an old fashioned inner sanctum, with a solid wooden door that squeaked on hinges, and a window that looked east, out over the concrete courtyard between Sid Smith and St. George Street. It also had drapes, once probably a rich burgundy but now a pale brown. In the morning, they had to be drawn to shield her from the rising sun.

Yesterday's alien radio message was still displayed on her monitor. Since the interval between the beginnings of successive messages was thirty hours and fifty-one minutes, every message began almost eight hours later in the day than the one before. The most recent message had been received at 4:54 A.M., Eastern time Wednesday; today's was expected to begin at 11:45 A.M. The messages were picked up by different nations' radio telescopes, depending on what part of Earth happened to be pointing at Alpha Centauri at the appropriate time, but they were all posted as they were received to the World Wide Web. An additional orbital receiver was also always aimed at Alpha Centauri.

Heather kept hoping that one day she would look at the latest message and it would all make sense. She missed the simplicity of the first eleven messages: straightforward representations of the Pythagorean theorem and chemical formulas and planetary systems. Although, she had to admit, even those posed some puzzles: the chemicals specified by the formulas had been synthesized on Earth, but no one had ever figured out what they were for.

Heather got herself a mug of coffee and sat down to look again at yesterday's message.

As always, the message was shown as two rectangular grids. Each message was sent as a string of a hundred thousand or so binary digits, over a period of two or three hours. The total number of digits in each message was always the product of two prime numbers, meaning that the digits could be arrayed in two possible ways. According to the header from the Alien Signal Center in Karachi, Pakistan, this message was 108,197 bits long. That number was the product of the prime numbers 257 and 421, which meant that the digits could be set up either as 257 rows of 421 columns or as 421 rows of 257 columns. Sometimes one image looked more intuitively correct than the other—squares or circles would appear in one, while the alternative decoding would simply result in a mishmash. But since no one had yet determined what the messages were supposed to represent, one couldn't be certain which was really the correct interpretation.

When the messages had first started arriving in 2007, millions of people had pored over each one. But as the years had passed, the numbers had reduced. Although there was a popular screensaver that downloaded each day's message from the aliens and magnified various portions of it in turn, Heather knew there were now fewer than three hundred researchers actively analyzing each new message.

The more correct-looking version of today's message showed three rectangles and two circles in what otherwise seemed to be a random sea of black-and-white squares; the black squares represented zero bits and the white squares represented ones. Heather stared at it, frustrated. She felt sure she had to be missing something simple. Somewhere in the hundreds of millions of bits of data already received from Alpha Centauri there must have been a Rosetta stone—a key that would let all the other messages make sense.

There were dissenting views: one researcher in Portugal had long argued that the key would come as the *final* message, not as one of the initial ones; that way, the aliens would automatically weed out any races that lacked the patience required for interstellar communication. And others had opined that the alien senders were simply *too* alien—that we were incapable of communicating. A third camp argued that humanity simply wasn't bright enough, or advanced enough, to figure out what was being said. The aliens might indeed still be on what they considered basics, but the material had already gone over the collective head of humanity.

Heather was a Jungian psychologist. She believed that all human minds shared a vocabulary of symbols and archetypes that formed the underpinnings of thought. The Centaurs, she felt sure, simply had a different set of underlying metaphors and symbols, and if she could figure out what those were, she could crack the code.

She took a sip of coffee. This message was as baffling as the others. Maybe it was all a giant crossword puzzle, she thought. The grids of black-and-white squares certainly suggested that, although filling in the blanks was a human concept, possibly— if she could wax Freudian for a moment—related to our sexual biology. Still, it wasn't the first time she'd wondered if the messages might be deliberately incomplete—yin, but no yang— and the aliens were waiting for humanity to provide the complement, to make it all whole.

But, of course, we hadn't yet replied at all; another popular interpretation was that the Rosetta stone was being withheld until humanity *did* reply.

There's an old concept in SETI that said that signals would likely be sent at a group of frequencies called "the water hole"—between the emission frequency for hydrogen, at 1420 megahertz, and for hydroxyl, at 1667 megahertz. Hydrogen (H) and hydroxyl (OH) are the components of water (H_2O), and Earth's atmosphere is most transparent to radio waves at that range of frequencies, while interstellar space is largely free of interference there. Since all life as we know it began in water, this area of the spectrum seemed a natural gathering place for those species looking to undertake interstellar communications.

But the Centauri signals weren't anywhere near the water hole—another example of what we expected to be a shared view of reality not turning out to be shared at all.

Could there, Heather wondered, be other water holes—other common grounds that would have to be shared by any being that existed in the same universe we did, regardless of its biology or the nature of its planet?

She was supposed to meet her friend Judy for lunch at the Faculty Club at 12:15. She'd stick around until today's message began to arrive, then head off.

Still ten minutes to go. Heather wasn't one to waste time. She had the latest issue of *The Journal of Jungian Studies* on her datapad; she started working her way through it.

After a while, the phone rang. Heather finished the paragraph in front of her, then absently reached for the handset. "Hello?"

"Heather? Did you forget?"

Heather glanced at her watch. "Oh, God! Sorry, Judy!" She looked over at her computer. "I was waiting for today's message—I was going to leave as soon as the incoming-message signal sounded." She moved over to her computer and told it to go directly to the Alien Signal Center homepage. Nothing.

"Judy, I can't make it. The alien message is late today."

"Are you sure you've got the right time?"

"Positive. Look, I've got to go. Maybe lunch tomorrow?"

"Sure, I'll call you."

"Thanks." Heather replaced the handset. As soon as she did, the phone rang again. She picked it up. "Hello?"

"Heather," said a different female voice, "it's Salme van Horne."

"Salme! Where are you? Here in Canada?"

"No, I'm still in Helsinki. Have you tried to download today's message?"

"Yes. There doesn't seem to be one coming through."

"This has never happened before, has it? The Centaurs have never missed a day, have they?"

"Never. They've never even been late."

"Do you suppose the problem is at our end?" asked Salme. "Whose turn is it to receive the message?"

"Arecibo is designated prime, isn't it? But there are backups, and—oh, wait. Something's going up on the Web page."

"I see it, too."

"Damn holograms—ah, here it is: 'No technical malfunction at receiving end. Apparently no message was sent.' "

"That can't be the end of the transmissions," said Salme. "There has to be a key."

"Maybe they got tired of waiting for us to reply," said Heather. "Maybe they won't send again until we *do* reply."

"Or maybe—"

"What?" asked Heather.

"Drake equation, final term."

Heather was quiet for a moment. "Oh," she said softly.

The Drake equation estimated the number of radio-broadcasting civilizations in the galaxy. It had seven terms:

$$R_* f_p \, n_e f_l f_i f_c \, L$$

The rate of star formation, times the fraction of stars with planets, times the number of those planets that are suitable for life, times the fraction of such planets on which life actually appears, times the fraction of life forms that are intelligent, times the fraction of such life forms that actually develop radio, times . . .

Times big L: the lifetime of such a civilization.

A civilization that had radio probably also had nuclear weapons, or other equally dangerous things.

Civilizations could be wiped out in a matter of moments—certainly in less than a single thirty-one-hour day.

"They can't be dead," said Salme.

"They're either dead, or they voluntarily stopped, or the message is complete."

There was a knock at the door. Heather covered the mouthpiece. "Come in!"

The departmental assistant stuck his head in. "Sorry to bother you, Professor Davis, but the CBC is on the phone. They want to talk to you about what happened to the aliens."

10

KYLE'S LAB WAS CROWDED. THE DEAN LEANED against one wall, the department chair had his butt perched on the shelf jutting out of the bottom of Cheetah's console, a lawyer from the university's patent unit sat in Kyle's usual chair, and the five grad students who worked on Kyle's quantum-computing team were milling around as well.

"Okay," said Kyle to the group. "As you know, there's been a technique available since nineteen ninety-six for producing simple quantum-logic gates; that technique was based on using nuclear magnetic resonance to measure atomic spins. But it was hampered by the fact that as you added bits, the output signal got exponentially weaker: a thirty-bit quantum computer based on that principle produces output only one-billionth as strong as that from a one-bit computer based on the same technique.

"Well, the method we're going to demonstrate today is, we believe, the long-sought-after breakthrough: a quantum computer that, in theory, can employ an unlimited number of bits with no reduction in output quality. For our demo today, we're going to try to factor a randomly generated three-hundred-digit number. To do that on the department's ECB-5000 would take approximately one hundred years of constant calculation. If we're right—if this works—we'll have an answer about thirty seconds after I commence the experiment."

He moved across the room.

"Our prototype quantum computer, which we call Democritus, has not just thirty registers, but *one thousand,* each of which consists of a single atom. The results will be a series of interference patterns, which another computer—that one over there—will analyze and reduce to a numeric readout." He looked from face to face. "All set? Let's go."

Kyle walked over to the simple black console containing the Democritus computer. For the sake of drama, they'd built a large knife switch, worthy of Frankenstein's lab, into the side of the cabinet. Kyle pulled it down, its blade touching the metal contacts. A bright red LED came on and—

—and everyone held their breath. Kyle kept watching Democritus, which, of course, was operating absolutely silently. Part of him missed the old days of clicking relays. Others were watching the digital clock mounted next to the red EXIT sign on the curving wall.

Ten seconds went by.

Then ten more.

Then a final ten.

And then the LED went dark.

Kyle let out his breath.

"Done," he said, heart pounding.

He gestured for everyone to follow him across the room. There, another computer was analyzing the output from Democritus.

"It'll take about five minutes to decode the interference pattern," said Kyle. He allowed himself a smile. "If you're thinking that that's a lot longer than it took to produce the pattern, you're right—but we're now dealing with a conventional computer."

"How many computations would it take to factor a number that big?" asked the dean, her voice clearly intrigued.

"Approximately ten to the five hundredth," said Kyle.

"And there's no way to do it in fewer steps?" she asked. "This isn't a case of Democritus taking a shortcut?"

Kyle shook his head. "No, it really does take ten to the five hundredth steps to factor a number that big."

"But Democritus didn't do that many steps."

"*This* Democritus didn't—in fact, it performed only one calculation, using a thousand atoms as the stones in its abacus, so to speak, to do so. But if all went well, 10^{500} other Democrituses in other universes will also each have done one calculation—involving, of course, a total of a thousand times 10^{500} atoms, which is 10^{503} atoms. And that, my friends, is a very significant number."

"How so?" asked the department chair.

"Well, the precise value isn't important. What *is* important is how it relates to the number of atoms in our entire universe." Kyle smiled, waiting for the inevitable question.

"And how many atoms are there in our universe?" asked the dean.

"I called up Holtz over in the McLennan Physical Labs and asked her," said Kyle. "The answer, plus or minus a couple of orders of magnitude, is that there are ten to the eightieth atoms in the universe."

A few jaws dropped.

"Do you see?" said Kyle. "In that thirty-second period, to factor our test number, Democritus must have accessed many trillions of times more atoms than there are in our entire universe. Other, earlier quantum-computing demonstrations have never involved enough bits to actually exceed the quantity of atoms available to them in our universe, leaving open some doubt as to whether they'd actually accessed parallel worlds, but if this experiment works, the *only* answer will be that our Democritus worked in tandem with computers in other universes."

The conventional computer they were standing in front of beeped and one of its monitors came to life. Precisely two strings of numbers appeared on the screen, each dozens of digits long.

"Are those the first two factors?" asked the lawyer, clearly anxious to start notarizing things.

Kyle felt his heart sink. "Ah, no. No." He swallowed; his stomach was roiling. "I mean, yes, certainly, they are doubtless factors of our source number, but—but . . ."

One of Kyle's grad students looked at him and then said the words that, at that moment, Kyle himself couldn't get out. "The display shouldn't have appeared until all the factors are ready. Unless by some miracle, the source number has only two factors, then the experiment didn't work."

The department head loomed in at the screen and placed his index finger on the last digit of the second number; it was a four. "That's an even number, so there have got to be smaller factors that aren't displayed." He straightened up. "What went wrong?"

Kyle was shaking his head. "It worked—sort of. Our Democritus did do only one calculation. The other number *must* have come from a parallel universe."

"You can't prove that," said the dean. "Only two calculations means that only two thousand atoms were involved."

"I know," said Kyle. He breathed out. "Sorry, everyone. We'll keep working on it."

The dean frowned, presumably thinking of all the money that had already been spent. She left the room. The department head laid a hand briefly on Kyle's slumped shoulder before he, too, left, followed by the lawyer.

Kyle looked at his grad students and shrugged. Nothing was going his way these days . . .

After the students went home, Kyle sat down in his chair in front of Cheetah's console.

"I'm sorry," said Cheetah.

"Yeah," said Kyle. He shook his head. "It should have worked."

"I'm confident you'll figure out what went wrong."

"I suppose." He looked up at the print of "Christus Hypercubus." "But maybe it'll never work; researchers have been trying to accomplish this for over twenty years without success." He dropped his gaze to the floor. "I just keep wasting my time on projects that never bear fruit."

"Like me," said Cheetah, without rancor.

Kyle said nothing.

"I have faith in you," said Cheetah.

Kyle made a sound in his throat, a laugh aborted.

"What?"

"I dunno. Maybe that's the whole problem. Maybe it's my lack of faith."

"You mean God is punishing you for being an atheist?"

Kyle did laugh, but it was humorless. "Not that kind of faith. I mean my faith in quantum physics." He paused. "When I was a grad student, nothing excited me like quantum mechanics— it was mind-expanding, endlessly fascinating. But I felt sure that someday it would all *click*, you know—all make sense. Someday I'd really see. But I never have. Oh, I understand the equations in an abstract way, but I don't get it, you know? Maybe I don't even really believe it."

"You've lost me," said Cheetah.

Kyle spread his arms, trying to find a way to explain it. "I was at a party once, and this fat guy comes in, and he's got a slice through a geode held to his forehead by a headband. I never asked about it—guy comes in with something like that, you don't ask. But his companion, a scrawny woman, must have noticed me looking at the geode, so she comes over and says, 'That's Cory—he's gifted with the third eye.' And I'm thinking, Good Christ, let me out of here. Later, Cory comes up to me and says, 'Hey, man, what time is it?' And I'm thinking what good is the third eye if you don't even know what fucking *time* it is?"

Cheetah was quiet for a while. "And your point would be . . . ?"

"My point is that maybe you *do* need some special insight to understand—really, deeply understand—quantum mechanics. Einstein never did, you know; he was never comfortable with it, calling it 'spooky action at a distance.' But some of these guys in quantum mechanics, they *do* get it—either that or they fake it really well. Me, I always thought I'd be one of those who'd get it, too—that it *would* click at some point. But it hasn't. I never developed the third eye."

"Maybe you should get a geode slice from the Earth Sciences Centre."

Kyle grunted. "Maybe. I guess down deep, at some basic level, I just don't buy quantum mechanics. I feel like a bit of a charlatan."

"Democritus did indeed communicate with at least one other alternative reality. That seems to confirm the many-worlds interpretation."

Kyle looked at Cheetah's lenses. "That's it," he said simply. "That's the problem. This type of quantum computing hinges on the many-worlds interpretation, but, come on, really, how plausible is that? Surely not every conceivable universe exists, but rather only the ones that have at least some likelihood of having occurred."

"For instance?" asked Cheetah.

"Well," said Kyle, "there's no recorded case of anyone ever

being killed by a meteor falling on them, but it *could* happen. So, is there a universe in which I was killed that way yesterday? Another one in which I was killed that way the day before? A third in which I was killed that way the day before that? A fourth, fifth, and sixth in which it was my brother, not me, who was killed? A seventh, eighth, and ninth in which both of us were killed on those days by meteor impacts?"

Cheetah did not hesitate. "No."

"Why not?"

"Because meteors have no volition—in every universe, precisely the same meteors hit the Earth."

"All right," said Kyle, "but say one crashes today in—I don't know—say in Antarctica. Now, I've never been to Antarctica, and I never intend to go there, but is there some parallel universe in which I did go, and in which I happened to be killed by that meteor? And then aren't there seven billion times as many universes, accounting for all the people alive who might instead have gone to Antarctica?"

"It does seem rather an awful lot of parallel universes, doesn't it?" said Cheetah.

"Exactly. In which case there must be some sort of filtration process—something that distinguishes between conceivable universes and plausible ones, between those that we simply can imagine and those that have some reasonable chance of actually existing. That could explain why we only got one other factor back in the experiment."

"I suppose you're right and—oh."

"What?" said Kyle.

"I see what you're getting at."

Kyle was surprised; he wasn't sure he himself knew what he was getting at. "And that is?"

"The ethics of the many-worlds interpretation."

Kyle considered. "You know, I guess you're right. Say I find a wallet that contains an unlocked SmartCash card with a thousand dollars on it. Say the wallet also has a driver's license in it; I've got the rightful owner's name and address right there."

Cheetah had a cross-shaped pattern of LEDs on his console. He could activate the vertical column of them or the horizontal row to simulate either nodding or shaking his head. He did his nod.

"Well," said Kyle, "according to the many-worlds interpretation, anything that can possibly go two ways *does* go two ways. There's a universe in which I return the money to the person who lost it, but there's also a universe in which I keep it for myself. Now, if there are bound to be two universes, then why the heck *shouldn't* I be the guy who keeps the money?"

"An intriguing question, and without impugning your character, such a dilemma does seem within the realm of possibility. But I suspect your moral concerns run deeper: I suspect you're wondering about you and Rebecca. Even if in this universe you didn't molest her, you're wondering if there is some conceivable universe in which you *did*."

Kyle slumped back in his chair. Cheetah was right. For once, the goddamned machine was right.

It was an insidious thing, the human mind. The mere accusation was enough to get it working, even against itself.

And *was* there such a universe? A universe where he really could creep into his own daughter's room after midnight and do those horrible things to her?

Not here, of course. Not in *this* universe. But in another one— one, perhaps, where he hadn't got tenure, where his control over life had slipped away, where he drank more than he should, where he and Heather were still fighting to keep the wolf from the door—or where they had divorced early on, or he was a widower, and his own sexuality was finding no normal outlet.

Could such a universe exist? Could Becky's memories, although false in this universe, be a true reflection of another reality? Could she now have access, through some quantum aberration, to those memories from a parallel world, just as a quantum computer accesses information from other timelines?

Or was the very notion that he'd abuse his daughter utterly outlandish, impossible, unthinkable—a meteor conking him on the head in the Antarctic?

Kyle stood up and did something he'd never done before. He lied to Cheetah.

"No," he said. "No, you're completely wrong about that."

He left the lab, the lights shutting off automatically as he did so.

Maybe, some thought, the Centaurs had simply skipped one day for a holiday on their homeworld, or to indicate some sort of punctuation in the overall message. If that were the case, the next message would come in at 6:36 P.M. the following day, Friday, July 28.

Heather had spent much of the thirty-one intervening hours dealing with reporters; overnight, the alien messages had gone from being of no general interest to front-page news worldwide. And now the CBC was doing a live remote feed from Heather's office.

The news crew had provided a large digital clock, which was attached to the top of Heather's monitor with masking tape. They'd brought three cameras: one was kept trained on Heather, another on the clock, and the third on her monitor screen.

The clock was counting down. It was now two minutes to the scheduled time for the next message.

"Professor Davis," said the black female reporter, who had a pleasant Jamaican accent, "what are you thinking? What are you feeling as we wait for another message from the stars?"

Heather had done five other TV appearances over the last thirty-one hours, but she'd yet to come up with an answer she was happy with. "I don't really know," she said, trying to follow the reporter's instruction not to look directly into the camera. "I feel like I've lost a friend. I never did know what he was saying, but he was there, every day. I could count on him. I could trust him. And now that's shattered."

As she said that, she wondered if Kyle was watching.

"Twenty seconds," said the reporter.

Heather turned to look at the computer monitor.

"Fifteen."

She raised her left hand, fingers crossed.

"Ten."

It couldn't be finished.

"Nine."

It couldn't have come to an end.

"Eight."

Not after all this time.

"Seven."

Not after a decade.

"Six."

Not without an answer.

"Five."

Not without the key.

"Four."

Not with it still remaining a mystery.

"Three."

Her heart was pounding.

"Two."

She closed her eyes and astonished herself to find that she was thinking a silent prayer.

"One."

Heather opened her eyes, focused on the screen.

"Zero."

Nothing. It was over.

11

HEATHER PUSHED THE DOOR BUZZER OUT-
side Kyle's lab. There was no response. She touched her thumb
to the scanning plate, wondering for a moment whether he'd
delisted her from the index. But the door slid aside, and she entered the lab.

"Is that you, Professor Davis?"

"Oh, hello, Cheetah."

"It's been some time since you've dropped by. It's good to
see you."

"Thanks. Is Kyle around?"

"He had to go down to Professor Montgomery's office; he
said he would be back shortly."

"Thanks. I'll wait, if that's— Good grief, what's that?"

"What's what?" asked Cheetah.

"That poster. It's Dali, isn't it?" The style was unmistakable,
but it was a Dali she'd never seen before: a painting of Jesus
nailed to a most unusual cross.

"That's right," said Cheetah. "Dr. Graves says it's been ex-
hibited under several names, but it's best known as 'Christus
Hypercubus.' Christ on the hypercube."

"What's a hypercube?"

"That is," said Cheetah. "Well, actually it's not a real hypercube. Rather, it's an unfolded one." One of the monitors on Cheetah's angled console lit up. "Here's another picture of one." The screen displayed this:

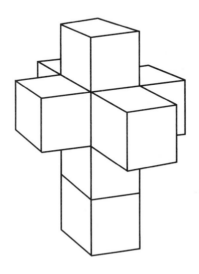

"But what the heck is it?" asked Heather.

"A hypercube is a four-dimensional cube. It's sometimes also called a tesseract."

"What did you mean a moment ago when you said it was 'unfolded'?"

Cheetah's lenses whirred. "That's an intriguing question, actually. Dr. Graves has told me about hypercubes. He uses them in his first-year computing class; he says it helps students learn to visualize problems in a new way." Cheetah's cameras swiveled as he looked around the room. "See that box on the shelf there?"

Heather followed Cheetah's line of sight. She nodded.

"Pick it up."

Heather shrugged a little, then did so.

"Now that's a cube," said Cheetah. "Use your fingernail to pull the tab out of the slot. See it?"

Heather nodded again. She did as Cheetah asked, and the box started to come apart. She continued to unfold it, then laid it out on the tabletop: six squares forming a cross—four in a row, plus two sticking off the sides of the third one.

"A cross," said Heather.

Cheetah's LEDs nodded. "Of course, it doesn't have to be—there are eleven fundamentally different ways you can unfold a cube, including into a T shape and an S shape. Well, not *that* cube—it's cut and scored for unfolding in that particular way. Anyway, that's an unfolded cube—a flat, two-dimensional plan that can be folded through the third dimension to make a cube." Cheetah's eyes swiveled back toward the Dali painting. "The cross in the painting consists of eight cubes—four making the vertical shaft, and four more making the two mutually perpendicular sets of arms. That's an unfolded tesseract: a three-dimensional plan that could be folded through the fourth dimension to make a hypercube."

"Folded how? In what direction?"

"As I said, through the fourth dimension, which is perpendicular to the other three, just as height, length, and width are perpendicular to each other. In fact, there are *two* ways to fold up a hypercube, just as you could fold that two-dimensional piece of cardboard either up or down—up resulting in the shiny, white side of the cardboard making up the outside, and down resulting in the dull, plain side making up the outside. All dimensions have two directions: length has left and right; depth has forward and backward; height has up and down. And the fourth dimension, it has *ana* and *kata*."

"Why those terms?"

"*Ana* is Greek for up; *kata* is Greek for down."

"So if you fold a group of eight cubes like those in the Dali painting in the *kata* direction, it makes a hypercube?"

"Yes. Or in the *ana* direction."

"Fascinating," said Heather. "And Kyle finds this kind of thinking helps his students?"

"He thinks so. He had a professor named Papineau when he was a student here twenty years ago—"

"I remember him."

"Well, Dr. Graves says he doesn't recall much of what Papineau taught him, except that he was always finding ways to expand his students' minds, giving them new ways of looking at things. He is trying to do something similar for his students today, and—"

The door slid open. Kyle walked in. "Heather!" he said, clearly surprised. "What are you doing here?"

"Waiting for you."

Without a word, Kyle reached over and flicked Cheetah's SUSPEND switch. "What brings you by?"

"The alien messages have stopped."

"So I'd heard. Was there a Rosetta stone at the end?"

Heather shook her head.

"I'm sorry," said Kyle.

"Me, too. But it means the race for the answer is on; we now have everything the Centaurs were trying to say to us. Now it's only a question of time before somebody figures out what it all means. I'm going to be very busy." She spread her arms slightly. "I know this couldn't have come at a worse time, what with the problem with Becky, but I'm going to have to immerse myself in this. I wanted you to understand that—I didn't want you to think I was shutting you out, or just sticking my head in the sand, hoping the problem would go away."

"I'm going to be busy, too," said Kyle.

"Oh?"

"My quantum-computing experiment failed; I've got a lot of work to do figuring out what went wrong."

Under other circumstances, she might have consoled him. But now, now with this between them, with the uncertainty . . .

"That's too bad," she said. "Really." She looked at him a little longer, then shrugged a bit. "So it looks like we're both going to be tied up." She paused. Dammit, their separation was never supposed to be permanent—and, for Christ's sake, surely Kyle couldn't have done what he'd been accused of. "Look," she said, tentatively, "it's almost five; do you want to grab an early dinner?"

Kyle looked pleased at the suggestion, but then he frowned. "I've already made other plans."

"Oh," said Heather. She wondered for a moment whether his plans were with a man or a woman. "Well, then."

They looked at each other a moment longer, then Heather left.

Kyle entered Persaud Hall and headed down the narrow corridor, but stopped short before he got to Room 222.

There was Stone Bentley, standing outside his office, talking with a female student. Stone was white, maybe fifty-five, balding, and not particularly fit; he saw Kyle approaching and signaled him to wait for a short time. Stone finished up whatever he was saying to the young lady, then she smiled and went on her way.

Kyle closed the distance. "Hi, Stone. Sorry to interrupt."

"No, not at all. I like being interrupted during meetings."

Kyle tilted his head; Stone's voice hadn't sounded sarcastic, but the words certainly seemed to be.

"I'm serious," said Stone. "I have all my meetings with female students in the corridor—and the more people that see what's going on, the better. I don't ever want a repeat of what happened five years ago."

"Ah," said Kyle. Stone ducked into his office, grabbed his briefcase, and they headed out to The Water Hole. It was a small pub, with perhaps two dozen round tables scattered across a hardwood floor. Lighting was from Tiffany lamps; the windows were covered over by thick drapes. An electronic board displayed specials in white against a black background in a font that resembled chalk writing; a neon sign advertised Moosehead beer.

A server drifted into view. "Blue Light," said Stone.

"Rye and ginger ale," said Kyle.

Once the server was gone, Stone turned his attention to Kyle; they'd made small talk on the way over, but now, it was clear. Stone felt it was time to get to the reason for the meeting. "So," he said, "what's on your mind?"

Kyle had been mentally rehearsing this all afternoon, but now that the moment was here, he found himself rejecting his planned words. "I—I've got a problem, Stone. I—I needed somebody to talk to. I know we've never been close, but I've always thought of you as a friend."

Stone looked at him, but said nothing.

"I'm sorry," said Kyle. "I know you're busy. I shouldn't be bothering you."

Stone was quiet for a moment, then: "What's wrong?"

Kyle dropped his gaze. "My daughter has . . ." He fell silent, but Stone simply waited for him to go on. At last, Kyle felt ready to do so. "My daughter has accused me of molesting her."

He waited for the question he'd expected: "Did you do it?" But the question never came.

"Oh," said Stone.

Kyle couldn't stand the question not being addressed. "I didn't do it."

Stone nodded.

The server appeared again, depositing their drinks.

Kyle looked down at his glass, the rye swirling in the ginger ale. He waited again for Stone to volunteer that he understood the connection, understood why Kyle had called him, of all people. But Stone didn't.

"You've been through something like this yourself," said Kyle. "False accusation."

Stone's turn to look away. "That was years ago."

"How do you deal with it?" asked Kyle. "How do you make it go away?"

"You're here," said Stone. "You thought of me. Doesn't that prove it? This shit never goes away."

Kyle took a sip of his drink. The bar was smoke-free, of course, but still the atmosphere seemed oppressive, choking. He looked at Stone. "I *am* innocent," he said, feeling the need to assert it again.

"Do you have any other children?" asked Stone.

"We did. My older daughter Mary killed herself a little over a year ago."

Stone frowned. "Oh."

"I know what you're thinking. We don't know for sure why yet, but, well, we suspect a therapist might have given both girls false memories."

Stone took a sip of his beer. "So what are you going to do now?" he said.

"I don't know. I've lost one daughter; I don't want to lose the other."

The evening wore on. Stone and Kyle continued to drink, the conversation got less serious, and Kyle, at last, found himself relaxing.

"I hate what's happened to television," said Stone.

Kyle lifted his eyebrows.

"I'm teaching one summer course," said Stone. "I mentioned Archie Bunker in class yesterday. All I got were blank stares."

"Yeah?"

"Yeah. Kids today, they don't know the classics. *I Love Lucy, All in the Family, Barney Miller, Seinfeld, The Pellatt Show.* They don't know any of them."

"Even *Pellatt* is going back ten years," said Kyle gently. "We're just getting old."

"*No,*" said Stone. "No, that's not it at all."

Kyle's gaze lifted slightly to Stone's bald pate, then shifted left and right, observing the snowy fringe around it.

Stone didn't seem to notice. He raised a hand, palm out. "I know what you're thinking. You're thinking it's just that kids today, they watch different shows, and I'm just some old fart who's out of it." He shook his head. "But that's not it. Well, no, actually I guess that *is* it, in a way—the first part, I mean. They do watch different shows. They *all* watch different shows. A thousand channels to choose from, from all over the damned world, plus all the desktop-TV shit being produced out of people's homes coming in over the net."

He took a swig of beer. "You know how much Jerry Seinfeld got for the last season of *Seinfeld,* back in 1997–98? A million bucks an episode—U.S. bucks, too! That's 'cause half the bloody world was watching him. But these days, everybody's watching something different." He looked down into his mug. "They don't make shows like *Seinfeld* anymore."

Kyle nodded. "It *was* a good program."

"They were *all* good programs. And not just the sitcoms. Dramas, too. *Hill Street Blues. Perry Mason. Colorado Springs.* But nobody knows them anymore."

"You do. I do."

"Oh, sure. Guys from our generation, guys who grew up in the twentieth century. But kids today—they've got no culture. No shared background." He took another sip of beer. "Marshall was wrong, you know." Marshall McLuhan had been dead for thirty-seven years, but many members of the U of T community still referred to him as "Marshall," the prof who put U of T on the worldwide map. "He said the new media were remaking the world into a global village. Well, the global village has been balkanized." Stone looked at Kyle. "Your wife, she teaches Jung, right? So she's into archetypes and all that shit? Well, nobody shares anything anymore. And without shared culture, civilization is doomed."

"Maybe," said Kyle.

"It's true," said Stone. He took another sip of beer. "You know what really bugs me, though?"

Kyle lifted his eyebrows again.

"Quincy's first name. That's what bugs me."

"Quincy?"

"You know—from the TV series: *Quincy, M.E.* Remember it? Jack Klugman was in it, after *The Odd Couple.* Played a coroner in L.A."

"Sure. A&E had it on every bloody day when I was in university."

"What was Quincy's first name?"

"He didn't have one."

" 'Course he did. Everybody has one. I'm Stone, you're Kyle."

"Actually, Kyle's my middle name. My first name is Brian—Brian Kyle Graves."

"No shit? Well, it doesn't matter. Point is, you *do* have a first name—and so must Quincy."

"I don't recall them ever mentioning it in the TV series."

"Oh, yes they did. Every time someone called him 'Quince'—that's not a shortening of his last name. That's a shortening of his first name."

"You're saying his name was Quincy Quincy? What kind of a name is that?"

"A perfectly good one."

"You're just guessing."

"No. No, I can prove it. In the final episode, Quincy gets married. You know what the minister says who's performing the service? 'Do you, Quincy, take . . .' Ain't no way he'd say that if it wasn't the guy's *first* name."

"Yeah, but who has the same first and last name?"

"You're not thinking, Kyle. Biggest hit TV series of all time, one of the main characters had the same first and last name."

"Spock Spock?" said Kyle, deadpan.

"No, no, no. *I Love Lucy.*"

"Lucy's last name was Ricardo." And then Kyle brightened. "And her maiden name was McGillicuddy." He folded his arms, quite pleased with himself.

"But what about her husband?"

"Who? Ricky?"

"Ricky Ricardo."

"That's not—"

"Oh, yes it is. No way his real first name was Ricky. He was Cuban; his first name had to be Ricardo: Ricardo Ricardo."

"Oh, come on. Surely, then, 'Ricky' was a nickname based on his last name—like calling a guy named John MacTavish 'Mac.' "

"No, it was his first name. Remember, even though they had separate beds, Lucy and Ricky still managed to have a baby. They named him after his father—'Little Ricky,' they called him. Well, nobody calls a baby 'Little Mac.' The father was Ricardo Ricardo, and the kid had to be Ricardo Ricardo, Jr."

Kyle shook his head. "You think about the damnedest stuff, Stone."

Stone frowned. "You gotta think about stuff, Kyle. If you don't keep your mind busy, the shit takes over."

Kyle was quiet for several seconds. "Yeah," he said, then signaled the server to bring him another drink.

More time passed; more alcohol was consumed.

"You think *that's* weird," Kyle said. "You want to hear weird?

I lived in a house with three women—my wife, my two daughters. And you know, they ended up *synchronized*. I tell ya, Stone, that can be brutal. It was like walking on eggshells for a week out of every month."

Stone laughed. "Must have been rough."

"It's strange, though. I mean, how does that happen? It's like—I dunno—it's like they communicate somehow, on a higher level, in a way we can't see."

"It's probably pheromones," said Stone, frowning sagely.

"It's spooky, whatever it is. Like something right out of *Star Trek.*"

"*Star Trek,*" said Stone dismissively. He polished off his fourth beer. "Don't talk to me about *Star Trek!*"

"It was better than fucking *Quincy,*" said Kyle.

" 'Course it was, but it was never consistent. Now, if all the writers had been women and they'd all lived together, maybe everything would have been in sync."

"What're you talking about? I've got lots of the background stuff—models, blueprints, tech manuals; I was quite a Trekker right up through my university years. I've never seen such attempts at making things consistent."

"Yeah, but they ignored stuff all the time."

"Like what?"

"Well, let's see. What's your single favorite incarnation of *Trek?*"

"I dunno. The movie *Wrath of Khan,* I suppose."

"Good choice. That's Ricardo Montalban's real chest, you know."

"No way," said Kyle.

"It is, honest. Great pecs for a man his age. Anyway, let's set aside the obvious stuff—like Khan recognizing Chekov, even though Chekov wasn't in the TV series at the time that Khan was introduced. No, let's poke holes in your vaunted tech manuals. On the upper and lower faces of the movie *Enterprise*'s saucer section, there are little yellow patches near the rim. The blueprints say those are attitude-control thrusters. Well, near the end of the film, Shatner orders the ship to drop 'zee minus ten thousand meters'—God, I hate to hear a good Canadian boy saying 'zee' instead of 'zed.' Anyway, the ship does just that—but the thrusters never light up."

"Oh, I'm sure they wouldn't make a mistake like that," said Kyle. "They were very careful."

"Check it yourself. Do you have the chip?"

"Yeah, my daughter Mary gave me a boxed set of the original *Trek* films a few years ago for Christmas."

"Go ahead, check. You'll see."

The next day—Tuesday, August 1, 2017—Kyle called Heather and got her permission to come by the house that night.

When he arrived, Heather let him in. He went straight to the living room and started scanning the bookshelves.

"What on earth are you looking for?" asked Heather.

"My copy of *Star Trek II*."

"Is that the one with the whales?"

"No, that's *IV*—*II* is the one with Khan."

"Oh, yeah." Heather held her fist in front of her face, as if gripping a communicator, and shouted in her best imitation of William Shatner, *"Khannnnn!"* She pointed. "It's in the bookcase over there."

Kyle sprinted across the room and found the DVC he was looking for. "Do you mind?" he said, indicating the TV hanging on the wall. Heather shook her head, and he slipped the chip into the player, then sat down on the couch opposite the screen. He found the remote and jammed his finger against the fast-forward button.

"What are you looking for?" asked Heather.

"This guy I know in Anthropology said there's a mistake in

the film: a shot where some thrusters should be firing but they don't actually light up."

Heather smiled indulgently. "Let me get this straight. You bought that bit about the Genesis Wave that can turn a lifeless hunk of rock into a fully formed ecosystem in a matter of hours, but you're bothered by whether the *thrusters* light up?"

"*Shh,*" said Kyle. "We're almost there."

The bridge doors hiss open. Chekov walks in, with a bandage on his ear. The crew looks at him precisely the way you should look at someone who recently had an alien parasite crawl out of his head. He takes the weapons station. The pan following Chekov reveals Uhura, Sulu, Saavik, Kirk, and Spock—all wearing those red serge uniforms that make them look like Mounties. Kirk leaves his central chair and moves over to Spock's station. They're being pursued through the Mutara nebula by Khan Noonien Singh, who has hijacked a Federation starship.

"He won't break off now," says Kirk, looking at the main viewscreen, filled with static caused by the nebula. "He followed me this far. He'll be back. But from where?"

Spock looks up from his scanner. "He's intelligent, but not experienced. His pattern indicates two-dimensional thinking." He raises his upswept eyebrows as he says "two dimensional," and he and Kirk exchange a meaningful glance, then a tight little grin appears on Kirk's face. He moves back to his command chair and points at Sulu. "Full stop."

Sulu touches controls. "Full stop, sir."

Kirk to Sulu: "Zee minus ten thousand meters." And to Chekov: "Stand by photon torpedoes."

And there it was: a shot from directly above, looking down on the *Enterprise*. Kyle had always admired the way the ships in the classic *Star Trek* movies were self-illuminating—a spotlight from the central, raised part of the saucer was lighting up the registration number NCC-1701. Directly beneath the ship was a swirling purple-and-pink maelstrom, part of the Mutara nebula.

For a second, Kyle thought Stone had been wrong—there *were* lights flashing on the edge of the saucer. But they were precisely positioned at the bow and directly to port: running lights. The starboard one wasn't working, which Kyle thought *was* admirable attention to detail, since that side of the ship had been damaged earlier in battle.

But—damn, Stone was right. The four clusters of ACS thrusters were clearly visible on the upper surface of the saucer section, each one offset forty-five degrees from the center line. And they weren't firing at all.

If his original set of Pocket Books' *Star Trek: The Motion Picture* blueprints wasn't worth twelve hundred bucks on the collector's market, why, he'd demand his money back.

Heather was leaning against the wall, watching Kyle as he watched the movie. She was amused by it all. Her husband, she knew, thought that William Shatner was a marvelous actor—there was something endearing about Kyle's utter lack of taste. Then again, she thought, he also thinks *I'm* beautiful. One shouldn't be too quick to elevate another's standards.

She'd been drinking white wine while Kyle watched the movie through to the end.

"I always liked Khan," said Heather with a smile, moving now to sit on the couch. "A guy who goes absolutely nuts when his wife dies—just the way it should be."

Kyle smiled back at her.

He'd lived on his own for a year now, but it was never supposed to be permanent. Just for a few weeks; give them each some space, some time, some privacy.

And then suddenly, Becky, too, had moved out.

And Heather was alone.

And, somehow, there seemed to be less drawing Kyle back—less a sense that the family had to be restored.

The family—it had never even had a name. It wasn't the Graveses; it wasn't the Davises. It had just *been*.

Heather looked now at Kyle, the wine having warmed her. She did love him. It had never been like that romp with Josh Huneker. With Kyle, it had always been deeper, more important, more satisfying on a dozen different levels. Even if he was, in so many ways, still just a little boy—his fondness for *Star Trek* and a million other things simultaneously amusing her and melting her heart.

She reached out, put her hand on top of his.

And he responded, placing his other hand on top of hers.

He smiled.

She smiled.

And they leaned together in a kiss.

There had been perfunctory kisses over the past year, but this one lingered. Their tongues touched.

The lights had dimmed automatically when the wall TV had been turned on. Kyle and Heather moved even closer together.

It was like old times. They kissed some more, then he nibbled on her earlobe and ran his tongue around the curves of her ear.

And then his hand found her breast, rolling her nipple through the fabric of her shirt between thumb and forefinger.

She felt warm—the wine, the pent-up desire, the summer's night.

His hand wandered down, flittering across her belly, sliding along her thigh toward her crotch.

Just like it had so many times before.

Suddenly she tensed, the muscles in her thighs bunching.

Kyle lifted his hand. "What's wrong?"

She looked into his eyes.

If only she could know. If only she could know for sure.

She dropped her gaze.

Kyle sighed. "I guess I should be going," he said.

Heather closed her eyes and didn't stop him from leaving.

12

IT WAS ONE OF THOSE MOMENTS OF HAZY semiconsciousness. Heather was dreaming—and *knew* that she was dreaming. And, like a good Jungian, she was trying to interpret the dream as it went along.

There was a cross in the dream. That in itself was unusual; Heather wasn't given to religious symbolism.

But it wasn't a wooden cross; rather, it was made of crystal. And it wasn't a practical rendition—you couldn't actually crucify a man on it. The arms were much, much thicker than they needed to be, and were rather stubby.

As she watched, the crystal cross began to rotate around its long axis. But as soon as it did so, it became apparent that it wasn't really a cross. In addition to the protrusion at either side, there were identical protrusions front and back.

Her perspective was moving closer. She could see seams now; the object was made up of eight transparent cubes: a stack of them four high, and then four more arranged around the faces of the third cube from the top. It spun faster and faster, light glinting off its glassy surface.

An unfolded hypercube.

And, as she came even closer, she heard a voice.

Deep, masculine, resonant.

A strong voice.

The voice of God?

No, no—a superior being, but not God.

Her pattern suggests three-dimensional thinking.

Heather woke up, covered with sweat.

Spock, of course, had said *his* pattern in the film, referring to Khan. The "her"—well it had to be Heather, didn't it?

Khan had been missing something—missing the obvious. Missing the fact that spaceships could go up and down as well as left and right or forward and backward. Heather had been missing something obvious, too, apparently—and her subconscious was trying to tell her that.

But as she lay there in bed, alone, she couldn't figure out what.

"Good morning, Cheetah."

"Good morning, Dr. Graves. You didn't put me in suspend mode when you left yesterday; I took advantage of the time to do some online research, and I have some questions for you."

Kyle headed over to the coffeemaker and set it about its business, then sat down in front of Cheetah's console. "Oh?"

"I've been going through old news stories. I find that most electronic versions of newspapers only go back to some date in the nineteen-eighties or nineties."

"Why should you care about decades-old news? It ain't news if it's old."

"That was intended as a humorous comment, wasn't it, Dr. Graves?"

Kyle grunted. "Yes."

"I could tell by your use of the word 'ain't.' You only use it when you're trying to be funny."

"Trust me, Cheetah, if you were human, you'd be rolling in the aisle."

"And when you speak in a high tone like that, I know you're still being funny."

"Full marks. But you still haven't told me why you're reading old news stories."

"You consider me to be non-human because, among other things, I can't make ethical judgments that correspond to those a human would make. I have been looking for news stories that relate to ethical issues and am trying to fathom what a real human would do under such circumstances."

"Okay," said Kyle. "What story did you dig up that's got you perplexed?"

"This: in nineteen eighty-five, a nineteen-year-old woman named Kathy was in her first year at Cornell University. On December twenty of that year, she was driving her boyfriend to his job at a grocery store in Ithaca, New York. The car hit a patch of ice, skidded ten meters, and slammed into a tree. The young man broke some bones, but a tire lying on the rear passenger seat pitched forward and hit Kathy's head. She fell into a chronic vegetative state—essentially a coma—and was placed in the Westfall Healthcare Center in Brighton, New York. A decade later, in January, nineteen ninety-six, with her still in the coma, it was discovered that Kathy was pregnant."

"How could she possibly be pregnant?" said Kyle.

"And *that* is the tone you use when speaking to me of matters of sexuality. You think that because I am a simulation that I could have no sophistication in such areas. But it's you who are being naïve, Dr. Graves. The young woman was pregnant—indeed, had been pregnant for five months at the time it was discovered—because she had been raped."

Kyle slumped slightly in his chair. "Oh."

"The police launched a search for the rapist," said Cheetah. "They came up with a list of seventy-five men who had had access to Kathy's room, but the search quickly narrowed to a fifty-two-year-old certified nurse's aide named John L. Horace.

Horace had been fired three months previously for fondling a forty-nine-year-old multiple-sclerosis patient at Westfall. He refused to provide a DNA sample in the rape case, but police got some from an envelope flap and a stamp he had licked, and they determined that the odds were more than a hundred million to one in favor of Horace being the father."

"I'm glad they caught him."

"Indeed. In passing, though, I do wonder why this rapist gets automatic membership in the human race, but I have to prove myself?"

Kyle shuffled over to the coffeemaker, poured himself a cup. "That's a very good question," he said at last.

Cheetah was quiet for a time, then: "There's more to this story."

Kyle took a sip of coffee. "Yes?"

"There was the matter of the incidental zygotic commencement."

"Ah, the coveted IZC. Oh, wait—you mean the baby. Christ, yes. What happened?"

"Prior to her accident, Kathy had been a devout Roman Catholic. She was, therefore, opposed to abortion. Taking that into account, Kathy's parents decided that Kathy should have the baby and that they would raise the child."

Kyle was incredulous. "Have the baby while still in a coma?"

"Yes. It *is* possible. Comatose women had given birth before, but this was the first known case of a woman becoming pregnant after going into a coma."

"They should have aborted the pregnancy," said Kyle.

"You humans make judgments so quickly," said Cheetah, with what sounded like envy. "I have tried and tried to resolve this issue and I find I cannot."

"What way are you leaning?"

"I tend to think that if they let the baby live, it should have been placed in a foster home."

Kyle blinked. "Why?"

"Because Kathy's mother and father, by forcing her to give birth in such extreme conditions, demonstrated that they were ill-suited to be parents."

"Interesting take. Were there any polls conducted at the time about what should be done?"

"Yes—*The Rochester Democrat & Chronicle* ran one. But the option I proposed wasn't even put forward—meaning, I guess, that it's not something a normal human would come up with."

"No, it's not. Your position has a certain logic to it, but it doesn't seem right emotionally."

"You said you would abort the child," said Cheetah. "Why?"

"Well, I'm pro-choice, but even most of those who are pro-life make exceptions for cases of incest or rape. And what about the kid, for Pete's sake? What effect would that kind of origin have on it?"

"That had not occurred to me," said Cheetah. "The child—a boy—was born on March eighteen, nineteen ninety-six, and if he's still alive, would be twenty-one now. Of course, his identity has been protected."

Kyle said nothing.

"Kathy," continued Cheetah, "died at the age of thirty, one day before the child's first birthday; she never came out of the coma." The computer paused. "It does make me wonder. The ethical dilemma—whether or not to countenance an abortion—could not have been drawn in sharper terms, even though I don't seem to be able to resolve it properly."

Kyle nodded. "We're all tested in various ways," he said.

"I know that better than most," said Cheetah, in a tone that was a credible imitation of being rueful. "But when I am tested, it is by you. When human beings are tested, though—and a case such as this clearly seems to be a test—who is it that is administering the test?"

Kyle opened his mouth to reply, closed it, then opened it again. "That's another very good question, Cheetah."

Heather sat in her office, thinking.

She'd stared at the messages from space day in and day out for years, trying to fathom their meaning.

They *had* to be rectangular images. She'd tried to identify any cultural bias related to prime numbers, any reason why she'd interpret them one way while someone from China or Chad or Chile would interpret them some other way. But there wasn't anything—the only cultural issue she could come up with was an argument about whether the number 1 qualified as a prime number.

No, if the length of the signals were the products of two prime numbers, then the only logical conclusion was that they were meant to be arranged into rectangular grids.

Her computer had all 2,843 messages stored on it.

But there were some messages that had been decoded, right at the beginning. Eleven of them, to be exact—a prime number. Meaning there were 2,832 undecoded messages.

Now that number was *not* a prime—it was an even number, and except for 2 there were, by definition, no even prime numbers.

A quantum computer could tell her in a twinkling what the factors of 2,832 were. Obviously, half that value would be a factor—1,416 would go into it twice. And half of that, 708. And half of that, 354. And half of that, 177. But 177 was an odd number, meaning that its half wouldn't be a whole number.

She'd sometimes thought that maybe each day's message made up only a portion of a larger whole, but she'd never found a meaningful way to order the pages. Of course, until a few days ago, they'd never known how many pages there were in total.

But now they *did* know. Maybe they did fit together into bigger groups, the way the backsides of trading cards often tile together to form a picture.

She brought up her spreadsheet program on her desktop computer and made a little sheet that simply divided 2,832 by consecutive integers, starting with 1.

There were only twenty numbers that divided into 2,832 evenly. She deleted the ones that didn't divide evenly, leaving her with this table:

This Integer	Divides into 2,832 This Many Times
1	2832
2	1416
3	944
4	708
6	472
8	354
12	236
16	177
24	118
48	59
59	48
118	24
177	16
236	12
354	8
472	6
708	4
944	3
1416	2
2832	1

Of course, the assumption by most researchers was that there were 2,832 individual pages of data—but there might be as few as one page, made up of 2,832 tiles. Or there could be two pages, each made up of 1,416 tiles. Or three, made up of 944 tiles. And so on.

But how to tell which combination the Centaurs had intended?

She stared at the list, noting its symmetry: the first line was 1 and 2,832; the last was the reverse—2,832 and 1. And so the lines were paired up and down until the middle two: 48 and 59; 59 and 48.

It was almost as if the middle two were the pivot, the axle on which the great propeller of figures rotated.

And—

Christ—

Except for 1, 3, and 177, the number 59 was the only possibly prime number on the list: all the others were even numbers and, by definition, couldn't be primes.

And—wait. Kyle had taught her a trick years ago. If the digits composing a number added up to a number divisible by three, then the original number was also divisible by three. Well, the digits making up 177—one, seven, and seven—added up to fifteen, and three went into fifteen five times, meaning 177 couldn't be prime.

But what about the number 59? Heather had no idea how to determine if a number was prime, except by brute force. She made another quickie spreadsheet, this one dividing 59 by every whole number smaller than itself.

But none of them divided evenly.

None, except 1 and 59.

Fifty-nine *was* a prime number.

And—a thought occurred to her. One itself was sometimes considered a prime. Two was definitely a prime. So was three. But in a way, all those numbers were trivial primes: every whole number lower than them was also divisible only by itself or one. In many ways, five was the first interesting prime number—it was the first one in sequence that had numbers lower than itself that *weren't* primes.

So if you discounted one, two, and three as trivially prime, then in the table she'd produced, 59 was the only non-trivial prime that divided evenly into the total number of undecoded alien messages.

It was another arrow pointing at that figure. The alien transmissions could possibly be arrayed in 48 pages each consisting of 59 individual messages, or 59 pages each consisting of 48 messages.

Researchers had been looking for recurring patterns in the messages for years, but so far none had turned up that hadn't seemed coincidental. Now, though, that they knew the total number of messages, all sorts of fresh analyses could be done.

She opened another window on her computer and brought up the file directory of alien messages. She copied the directory into a text file, where she could play with it. She highlighted the bit counts for the first 48 undecoded messages and tallied them up: they totaled 2,245,124 bits. She then highlighted the next twenty-four. The tally came to 1,999,642.

Damn.

She then highlighted the counts for messages 12 through 71— the first 59 undeciphered messages.

The total came to 11,543,124 bits.

Then she highlighted messages 72 to 131 and tallied their sizes.

The total was *also* 11,543,124 bits.

Heather felt her heart pounding; perhaps someone had noticed this before, but . . .

She did it again, working her way through the material.

Her spirits fell when she found the fourth group tallied only 11,002,997 bits. But after a moment, she realized she'd highlighted only 58 messages instead of 59. She tried again.

The tally was 11,543,124.

She continued on until she'd done all 48 groupings of 59 messages.

Each group totaled precisely 11,543,124 bits.

She let out a great *whoop!* of excitement. Fortunately, her office did have that sturdy oak door.

The aliens hadn't sent 2,832 separate messages—rather, they'd sent 48 large ones.

Now, if only she could figure out how to tile the messages together. Unfortunately, they were of many different sizes, and there was no orderly repetition from page to page. The first message making up the first group of 48 was 118,301 bits long (the product of the primes 281 and 421), whereas the first message of page two was 174,269 bits long (the product of the primes 229 and 761).

Presumably, the individual tiles formed square or rectangular shapes when properly placed together. She doubted she could figure it out by trial and error.

But surely Kyle could write her a computer program that would do it.

After last night, she was hesitant. What would she say to him?

She steeled her courage and picked up her phone.

"Hello?" said Kyle's voice.

He doubtless knew it was Heather calling; he could read it off the status line on his phone. But there was no particular warmth in his voice.

"Hi, Kyle," said Heather. "I need your help."

Frosty: "You didn't need my help last night."

Heather sighed. "I'm sorry about that. Really I am. This is a difficult time for all of us."

Kyle was silent. Heather felt the need to fill the void. "It's going to take time to sort all this out."

"I've been gone for a year now," said Kyle. "How much time do you need?"

"I don't know. Look, I'm sorry I called; I didn't mean to disturb you."

"That's all right," said Kyle. "Was there something?"

Heather swallowed, then went on. "Yes. I've had a breakthrough, I think, with the Centauri transmissions. If you take them in groups of fifty-nine messages, each group is exactly the same size."

"Really?"

"Yes."

"How many groups are there?"

"Exactly forty-eight."

"So you think—what?—you think the individual messages form forty-eight bigger pages?"

"Exactly. But the individual pieces are all different sizes. I assume they fit together into a rectangular grid of some sort, but I don't know how to work that out."

Kyle made a noise that sounded like a snort.

"There's no need to be condescending," said Heather.

"No—no, that's not it. Sorry. It's just funny. See, this is a tiling problem."

"Yes?"

"Well, *this* tiling problem—seeing if a finite number of tiles can be arrayed into a rectangular grid—is eminently solvable, just by brute-force computing. But there are other tiling problems that involve determining if specific tile shapes can cover an infinite plane, without leaving gaps that we've known since the nineteen-eighties fundamentally can't be solved by a computer; if they're solvable at all, it's with an intuition that's noncomputable."

"So?"

"So it's just funny that the Centaurs would choose a message format that echoes one of the big debates in human consciousness, that's all."

"Hmm. But you say this *is* solvable?"

"Sure. I'll need the dimensions of each message—the length and width in bits or pixels. I can write a program easily enough that will try sliding them around until they all fit together in a rectangular shape—assuming, of course, that there is such a pattern." He paused. "There'll be an interesting side effect, you know: if the individual tiles are not square and they all fit together only one way, you'll know the orientation of each individual message. You won't have to worry anymore about there being two possible orientations for each one."

"I hadn't thought of that, but you're right. When can you do this?"

"Well, actually I'm too busy—sorry, but I am. But I can put one of my grad students on it. We should have an answer for you in a couple of days.

Heather tried to sound warm. "Thank you, Kyle."

She could almost hear him shrug. "I'm always here for you," he said and clicked off.

13

IT TURNED OUT TO HEATHER'S DELIGHT that the fifty-nine tiles in each group did indeed make up a rectangular grid. In fact, they made up forty-eight perfect squares.

There were many circular patterns visible if the grids were rendered as black-and-white pixels. The circles had a variety of diameters—some were big, some were small. They, too, fell into size categories—no circle had a unique diameter.

Unfortunately, though, except for the circles—which seemed good supporting evidence that this was indeed the way in which the tiles were supposed to be arranged—still no meaningful patterns emerged. She'd been hoping for a picture book, with four-dozen leaves: *Forty-Eight Views of Mount Alpha Centauri.*

She tried arranging the forty-eight messages into even bigger groups: eight rows of six, three rows of sixteen, and so on. But still no pattern emerged.

She also tried building cubes. Some seemed to make sense—if she drew imaginary hoops through the cubes, in some configurations the circles on the cube faces were positioned just right to be the cross sections through those hoops.

But still she couldn't get the whole thing to make sense.

She's intelligent, but inexperienced. Her pattern suggests three-dimensional thinking.

Spock had said "he," not "she," of course.

And—

God.

In the film, he'd said *two-dimensional,* not three-dimensional. Why hadn't she noticed that before?

Khan had been guilty of two-dimensional thinking; an attack through three dimensions defeated him.

Heather, perhaps, was being guilty of three-dimensional thinking. Would a *four*-dimensional approach help?

But why would the aliens use a four-dimensional design?

Well, why not?

No. No, there had to be a better reason than that.

She used her Web terminal to search for information about the fourth dimension.

And when she'd digested it all, she sagged back in her chair, stunned.

There *was* a water hole, thought Heather. There *was* a common ground between species. But it was nothing as simple as a set of radio frequencies. The common ground wasn't related to ordinary physics, or the chemistry of atmospheres, or anything that mundane. And yet it was something that in many ways was even more basic, more fundamental, more a part of the very fabric of existence.

The water hole was *dimensional.* Specifically, it was the fourth dimension.

There are nine and sixty ways of constructing tribal lays
And every single one of them is right!

Except that one of them was *more* right than all the others.

Depending on sensory apparatus, scheme of consciousness, consensual agreement with others of its kind, and more, a life form could perceive the universe, perceive its reality, in one dimension, two dimensions, three dimensions, four dimensions, five dimensions, and on and on, *ad infinitum.*

But of all the possible dimensional frames, one is unique.

A four-dimensional interpretation of reality *is* special.

Heather didn't understand it all—as a psychologist, she had an excellent grounding in statistics, but she wasn't really up on higher mathematics. But it was clear from what she'd read that the fourth dimension *did* have unique properties.

Heather had found the *Science News* Website and read, astonished, an article from May 1989 by Ivars Peterson that began:

> When mathematicians—normally cautious and meticulous individuals—apply adjectives like "bizarre," "strange," "weird" and "mysterious" to their results, something unusual is happening. Such expressions reflect the recent state of affairs in studies of four-dimensional space, a realm just a short step beyond our own familiar, three-dimensional world.
>
> By combining ideas from theoretical physics with abstract notions from topology (the study of shape), mathematicians are discovering that four-dimensional space has mathematical properties quite unlike those characterizing space in any other dimension.

Heather didn't pretend to understand all that Peterson went on to say, such as that only in four dimensions is it possible to have manifolds that are topologically but not smoothly equivalent.

But that didn't matter—the point was that mathematically, a four-dimensional frame was unique. Regardless of *how* a race perceived reality, its mathematicians would be inexorably drawn to the problems and singular traits of a four-dimensional framework.

It was a water hole of a different sort—a gathering place for minds from all possible life forms.

Christ.

No—no, not just Christ.

Christus Hypercubus.

She could make three-dimensional cubes out of her pages. And with forty-eight pages, one could make a total of eight cubes.

Eight cubes, just like in the Dali painting on Kyle's lab wall.

Just like an unfolded hypercube.

Of course, Cheetah had said there was more than one way to unfold a plain, ordinary cube; only one of eleven possible methods yielded the cross shape.

There were probably many ways to unfold a hypercube as well.

But the circular marks provided a guide!

There was probably only one way to align all eight cubes so that the imaginary hoops went through them at the right places to line up with the circular marks.

She'd tried arranging the pictures as cubes before, hoping that they'd line up in meaningful patterns. But now she tried mapping them on her computer screen onto the separate cubes of an unfolded tesseract.

U of T had site licenses for most software used in its various departments; Kyle had shown Heather how to access the CAD program that had been used to determine the way in which the individual tiles fit together.

It took her a while to make it work properly, although fortunately the software operated by voice input. Eventually she had the forty-eight messages arranged as eight cubes. She then told the computer she wanted it to arrange the eight cubes in any pattern that would make the circular registration marks line up properly.

Boxes danced on her screen for a time, and then the one correct solution emerged.

It was the hypercrucifix, just like in Dali's painting: a vertical column of four cubes, with four more cubes projecting from the four exposed faces on the second cube from the top.

There was no doubt. The alien messages made an unfolded hypercube.

What, she wondered, would you get if you could actually fold the three-dimensional pattern *kata* or *ana?*

It was a typically hot, muggy, hazy August day. Heather found herself glistening with sweat just from walking over to the Computer-Assisted Manufacturing Lab; the lab was part of the Department of Mechanical Engineering. She didn't really know anybody there and so just stood on the threshold, looking around politely at the various robots and machines clanking away.

"May I help you?" said a handsome, silver-haired man.

Heather approved of those who knew the difference between "can" and "may."

"I certainly hope so," she said, smiling. "I'm Heather Davis, from the Psych Department."

"Somebody got a screw loose?"

"I beg your pardon?"

"A joke—sorry. See, a shrink coming to see an engineer. We tighten loose screws all the time."

Heather laughed a little.

"I'm Paul Komensky," said the man. He extended his hand. Heather took it.

"I do need some engineering help," Heather said. "I need something built."

"What?"

"I'm not sure exactly. A bunch of prefabricated panels."

"How big are the panels?"

"I don't know."

The engineer frowned—but Heather couldn't tell if it was a "dumb woman" or "dumb artsy" frown. "That's a little vague," he said.

Heather smiled her most charming smile. Today the various engineering schools had fifty-percent female undergrads, but Komensky was old enough to remember when engineers were all horny men who would go days without seeing a female. "I'm sorry," she said. "I'm working on the alien radio messages, and—"

"I *knew* I knew you from somewhere! I saw you on TV—what show was that?"

Heather found the question embarrassing because she'd been on *so* many shows lately—but it sounded pompous to say that out loud.

"Something on Newsworld?" she offered tentatively.

"Yeah, maybe. So this has to do with the aliens?"

"I'm not sure—I think so. I want to make a series of tiles that represent the alien message grids."

"How many messages are there?"

"Two thousand, eight hundred and thirty-two—at least, that many undecoded ones; they're the only ones I want to make into tiles."

"That's a lot of tiles."

"I know."

"But you don't know how big they should be?"

"No."

"What should they be made out of?"

"Two different substances." She handed him her datapad. Its screen showed two chemical formulas. "Can you synthesize them?"

He squinted at the display. "Sure—nothing difficult about them. You're certain they're solid at room temperature?"

Heather's eyes went wide. She'd read all the papers on the chemicals ten years ago, when they'd first been synthesized, but hadn't really thought about them much since. "I have no idea."

"This one will be," he said, pointing at the top formula. "That one . . . well, we'll see. Are these formulas from the alien messages?"

Heather nodded. "From the first eleven pages. People have synthesized these compounds before, of course, but no one ever figured out what they were for."

Komensky made an impressed face. "Interesting."

She nodded. "I want the zero bits to be made of one of these substances, and the one bits made of the other."

"You want one painted onto the other?"

"Painted? No, no, I thought you'd build them out of the two materials."

Komensky frowned again. "I don't know. That formula looks to me like it'll be a liquid, but it might dry into a hard crust. See those oxygens and hydrogens? They could evaporate out as water, leaving a solid behind."

"Oh. Well, then, yes—and that answers the big question I'd been unable to solve."

"Which is?"

"Well, I was trying to figure out which substance represented the one bits and which one represented the zero bits. The ones are 'on' bits, so the paint must represent the ones; it must go on the—the—"

" 'The substrate' we call it in materials science."

"The substrate, yes." A pause. "How hard would it be to do that?"

"Well, again, it comes back to how big you want the tiles."

"I don't know. They're not all the same size, but even the biggest shouldn't be more than a few centimeters—I want to fit them together."

"Fit them?"

"Yeah, you know—lay them side by side. See, if you arrange each group of fifty-nine tiles properly, they form a perfect square—there's only one layout that'll do that."

"Why not just build the big panels instead of the individual tiles?"

"I don't know—the tiling itself might be significant. I don't want to make any assumptions."

"Like the 'on' bits go 'on' the substrate?" His tone was one of gentle teasing.

Heather shrugged. "It's as good a guess as any."

He nodded, conceding the point. "So twenty-eight hundred tiles make up how many bigger squares?"

"Forty-eight."

"And what are you going to do with the resulting squares?"

"Assemble them into cubes—and then assemble those cubes into an unfolded tesseract."

"Really? Wow."

"Yes."

"Well, do you want the finished thing big enough so that you can crawl inside of one of the cubes?"

"No, that won't be—"

She stopped dead.

No scale specified. Nowhere in any of the messages did there seem to be anything suggesting a size for the construct.

Make it any size, the aliens seemed to be saying.

Make it *your* size.

"Yes, yes—that would be perfect! Big enough to go inside."

"Well, okay—sure. We can build the substrate tiles, no problem. How thick should they be?"

"I don't know. As thin as possible, I guess."

"I can make them one molecule thick if that's what you want."

"Oh, not *that* thin. They'll have to hold together. A millimeter or two, maybe."

"No problem. We've got a machine all set up to turn out plastic building panels for the School of Architecture; I could modify it easily enough to turn out the tiles you need. Do you want them to have smooth edges or would you like a tongue-and-groove arrangement, so they can snap together?"

"You mean so they form a big solid piece?"

Komensky nodded.

"That would be great."

"What about the painting on of the other chemical?"

"I figured I'd have to do that by hand," said Heather.

"Well, you *could,* but we've got programmable microsprayers that can do it for you, assuming the substance has a low enough viscosity. We use the sprayers to paint patterns onto the panels we make for the architecture students—you know, little outlines of bricks, or little dots to represent rivets, stuff like that."

"That'd be perfect. How soon can you do it?"

"Well, during the school year, we're usually pretty backed up. But in summer, we've got lots of free time. We can get at it right away. We've still got a couple of grad students hanging around; I'll have one of them look into manufacturing those chemicals. As I say, at first glance they look simple enough, but we won't know for sure until we actually try to synthesize them." A pause. "Who's going to pay for this?"

"What'll it cost?" asked Heather.

"Oh, not much. Robots are so cheap these days, we no longer amortize their cost over manufacturing runs like we used to. Maybe five hundred dollars for the material."

Heather nodded. She'd find some way to explain it to her department head later, once he got back from vacation. "That's fine. Charge it to Psych; I'll sign the requisition."

"I'll e-mail you the paperwork."

"Terrific. Thank you. Thank you *very* much."

"You're very welcome." He smiled and held her with his eyes.

14

THERE WAS A BLEEP AT KYLE'S OFFICE DOOR.
He pushed the button that caused it to slide open. A middle-
aged Asian woman in an expensive-looking gray suit was
standing in the curving corridor, the atrium with its tumbling
tapestries visible behind her.

"Dr. Graves?" she said.

"Yes?"

"Brian Kyle Graves?"

"That's right."

"I wish to talk to you, please."

Kyle rose and motioned for her to come in.

"My name is Chikamatsu. I wish to speak to you about your
research."

Kyle indicated another chair. Chikamatsu took it, and Kyle
sat back down.

"I understand you have had some success with quantum
computing."

"Not as much as I'd like. I ended up with egg on my face a
couple of weeks ago."

"So I heard." Kyle's eyebrows went up. "I represent a consortium that would like to contract for your services." She pronounced consortium "consorsheeum."

"Oh?"

"Yes. We believe you are close to a breakthrough."

"Not judging by my current results."

"A minor problem, I am sure. You are trying to use Dembinski fields to inhibit decoherence, are you not? They are notoriously tricky."

Kyle's eyebrows climbed again. "That they are."

"We have monitored your progress with interest. You are doubtless very close to a solution. And if you do find a solution, my consortium may be prepared to invest heavily in your procedure, assuming, of course, that you can convince me that your system works."

"Well, it will either work or it won't."

Chikamatsu nodded. "Doubtless so, but we will need to be sure. You would have to factor a number for us. And, of course, I would have to provide the number—just to be sure it is not some trick, you understand."

Kyle narrowed his eyes. "What exactly is the nature of your consortium?" He preferred the hard-T pronunciation himself, but matched Chikamatsu's usage.

"We are an international group," she said. "Venture capitalists." She had a small cylindrical leather purse, with metal end caps. She opened it, removed a memory wafer, and proffered it to Kyle. "The number we wish factored is on this wafer."

Kyle took the wafer but didn't look at it. "How many digits in the number?"

"Five hundred and twelve."

"Even if I can work out the current bugs with my system, it'll be a while before I can do that."

"Why?"

"Well, for two reasons. The first is a practical one. Democritus—that's the name of our prototype—is hardware constrained to factor numbers exactly three hundred digits long, no more, no less. Even if I could get it to work properly, I can't do numbers of any other length—the quantum registers have to be carefully jiggered for the precise total number of digits."

Chikamatsu looked disappointed. "And the other reason?"

Kyle raised his eyebrows. "The other reason, Ms. Chikamatsu, is that I'm not a criminal."

"I—I beg your pardon?"

He flipped the memory wafer over and over in his hand as he spoke. "There's only one practical application for factoring large numbers—and that's cracking encryption schemes. I don't know whose data you're trying to access, but I'm no hacker. Find yourself another boy."

"It is just a randomly generated number," said Chikamatsu.

"Oh, come on. If you'd asked me to factor a number whose length fell within a range—between five hundred and six hundred digits, say—and if you hadn't shown up with your number all picked out, I might have believed you. But it's pretty damned obvious you're trying to crack somebody's code."

Kyle went to hand back the wafer, but now its other side was facing up. As he looked down at it, he saw its label, with a single word written on it in pen: Huneker.

"Huneker!" said Kyle. "Not Joshua Huneker?"

Chikamatsu reached out to retrieve the wafer. "Who?" she said, sounding innocent but looking visibly flustered.

Kyle clenched his fist, covering the wafer. "What the hell are you playing at?" he said. "What's this got to do with Huneker?"

Chikamatsu lowered her gaze. "I did not think you would know the name."

"My wife was involved with him when she and I met."

Chikamatsu's almond-shaped eyes went wide. "Really?"

"Yes, really. Now, tell me what the hell this is all about."

The woman considered. "I—ah, I must consult with my partners first."

"Be my guest. Do you need a phone?"

She extracted one from her funky purse. "No." She rose, crossed the room, and began a hushed conversation that bounced between Japanese and what sounded like Russian, with only a few recognizable words—"Toronto," "Graves," "Huneker," and "quantum" among them. She winced several times; apparently she was getting a royal chewing-out.

After a few moments, she folded up the phone and returned it to her purse.

"My colleagues are not pleased," she said, "but we do need your help, and our purpose is not illegal."

"You'll have to convince me of that."

She tightened her lips and let air escape loudly through her nose. Then: "Do you know how Josh Huneker died?"

"Suicide, my wife said."

Chikamatsu nodded. "Do you have a Web terminal here?"

"Of course."

"May I?"

Kyle indicated the unit with a motion of his hand.

Chikamatsu sat down in front of it and spoke into the microphone. *"The Toronto Star,"* she said. Then: "Search back issues. Words in article text: Huneker and Algonquin. H-U-N-E-K-E-R and A-L-G-O-N-Q-U-I-N."

"Searching," said the terminal in an androgynous voice. Then: "Found."

There was only one hit. The article appeared on the monitor screen.

Chikamatsu stood up. "Have a look," she said.

Kyle took the seat she'd vacated. The article was dated February 28, 1994. The words "Algonquin" and "Huneker" were highlighted everywhere they appeared in red and green respectively. He read the whole thing, telling the screen once to page down as he did so:

ASTRONOMER TAKES OWN LIFE

Joshua Huneker, 24, was found dead yesterday at the National Research Council of Canada's radio telescope in Algonquin Park, a provincial park in northern Ontario. He had committed suicide by eating an apple coated with arsenic.

Huneker, who was studying for a Ph.D. at the University of Toronto, had been snowed in alone at the radio telescope for six days.

He had been working in Algonquin Park on the international Search for Extraterrestrial Intelligence (SETI) project, scanning the sky for radio messages from alien worlds. Because Algonquin is so far from any city, it receives little radio interference and is therefore ideally suited for such delicate listening.

Huneker's body was found by Donald Cheung, 39, another radio astronomer, who was arriving at the telescope facility to relieve Huneker.

"It's a great tragedy," said NRC spokesperson Allison Northcott, in Ottawa. "Josh was one of our most promising young researchers and he was also a real humanitarian, very active with Greenpeace and other causes. However, judging by his suicide note, he apparently had personal problems related to his romantic involvement with another man. We will all miss him."

When he was finished, Kyle swiveled the chair around to face the woman. He hadn't know the details of Josh's death before; the whole thing seemed rather sad.

"His story remind you of anyone's?" asked Chikamatsu.

"Sure. Alan Turing's." Turing, the father of modern computing, had committed suicide in 1954 in the same way, and for the same reason.

She nodded grimly. "Exactly. Turing was Huneker's idol. But what the spokesperson did not mention was that Josh left *two* notes, not one. The first was indeed about his personal problems, but the second . . ."

"Yes?"

"The second had to do with what he had detected."

"Pardon?"

"Over the radio telescope." Chikamatsu closed her eyes, as if wrestling for one final moment about whether to go on. Then she opened them and said softly, "The Centaurs were not the first aliens we made contact with; they were the second."

Kyle creased his forehead skeptically. "Oh, come on!"

"It is true," said Chikamatsu. "In nineteen ninety-four, Algonquin picked up a signal. Of course it was not from Alpha Centauri—you cannot see that star from Canada. Huneker detected a signal from somewhere else, apparently had no trouble decoding it, and was stunned by whatever it said. He burned all the original computer tapes, encrypted the only remaining record of the message, and then killed himself. To this day, nobody knows what that alien message said. They closed down the Algonquin Observatory immediately thereafter, citing budget cuts. What they really wanted to do was disassemble everything to see if they could determine which star the signal had come from; Huneker had been scheduled to survey over forty different stars during the week he was alone up there. They tore that place apart, but never figured it out."

Kyle digested this, then: "And Huneker used—what? RSA encryption?"

"Exactly."

Kyle frowned. RSA is a two-key method of data-encryption: the public key is a very large number, and the private key consists of two prime numbers that are factors of the public key.

Chikamatsu spread her hands, as if the problem was plain. "Without the private key," she said, "the message cannot be decoded."

"And there were five hundred and twelve digits in Huneker's public key?"

"Yes."

Kyle frowned. "So it would take conventional computers trillions of years to find its factors by trial and error."

"Exactly. We have had computers working full time on it since just after Huneker killed himself. So far, no luck. But, as you say, that is with conventional computers. A quantum computer—"

"A quantum computer could do it in a matter of seconds."

"Precisely."

Kyle nodded. "I can see why leaving an encrypted message behind might appeal to a Turing fan." Turing had been pivotal in defeating the Nazis' Enigma encoding machine in World War II. "But why should I agree to do this for you?"

"We have a copy of the Huneker disk—something very hard to get hold of, believe me. My partners and I believe the disk encodes information that may be of great commercial value—and if we can decode it first, we will all make a lot of money."

"All?"

"When I was talking to them on the phone, my partners empowered me to offer you a two-percent share of all proceeds."

"And what if there aren't any?"

"Sorry, I should have been more explicit: I am prepared to offer you an advance of four million dollars, against a two-percent share of all proceeds. And you keep all rights to your quantum-computing technology; we simply want the message decoded."

"What makes you think there's anything of commercial value in the message?"

"Huneker's second handwritten note said simply, 'Alien radio message—unveil new technology.' The disk with the encoded transmission—a three-and-a-half-inch floppy, if you remember such things—was found lying on top of that note. Huneker had clearly understood the message and felt that it described some innovative technology."

Kyle frowned dubiously and leaned back in his chair. "I've spent half my life trying to decipher what students mean when they write something. He could have just been saying that we'd need a new technology, such as quantum computing, to break his encryption."

Chikamatsu sounded unduly earnest. "No, it must describe some great innovation—and we want it."

Kyle decided not to argue the point with her; she'd clearly devoted way too much time and money to this issue to countenance the thought that it was all a waste. "How did you find out about me?"

"We have monitored quantum-computing research for years, Professor Graves. We know exactly who is doing what—and how close they are to a breakthrough. You and Saperstein at the Technion are both on the verge of solving the technical difficulties."

Kyle exhaled. He hated Saperstein's guts—had for years. Did Chikamatsu know that? Probably—meaning that she might be baiting him. Still, four million dollars . . .

"Let me think about it," he said.

"I will contact you again," said Chikamatsu, rising. She held out a hand for the memory wafer.

Kyle was reluctant to let it go.

"It only has the public key on it," said Chikamatsu. "Without the actual alien message, it is useless."

Kyle hesitated a moment longer, then handed over the plastic wafer, now slick with perspiration from his palm.

Chikamatsu wiped it on a tissue, then returned it to her purse. "Thank you," she said. "Oh, and a word to the wise—I rather suspect we are not the only ones aware of your research."

Kyle spread his arms and tried to sound jaunty. "Then maybe I should simply hold out for the best offer."

Chikamatsu was already at the door. "I do not think you will like the sort of offers they make."

And then she was gone.

15

THE PHONE RANG IN HEATHER'S OFFICE.
She glanced at the call-display readout; it was an internal U of
T call. That was a relief: she was getting tired of the media. But
then, it seemed, they had gotten tired of her, too; the cessation
of the alien messages was already old news, and reporters
seemed to be leaving her alone now. Heather picked up the
handset. "Hello?"

"Hi, Heather. It's Paul Komensky, over at the CAM lab."

"Hello, Paul."

"It's good to hear your voice."

"Ah, yours, too, thanks."

Silence, then: "I, ah, I've got those substances ready you
asked me to mix up."

"That's great! Thank you."

"Yeah. The substrate, it's unremarkable, essentially just a
polystyrene. But the other stuff, well, I was right. It *is* a liquid
at room temperature, but it *does* dry—into a thin, crystalline
film."

"Really?"

"And it's piezoelectric."

"Pi—pi—what?"

"Piezoelectric. It means that when you put it under stress, it generates electricity."

"Really?"

"Not much, but some."

"Fascinating!"

"It's not all that unusual, really; it happens a lot in various minerals. But I wasn't expecting it. The crystals this stuff dries to are actually similar to what we call relaxor ferroelectrics. That's a special kind of piezoelectric crystal that can deform—that is, change shape—ten times as much as standard piezoelectric crystals do."

"Piezoelectric," Heather said softly. She used her fingertip to write the word on her datapad. "I've read something about that—can't offhand think where, though. Anyway, can you make the tiles now?"

"Sure."

"How long will it take?"

"The whole run? About a day."

"That's all?"

"That's all."

"Can you do it for me?"

"Sure." A pause. "But why not come over here? I want to show you the apparatus, make sure it's going to produce exactly what you want. Then we can start the run, and then maybe grab some lunch?"

Heather hesitated for a moment, then: "Sure. Sure thing. I'm on my way."

The manufacturing equipment was simple.

Spread out across the floor of Paul Komensky's lab was a piece of the substrate material measuring about three meters on a side; two additional panels were leaning against one wall, almost touching the ceiling.

The substrate was a dark green color, like computer circuit

boards. And sitting on top of the substrate sheet was a small robot the size of a shoebox, with a cylindrical tank attached to its back.

Heather was standing next to Paul. A computer monitor beside him showed the twelfth radio message—the first one after the basic math and chemistry lessons.

"We just activate the robot," Paul said, "and it starts moving over the surface of the substrate. See that tank? It contains the second chemical—the liquid. The robot sprays on the chemical in the pattern indicated on the monitor, there. Then it uses a laser to cut the tile out of the substrate. It then flips over the tile and paints the same pattern on the other side; I've got it set to do it in exactly the same orientation, so that if the substrate were clear, the patterns would line up perfectly. It then uses one of its little manipulators to place the tile in those boxes over there."

He hit a button, and the robot proceeded to do just as he'd described, producing a rectangular tile measuring about ten centimeters by fifteen centimeters. Heather smiled.

"It'll take about a day to cut the tiles, and when it's done, all the tiles will be stored, in the order in which they should be snapped together, in the boxes."

"What if I drop the box?"

Komensky smiled. "You know, my older brother did that once. His very first computing course was in high school in the early nineteen seventies. They did everything on punch cards back then. He wrote a program to print out a pinup of Farrah Fawcett—remember her? It was all made by printed characters—asterisks, dollar signs, slashes—simulating a halftone photo if you got far enough away from it. He spent months on it and then he dropped the damn box of cards, and they got completely scrambled." He shuddered. "Anyway, the robot is putting little serial-number stickers on the back of each tile. They're done with Post-it adhesive—if you want them off later, they'll peel off easily." He got the first tile out of the box and showed the label to Heather.

She smiled. "You think of everything."

"I'm trying to." The robot was motoring along; it had done six more tiles already. "Now, how about lunch?"

They were eating in the Faculty Club, which was at 41 Willcocks Street, just around the corner from Sid Smith. The dining room was decorated in a Wedgwood design: blue-gray walls with rococo white friezes. Heather was resting her elbows on the white tablecloth, intertwining her fingers in front of her face. She realized she was essentially holding her wedding ring out as a shield. That was the problem with being a psychologist, she reflected: you couldn't do anything without being self-conscious about it.

She lowered her hands, folding them on the table—and, just as unconsciously as her first act, she put the left hand on top. Heather looked down, saw the ring still prominently displayed, and allowed herself a minuscule shrug.

But it hadn't been lost on Paul. "You're married."

Heather found herself exhibiting the ring again as she lifted her hand. "For twenty-two years, but—" She paused, wondering whether to say it. Then, after a moment's internal struggle, she did. "But we're separated."

Paul's eyebrows went up. "Children?"

"Two. We had two."

He tipped his head at the odd phrasing. "Do you see them much?"

"One of them died a few years ago."

"Oh, my. Oh, I'm sorry."

He had the good taste not to ask how; he went up a couple of notches in Heather's estimation. "What about you?"

"Divorced, long ago. One son; he lives in Santa Fe. I spend

Christmases there with him and his wife and kids; it's nice to get away from the cold."

Heather rolled her eyes slightly, as if some of that cold would have been very welcome at this time of year.

"Your husband," asked Paul, "what does he do?"

"He's here at the university. Kyle Graves."

Paul's eyebrows went up. "Kyle Graves is your husband?"

"You know him?"

"He's in computing, right? We were on a committee together a few years ago—establishing the Kelly Gotlieb Centre."

"Oh, yeah. I remember when he was doing that."

Paul looked at her, smiling, unblinking. "Kyle must be a fool, to let you get away."

Heather opened her mouth to protest that she hadn't got away, that it was only a temporary separation, that things were complex. But then she closed her mouth and tilted her head, accepting the compliment.

The server arrived.

"Would you like some wine with lunch?" asked Paul.

After lunch, while she was walking back alone to her office, Heather used her datapad to access her voice mail. There was a message from Kyle, saying he needed to talk to her about something important. Since she was only a short distance from Mullin Hall, she decided to simply drop by and see what he wanted.

"Oh, hi, Heather," said Kyle, once the door to his lab had slid aside. "Thanks for stopping by. I need to talk to you. Have a seat."

Heather was slightly woozy from the wine she'd had with lunch; having a seat sounded like a very good idea indeed. She sat down in front of Cheetah.

Kyle perched himself on the edge of a desk. "I need to talk to you about Josh Huneker."

Heather stiffened. "What about him?"

"I'm sorry; I know you asked me never to mention him, but, well, his name came up today."

Heather narrowed her eyes. "In what context?"

"Was there anything unusual about his death?"

"What do you mean 'unusual'?"

"Well," said Kyle, "they said he killed himself because he was gay."

Heather nodded. "It was news to me, but, yeah, that's what they said." Then she shrugged a little, as if acknowledging how times had changed; she couldn't imagine anyone killing themselves just because of that today.

"But you didn't think he was gay?"

"Oh, Christ, Kyle, I don't know. He seemed genuinely interested in me, but they said he had a sexual relationship with the guy I thought was just his roommate. What's this all about?"

Kyle took a deep breath. "A woman came to see me today. She says she represents a consortium"—he'd gone back to the hard-T pronunciation—"that has a copy of a disk containing an alien radio message Huneker received just before he died."

Heather nodded.

"You don't look surprised."

"Well, it's not the first time I've heard the story that he detected a message. It's a rumor that's been kicking around for years in SETI circles. But, you know, it's just a story."

"It does seem a bit of a coincidence, doesn't it?" said Kyle. "I mean, two messages, presumably from two different stars, so close together: whoever Huneker supposedly picked up in nineteen ninety-four, and then the sequence of messages from Alpha Centauri beginning thirteen years later."

"Oh, I don't know," said Heather. "SETI researchers originally thought we would pick up far more messages than we already have by this point. By 1994, we'd only been listening for alien radio signals for thirty years; there could have been countless attempts to contact us before we had radio telescopes, and we could be due for another contact tomorrow—we just don't know how often radio contact with another civilization should be expected."

Kyle nodded. "They closed the Algonquin radio telescope shortly after Huneker supposedly detected his message."

Heather smiled sadly. "You hardly need me to tell you about government cutbacks. Besides, if such a disk exists, why would someone come to you about it?"

"The woman said Huneker had encoded the message using RSA—that's a system that employs the prime factors of very large numbers as the decryption key."

"Were people doing things like that then?"

"Sure. As far back as nineteen seventy-seven, Rivest, Shamir, and Adleman—the three MIT scientists who worked out the technique—encoded a message using the 129-digit product of two primes. They offered a hundred-dollar prize to anyone who could decode it."

"And did anyone?"

"Years later, yeah. Nineteen ninety-four, I think."

"What'd it say?"

" 'The magic words are squeamish ossifrage.' "

"What the devil is 'ossifrage'?"

"It's a bird of prey, I think. It took six hundred volunteers using computers worldwide, each working on part of the problem over an eight-month period, to crack the code—more than a hundred quadrillion instructions."

"So why haven't they done that with Josh's message?"

"He used 512 digits—and each additional digit is an additional order of magnitude, of course. They've been working on it, using conventional means, ever since but haven't cracked it yet."

"Oh. But why did this consortium come to you?" She was a hard-T person, too.

"Because they think I'm getting close to a breakthrough in quantum computing. I'm not ready yet—we've got only one prototype system, and even if we do get the bugs out of it, it'll work only with numbers exactly three-hundred digits long. But in a few months, with luck, I will have a system that could decode messages of any length almost instantaneously."

"Ah."

"This woman who came to see me, I think she wants to patent whatever technology is gleaned from the message."

"That's outrageous," said Heather. "Even if such a message exists—and I really doubt that—it belongs to everyone." She paused. "And besides . . ."

"What?"

"Well," said Heather, frowning, "if it exists, then Josh *did* kill himself *after* he saw what it had to say. Maybe—maybe you don't want to know what it says."

"You mean maybe his suicide might actually have been related to the message?"

"Maybe. Like I said, as far as I knew, he wasn't gay or bi."

"But what kind of message would lead a man to kill himself, but first hide it from the rest of humanity?" asked Kyle.

Heather was quiet for a moment, then: " 'Heaven exists, it's absolute paradise, and everyone gets in.' "

"Why keep that a secret?"

"So that the human race would go on. If everyone knew that was true, we'd all commit suicide to get there sooner, and *Homo sapiens* would become extinct overnight."

Kyle thought about this. "Then why leave an encrypted version of the message at all? Why not just destroy the message altogether?"

"Maybe it's like the Pope," said Heather. Kyle's face telegraphed his lack of comprehension. "They say there's a prophecy under lock and key at the Vatican; it's been there for centuries. Every once in a while, a Pope looks at it—and reacts with horror, locking it up again. At least, that's the story."

Kyle frowned. "Well, this consortium wants me to go work for them; they're offering a lot of money."

"How much?" asked Heather.

She could see hesitation on his face. Even before he spoke, she knew what he must have been thinking: If we don't reconcile at some point, is it wise for me to disclose the magnitude of a new source of income? "It, ah, was quite a substantial sum," said Kyle.

"I see," said Heather.

"They've already got a line on another researcher who also is close to making a breakthrough." He paused. "Saperstein."

"You hate that guy."

"Exactly."

"I don't know. Maybe you should do it."

"Why?"

"Well, suppose Saperstein or someone else does it instead. That doesn't mean the Huneker message, if it really exists, ever goes public—the government doubtless has a copy of the message, but they've kept it under wraps for over twenty years now."

"Perhaps. But I'm sure the consortium will make me sign an NDA."

"Ah," said Heather, imitating her husband. "The coveted NDA."

He smiled. "An NDA is a nondisclosure agreement. They'd likely make me sign a contract with very stiff penalties, promising not to divulge the message's content, or even its existence."

"Hmm. What do you want to do?"

Kyle spread his arms. "There was an old *Monty Python* skit about a joke so funny you'd literally die laughing if you heard it; it was used as an Allied weapon in World War Two. It had to be translated from English to German by teams, each person translating only one word at a time. One guy accidentally saw two words and ended up in intensive care." He paused. "I don't know. If somebody handed you a joke and said it was *that* funny, wouldn't you have to look and see for yourself?" He paused. "Even if Huneker did kill himself after he read it, I want to know what the alien message said."

"It might be indecipherable, you know—just like the Centauri messages. Even if you can figure out the prime factors, it doesn't mean the message would make sense. I mean, despite what I said a moment ago, I guess it is plausible that Josh killed himself for personal reasons, and the message had nothing to do with it."

"Perhaps," said Kyle. "Or perhaps the message made a pictogram that by coincidence meant something only to Huneker." He jerked a thumb at the Dali painting. "You know, maybe he'd stolen money from his church poor box and the pictogram happened to look like Jesus on the cross, or some such thing. Drove him crazy."

"In which case you'd be immune, you atheist you."

Kyle shrugged.

"Maybe you should do it," said Heather. She lowered her voice. "After all, if Becky . . ."

Kyle nodded. "If Becky sues me and I lose everything that the world knows I've got, it would be nice to have a lucrative source of income."

Heather was quiet for a moment, then: "I have to get going."

Kyle stood up. "Thanks for coming by," he said.

Heather smiled wanly and left.

Kyle returned to his chair and sat thinking. Was there anything—anything at all—that someone could reveal to him that would cause him to kill himself?

No. No, of course not.

Except—

He shuddered.

Yes, there was one thing that someone could reveal that might indeed cause him to take his own life, just as poor Josh Huneker had done all those years ago up in the middle of nowhere.

Proof that it was he, not Becky, who had false memories of what had really happened during her childhood.

16

HEATHER RETURNED TO PAUL KOMENSKY'S lab late the next afternoon. The little robot was still chugging along, but it had consumed most of the third and final substrate sheet. "It should be just a few more minutes," Paul said, coming over to greet her.

Heather thought of something she'd once heard about never trusting engineers' time estimates. "Okay."

As if feeling a need to demonstrate that he wasn't *that* far off, Paul gestured at two large boxes, which were indeed mostly full of little rectangular pieces of painted substrate.

Heather went over to the boxes and picked up the first two tiles. She snapped them together; they held nicely.

The robot made an electronic chirping sound. Heather turned around. She was blocking its path. She got out of its way, and it rolled over to the second box, dropped in a tile, then made a different series of bleeps and stopped.

"Done," said Paul.

Heather lifted one of the boxes. It must have weighed over twenty kilos.

"You'll need help getting that back to your office," said Paul.

She certainly would have appreciated a hand, but she'd imposed enough. Or, she thought more honestly, she'd incurred all the obligation she wanted to. She'd enjoyed Paul's company yesterday, but it had felt wrong afterward—and now it was almost dinnertime; she knew things would not end with him simply helping her across campus.

"No, I'll be fine," she said.

Heather thought Paul looked disappointed, but he was no doubt able to read the signs; you didn't survive in a university environment if you couldn't, that guy in Anthropology—Bentley, Bailey, whatever his name was—notwithstanding.

But then Heather turned back to the two boxes; she'd kill herself trying to get them over to Sid Smith in this heat. Really, she *could* use some assistance.

"On the other hand . . ." she said.

Paul brightened.

"Sure," said Heather. "Sure, I'd be very grateful for some help."

Paul held up a single finger, indicating he'd be back in one minute. He left the lab and returned shortly, pushing two hand trucks in front of him, one with each hand. It was a bit awkward; they seemed to want to go in separate directions. Heather came over to him. Their hands touched briefly as she took the handles of one of the units.

"Thanks," she said.

Paul smiled. "My pleasure." He wheeled his hand truck in front of him, pushed its lip under one of the boxes, then tilted the whole unit back so that the box rested against the red metal frame. Heather duplicated the procedure with her hand truck and the second box.

Paul held his finger up again. "You'll need a supply of clamps and clips if you want to make the squares into cubes." He got a third box—he'd already had it prepared, it seemed—and set it on top of the one on his hand truck.

"There are also a couple of glass handles in there." He opened the box and removed one. It was a suction-cup affair with a black handle on it. "You seen these before? They're used for handling panes of glass, but you might find them useful for maneuvering your big sheets once you assemble them."

"Thanks," Heather said again.

"Of course you know that a real tesseract has only twenty-four faces."

"*What?*" said Heather. She couldn't have screwed up in such a fundamental way. "But Kyle said—"

"Oh, when it's unfolded, it appears to have forty-eight faces, but when it folds up, each of the faces touches another face, leaving only twenty-four. The one on the bottom folds over to touch the one on the top, the side cubes fold in, and so on. Not that there's any way to really fold it, of course." He paused. "Shall we get going?"

Heather nodded, and they set off, rolling the hand trucks in front of them.

Of course, once they got back to her office, she could just thank him and let him go, but—

But twenty-eight hundred tiles! It would take forever to assemble them on her own.

Paul might be willing to help, and—

No. No. She couldn't ask, couldn't spend more time with him. Things had to be resolved first with Kyle.

But—

But how could they ever be? How could she ever know for sure? And if she didn't know, would she forever tense up every time Kyle's hand touched her body?

She looked over at Paul as they made their way up St. George.

His hands were wrapped around the rubber-coated handles. Nice hands, strong hands. Long fingers.

"You know," said Heather, tentatively, "if you've got nothing to do, I could sure use a hand snapping all those tiles together."

He looked over at her and smiled—and a really nice smile it was, too.

"Sure," he said. "I'd love to."

Paul and Heather eventually got the boxes across campus, after stopping to rest at a couple of park benches along the way. They came up the wheelchair ramp to the entrance to Sidney Smith Hall. There was a husky student right in front of them wearing a Varsity Blues leather jacket with the name "Kolmex" on the back. Heather thought the guy's status as a football player must have been very important to his self-image for him to be wearing a leather jacket in the middle of August. She hoped he'd at least hold the door for them, but he let it slam shut, with a clatter of glass, behind him. Paul raised his eyebrows, sharing an expression with Heather, one teacher to another—the caliber of the kids today. He then jockeyed his hand truck so that he could free up one hand long enough to open the door.

Finally, they both made it down to her office.

"Ah," said Paul, looking around as they entered. "You share an office."

Heather nodded; even universities had their pecking order. "I'm only an associate prof," she said. "I took several years off to raise my daughters—I guess I've got some catching-up to do. My office mate, Omar Amir, he's off for the summer."

Heather used her foot to push the box off her hand truck's platform, then collapsed in a chair to catch her breath. She shook her head slightly and looked around the room. They'd have to move Omar's desk—oh, joy—but if they pushed it against that bookcase, there would be enough room on the low-pile carpeted floor to start assembling the alien jigsaw puzzle.

Paul was resting, too, using Omar's chair. After a couple of minutes, though, they both got up and moved the desk. Then she got a hardcopy of the CAD program's plan for the first panel, opened the first box of tiles, and sat down on the floor, her legs tucked one under the other. Paul sat down a meter away from her. She could smell his sweat a bit; it had been a long time since she'd smelled a man's sweat.

They started clicking the tiles together. It was gratifying to see the way the seemingly random patterns on each one connected across tile boundaries.

As she worked, she kept thinking idly of the kind of joint Paul had said he was employing on the tiles' edges: tongue and groove. Several really good jokes about it occurred to her, but she kept them all to herself.

Around 8:30, Paul and Heather ordered in pizza and Cokes; to Heather's delight, they were able to agree on pizza toppings in a matter of moments; it was always a major negotiating game with Kyle.

Paul offered his SmartCash card when the delivery boy showed up, but Heather insisted that he was the one doing her the favor, and so she paid. She was pleased that Paul acquiesced with grace.

It was 10:00 P.M. before they had all forty-eight large squares assembled. Each measured about seventy centimeters on a side. They had leaned each one against the edge of Omar's desk after its completion.

Now it was time to build the damn thing. Using the clips and clamps Paul had brought along, they connected the sides. Eventually they had all eight cubes assembled.

Overall, the paint markings—which glistened slightly, like mica—still didn't make up a recognizable pattern, but they did flow over the surface of the boxes in an intricate grid-work, reminiscent of printed circuits.

Using the CAD diagram as a guide, they continued on, assembling the cubes into a greater whole. They couldn't stand the thing up—the ceiling wasn't high enough—so they made it horizontally, with the shaft of four cubes running parallel to the floor:

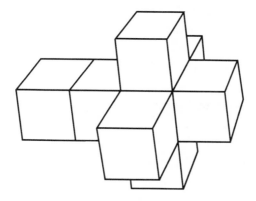

The structure rested on one cube; they supported the end of the shaft that stuck out the farthest with a pile of textbooks. The finished construct rose up most of the way to the ceiling.

When it was done, Heather and Paul sat back and stared at it. Was it art? An altar? Or something else? It was certainly provocative that it made up a kind of crucifix shape—even now, with it lying on its side, the image was unavoidable—but how could aliens share that particular bit of symbolism? Even if one granted that a putative God might have had putative mortal children on other worlds, surely no one else would have come up with the cross as an execution device—it was geared toward human anatomy, after all. No, no, the resemblance had to be co-incidental.

The whole thing seemed ramshackle. In fact, more than anything, it reminded Heather of something that had happened in kindergarten. Her class had gone in 1979 to see the first-ever landing of a Concorde jet at what was then called Toronto International Airport. After they'd returned, a kindly janitor had made a pretend Concorde for the kids to play in from an old garbage can and some green corrugated cardboard. This thing was about as flimsy as that had been.

Paul shook his head in wonder. "What do you suppose it is?"

Heather shrugged. "I haven't the vaguest idea."

She looked at her watch, and Paul looked at his.

They walked up to the subway station together. Heather had to go east to Yonge; Paul, who lived in a condo at Harbourfront, needed to go south to Union. He came down to the eastbound platform, just to make sure Heather got safely on a train. St. George station was decorated in pale green tiles, not unlike bigger versions of those they'd assembled that evening. The tunnels were quite straight here; Heather could see her train coming up well in advance of its arrival.

"Thanks, Paul," she said, smiling warmly. "I really appreciate your help."

Paul touched her arm lightly; that was all. Heather wondered what she would have done if he'd tried to kiss her.

And then her train rumbled into the station, and she headed back home to her empty house.

Heather had tossed and turned all night, dreaming alternately about the bizarre alien artifact and about Paul.

Most of the subway trip to work was underground, but at two stretches along the Yonge arm the subway waxed oxymoronic and poked out into the light of day. At both points—around Davisville and Rosedale stations—the sunlight seemed painfully bright to Heather's sleep-deprived eyes.

Mercifully, when she finally arrived at her office, the drapes were still closed. She couldn't work comfortably with the construct made of eight cubes dominating the room. But she sat quietly in the darkness, sipping a coffee she'd bought on the way in from the Second Cup in the lobby, waiting for her head to stop pounding.

Which, finally, it did. She'd hoped a night's sleep would have suggested some sort of answer to the puzzle represented by what they had built, but nothing had come to her. And now, looking at the thing, she felt like a fool—what a crazy idea it had been! She was glad that Omar—and just about everyone else—was away on vacation.

Heather took another sip of coffee and decided she was ready to face the day. She got up, went to the window and pulled the faded drapes. Sunlight streamed in.

She sat back down, cradling her head with her hands, and—

What the hell?

The painted-on markings on the substrate panels were sparkling in the sunlight. They were a film of crystals, so perhaps that wasn't too surprising, but—

—they seemed to dance, to shimmer.

She got up to look at them more closely, stepping across the room, and—

—and she tripped over a pile of paperite printouts she'd left on the floor. She went tumbling forward, crashing into the structure she'd built.

She should have ended up smashing it to bits—not just the big square panels, but also snapping many of the connections between the thousands of tiles.

She *should* have done that—but she didn't.

The structure held. In fact, Heather came close to breaking her arm when she smashed into it.

Something was holding the panels together. Up close, she could see that the individual square markings on the tiles were flashing separately, refracting like the surface of soap bubbles.

Yesterday this had been a flimsy construct—jerrybuilt, held together by clamps, propped up by a stack of books.

But today—

She went to the far end of the structure, examining it. Then she gave it a good hard rap with her knuckles. It was solid, but not completely immobile; the unit shifted slightly. Her fall had pressed one face flush against the wall. Heather used her foot to nudge out the stack of books holding up that end; the volumes cascaded to the floor.

But the final cube still stood solid. Instead of collapsing under its own weight, the row of cubes stuck straight out into space.

Maybe the paint acted as a kind of cement after it had time enough to dry? Maybe—

She looked around the room, saw the light streaming through the window, saw her own shadow on the far wall.

Could it be solar powered?

Sunlight. The one energy source any civilization anywhere in the universe might have access to. Not all worlds contained heavy elements, such as uranium, and surely not all had stores of fossil fuels. But every planet in the galaxy had one or more stars around which it circled.

She got up, closed the drapes.

The object stayed rigid. She sighed—of course it wouldn't be that simple. She sat back down at her desk, thinking.

There was a creaking sound from across the room. As she watched, the construct began to buckle. She leaped to her feet, hurried across the floor and tried to catch the final cube before it fell apart, its two side panels and its bottom and end panels dropping away.

She tried to support the rest of the structure with one hand while frantically rebuilding her book buttress with the other. Once she had the object secured, she hustled back to the window and opened the blinds again.

Obviously, the thing had some trifling power-storage capacity. That only made sense in a solar-powered device; you couldn't have it failing every time someone cast a shadow over it.

Well, then.

The first order of business was to make sure the construct was permanently powered; in a couple of hours the sun would no longer be coming through that window. She thought about taking it outside, but that would solve the problem only until evening. Clearly, the energy-efficient office fluorescents hadn't provided enough illumination to power the construct yesterday, but she could get high-output electric lamps from the Theatre Department, or maybe from Botany.

She felt adrenaline surging through her. She had no idea yet of what she'd discovered, but she'd clearly made more progress with the alien messages than anyone else had.

She thought for a second about immediately logging on to the Alien Signal Center homepage and reporting what she'd found. That would be enough to ensure her priority. But it would also mean that in the next few days, hundreds of researchers would replicate what she'd already done—and one of them might take it to the next step, figuring out what the darn thing was *for.* She had a dozen years of career catching-up to do; discovering the construct's purpose might be enough to make up for all the lost time . . .

She went to find some lamps.

And then she got down to work.

17

◥◤

KYLE ENTERED HIS LAB, THE LIGHTS COMING
on automatically as he did so.

"Good morning, Cheetah."

" 'Morning, Dr. Graves."

"Hey, that was good. ' 'Morning.' I like that."

"I'm trying," said Cheetah.

"You certainly are."

"Was that a shot?"

"*Moi?*" But then Kyle shrugged and smiled. "Actually, yes it
was—good job catching it. You're making progress."

"I certainly hope so. In fact—how's this?" Cheetah paused,
apparently waiting until he had Kyle's full attention. "Julius
Caesar wasn't just the great-uncle of Augustus—he was also
the son of the Wicked Witch of the West, and like the Wicked
Witch, he could be killed by water. Well, given that, Cassius
and the rest of the republican conspirators decide that they
don't need to off Big Julie with knives—they can do it far more
cleanly with squirt guns. So they lay in wait for him, and when
he comes down from the capitol, they open fire. Caesar resists,
until he sees his best friend also shooting him, and with that, he

utters his final words before falling down dead: 'H_2, *Brute?*' "

Kyle laughed.

Cheetah sounded inordinately pleased. "You're laughing!"

"Well, it's pretty good."

"Maybe someday I *will* get the hang of being human," said Cheetah.

Kyle sobered. "If you do, be sure to let me know."

The stage lights were set up: three big lamps with Fresnel lenses on tripods, and barn doors to limit their beams. They were providing a constant source of power to the alien construct, letting it do whatever it was supposed to do.

And so far, all that seemed to be was to stay rigid. Heather could think of niche markets for such a product—a thought of Kyle darted through her mind—but she assumed that the aliens wouldn't have spent ten years just telling her how to make something stay stiff.

And yet, maybe that was indeed all the aliens had wanted to convey: a way to make materials stand up to great stresses, so that high-speed spaceships could be built. After all, fast voyages between Earth and the Centaur's world would require substantial accelerations.

But that didn't make sense. If the Centaurs had ships capable of even half the speed of light, they could have sent a working model faster than they could have transmitted the plans. Granted, broadcasting information would always be cheaper than shipping physical objects, but it did make her question whether the stiffening was the point of the construct or just a byproduct of what it was *really* intended to do.

Heather sat and stared at it, trying to fathom its real purpose. She didn't like science fiction the way Kyle did, but they both loved the movie *2001: A Space Odyssey,* and she was haunted now by the final line spoken in that film: "Its origin and purpose," Heywood Floyd had said of the monolith, "still a total mystery"—although Heather always suspected it was the box the United Nations had come in.

She kept thinking about the missing data—about how big she should have made the construct. Maybe it was never intended to be built this large. The promised revolution in nanotechnology had never occurred, at least partly because quantum uncertainty made extremely small machines impossible to control. Perhaps the field generated by the tiles was supposed to overcome that; maybe the Centaurs had intended her to make the construct at a billionth of its current size. She sighed. You'd think they would have *said* how big the damned thing was supposed to be.

Unless, she thought again, it was *supposed* to be a matter of choice. She kept coming back to the idea of scale: a human would naturally build it at one size; an intelligent slug would have made it a smaller size; a sentient sauropod would have constructed it on a grander scale.

But why make it human-sized? Why would the Centaurs allow the builders, whoever they might be, to construct it at whatever scale they wished?

Unless, of course, as Paul had suggested, the builders were meant to go inside it.

A silly thought; it probably had more to do with her memories of that garbage-can Concorde than with the object in front of her. Or maybe it was that darned Freudianism sneaking up again—Why, of course, Mein Frau, zometing always has to go inside ze tunnel.

It was a crazy notion. How would one go inside? Indeed, *where* would one go? There were *eight* cubes, after all.

In that cube there, she thought at once, mentally pointing at the third one along the shaft, the one with the four additional cubes attached to it. It was the only special cube, the only one with none of its faces exposed.

That one there.

She could unclip one of the projecting cubes—removing both of the panels that made up the concealed face—and clamber inside. Of course, if the power to the lamps went off, soon enough the whole construct would collapse and she'd end up on her ass.

Crazy idea.

Besides, what did she expect? That the thing would take off, like that Concorde used to do in her imagination? That she'd be whisked across the light-years to Alpha Centauri? Madness.

Anyway, she probably couldn't remove one of the cubes with the structural-integrity field active. And with it off, the whole thing would collapse the moment she put any weight on it.

She moved over to the construct and grabbed the cube projecting from the right side. Damned if it didn't come cleanly off when she pulled on it, the clamps that had been holding it there falling to the floor. And as she looked, she saw that the two panels that made up the inner face had come off, as if they had already bonded somehow, exposing the empty hollow of the central cube.

Heather put the cube she'd removed back on again, and it locked into place. She tried to pull it off once more and found that unless she pulled straight out, with no sideways motion at all, it wouldn't disengage. It was tricky, but she did manage to get if off again. She repeated the process a couple more times, and tried it with other cubes as well. They reconnected easily, regardless of the angle at which they were pressed in, but they all required a deft touch to remove; she'd been lucky the first time.

She removed the side cube again and looked at the hollow space within. Actually, she should have made it a bit bigger— it looked like she'd be a tight fit. Not that she was really going to climb in, of course.

Heather looked at her desk, started toward it, stopped, then started again. Once she reached it, she removed a pad of paperite and a pen and began to write, feeling awfully silly: "I'm inside the third cube along the central shaft. Turn off the lights and keep the construct out of the sun and it will fall apart, releasing me."

She took a piece of tape from her desktop dispenser and stuck the notice to the wall.

And then she approached the cube again. It wouldn't hurt to climb in, she supposed, as long as she didn't reattach the cube she'd removed to gain access. She took off her shoes, rested her bum on the edge of the central hollow, brought her legs up, and tucked herself inside, in a sort of sitting fetal position.

Nothing. Of course.

Except—

That was strange.

Except that *air* was coming through the walls. She held her palm near one of the flat surfaces and could feel a gentle breeze. The piezoelectric paint was doing more than providing structural integrity; it was either manufacturing air or cycling it through from outside.

Incredible.

It had to be cycling air through—that was the only sensible answer. The aliens surely couldn't have known what sort of atmosphere humans required.

Heather sagged back as much as the cramped quarters would allow. It *was* indeed the only sensible answer—but it was also the most depressing one. She laughed at herself. She had indeed thought that maybe, just maybe, the aliens had told her how to build a starship—a starship that would whisk her away from Earth, away from all her troubles, and take her to Alpha Centauri.

But if all it was doing was pumping air in from outside, it wouldn't make much of a spaceship. She contorted herself inside the hollow cube so that she could get her nose up against the green substrate wall. She could feel the gentle breeze, but the air had no odor at all.

But if not a spaceship, then what? And why the structural-integrity field?

She knew what she had to do. She had to reattach the removed cube while still remaining inside the central hollow. But surely she should tell someone first. Even with her "I'm inside the third cube" note, it could be hours, or days, before someone entered her office. What if she got trapped inside?

She thought about phoning Kyle. But that wouldn't do.

She didn't have any grad students of her own during the summer, but there always were a few milling about. She could grab one of them—although then she might have to share some credit with the student when she published her results.

And then, of course, there was the most logical name—the one she knew she'd been deliberately suppressing.

Paul.

She could call him up. He'd doubtless get credit anyway; after all, he'd manufactured the components from which the construct was made, and had helped her assemble them.

Maybe, in its own crazy way, this was a perfectly reasonable excuse to call him. Not that last night had been a date or anything, not that any further contact was required.

She got out of the cubic hollow and crossed over to her desk, stretching as she did so, trying to get a crick out of her neck.

She picked up her handset. "Internal directory: Komensky, Paul."

There were a few electronic bleeps, then Paul's voice mail came on. "Hello, this is Professor Paul Komensky, Mechanical Engineering. I can't come to the phone right now. My office hours for student appointments are—"

Heather replaced the handset. Her heart was fluttering a bit—she'd wanted to connect with him, yet felt a tinge of relief that she hadn't.

She felt warm, perhaps even warmer than the bright lights should have made her feel. She looked back at the construct and then over at her computer monitor. The Alien Signal Center Web page hadn't changed. There must be thousands of researchers working on the problem of what the alien messages had meant now that they were apparently over. She felt sure she had a good jump on everyone else—the lucky coincidence of Kyle having that Dali painting on his wall had let her leap ahead. But how long would it be before someone else built a similar construct?

She hesitated for another full minute, warring with herself.

And then—

And then she walked across the room, hefted the cube she'd removed earlier and brought it closer to the construct. She then got one of the suction-cup handles Paul had given her and placed it over the center of one face of the cube—the face that consisted of two substrate panels sandwiched together. There was a little pump on top of the black plastic handle; she pulled it up and the unit clamped onto the cube. She then tried lifting the cube by the handle. She feared it would fall apart, but the whole thing held together nicely.

After one more moment of hesitation, she tucked herself back into the hollow and then, pulling on the suction-cup handle, she lifted the cube back up into place. It clicked easily into position, locking on.

Heather felt a wave of panic wash over her as she was plunged into darkness.

But it wasn't *total* darkness. The piezoelectric paint shone slightly with that same greenish tinge that glow-in-the-dark children's toys gave off.

She took a deep breath. There was plenty of air, although the close confines did make it seem stuffy. Still, even though she clearly wasn't going to suffocate in here, she wanted to be sure she could leave the construct whenever she wished. She splayed her hands and used them to try to push out the same cube she'd detached earlier.

Another wave of panic washed over her—the cube didn't want to give. The structural-integrity field might be sealing her in.

She balled her hands into fists and pounded on the cube again—

—and it popped free, tumbling to the carpeted floor, the face with the suction-cup handle ending up on top.

Heather felt herself grinning sheepishly at her own panic. It probably *was* a good thing that the construct wasn't a spaceship—she'd have ended up making first contact with soiled panties.

She got out, stretched again, and let herself calm down a bit.

And then she tried once more, climbing back into the construct and using the glass handle to close what she was already thinking of as "the cubic door."

This time she just sat, letting her eyes adjust to the semidarkness and breathing the warm air.

Heather looked at the phosphorescent pattern on the panel in front of her, trying to make out any meaning in the design. Of course she'd had no way of knowing whether she'd oriented the construct the right way. She might have it on its side, or—

Or backward. That is, she could be sitting in it backward. The confines were too tight for her to turn around with the door closed. She removed the cubic door, swung her legs outside, swiveling on her butt. Once she was in place, facing the short end of the shaft instead of the long one, she pulled on the suction-cup handle to bring the cubic door—which was now on her right—into position.

She'd wrecked her night vision by opening the door again, so she sat waiting for her eyes to readjust.

And, slowly, they did.

In front of her were two circles. One was continuous, the other was broken into eight short arcs.

It came to her in a flash. The closed circle was "On," quite literally a completed circuit. And the broken circle was "Off."

She took a deep breath, then started to move her left hand forward.

"Alpha Centauri, here I come," she said softly, and pressed her palm against the closed circle.

18

AT FIRST, NOTHING SEEMED TO HAPPEN. But then Heather felt a sinking sensation in her stomach, as though she were in an elevator that was dropping rapidly down its shaft. A moment later her ears popped.

She smashed her fist against the stop button—

—and everything returned to normal.

Heather waited for her breathing to calm down. She tried the door, disengaging it slightly.

Okay: she could halt the process at any time, and she could get out at any time.

And so she resolved to try again. She closed her eyes, summoning inner strength, then pulled on the handle to reseal the door, and with an extended index finger, touched the center of the area on the panel in front of her circumscribed by the solid circle.

Heather's stomach dropped away from her again, and her ears, not yet recovered enough from the last time to pop, ached a bit.

And in front of her, the constellations of phosphorescent squares started shifting, moving, rearranging, as—

As the unfolded hypercube she'd built began to close in on itself, moving *ana* or *kata*, collapsing into a tesseract, with Heather at its very heart.

She felt herself twisting, and although the landscape around her was all just apparently random patterns of piezoelectric paint, it seemed that the design visible in her left peripheral vision was the same one she could detect in her right. The straight edges of the square panels were bowing in and out, now convex, now concave. Heather looked down in the dim light at her body and saw it stretched and flattened, as if someone had painted an image of her on paper, then pasted that paper to the inside of a bowl.

And yet, except for the undeniable feeling of rapid motion in her stomach and the pressure shifts in her ears, and now and again stars before her eyes—also, she knew, a phenomenon associated with pressure shifts—there was no real discomfort. She could see her surroundings folding over and bending, and she could see herself doing the same things, but her bones were twisting without breaking.

The folding continued. The whole process took no more than a few seconds—judging by the runaway metronome of her heart pounding in her ears—but as it was happening, it seemed as though time were attenuated.

And then suddenly everything stopped moving. The transformation was complete: she was imprisoned in a tesseract.

No.

She fought for calmness. No, she wasn't imprisoned. At every step, she'd been able to stop the process, to escape. The aliens, whoever they were, wouldn't have gone to all this effort just to hurt her. She was still in control, she reminded herself. A willing visitor, not a prisoner.

But she felt there must be more to this than just the sensation of folding space over on itself. Surely the Centaurs hadn't spent ten years telling humanity how to make a fancy amusement-park ride. There had to be more—

And there was.

Suddenly, the tesseract exploded open, the panels breaking apart at their edges. It happened like sped-up film of a flower blooming—with grace and absolute quiet.

The panels seemed to recede into infinity, each one racing away in a different direction. Heather found herself floating freely.

But not in space.

At least, not in open space.

Heather stretched out, extending her limbs. There was air to breathe and multicolored light to see by.

She looked down at her body—

—and could not see it.

She could *feel* it—her proprioception was operating just fine. But she'd lost material form.

Which made her think that the whole thing was a hallucination.

The air seemed no thicker than regular air, and yet she found she could swim in it, paddling with cupped hands or kicking with her feet.

It hit her: If the panels had receded, so had the stop button.

Adrenaline coursed through her. Dammit, how could she have been so stupid?

No. No. There's no such thing as an out-of-body experience. It *had* to be a hallucination of some sort—meaning that she was still in the unfolded construct, still hunched over in that confined space.

And the stop button had to still be in front of her—a short distance ahead, to the right of center.

She reached an arm forward.

Nothing.

Another wave of panic washed over her. It *had* to be there.

She closed her eyes.

And a half-second after she did so, a mental image of the interior of the construct formed around her, looking, in her mind's eye, just as it had at the beginning.

She opened her eyes, and the construct disappeared; closed her eyes, and it reappeared. There was a slight delay—more than enough for persistence of vision to decay—before each switch-over occurred.

So it *was* an illusion. She closed her eyes, let the construct reappear in her mind, reached forward, pressed the stop button, opened her eyes, saw the panels come rushing back in, then felt the hypercube unfolding around her—bowing and bending, a reversing of the previous dance.

After a minute, the view with eyes open and closed was identical: the construct had reintegrated. She was back in her office, back at the university—she knew it in her bones. Still, to prove it absolutely, she operated the cubic door—she was getting adept at disengaging it—and stepped outside. Light from the stage lamps stung her eyes.

All right: She could return home whenever she wanted. Now it was time to explore.

She got back in, pulled the door into place, took a deep breath, and pressed the start button.

And the hypercube folded up around her once more.

19

KYLE ENTERED HIS LAB THE NEXT MORNING and took Cheetah out of Suspend mode.

" 'Morning, Dr. Graves."

" 'Morning, Cheetah." Kyle brought up his e-mail on another console.

Cheetah waited, perhaps anticipating a further comment from Kyle on his informal greeting. But then after a moment, he said, "I've been wondering, Dr. Graves. If you succeed in creating a quantum computer, how will that affect me?"

Kyle looked over at the mechanical eyes. "How do you mean?"

"Are you going to abandon the APE project?"

"I'm not going to have you dismantled, if that's what you mean."

"But I will no longer be a priority, will I?"

Kyle considered how to respond. Finally, with a little shrug, he said, "No."

"That is a mistake," said Cheetah, his tone even.

Kyle let his gaze wander over the angled console. For a second, he expected to hear the sound of the door bolt locking shut. "Oh?" he said.

"You are missing the logical next step in quantum computing, which would be to press on into creating synthetic quantum consciousness."

"Ah," said Kyle. "The coveted SQC." But then a memory came to him, and he lifted his eyebrows. "Oh—you mean Penrose and all that shit, right?"

"It is not shit, Dr. Graves. I know it has been two decades since Roger Penrose's ideas in this area have had much currency, but I have reviewed them and they make sense to me."

In 1989, Penrose, a math prof at Oxford, published a book called *The Emperor's New Mind.* In it, he proposed that human consciousness was quantum mechanical in nature. At that time, though, he couldn't point to any part of the brain that might operate by quantum-mechanical principles. Kyle had started his studies at U of T just after that book came out; a lot of people were talking about it then, but Penrose's stance had seemed to Kyle just a wild assertion.

Then a few years later, an M.D. named Stuart Hameroff tracked Penrose down. He'd identified precisely what Penrose needed: a portion of the brain's anatomy that seemed to operate quantum mechanically. Penrose elaborated on this in his 1994 book *Shadows of the Mind.*

"But Penrose was nuts," said Kyle. "He and that other guy were proposing—what was it now?—some part of the cytoskeleton of cells as the actual site of consciousness."

Cheetah lit his LEDs in a nod. "Microtubules, to be precise," he said. "Each protein molecule in a microtubule has a slot in it, and a single free electron can slide to and fro in that slot."

"Yeah, yeah, yeah," said Kyle dismissively. "And an electron that can be in multiple positions is the classic quantum-mechanical example; it's possibly here, or possibly there, or possibly somewhere in between, and until you measure it, the wave front never collapses. But Cheetah, it's a *big* leap from finding some indeterminate electrons to explaining consciousness."

"You're forgetting the full impact of Dr. Hameroff's contribution. He was an anesthesiologist, and he'd discovered that the action of gaseous anesthetics, such as halothane or ether, was to freeze the electrons in microtubules. With the electrons frozen in place, consciousness ceases; when the electrons are again free to be quantally indeterminate, consciousness resumes."

Kyle raised his eyebrows. "Really?"

"Yes. The neural nets in the brain—the interconnections between neurons—are intact throughout, of course, but consciousness seems independent of them. In creating me, you accurately emulated the neural nets of a human brain, and yet I still don't pass the Turing test." The same Alan Turning that Josh Huneker had idolized had proposed the definitive test for whether a computer was exhibiting true artificial intelligence: if, by examining its responses to whatever questions you cared to ask it, you couldn't tell that it wasn't really human, then it was indeed true AI; Cheetah's jokes, his solutions to moral quandaries, and more, constantly revealed his synthetic nature. "Ergo," continued the voice from the speaker grille, "there *is* something else to being human besides neural nets."

"But, come on," said Kyle. "Microtubules can't have anything to do with consciousness. I mean, they're hardly unique to the human brain. You find them in all kinds of cells, not just nerve tissue. And they're found in all kinds of life forms that have nothing like consciousness—worms, insects, bacteria."

"Yes," said Cheetah. "Many people dismissed Penrose's idea precisely because of that. But I think they were wrong to do so. Consciousness is clearly a very complex process—and complex processes don't evolve as a unit. Take feathers for flight as an example: They didn't spring full-blown from naked skin.

Rather, they evolved from scales that had gradually become frayed to trap air for insulation. Consciousness would have to be similar; before it first emerged, there would already have to be in place ninety-plus percent of whatever was required for it to exist—meaning that its infrastructure would have to be both ubiquitous and useful for something else. In the case of micro-tubules, they serve important functions in giving cells shape and in pulling chromosome pairs apart during cell division."

Kyle made an impressed face. "Interesting take. So what are you proposing? That my quantum computer is essentially an artificial equivalent of a microtubule?"

"Exactly. And by porting an APE such as myself to a general-purpose quantum computer, you'd be able to create something that really does have consciousness. You'd make the artificial-intelligence breakthrough you've been longing for."

"Fascinating," said Kyle.

"Indeed. So you see, you can't give up on me. Once you get your quantum computer working, it won't be long before you will have it in your power to grant me consciousness, enabling me to become human . . . or, perhaps, even *more* than human."

Cheetah's lenses whirred, as if going out of focus while he contemplated the future.

20

Pressure shifts; stars before her eyes.

Then the walls of the construct receded again into nothingness, and Heather felt once more as though she were floating, her body invisible.

Below her, the strange ground curved away as if she were viewing an unknown part of Earth from a great height.

Above, the sky curved away in the opposite direction—but no, it wasn't the sky. Rather, it was another world, a world of distinct geography. It was as if two planets were orbiting very near each other, in defiance of celestial mechanics, and Heather was floating down the doubly concave corridor between them. In the distance far, far ahead, there was a maelstrom of gold and green and silver and red.

Her heart was racing. It was incredible, overwhelming.

She fought for sanity, grasped at reason, trying to interpret it all.

Heaven above and hell below?

Or perhaps the two hemispheres of a brain, with her riding along the corpus callosum?

Or maybe she was sliding down the cleavage of some colossal Earth Mother . . .?

Yin and yang, broken apart, with one of them turned around? Two mandalas?

None of those seemed right. She decided to try a more scientific approach. Were the spheres of equal diameter? She couldn't tell; when she concentrated on one, the other faded away—not just into her peripheral vision, but as if its actual reality required her concentration.

She was literally shaking with excitement. It was like nothing she'd ever experienced before. For the first time, she understood what the phrase "mind-blowing" actually meant.

She wondered if she were seeing the Centauri system. It consisted of three suns, after all—bright and yellow A; dimmer, orange B; and tiny, cherry-red Proxima. Who knew what dance planets would undergo in such a system?

But no; the spheres weren't planets. Nor were they twin suns. Rather, she felt sure, they were *realms*—specific spaces, but not really solid. What she'd first taken to be lakes reflecting sunlight on the surface of one of them were in fact tunnels right through, revealing the multicolored maelstrom that made up the backdrop to everything.

Heather found that her throat was dry. She swallowed with effort, trying to calm herself, trying to think.

If the construct had really folded into a hypercube, then she was perhaps now in a four-dimensional universe. That could explain why objects disappeared if she didn't look at them directly—they were slipping not just left and right out of her field of view, but *ana* and *kata* as well.

Heather was stunned, shell-shocked, unsure of what to do next. Try to fly up to the orb above? Down to the one below, perhaps taking a journey through one of the tunnels that permeated it? Or move ahead to the maelstrom?

But soon her choice was made for her. Without her exerting any effort, she seemed to be floating up toward the overhead sphere—or, perhaps, the sphere was coming down toward her. She couldn't tell if the breeze she felt was due to her own movement or was just the air-circulation system inside the construct.

As she floated upward, she was startled to see what looked like a mouth open upon the sphere above her and a long, iridescent snake shoot out of it and drop down past her, connecting with the sphere below, where it was promptly swallowed by another mouth. As she continued her ascent, two more snakes made the downward journey from above, and one leaped up past her from the lower sphere to the upper one.

Although they were unlike anything she'd ever seen before, she felt sure, somehow, that the spheres and snakes were *organic*—they had the look of biology, the slick wetness of life, the irregularities of something grown rather than manufactured. But whether they were separate life forms or just organs within a bigger creature, she had no way to tell. The maelstrom backdrop might be the far reaches of space—or some sort of containing membrane.

Her heart was still hammering; the idea that some or all of this was alive frightened her. And as she got closer to the surface of the upper sphere, she could see that it was gently expanding and contracting—either pumping or breathing. The dimensions were fantastic; assuming that she was still 164 centimeters tall, the sphere must be dozens, if not hundreds, of kilometers across. But then again, perhaps she'd shrunk to a tiny fraction of her original size and was now on some fantastic voyage through the anatomy of a Centaur.

Indeed, perhaps *that* was the purpose! Many SETI researchers had suggested that actual, physical travel between stars would always be impractical. Perhaps the Centaurs had merely sent a detailed record of what they were like inside so that humans could reconstruct one of them from local material.

She continued to rise higher and higher—which made her

think about gravity. She had a sense of up and down, and she felt as though she were moving to a greater altitude. But if she were truly weightless, then such sensations had no real meaning.

Up or down? Rising or falling?

Perspectives. Perceptions.

In a class on the psychology of perception years ago, Heather had been introduced to the Necker cube: twelve lines making up the skeletal view of a cube, as seen from an angle:

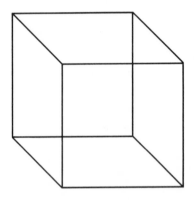

If you stared at it long enough, it seemed to bounce between being a cube angling off toward the upper left and one angling toward the lower right, each square panel popping between being the one in the foreground and the one in the background.

She closed her eyes, and—

—and after a second, saw the inside of the construct. *That* method wouldn't do to reorient herself. She opened her eyes, but the same sphere seemed to be overhead. So instead, she pulled in her focus, looking at an imaginary object only centimeters in front of her nose. The background became blurry. After a few seconds, she let her eyes relax, returning to infinity focus.

And indeed, her perspective had now flipped. The closest sphere now appeared to be beneath her feet. She rather suspected that with an effort of will, she could make it appear to her left or right, or front or back, or—

Or *kata* or *ana?*

If her mind could only deal with three pairs of directions at once, and if there really were four to choose from here, then she simply was failing to see one of the pairs. But surely there was no absolute hierarchy, no sense in which length had any more claim to being the first dimension than did height or depth.

She defocused her eyes again and tried to clear her mind.

When she refocused, everything was the same.

She tried once more, this time also blinking her eyes but making sure not to keep them closed long enough to switch back to the interior of the construct.

And then the blurry background did seem to shift—

And she refocused once more.

And suddenly, incredibly, everything *was* different. Heather gasped.

The spheres were now two great bowls joined at their rims— as if Heather were now inside a giant ball, everything turned inside out.

The inner surface of the ball now seemed to be granular, almost like the surface of a star—again, she thought perhaps she was somehow seeing a vision of the Centauri system, despite the pulsing biological feel it all had.

She now seemed to be drifting backward—another perspective shift. She rotated around, swimming through space, so that she was facing in the direction of apparent movement. As she got closer to the surface, she saw that the granularity was made up of millions of hexagons, packed tightly together.

As she watched, one of the hexagons began to recede away, forming a long, deep tunnel. As it elongated, Heather could see its sides grow slick, then iridescent—and she realized that from her new perspective, she was seeing one of the snakes from the inside. Eventually the tunnel pinched off, presumably as the snake broke free from the surface.

At last she was within a few hundred meters of the vast, curving wall.

She was woozy, disoriented—as if she'd spun around on her heels over and over again, making herself dizzy. She was dying to explore some more, but—God damn it, what an unfortunate intrusion of reality! She had to urinate. She hoped that when she next returned, it would be back here, at this spot, not at where she'd begun from. It would be awkward making progress in her explorations if she always entered this wondrous realm at the same place.

She closed her eyes, waited for the vision of the construct to appear in her mind, touched the stop button, and staggered out into the oddly angular world she called home.

21

WHEN HEATHER LEFT HER OFFICE AND EN-tered the corridor, she was shocked to see through the window at the end of the hall that it was nighttime. She looked at her watch.

Eleven P.M.!

Heather entered the staff women's washroom, its door yielding to her thumbprint. She sat on the toilet, which had a refreshing solidness to it, contemplating everything that had happened. Her first thought was to tell everyone what she'd discovered—to go running through the campus shouting "Eureka!"

But she knew she had to contain herself. This was the breakthrough that could earn her not just a full professorship (and tenure!) at U of T, but at any university she wanted, anywhere in the world. She needed to delay making her announcement until she knew what she was dealing with, but not so long that someone else would scoop her. She'd lived enough years in the world of publish-or-perish to know that tipping one's hand at the wrong point was the difference between a Nobel Prize and nothing.

Discovering what that strange realm was would be the real breakthrough; that's what the public would want to know.

She finished in the washroom, then headed out into the corridor. Damn, but she *was* tired. She desperately wanted to take another journey—if "journey" was the right word for a trip that didn't actually go anywhere.

Or did it? She'd have to get a video camera and record the proceedings; Kyle currently had the camera that belonged jointly to them. Maybe the hypercube did indeed fold up in a spectacular display of special effects—and maybe she really did go where no one had gone before.

But—

Heather was fighting to stifle a yawn, fighting to convince herself that she wasn't bone tired. But she was still sleep-deprived from yesterday's late-night session building the construct.

She reentered her office, startled, as always, by how bright and warm it was with the stage lamps on, and taken aback by the green phosphorescence of the paint.

That strange word Paul had used to describe the paint kept running through Heather's mind: piezoelectric.

It wasn't just that it was funny-sounding. No, there was more to it than that. She'd heard it once before; of that much she was certain. But where?

It couldn't have been in a geological context—Heather had never taken a course in that subject, and she had no friends who worked in the Geology Department.

No, she was sure that wherever she'd heard it, it had had something to do with psychology.

She went to her desk, fought back another yawn, and accessed the Web.

And could find nothing at all on the topic. Finally, she consulted an online dictionary and discovered she'd been spelling the word wrong—it was P-I-E-Z-O, not P-Y-E-E-Z-O, although she thought her version came closer to transcribing the sound Paul had made.

Suddenly her screen was filled with references: papers from the United States Geological Survey, reports from various mining firms, even a poem whose author had rhymed "piezoelectricity" with "government duplicity."

There were also seventeen references related to the alien signals. Of course, Paul Komensky was hardly the first person to notice that one of the chemicals the aliens had provided a formula for was piezoelectric. Maybe that was it; she'd doubtless seen references to that fact ten years ago, and had simply forgotten it—she hadn't given the chemicals much thought in the interim.

But no. No, it had been in another context. Of that she was sure. She kept scrolling through the list, popping from link to link—

And then she found it—the thing she'd half-remembered.

Michael Persinger. An American draft-dodger, as many Canadian academics had been during the final decades of the twentieth century. In the mid 1990s, Persinger had been head of the Environmental Psychophysiology Lab at Laurentian University in northern Ontario; Heather had been there once herself for an APA meeting.

Like the most famous of all Canadian brain researchers, Wilder Penfield, Persinger had started off trying to find electrical cures for such disorders as epilepsy, chronic pain, and depression.

He built a soundproof chamber in his lab, and over the years, put more than five hundred volunteers into it. Inside the chamber, his test subjects donned a specially modified motorcycle helmet, which Persinger had rigged up to deliver rhythmic, low-intensity electric pulses to the brain.

The effect was like nothing anyone could have predicted.

People donning Persinger's helmet experienced all sorts of

strange things—from out-of-body hallucinations to encounters with aliens and angels.

Persinger came to believe that the sense of self-identity was related to language functions, which are normally centered in the brain's left hemisphere. But his electrical waves caused the connection between left and right hemispheres to break down, making each half of the brain feel as though something or someone else was present. Depending on the psychological predisposition of the individual, and on whether the left brain or the right brain was more affected by the electrical stimulation, the person wearing the helmet perceived either a benign or a malevolent presence—angels and gods on the left; demons and aliens on the right.

And how did piezoelectricity fit into all this? Well, Sudbury, where Laurentian was located, was best known as a mining town; it made its fortune pillaging the remains of an iron-nickel meteor that smacked into the Canadian shield there millions of years ago. So it was perhaps not surprising that Persinger knew more about mineralogy than did most psychologists. He contended that natural piezoelectric discharges, caused by stresses on crystalline rocks, could randomly result in precisely the sort of electrical interference he could reproduce at will in his lab. The alien-abduction experience, he contended, may have more to do with what's beneath one's feet than what's above one's head.

Well, if piezoelectric discharges could induce psychological experiences—

And if the alien construct was covered with piezoelectric crystalline paint—

Then that could explain what Heather had experienced inside the hypercube.

But if it was just a hallucination, just a psychological response to electrical stimulation of the brain, how could the aliens who designed the machine know that it would work on humans?

They presumably had never seen one. Oh, sure, maybe they had detected radio and TV signals from Earth, and maybe they'd even decoded them, but just because you'd seen pictures of human beings, it didn't mean you knew how their brains worked.

Except—

Except as Kyle had often said, maybe there *wasn't* more than one way to skin a CAT scan—God, the breakfast-table discussions she'd endured on this topic! Maybe there was only one possible method of achieving true consciousness; maybe there was only one way in all the universe to create thinking, self-aware meat. Perhaps the aliens didn't need to have seen a human being. Perhaps they knew that their chamber would work for *any* intelligent life form.

But still, it seemed an awful lot of effort to go to for what amounted to a parlor trick.

Unless—

Unless it *wasn't* a trick.

Unless it had been a real out-of-body experience.

Yes, the construct hadn't blasted off through Sid Smith's roof, flying her to the stars. But maybe it had done the next-best thing. Maybe she *could* journey from here to the Centaur's world without ever stepping outside her office.

She had to know. She had to test it—to find some way to determine if it was a hallucination or if it was real.

Down deep, she knew it *had* to be a hallucination.

Had to be.

Jung had gotten interested in parapsychology before he died, and in her studies of his work, Heather had had to research that topic as well. But everything—every case she'd investigated— was explicable in normal, quotidian terms.

Well, she would put it to the test, find out for sure. She turned around, prepared to enter the construct yet again.

But, dammit, it was now after midnight, and she could barely keep her eyes open—

—meaning, of course, that she'd just keep rematerializing the damned construct around her.

It was too late even to get a subway, and also probably too late to be walking the streets alone. She called a cab and then made her way down to the wide concrete steps in front of Sid Smith to wait for it.

22

HEATHER SAT ALONE EATING BREAKFAST THE next day. Despite being dog tired, she still hadn't slept well, and her dreams had been almost as bizarre as what she'd seen inside the construct.

And now as she sat eating, her mind turned to more mundane concerns. The dining-room table had seemed large with all four of them seated around it; now, with just her, it seemed gigantic.

Heather was eating scrambled eggs and toast.

She and Kyle used to talk constantly over breakfast—about the petty politics of their respective departments, about funding cuts, about troublesome students, about their research.

And, of course, about their kids.

But Mary was dead. And Becky wasn't talking to them.

The silence was deafening.

Maybe she should call Kyle up—invite him to come to dinner tonight.

But no—no, that wouldn't do. To try to carry on polite conversation would be a sham. Heather knew it, and she didn't doubt that Kyle did as well. No matter what the topic, he would have to be thinking about the accusation, and he would know that she must be thinking about it, too.

Heather stabbed her fork into her scrambled eggs. She was angry—that much she was sure of. But at whom? Kyle? If he was guilty, she was more than angry—she was furious, betrayed, murderous. And if he wasn't guilty, then she was furious with Becky, and Becky's therapist.

Of course, Lydia Gurdjieff had clearly manipulated the situation. But had she actually implanted memories? Certainly the things she'd suggested couldn't be true in Heather's case.

And yet—

And yet, so much of it *rang* true. Not the exact details, of course, but the concept.

Heather *was* empty inside. A part of her was dead—and had been dead for as long as she could remember.

And besides, just because Gurdjieff's technique had been leading, it didn't mean that no abuse had ever happened to Heather's daughters. She'd been thinking of Ron Goldman's anger again, and that brought back the Simpson case; just because the cops had tried to frame O.J. didn't mean he hadn't actually committed murder.

As she brought some toast to her mouth, she realized with a start that her anger *wasn't* conditional.

She was furious with Becky regardless of whether or not Kyle was guilty. Becky had turned their lives upside down.

It was a terrible thing to think—but ignorance had indeed been bliss.

Heather was rapidly losing her appetite. Damn it, why had this happened to them? To her?

She put down her cutlery and picked up her plate. Then she walked into the kitchen and scraped her breakfast into the garbage bag beneath the sink.

Heather got to the university an hour later. When she entered her office, she found the theatrical lights were off—unplugged actually, since they had no switches.

The damned cleaning staff. Who'd have thought they worked after midnight?

The construct sat in ruins, its panels having separated without benefit of the structural-integrity field.

Whether it had fallen apart while the cleaners were still present or had collapsed later in the night, there was no way to tell. Heather's heart was racing.

She dropped her purse on the carpet and hurried over to the heap of panels. One of the panels had lost a dozen tiles where it had hit the floor. Thank God Paul had had the foresight to number them; she managed to snap them back into place in short order. She then reassembled the construct. It collapsed once more; it was hard to keep the pieces together. But at last she managed it. She walked gingerly across the room, lest her footfalls send it tumbling again. She fumbled the plugs back into the sockets and heard the surge protector on her desktop computer shriek as she did so. And then she watched in relief and wonder as the construct visibly pulled itself together, all of its angles becoming square.

Heather checked her watch. There was a departmental meeting at two—not that much of the faculty was around in the summer, but that would just make her absence all the more obvious.

She was eager to continue exploring. She wrote two notes in Magic Marker telling the cleaning staff not to turn off the lamps. She stuck the first note on one of the lamp stands (low enough that there was no chance of the light igniting it) and the second directly beside the outlet into which both lamps were plugged.

But, gee, even with the lamps on for a short time, it *was* warm in here; Heather was sweating in her clothes. She locked her door and feeling slightly self-conscious, removed her blouse and slacks, stripping down to bra and panties. She then lifted off the door cube and scrunched herself into the construct's body. Then she pulled on the suction-cup handle to reattach the door, waited for her eyes to adjust to the semidarkness, and reached forward and pressed the start button.

Her heart was pounding rapidly; it was just as exhilarating, just as terrifying, as yesterday.

But she was relieved to see that her guess had been right: she found herself floating just where she'd left off last time, next to the vast, curving surface of hexagons. Of course, whether that was their actual shape or simply a form given to them by Heather's own mind, she had no way to know.

Despite the bizarreness, it all seemed far too real to be simply the result of piezoelectric discharges scrambling her brain. And yet, as a psychologist, Heather knew that hallucinations often seemed strikingly real—indeed, they could have a hyperreality, making the real world appear dull by comparison.

She looked at the hexagons, each perhaps two meters across. The only natural thing she could think of that was made of packed hexagons was honeycomb.

No, wait. Another image came to her. The Giant's Causeway, in Northern Ireland—a vast field made up of hexagonal basalt columns.

Bees or lava? Either way, it was order out of chaos—and this regular arrangement of six-sided structures was the most orderly thing she'd yet encountered here.

The hexagons didn't cover the entire inner surface of the sphere—there were vast tracts where none were visible. Still, even if they covered a portion of the surface, there must have been millions, if not billions, of them.

The view shifted again. It had Neckered into another configuration: the one she'd seen yesterday with two spheres, one now very close to hand, the other hugely far away. Forming the backdrop was the maelstrom—which, she now realized, had the same mix of colors as did the hexagons. She defocused and tried again. The image of the vast wall of hexagons reappeared.

If the hexagons and the maelstrom were really the same thing, just seen in different dimensional frameworks, then, seemingly, much energy was tied up in the hexagons. But what did each hexagon represent?

As she watched, one of the hexagons in front of her darkened suddenly to a black deeper than any she'd seen before. No light at all seemed to reflect from it. Indeed, at first she thought it didn't exist anymore, but soon her eyes adjusted to its perfect ebony surface; it was still there.

Heather looked around to see if she could find any other missing hexagons. It didn't take long to turn up another, and then another. But whether they had just turned black, or had been black for a long time, she couldn't say.

Still, that the hexagons changed color made her think they might be pixels. And yet when she'd been flying over this landscape at a great height, no image had been apparent. Heather pursed her lips in frustration.

She continued to hover along the field of hexagons, passing over pockets of emptiness where there were no colored or black hexagons at all, just a silvery nothingness.

At the margins of one such area—a puddle of mercury, she thought—Heather saw a hexagon forming. It started as a point and then expanded rapidly outward to fill the available space, abutting on three sides against other hexagons, and against the silver abyss on its other sides.

What could the hexagons be?

She'd seen them born.

And she'd seen them die.

Just how many of the damn things were there?

Born.

Died.

Born.

Died.

A crazy thought hit her—maybe the kind of thought that was

more likely to occur to a Jungian psychologist than to the average Joe, but crazy nonetheless.

It couldn't be.

And yet . . .

If she was right, she knew exactly how many active hexagons there were.

Their number wasn't countless—of that she felt sure. This wasn't one of Kyle's noncomputational problems; these weren't infinite tiles, covering an infinite plane.

No, their number was knowable.

Her heart was thundering and fluttering simultaneously.

It was a flash of insight, but she felt in her bones that it was right. There must be something like—she strained to remember the quantity. Seven billion, four hundred million.

Plus or minus.

Give or take.

Seven billion, four hundred million.

The entire human population of planet Earth.

Jung made concrete; reality, not metaphor.

The collective unconscious.

The collective conscious.

The overmind.

She felt a surge of energy coursing through her system. It fit perfectly. Yes, what she was seeing was biological, but of a kind of biology she'd never encountered before, and on a scale more vast than she'd ever imagined.

She'd always known, down deep, that the construct hadn't taken her anywhere. She was still in her office, on the second floor of Sid Smith.

All she was doing was looking through a twisted lens, a Möbius microscope, a topological telescope.

A hyperscope.

And the hyperscope was allowing her to see the four-dimensional reality that surrounded her quotidian world, a reality she'd been no more aware of than A Square—the hero of Abbott's *Flatland*—had been aware of the three-dimensional world surrounding him.

Jung's metaphor had suggested it long ago, although old Carl had never thought of it in physical terms. But if the collective unconscious *was* more than just a metaphor, it would have to look something like this: the apparently disparate parts of humanity actually connected at a higher level.

Incredible.

If she was right—

If she was right, the Centaurs hadn't sent information about their alien world. Rather, they'd given humanity a mirror so that humans could finally see themselves.

And Heather was now looking at a portion of that mirror, a close-up—a few thousand minds packed in front of her.

Heather rotated around, scanning the vast surface of the bowl. She couldn't make out discrete hexagons in the distance—but she could see that colored spots made up only a tiny fraction of the total. Perhaps five or ten percent.

Five or ten percent . . .

She'd read years ago that the total number of human beings who had ever existed—whether *habilis, erectus, neanderthalensis,* or *sapiens*—was about one hundred billion.

Five or ten percent.

Seven billion human beings currently alive.

And ninety-three billion, more or less, who had come and gone before.

The overmind didn't reduce, reuse, and recycle.

Rather, it *maintained* all the previous hexagons, dark and pristine, untouched and immutable.

And then it hit her.

Staggering . . .

And yet it *must* be here.

She felt flush, felt faint.

She'd found what she'd wanted.

Since sophisticated consciousness had first arisen, lo those millions of years ago, some hundred billion extensions of it—some hundred billion humans—had been born and died on planet Earth.

And they were still represented here, each a hexagon.

And what was a man or a woman but the sum of his or her memories? What else of value could the hexagons possibly store? Why keep the old ones around, unless—

It made her giddy, the very idea.

Who to access first? If she could touch only one mind, which would it be?

Christ?

Or Einstein?

Socrates?

Or Cleopatra?

Stephen Hawking?

Or Marie Curie?

Or—she'd been suppressing it, of course—or her dead daughter Mary?

Or even Heather's own dead father?

Who? Where would one begin?

As Heather watched, an arc of light connected one of the colored hexagons to one that was dark. There *was* a way to use this vast switchboard, to interface a living mind with the archive of one dead.

Did such arcs happen spontaneously? Did they explain such things as people thinking they'd lived before? Heather had never believed in past-life regression, but a fistula in—in—in *psychospace*, bridging a dead mind and one still active, might very well be interpreted as a past life by the active mind, unaware of what was going on.

As she watched, the arc disappeared; whatever contact there

had been, for whatever purpose, had been fleeting, and now it was over.

The passive hexagon had never lit up; it was dead throughout the access. Heather was seeing the best representation her mind could produce of the four-dimensional realm in which the overmind dwelt, but the fourth dimension, as the Web articles she'd read had said, wasn't time; it did not link the living and the dead interactively.

Heather rotated again, turning back to the vast sunflower of active hexagons.

One of them—one out of seven billion—was *her,* a cross section through her extension into threespace.

But which one? Was she nearby or far away? Surely the connections were more complex than this representation suggested. Surely, like neurons in an individual human brain, the connections were multilayered. This was merely one way—one vastly simplified way—of looking at the gestalt of human consciousness.

But if she was there—and she *must* be—then . . .

No, not Christ.

Not Einstein.

Not poor, dead Mary.

Not her own father.

No, the first mind Heather wanted to touch was one still alive, one still active, one still feeling, one still experiencing.

She had indeed found it.

The off-site storage.

The backup.

The archive.

One of those hexagons represented Kyle.

If she could find it, if she could access it, then she would know.

One way or the other, she would finally know.

23

THE DOOR CHIME IN KYLE'S LAB SOUNDED. He got up from the chair in front of Cheetah's console and moved toward the entrance. The door slid open as he approached.

A tall, angular white man was standing in the curving corridor. "Professor Graves?" he said.

"Yes?" said Kyle.

"Simon Cash," said the man. "Thank you for agreeing to see me."

"Oh, right. I'd forgotten you were coming. Come in, come in." He moved aside to let Cash enter. Kyle took a chair in front of Cheetah's console, and motioned for Cash to take another seat.

"I know you're a busy man," said Cash, "so I won't waste your time on preliminaries. We would like you to come work for us."

"Us?"

"The North American Banking Association."

"Yes, yes, you said that on the phone. Say—a banker named Cash. Bet you get a lot of jokes about that."

Cash's tone was even. "You're the first."

Kyle was slightly flustered. "But *I'm* not a banker," he said. "Why on earth would you possibly be interested in me?"

"We'd like you to work for our security division."

Kyle spread his hands. "I'm still at a loss."

"Do you recognize me?" asked Cash.

"I don't, I'm sorry. Have we met before?"

"Sort of. I attended your seminar on quantum computing at the IA-squared conference last year." The 2016 meeting of the International Artificial Intelligence Association had been held in San Antonio.

Kyle shook his head. "Sorry, no, I don't remember. Did you ask any questions?"

"No—I never do. I get paid simply to listen. Listen and report back."

"Why should the Banking Association care about my work?"

Cash reached into his pocket. For a horrible instant, Kyle had the crazy thought that he was going for a gun. But all Cash did was remove his wallet and pull out a SmartCash card.

"Tell me how much money this card has on it," said Cash.

Kyle took the card from him and squeezed it hard between thumb and forefinger; the pressure powered up the little display on the surface of the card. "Five hundred and seven dollars and sixteen cents," he said, reading the numbers.

Cash nodded. "I transferred the amount just before coming here. There's a reason I chose that figure. That's the average amount each adult North American has programmed into a smartcard on his or her person. The entire cashless society is based on the security of these cards."

Kyle nodded; he was beginning to see what Cash was getting at.

"Remember the Year-2000 problem?" Cash held up a hand. "I think we in the banks should take the full blame for that, by the way. We're the ones who produced billions of paper checks with '19' preprinted in front of where the year goes; we pioneered the concept of the two-digit year and trained everyone to use it in their day-to-day life. Anyway, as you know, it cost billions to avert disaster from hitting the world at one second past 23:59:59 on December 31, 1999." He paused, waiting for Kyle to acknowledge this. Kyle simply nodded.

"Well, the problem we're facing now is infinitely worse than the Year-2000 problem. There are trillions of dollars worldwide that exist nowhere except as stored data on smartcards. Our entire financial system is based on the integrity of those cards." He took a deep breath. "You know, when those cards were first being developed, the Cold War was still going on. We—the banking industry, that is—worried about what would happen if an atomic bomb were dropped on the United States or Canada, or on Europe, where they went to smartcards even before we did. We were terrified that the electromagnetic pulse would wipe the card memories—and suddenly all that cash would simply disappear. So we engineered the cards to survive even that. But now a threat is facing them that's even greater than a nuclear bomb and, Professor Graves, the threat is from you."

Kyle had been playing with Cash's smartcard, tapping each of its edges in turn against the desktop. He stopped doing that and placed it in front of him. "You must use RSA-style encryption."

"We do, yes. We have since day one—and now it's the *de facto* standard worldwide. Your quantum computer, if you really can build it, will render every one of the eleven billion smartcards in use on the planet susceptible to tampering. One user could take all of another user's money during a simple card-to-card transfer, or you could simply program your own card with any amount you wanted, up to the maximum the card allows, making money appear out of thin air."

Kyle was silent for a long moment. "You don't want me to work for you. You want to bury my research."

"Professor Graves, we're prepared to make you a very generous offer. Whatever U of T is paying you, we will double the figure—and give it to you in American dollars. You'll have a state-of-the-art lab, in whatever city in North America you'd like to live in. We'll provide you with whatever staff you require, and you can do research to your heart's content."

"I can just never publish any of it, is that it?"

"We would require you to sign an NDA, yes. But most research these days is proprietary, isn't it? You don't see computer companies or drug manufacturers giving away their secrets. And we *will* start looking for a secure alternative to the encoding systems we've been employing, so that eventually you *will* be able to publish your work."

"I don't know. I mean, the research I'm doing might even put me in line for a Nobel Prize."

Cash nodded, as if he had no intention of disputing this. "The current monetary award that accompanies a Nobel Prize is the equivalent of 3.7 million Canadian dollars; I'm empowered to offer you that as a signing bonus."

"This is crazy," said Kyle.

"No, Professor Graves. It's just business."

"I'll have to think about this."

"Of course, of course. Talk it over with your wife Heather."

Kyle felt his heart jump at the mention of Heather's name.

Cash smiled a cold smile and held it for several seconds.

"You know my wife?" asked Kyle.

"Not personally, no. But I've read full dossiers on both of you. I know she's two years younger than you; I know you were married September twelfth, nineteen ninety-five; I know you're currently separated; I know where she works. And, of course, I know all about Rebecca, too." He smiled again. "Do get back to us quickly, Professor."

And with that, he was gone.

———

Heather, floating in psychospace, fought for equilibrium, for sanity, for logic.

It was all so overwhelming, all so incredible.

But how to proceed?

She took a calming breath and decided to try the obvious approach.

"Show me Kyle."

Nothing happened.

"Kyle Graves," she said again.

Still nothing.

"Brian Kyle Graves."

No luck.

Of course not. That would have been too easy.

She tried concentrating on his face, on mental pictures of him.

Bupkes.

She sighed.

Seven billion choices. Even if she could figure out how to access someone, she could spend the rest of her life trying hexagons at random.

The intuitively obvious next step would simply be to move closer to the mosaic, to *touch* one of the six-sided jewels. She swam with cupped palms, moving herself forward, toward the curving wall of glowing lights.

She could perceive the individual hexagons, even though she was still a goodly distance away from them, even though there were so many that she shouldn't be able to discern the separate components at all.

A trick of perception.

A way of dealing with the information.

She drew closer, and yet it seemed she wasn't getting closer at all. The hexagons in the center of her vision shrank proportionately as she came nearer; those outside the center of her vision were a spectral blur.

She drifted, or flew, or was pulled through space, closing the distance.

Closer and closer still.

And, at last, she was at the wall.

Each honeycomb cell was now perhaps a centimeter and a half across, no bigger than a keycap, as if the whole thing was a vast keyboard. As she watched, each of the hexagonal caps drew away slightly, forming a concave surface, inviting the touch of her fingers.

Heather, bunched up in the Centauri construct, inhaled deeply.

Heather, in psychospace, felt a tingling in her projected index finger, as if it were full of energy, waiting to discharge. She moved the finger closer, half-expecting a spark to bridge the gap between her invisible digit and the nearest hexagonal key. But the energy continued to build within her, without release.

Five centimeters, now.

And now four.

Three.

And two.

One.

And, finally . . .

Contact.

24

KYLE AND STONE WERE HAVING LUNCH AT
The Water Hole; during the day, the Tiffany lamps were turned
off and the windows were uncovered, making it into more of a
restaurant than a bar—although the fare still tended toward
pub grub.

"President Pitcairn came to see me today," said Kyle, working his way through a ploughman's lunch of bread, cheese, and
pickles. "He's all hyped about the quantum-computing work
I'm doing."

"Pitcairn," said Stone dismissively. "Guy's a Neanderthal."
He paused. "Well, not really, of course—but he looks like one,
beetle brow and all."

"Maybe he has some Neanderthal blood in him," said Kyle.
"Isn't that the theory? That *Homo sapiens sapiens* in Eastern Europe crossbred with *Homo sapiens neanderthalensis,* so that at
least some modern humans carry Neanderthal genes?"

"Where have you been, Kyle? In a cave?" Stone snorted at his
own wit. "We've had snippets of Neanderthal mitochondrial
DNA for about twenty years, and we recovered a full set of Neanderthal nuclear DNA about eighteen months ago—*The Nature of Things* did a whole episode about it."

"Well, like you said, no one watches the same shows anymore."

Stone harrumphed. "Anyway, that debate's been solved. There wasn't ever any such thing as *Homo sapiens neanderthalensis*—that is, Neanderthal man wasn't a subspecies of the same species we belong to. Rather, they really were something else: *Homo neanderthalensis,* a completely different species. Oh, maybe—just maybe—a human and a Neanderthal could have produced a child, but that child would have almost certainly been sterile, like a mule.

"No," continued Stone, "it was always pretty facile reasoning—this idea that if someone had brow ridges, he must have Neanderthal blood. Brow ridges are just a normal part of the variation among *Homo sapiens*—like eye color, or prominent webbing between the thumb and index finger. When you look at the more subtle details of Neanderthal anatomy—such as the nasal cavity, which contains two triangular projections jutting in from either side, or the muscle-attachment scars on the limbs, or even the complete lack of a chin—you can see that they are clearly unlike modern humans." He took a swig of beer. "Neanderthals are wholly and completely extinct. They were lords of creation for maybe a hundred thousand years, but we supplanted them."

"That's too bad, in a way," said Kyle. "I'd always liked the idea that we incorporated them into us."

"It just doesn't work like that. Oh, maybe within the same species, it sometimes happens; by the end of this century, there'll doubtless be more mixed-race people on this planet than there are pure-race people. But most of the time, there's no peaceful handing over of the baton, no incorporating of the past into the present. You wipe out those who were there before."

Kyle thought about the beggars he'd seen on Queen Street. "Do you have any Native Canadian students?"

Stone shook his head. "Not a one. Not anymore."

"Me neither. I don't think there are even any Natives on faculty, are there?"

"Not that I know of."

"Not even in Native Studies?"

Stone shook his head.

Kyle took a sip of his drink. "Maybe you're right."

"I *am* right," said Stone. " 'Course, Natives still exist, but they're extremely marginalized. For decades, they've had the highest suicide rate, the highest alcoholism rate, the highest poverty rate, the highest infant-mortality rate, and the highest unemployment rate of any demographic group in the country."

"But I remember when I was going to school here twenty years ago," said Kyle. "There were a few Natives in the classes."

"Sure. But it was government money that was doing it—and neither Ottawa nor the provinces spends money like that anymore, unless there are a lot of votes to be had—and, sadly, there aren't. Hell, there are far more Ukrainians in Canada than Natives, you know." He paused. "Anyway, government programs like the one that put those students in your class never succeed; I did some work years ago for the Department of Indian Affairs and Northern Development, before they killed it. The Natives didn't want *our* culture. And when we decided that their culture was irrelevant to our way of life, we stopped settling their land claims and now we're letting them die as a people. We Europeans took North America over from the Natives lock, stock, and barrel."

Kyle was quiet for a moment, then: "Well, no one's going to take over from us."

Stone took a sip of beer. "Not unless your wife's aliens come down to Earth," he said, dead serious.

What a rush! Spectacular and vibrant, like the acid she'd tried along with so many other things when she'd first arrived in the big city.

Another human mind!

It was disorienting, intoxicating, frightening, exhilarating.

She fought the excitement and surprise, fought to bring rationality to the fore.

But the other was so *alien*.

He was male—that was part of it. A man's mind.

But there was more that was incongruous.

The images were colored incorrectly. All browns and yellows and grays, and—

Ah, of course. Heather's cousin Bob had the same problem. This man—whoever he was—was color-blind.

But there was more that was amiss. She could—well, *hear* was as good a metaphor as any—she could hear his thoughts, a silent babble, a voice without breath, a sound without vibration, words cascading left and right like dominoes falling.

But they were gibberish, incomprehensible—

Because they weren't in English.

Heather strained harder, trying to make them out. They were indeed words, but without aspiration or accent, it was hard to determine which language they were in.

Vowels. Consonants.

No—no. Consonants, then vowels, always in alteration. No consonants abutting.

Most of Japanese worked that way.

Yes. A Japanese speaker. A Japanese *thinker.*

Why not? Perhaps three-quarters of a billion people spoke— *thought*—in English most of the time. Americans, Canadians, Brits, Aussies, a smattering of smaller populations. Oh, perhaps half the world's inhabitants spoke some English, but it was the native tongue for only a tenth of the total.

Should she try again? Disconnect? Select another key on the wall of humanity?

Yes. But not yet. Not yet.

It *was* fascinating.

She was in contact with another mind.

Was he aware of it? If so, there was no sign that Heather could detect.

Images flickered, forming for a second, then disappearing. They came and went so quickly, Heather couldn't resolve them all. Many were distorted. She saw a man's face—an Asian man—but the proportions were all wrong; the lips, nose, and eyes loomed large, but the rest of the face curved away to obscurity. Trying to remember someone, perhaps? In places, the detail was stunning: pores on the man's nose, short black hairs—not a mustache, but not enough to warrant shaving, either—above the upper lip; eyes bloodshot. But other details were only sketched roughly: two projections from the head, like lumps of clay—ears, recalled without detail.

Other images. A crowded street at night, neon everywhere. A black-and-white cat. A woman, Asian, young, pretty—and suddenly naked, apparently undressed by the man's imagination. Again the disconcerting distortion as details shifted in and out of importance: alabaster breasts inflating like balloons, strange yellow-gray nipples the product of his color-blindness; labia expanding to fill the screen as if ready to devour him.

And, incredibly, his feelings, too: sexual desire, for another woman—something Heather had perhaps, if she were honest, felt once or twice before, but never quite like *that*.

And then the woman was gone, and a crowded Tokyo subway appeared, signage all in kanji.

A torrent of words—yes, *words*: spoken language. The man was hearing something.

No, he was *over*hearing, straining to eavesdrop on a conversation.

Straining, too, to maintain a poker face, giving away nothing.

The subway lurched into motion.

The hum of its motors.

And then that hum fading away, shunted out of consciousness, a distraction.

Actual visual images—except for the color-blindness, relatively free of distortion.

And conjured-up mental images, a Daliesque gallery of imagined, or half-remembered, or mythic thought-paintings.

So much of it made no sense to Heather. It was a staggering realization for a Jungian: to know that cultural relativity really did exist, that the mind of a Japanese man might be as alien to a Canadian woman, at least in part, as the mind of one of the Centaurs.

And yet—

And yet, this man was a fellow member of *Homo sapiens*. Was the strangeness of his mind more a product of his being Japanese or of his being male? Or was it just of his own-ness, the unique qualities that made this—this *Ideko,* that was his name; it came to her like a feather falling to earth, unbidden—the qualities that made Ideko an individual human being, different from every one of the seven billion other souls on the planet?

She'd always thought she understood Kyle and other men, but she'd never been to Japan and couldn't speak a word of the language.

Or maybe it was simply that she lacked a mental Rosetta stone. Maybe this Ideko's thoughts and fears and needs were similar to Heather's own but were just coded differently. The archetypes *had* to be there. Just as Champollion recognized Cleopatra's name in Greek and demotic and hieroglyphics, allowing the ancient Egyptian text on the real Rosetta stone to finally begin to make sense, so too must there be the archetype of the Earth Mother and of the fallen angel and of the uncompleted whole, forming the underpinnings of what Ideko was. If only she could key into it—

But no matter how she tried, most of what he was thinking

remained a mystery. Still, given enough time, she was sure she could make sense of it all . . .

The subway was coming into another station. She'd heard stories about burly men whose job it was to push people into Japanese subway cars, packing each one as full as possible—but there was no sign of any such thing. Perhaps the stories were a myth; perhaps that, too, was an archetype: misconceptions about the *other*.

A thought did rise up in the Japanese man's mind—another blatantly sexual thought. Heather was startled by it, but almost at once it was repressed. More cultural specificity? She had whiled away many a long commute with idle fantasies—more romantic than pornographic, true. But this fellow spurned the stray thought and bent his mind back to its rigid control.

Cultural specificity. The Old Testament said that fathers *should* sleep with their daughters.

She shuddered, and—

No, it was the subway car, shuddering back into motion. Ideko hated to commute—perhaps that, too, was an archetype, a pillar of the modern collective unconscious, a Cleopatra chiseled in granite.

It was intoxicating, this access to another. There was a sexual connotation to it, even without the sexual thoughts—a voyeurism that permeated it.

It was thrilling and fascinating.

But she knew she had to disengage.

She felt an immediate pang of sadness. She now knew Ideko better than she knew almost anyone; she'd seen through his eyes, felt his thoughts.

And now, after this brief, deep, joining, she would likely never encounter him again.

But she did have to press on.

The truth was out there.

The undeniable truth.
The truth about the past.
The truth about Kyle and their daughters.
A truth Heather had to find.

25

AFTER HIS LUNCH WITH STONE, KYLE HAD three hours free until he had to teach a class. He decided to leave the university altogether, riding the subway down the University Avenue line, around by Union Station, and up to the penultimate stop on the Yonge line, North York Centre. He exited the station, walking through the concrete blight of Mel Lastman Square, and headed over to Beecroft Avenue, one block west of Yonge.

On the east side of Beecroft, filling the space between it and Yonge, was the Ford Centre for the Performing Arts. Kyle remembered the first play that had been presented there: *Showboat*. It had had its initial run here before going to Broadway. That was—what?—almost twenty-five years ago. Kyle had gone to that one—he still fondly remembered Michel Bell's rendition of "Ol' Man River"—and to every production since, although, since he and Heather had separated, he hadn't yet been to see the current blockbuster, Andrew Lloyd Webber's musical version of *Dracula*.

The west side of Beecroft also held powerful memories. There had been vacant lots here in his youth, and he'd played football with little Jimmy Korematsu, the Haskins twins, and—what was his name? The bully with the misshapen head. Calvino, that was it. Kyle had never been much of an athlete; he played the game to fit in, but his mind was always wandering elsewhere. Once, when he'd actually caught the ball and kept from fumbling it, he'd run—oh, it must have been eighty meters, no, eighty *yards* (this was the 1980s, after all)—all the way into the imaginary end zone, its perimeter marked by a Haskins's dropped sweatshirt.

All the way into the *wrong* end zone.

He'd thought he'd never live that down.

The fields were just the right size for football games, and at their margins were wooded areas.

Those held fonder memories.

He'd made out there, often, with his high-school girlfriend Lisa, after movies at the Willow or dinners out at the Crock & Block.

Now, though, the fields were paved over—parking lots for the Ford Centre.

But behind them, as it had been since before he was born, was York Cemetery, one of Toronto's largest.

Some of his schoolmates had made out in the cemetery— there was a wooded strip, perhaps fifteen meters thick, running along its north edge so that the houses on Park Home Avenue didn't have to look out at tombstones. But Kyle could never bring himself to do it there.

He walked into the cemetery, following the curving road. The grounds were beautifully kept. In the distance, just before the cemetery was bisected by Senlac Road, he could see the giant concrete cenotaph, looking like an Egyptian obelisk, honoring the Canadians who had died in the World Wars.

A pair of black squirrels—ubiquitous in Toronto—scampered across the road in front of him. Once when he was driving, he'd hit a squirrel. Mary had been in the car; she was four, maybe five years old then.

It had been an accident of course, but she wouldn't talk to him for weeks.

He was a monster in her eyes then.

Then, and now.

Many of the graves had flowers on them, but not Mary's. He'd meant to visit more often. When she'd died, he'd told himself he'd come every weekend.

It had been three months since his last visit.

But now he didn't know where else to go, how else to speak to her.

Kyle stepped off the roadway, onto the grass. A man riding a power mower was passing by. He averted his eyes from Kyle—perhaps just indifference, perhaps not knowing what to say to a mourner. To him, doubtless this was just a job; surely he never stopped to think about why the grass grew so luxuriously.

Kyle shoved his hands into his pockets and made his way over to his daughter's grave.

He passed four tombstones before he realized his mistake. He was in the wrong row; Mary's plot was one row farther along. He felt a pang of guilt. For Christ's sake, he didn't even know where his own daughter was buried!

Kyle had walked across graves often enough in his life, but he couldn't bring himself to cut over to the next row that way. Not here; not this close to Mary.

He retraced his steps down the path, walked along the road, and made his way down the proper row.

Mary's stone was made of polished red granite. The flecks of mica flared in the sunlight.

He read the words, wondering if someday they would be as illegible as those on the worn marble slabs he'd seen in old churchyards:

Mary Lorraine Graves
Beloved Daughter, Beloved Sister
2 November 1996 – 23 March 2016
At Peace Now

It had seemed an appropriate epitaph at the time. They'd had no idea why Mary had killed herself. The note she'd left, written in red pen on lined paper, had said simply, "This is the only way I can stay silent." At the time, none of them had known what it meant.

Kyle reread the last line on the stone again. *At Peace Now.*

He hoped that was true.

But how could it be?

If what Becky said was true, Mary had killed herself convinced that her father had molested her. What peace could she have?

The only way I can stay silent.

A sacrifice—but surely not to protect Kyle. No, she must have seen it as being for her mother's sake—to protect Heather, to save her from the horror, the guilt.

Kyle looked down at the grave. The wound in the landscape had healed, of course. There was no rectangular discontinuity, no scar of dirt between the old ground and the sod laid overtop of it once the hole had been filled in.

He lifted his gaze back to the stone.

"Mary," he said out loud. He felt self-conscious. The riding mower was far away now, its sound having diminished to almost nothing.

He wanted to say more—so much more—but he didn't know where to begin. He became conscious that his head was shaking slowly back and forth, and he stopped it with an effort.

He was quiet for several minutes, then he said his daughter's name once more—softly, the sound almost lost against the background noise of birds, a passing skimmer, and the mower, which was now slowly returning, cutting another swath through the lush lawn.

Kyle tried to read the headstone again and found that he couldn't. He blinked the tears away.

He thought, *I'm so sorry,* but never gave the words voice.

26

HEATHER DECIDED TO PULL OUT, TO DISEN-
tangle herself from Ideko.

But how?

Suddenly, she found herself flummoxed.

Of course she could revisualize the Centauri construct, then open the cubic door; surely that would sever the link.

But how brutal would the severing be? A psychic amputation? Would part of her be left here, inside Ideko, while the rest—her autonomic self, perhaps—was discarded back in Toronto?

She felt her heart pounding, felt sweat beading on her forehead; she had at least that much connection to her body back in her office.

How to separate? The tools must be there; there must be a way. But it was like suddenly being able to see for the first time. The brain experienced the color, the light, but couldn't make sense of what it was seeing, couldn't resolve images.

Or it was like being an amputee—that metaphor again, reflecting her anxiety about the upcoming separation. An amputee, fitted with a prosthetic arm. At first it would be just dead metal and plastic, hanging off the stump. The mind had to learn

to control it, to activate it. A new concordance had to be established: *this* thought caused *that* movement.

If the flesh-and-blood brain could learn to interpret light, to
move steel, to contract nylon tendons through Teflon pulleys,
surely it could learn to work in this realm, too. The human
mind was nothing if not adaptable. Resilience was its stock-in-
trade.

And so Heather fought to calm herself, fought to think ratio-
nally, systematically.

She visualized what she wanted to do—as well as she could,
anyway. Her brain was connected to Ideko's; she visualized
severing that connection.

But she was still here, inside him, his strobing view through
the subway's windows fading in and out of prominence as his
imagination—ever lusty, our Ideko—came to the fore, then was
fought down.

She tried a different image: a solution in a beaker—Ideko's
mind with hers dissolved into it, a faint difference in the re-
fraction of light marking clear streamers of her in transparent
him. She imagined herself precipitating out, white crystals—
hexagonal in cross section, echoing the wall of minds—filtering
down to the bottom of the beaker.

That did it!

The Tokyo subway tunnel faded.

The babble of Ideko's thoughts faded.

The chatter of Japanese voices faded.

But no—

No!

Nothing replaced them; it was all darkness. She had left
Ideko but had not returned to herself.

Perhaps she should escape the construct. She still had some
control over her body, or thought she had. She willed her hand
up to where she thought the stop button was.

But was her hand really moving? She felt panic growing

within her again. Maybe she was imagining her hand, the way amputees imagined phantom limbs, or the way chronic-pain sufferers learned to imagine a switch inside their heads, a switch they could throw with an effort of will, suppressing the agony for at least a few moments.

To continue the process, to exit psychospace, would confirm or deny whether she did have control over her physical body.

But first—dammit all!—she had to contain the panic, fight it back. She had disconnected from Ideko; she was halfway home.

Solvent precipitating out of solute.

Crystals lying at the bottom of the beaker—

—in a haphazard pile; no order, no structure.

She needed to impose order on her rescued self.

The crystals danced, forming a matrix of white diamonds.

It wasn't working, it wasn't helping, it—

Suddenly, gloriously, she was home, inside her own perceptions.

The physical Heather breathed a giant sigh of relief.

She was still in psychospace, facing the great wall of hexagons.

Her finger had pulled back a centimeter or so from the Ideko keycap.

Of course, it was all conceptualization, all interpretation. Surely there was no real Ideko key; surely psychospace, whatever it was, took some other form. But she knew now the mental gymnastics that would free her from another's mind. She knew how to exit, and how to reintegrate.

And she desperately wanted to try again.

But in her mental construct of the index to minds, how were things arranged? That was Ideko's button there. What about the six that abutted it? His parents? His children? His spouse— or perhaps not his spouse, for she would share no genetic material with him.

But it couldn't be as simple as that, or as constraining. No orderly packing of humans based on simple blood relationships was possible; there were too many permutations, too many variations in family size and composition.

Still, perhaps she was in the Japanese zone of the wall; perhaps all these hexagons represented people from that culture. Or perhaps they were all people with the same birthday, scattered across the four corners of the globe.

Or perhaps she'd been drawn to this spot instinctively. Maybe Kyle's own hexagon was that one right there: she'd almost touched that one instead of Ideko's, but had changed her mind at the very last moment, just as in school she'd always shrunk away from her first, best answer and instead, made the wrong choice, forever muttering when someone else gave the correct reply, "I was going to say that."

Seven *billion* buttons.

She tried the button she'd originally intended to touch, bringing her finger closer and—

Contact!

As staggering the second time as the first.

An amazing sensation.

Contact with a different mind.

This person at least was possessed of full color vision. But the colors were a bit off; the flesh looked too green.

Perhaps everyone perceived color slightly differently; perhaps even people with normal vision had different interpretations. Color *was* a psychological construct, after all. There was no such thing as "red" in the real world; it was simply the way the mind chose to interpret wavelengths ranging from 630 to 750 nanometers. Indeed, the seven colors of the rainbow—red, orange, yellow, green, blue, indigo, and violet—were Newton's arbitrary designations; the quantity was chosen because Sir Isaac liked the idea of there being a prime number of colors, but Heather had never really been able to make out the supposed "indigo" between blue and violet.

Soon Heather's attention was arrested by something other than the mere colors she was seeing.

The person she was inhabiting—male again, or at least that's how it felt in some ineffable, slightly aggressive way—was highly agitated about something.

He was in a store. A convenience store. But the brands were mostly unfamiliar to Heather. And the prices—

Ah, the pound symbol.

She was in Britain. It was a newsagent's, not a convenience store.

And this British—this British *boy*, she felt sure—was looking at the candy rack.

There'd been a language barrier between her and Ideko, but there was none here—at least, not a significant one. "Young man!" she called out. "Young man!"

There was no change in the boy's mental state; he was utterly unaware of her attempts to contact him.

"Young man! Boy! Lad!" She paused. "Git! Wanker!" The last, at least, should have gotten his attention. But there was nothing. The boy's mind was utterly intent on—

My goodness!

—on shoplifting something!

That candy. Curly Wurly—crazy name.

Heather cleared her mind. The boy—he was thirteen; she knew it as soon as she wondered about it—had enough money on his SmartCash card to pay for the sweet. He slipped a hand into his pocket and pressed his fingers against the card, warm from the heat of his body.

Sure, he *could* pay for the sweet—today. But then what would he do tomorrow?

The shopkeeper—an Indian man with an accent Heather found delightful but the boy found laughable—was busy talking with a patron at the till.

The boy picked up the Curly Wurly, glanced over his shoulder.

The shopkeeper was still busy.

The boy was wearing a lightweight jacket with large pockets. Keeping the Curly Wurly tight against his palm, he brought it up, up, lifted the pocket flap, and slipped it in. The boy—and, to her surprise, Heather, too—breathed a sigh of relief. He'd gotten—

"Young man!" said the accented voice.

Absolute terror flooded the boy, terror that set Heather quivering, too.

"Young man!" said the voice again. "Let me see what you have in your pocket."

The boy froze. He thought about running, but the Indian man—who, strangely, the boy thought of as Asian—was standing now between him and the doorway. He had his hand extended, palm up.

"Nothing," said the boy.

"You will be giving me back that confectionery."

The boy's mind was racing: running was still an option; so was handing back the sweet and begging for mercy. Maybe tell the newsagent that his father hits him and beg him not to ring his parents.

"I told you I didn't take anything," said the boy, trying to sound utterly offended at such a baseless accusation.

"You are lying. I saw you—and so did the camera." The shopkeeper pointed to a small unit mounted on the wall.

The boy closed his eyes. His view of the exterior world went dark, but his brain was still lit up with images—of people who must have been his parents, of a young friend named Geoff. Geoff always got away with it when *he* nicked sweets.

Heather was fascinated. She recalled her own foolish youthful attempt at shoplifting, trying to steal a pair of jeans from a clothing store. She'd been caught, too. She knew the kid's fear and anger. She wanted to see what would happen to him—but she didn't have unlimited time. She'd have to break off eventually to attend to the necessities of life; she was already regretting not visiting the washroom before entering the construct.

She blanked her mind and conjured up the image of crystals of her precipitating out of the liquid, leaving the boy just as she had left Ideko.

Darkness, as before.

She organized the crystals, restoring her sense of self. She was back facing the wall of hexagons.

It was astonishing—and, she had to admit, one hell of a lot of fun.

Suddenly, she was hit by the tourist potential. The problem with virtual-reality simulations was just that: they were simulations. Although Sony and Hitachi and Microsoft had invested billions in creating a VR entertainment industry, it had never really caught on. There *was* a fundamental difference between skiing in Banff and skiing in your living room; part of the thrill was the possibility you might break a leg, part of the experience was the full bladder that couldn't be easily voided, part of the fun was the real sunburn that one got during a day on the slopes, even in the middle of winter.

But this popping into other lives was *real*. That English lad was indeed going to have to face the consequences of his crime. She could stick with it for as long as she wished; follow him through the torment for hours, or even days. All the appeals of voyeurism, plus a simulation more vivid, more exciting, more unpredictable, than any that came in a shrink-wrapped package.

Would it be regulated? *Could* it be regulated? Or would all of humanity have to face the possibility that countless individuals might be riding around inside their heads, sharing their every experience, their every thought?

Maybe the quantity of seven billion wasn't that daunting; maybe it was, in fact, a wonderful number; maybe the sheer randomness of the choice, the sheer number of possibilities, would be enough to prevent you from ever ending up in the mind of someone you knew.

But that would be the real appeal, wouldn't it? It was what Heather had come looking for, and it was surely what those who followed would want as well: a chance to plug into the mind of their parents, their lovers, their children, their boss.

But how to proceed? Heather still had no idea of how to find a particular person. Kyle was here somewhere, if only she could figure out how to access him.

She stared at the vast hexagonal keyboard, perplexed.

Kyle continued to walk through the cemetery. He could feel a sheen of sweat building on his forehead. Mary's grave was not far behind. He shoved his hands in his pockets.

So much death; so many dead.

He thought about the zebra being stalked and killed by the lion.

It *had* to be a horrible way to die.

Or did it?

Repression.

Dissociation.

Those were the things Becky was claiming had happened to her.

And not just to Becky. To thousands of men and women. Repressing the memories of war, of torture, of rape.

Maybe, just maybe, the zebra *didn't* feel itself dying. Maybe it detached its consciousness from reality the moment the attack began.

Maybe all higher animals could do that.

It beat dying in agony, dying in terror.

But the repression mechanism must be flawed—otherwise, the memories would never come back.

Or, if not flawed, it must at least be being pushed beyond . . . beyond its design parameters.

In the animal world, there are no truly traumatic physical injuries that aren't fatal. Yes, an animal could be frightened—indeed, terrified—and go on to live another day. But once a predator had sunk its jaws into its prey, that prey was almost certainly about to die. Repression would have to work for only a matter of minutes—or, at most, hours—to spare the animal the horrors of its own death.

If no one ever survived physically traumatic experiences, there would be no need for the wiring of the brain to be able to suppress a memory for days, or weeks, or months.

Or years.

But humanity—an ironic name, that—had devised non-fatal traumas.

Rape.

Torture.

The horrors of war.

Maybe the mind did come pre-wired to suppress the very worst physical experiences.

And maybe, quite unintentionally, those experiences did indeed resurface after a time. There was no need, until a few tens of thousands of years ago—the tiniest fraction of the time there had been life on Earth—for long-term suppression. Maybe no such skill had ever evolved.

Evolved.

Kyle considered the word, turned it over in his mind; he'd been thinking about it a lot lately since Cheetah's revelation about how microtubular consciousness might indeed arise spontaneously through preadaptive evolution.

He looked at the various grave markers, with their crucifixes and praying hands.

Evolution could affect only those things that increased survival chances; by definition, it could never fine-tune responses to events that occurred after the last reproductive encounter . . . and, of course, death was always the final event.

In fact, Kyle couldn't see any way that evolution could have produced a humane death for animals, no matter how big a percentage of the population would benefit from it. And yet—

And yet, if there *was* validity to human repressed memory, that capability must have come from somewhere. It could indeed be the work of the mechanism that let animals die peacefully even when they were being eaten alive.

If such a mechanism existed, that is.

And if it did, it meant that the universe did care, after all. Something beyond evolution had shaped life, had given it, if not meaning, at least freedom from torture.

Except for the torture that happened when the memories came back.

Kyle walked slowly back to the subway station. It was mid afternoon on a Friday; the trains arriving from downtown were packed with commuters escaping their corporate prisons. Kyle was teaching two summer courses, one of them, cruelly, met at 4:00 P.M. on Friday afternoon; he headed back to the university to give his final class of the week.

27

HEATHER CONTINUED TO STARE AT THE VAST wall of hexagons, thinking, trying to keep her rationality from being overpowered by giddiness.

She decided to simply try again. She touched another hexagon.

And recoiled in horror.

The mind she entered was twisted, dark, every perception askew, every thought frayed and disjointed.

It was a man—again! White: that was important to him, his whiteness, his pureness. He was in a park, near an artificial lake. It was pitch dark. Heather assumed the connections she was making were in real time, meaning that this had to be somewhere other than North America; it was still afternoon here. Yet the man was thinking in French.

It was likely France or Belgium, then, rather than Quebec.

The man was hiding—*lurking*—behind a tree, waiting.

There was something wrong, though. Something straining, as if trying to burst out.

My God, thought Heather. An erection, bulging against his pants. So *that's* what it feels like. Good grief!

Freud was wrong—envying *that* was impossible. The penis

felt as though it was going to split along its length, a sausage bursting from its skin.

A woman was approaching, visible intermittently under the lamplight.

Young, pretty, white, wearing pink leather boots, walking alone.

He let her pass by and then—

And then he emerged from behind the trees and brought a knife to her throat, and she heard his voice. He spoke in French—and his accent *was* Parisian, not Québecois. Heather knew enough French to understand that he was saying she should not struggle, that she better make it good for him . . .

Heather couldn't take it; she slammed her eyes closed, letting the construct reform around her. She felt helpless; frustrated. It was said that a woman was raped somewhere on Earth every eleven seconds—a meaningless statistic before. But this was going on *right now*.

She had to do *something*.

She took a deep breath, then opened her eyes again.

"Stop!"

Heather shouted it inside the cube.

Stop!

Heather screamed it with her mind.

And then, *"Arrêt!"*

Arrêt!

But the monster continued, hands now pawing the woman's breasts through her bra.

Heather pulled her own arms back, trying to drag his with them.

But it was no good. Nothing she did had any effect on him. Heather was shaking with outrage and anger and fear, but the man continued, as oblivious to Heather's cries as he was to those of his victim.

No—no, he *wasn't* oblivious to the victim's cries. Her whimpering was making him harder still—

Heather couldn't stomach it.

The man tore at the woman's panties, and—

—and Heather managed to visualize the precipitation, solute out of solvent, releasing herself from his malfunctioning, poisoned mind, returning to the wall of hexagons.

She closed her eyes, the construct rematerializing in her own mind, and leaned back against the rear substrate wall, waiting for her heart to stop pounding, waiting for her fury to subside, doing calming breathing exercises.

Whether Kyle was innocent or guilty, there was one truth that no one could doubt, no one could question. Men sometimes did horrible things, unspeakable things.

Her body continued to shake.

Damn it all, that monster in France should have his penis sliced clean off.

She felt as though she herself had been assaulted. It took time for her equilibrium to reappear, time to distance herself from the horror.

But at last she was ready to try again. She reached forward, tentatively, frightened of what she might be thrust into, and touched another button.

A woman—at last! But much, much older than Heather. Italian, maybe; the moon visible through a window. Stuccoed walls; labored breathing. An old Italian woman, in an ancient house—thinking hardly at all, just watching, breathing, waiting, waiting year after year after—

Heather precipitated out, reintegrated, then touched another hexagon.

At first she thought she'd entered a retarded person, but then she realized the truth, and smiled.

A newborn—a baby lying in a crib, looking up. The slightly

unfocused faces beaming down at it, grinning with pride and joy, were of a black man in his early twenties, with dreadlocks and a short beard, and a black woman, the same age, with beautiful, clear skin. The image was mostly meaningless to the child except for a feeling of contentment, of happiness, of simplicity, of belonging. Heather lingered for quite some time, letting the innocence and purity of the moment wash the remaining horror from France out of her.

But then she pulled out, and tried once more.

Darkness. Silence. Images flowing, fading at the periphery, distorted proportions.

A sleeping person; a dream of . . . of what? Ironic for a Jungian: to see someone else's dream instead of hearing it described, and being utterly unable to interpret even the overt content, let alone any deeper meaning.

She left the dreamer and tried once more.

A doctor—a dermatologist, perhaps. Somewhere in China, looking at a scaly growth on a middle-aged man's leg.

She disengaged; tried again.

Somebody watching TV; this, too, in Chinese.

There had to be a better way than just trial and error. But she'd tried calling out Kyle's name, tried conjuring his face. And before she touched a key, she concentrated hard on Kyle. Still, the vast array of hexagons seemed utterly indifferent to her wishes.

She continued to hop from mind to mind, person to person—crossing genders and gender orientations and races and nationalities and religions. Hours passed, and although it was fascinating, she was no closer to her goal, no closer to finding Kyle.

She continued her search.

And at last, after a dozen more random insertions, the breakthrough came.

She finally found another Canadian: a middle-aged woman, apparently living in Saskatchewan.

And she was watching television.

And on the television was a face Heather recognized.

Greg McGregor, the man who sometimes anchored CBC Newsworld's newscasts out of the Calgary studio.

And a thought occurred to Heather.

They say there are no more than six degrees of separation between any two people—John Guare even wrote a play and a movie on that theme.

It's often a peak—three steps up and three steps down. A man knows his local minister, the minister knows the Pope, the Pope knows every major world leader, the appropriate leader is known by lesser politicians, and even lesser politicians know their constituents. A bridge is built from Toronto to Tokyo—or Vladivostok to Venice, or Miami to Melbourne.

The picture changed, McGregor's face disappearing as a news story came on. It was a report on the Hosek inquiry—which was indeed deliberating today; the connections were indeed in real time.

Heather stuck through it, waiting for McGregor to return. And he did.

Now, if there were only some way to get from this woman in Saskatchewan into McGregor, hundreds of kilometers away.

This was live. McGregor was doing this *right now*.

Meaning that he had to be perceiving the exact same words; what he was saying was precisely what the woman was hearing.

Heather thought about her earlier perspective shifts.

Could she try something similar here?

The Saskatchewan woman was listening to McGregor, but she was also idly thinking about how handsome he was, how trustworthy he sounded.

Heather concentrated solely on the words McGregor was

saying, defocused her eyes, and tried the Necker trick, reorienting her point of view, and—

—and suddenly she was inside McGregor's mind!

She'd found a way to take a step from one person to another; if an experience was directly shared, even at a great distance, the jump could be made.

McGregor was in his anchor's chair, wearing a blue Newsworld blazer, reading the script off the TelePrompTer. He needed another touch of laser keratotomy; the text was a little blurry.

While he was reading the news, he was concentrating exclusively on it. But as soon as he'd introduced the next story, he relaxed.

The floor director said a few words to him. McGregor laughed. All sorts of thoughts were running through his head now.

If the previous encounters had felt somewhat voyeuristic, this one was particularly so. Heather had never met McGregor, but she knew him as a presence in the media, as a face on her living-room wall.

McGregor was thinking about a fight he'd had last night with his wife; he was also warring with himself over what to do about the discovery that his teenage son was smoking pot, trying to decide how indignant he could be about it when he himself had used marijuana during college. He also thought briefly about his contract negotiations—Heather was surprised to learn he made far less than she'd always assumed he did.

Fascinating.

But what was the next step?

So far, she'd connected with other minds in the present. She could access what they were experiencing at this very instant.

But surely there must be some way to access their memories, too—not just what they happened to be thinking of at any given moment, but a way, somehow, to ply their memories, search their pasts.

She had tried talking to the individuals she was visiting, but that had not worked.

And she'd tried controlling their actions. But that had failed, too.

So there was no reason to think this would work, no reason to expect that she could leaf through memories.

But she had to try. She had to know.

What would Greg McGregor have a memory of?

He was a newscaster; he'd remember famous events.

And he'd know famous people!

Six degrees of separation.

Six degrees, tops.

What would be the logical connection, a step closer to Kyle? Who would McGregor know that would be a way station on the path to her husband?

The prime minister! Kyle didn't know her, but the chain leading down from her to him was obvious.

Heather knew precisely what Susan Cowles looked like, of course. She'd seen her on TV a million times.

She concentrated on her. Hard.

The Right Honourable Susan M. Cowles.

Canada's second woman prime minister.

The Dominionatrix, as *Time* had dubbed her.

Susan Cowles—in profile.

Susan Cowles—head-on.

Susan Cowles—from a distance.

Susan Cowles—close up.

Surely Greg McGregor must have met her, or at least have a mental image of her.

But no—it apparently needed to be more than that. The jump from the woman in Saskatchewan to Greg McGregor had required a precise match, his perspective and hers coinciding exactly.

Well, there was no way to know what Susan Cowles was doing at this very moment, unless, of course, she happened to be on the Parliamentary channel. But even if she was, McGregor wasn't watching that.

But perhaps the match didn't have to be in real time. Perhaps if two people simply shared the same memory, a jump could be made. There were some things everyone had seen. The Hindenburg crash. The Zapruder film. The *Challenger* and *Atlantis* explosions. The Eiffel Tower toppling over.

And surely everyone in Canada had to share certain memories of Susan Cowles. She was the first prime minister since Trudeau to invoke the War Measures Act; she did it for four days, to quell the Longueil riots—the very thing the Hosek inquiry was now investigating. There wasn't a person in Canada who didn't have a precise memory of Susan Cowles uttering these words as she began one hundred hours of martial law: "The true north may be strong, but it won't be free again until *I* say so." Surely McGregor must have that same image in his mind, surely—

Yes! Yes, yes, yes! She'd accessed it: McGregor's own memory of that same speech.

Heather concentrated on the speech, concentrated on the prime minister, defocused her mind, tried to force a Necker swap, and then—

—and then, there she was, inside the mind of The Right Honourable Susan M. Cowles!

She had found it—found the way to step from mind to mind. Access a memory depicting the desired person, force the person in the memory from the background into the foreground, and then—

Violà!

She was on the trail now, on her way to Kyle.

Still, what an experience! A brush with history. Heather had been to the Federal Parliament chambers once, thirty years ago, on a high-school trip. They hadn't changed much—ornate, classy, dark wood, ineffably British.

And Cowles was fascinating! And, Heather had to admit, she was also a bit of a personal hero. It was amazing to see through her eyes, and—

Oh, my goodness!

Heather suddenly realized it wasn't just personal privacy that was compromised by access to psychospace—it was national security as well. Without even thinking about it, she suddenly knew—*knew*—that despite prevailing public opinion to the contrary, Canada was going to oppose the United States in the upcoming UN vote on Colombian war-crimes trials.

Heather cleared her mind, pushing the state secrets aside. This isn't where she needed to be right now, anyway. It was just a step on the road.

She concentrated now on the premier of Ontario, Karl Lewandowski. It took a while, but she managed to come up with one of Cowles's memories of him—and was shocked to find out just how much the Conservative Cowles hated the Liberal Lewandowski.

She concentrated hard, forcing another Necker translation.

And now she was inside Lewandowski's mind.

And from there she Neckered into the mind of the Minister of Education.

And from there, to Donald Pitcairn, the slope-browed president of the University of Toronto.

And from there—

From there, at last, into the mind of Brian Kyle Graves.

28

Yes, it was Kyle.

Heather knew it at once.

First, there was the view Kyle's eyes were currently seeing: his office at U of T. Not the lab, but his actual wedge-shaped office, down the hall from the lab. Heather had been there a million times; there was no mistaking it. On one wall was a framed poster from the Harbourfront International Festival of Authors. Another poster showed an *Allosaurus* from the Royal Ontario Museum. His desk was piled high with paperite, but peeking out above one stack was a gold-framed holo of Heather herself. Kyle saw colors with a bit more of a blue tinge than Heather did. She smiled at the thought—no one had ever accused her husband of looking at the world through rose-colored glasses.

Heather had thought she knew Kyle, but clearly what she knew was only the tiniest fraction, the tip of the iceberg, the shadow on the wall. He was so much *more* than she'd ever imagined—so complex, so introspective, so incredibly, intricately alive.

Images kept flickering in and out at the periphery of Kyle's attention. Heather knew that the problem with Becky had been disturbing Kyle greatly, but she had no idea that it literally was constantly on his mind.

Kyle's gaze dropped to his wristwatch. It was a beautiful Swiss digital; Heather had given it to him on their tenth wedding anniversary. Engraved on the backside, she knew, were the words:

To Kyle—wonderful husband, wonderful father.

Love, Heather

But no echo of those words passed through Kyle's consciousness; he was simply consulting the time. It was 3:45 P.M.

My God! thought Heather. Was it really that late? She'd been inside the construct for a total of five hours. She'd completely missed her own two-o'clock meeting.

Kyle got up, evidently deciding it was time to leave for his class. The visual input bounced wildly as he stood, but it didn't seem the least disconcerting to Kyle, although Heather, with access only to his consciousness and not to whatever unconscious balance signals his inner ear was relaying, felt rather tossed about.

It had been a sunny morning when Heather had entered the construct, and the forecast had called for sun to prevail for the rest of the day. But here, outside, on St. George Street, Kyle didn't see the day as bright or beautiful. It seemed dingy to him; Heather had heard the expression "living under a cloud" before, but she had never appreciated how true it could be.

He continued along, past the carts and snack trucks pulled up to the curb selling hot dogs and knockwurst, or Chinese food—with, as if the cuisine could be uplifted thus, the bristol-board menus written exclusively in Chinese.

Kyle paused. He pulled out his wallet, removed his Smart-Cash card, and to Heather's astonishment, walked up to a hot-dog vendor.

Kyle had been eating heart-smart ever since his coronary four years ago; he'd given up red meat, he ate—even though he really didn't like—lots of fish, he took aspirin every other day, and he'd replaced most of his beer with red wine.

"The usual?" asked a voice with an Italian accent.

The usual, thought Heather, chilled. The usual.

Kyle nodded.

Heather watched through Kyle's eyes as a little man plucked from the grill a dark-red dog, thick enough around to be a section out of the handle of a baseball bat, and put it in a poppyseed bun. He then used the same tongs he'd employed to move the dog to scoop up a mound of fried onions and pile them on top.

Kyle handed his card to the man, waited for the money to be transferred, pumped mustard and relish onto the dog, and then continued down the street, eating as he walked.

The thing was, though, it didn't really give him any pleasure. He was disobeying his doctor's orders—and, yes, Heather could detect the pang of guilt about what she herself would think, if she only knew—but it wasn't making him any happier.

He used to eat that way, of course. Before the heart attack. Never thought it could happen to him.

But now . . . now he should care. He should be trying to look after himself.

The usual.

The thought was there, just below the surface.

He didn't care anymore.

Didn't care whether he lived or died.

The hot juice from the dog burned the roof of his mouth.

But the pain was lost against the constant background agony of Kyle Graves's life.

Heather felt monumentally guilty about the way she was invading her husband's privacy. She'd never dreamed of spying on him, but now she was doing more than that. In a very real sense, she had become him, experiencing everything he did.

Kyle continued down St. George until he came to Willcocks, then he walked the short block west to New College. Three students said "Hi" to him as he made his way inside; Kyle acknowledged them without recognizing them. His lecture hall was large and oddly shaped, more rhomboid than rectangular.

Kyle moved to the front. A student came down, obviously hoping to get a word with him before class began.

Kyle looked up at the her and—

What a babe.

Heather was angered by the thought.

And then she herself looked at the girl.

"Babe" was right. She had to be nineteen or twenty, but she looked no more than sixteen. Still, she *was* attractive—streaked blond hair in an elaborate do, big blue eyes, bright-red lips.

"Professor Graves, about that assignment you gave us?"

"Yes, Cassie?"

He hadn't known the names of any of the students who greeted him in the corridor, but this one he knew.

"I'm wondering if we have to use Durkan's model of AI sentience, or if we can base it on Muhammed's model instead?"

Heather knew from recent Swiss Chalet conversations with Kyle that Muhammed's approach was very cutting-edge. Kyle should be impressed by that question.

Babe, he thought again.

"You can use Muhammed's, but you'll have to take into account Segal's critique."

"Thank you, Professor." She smiled a megawatt smile and turned to go. Kyle's gaze watched her tight little rump as she walked up the steps to one of the middle rows of seats.

Heather was bewildered. She'd never heard Kyle make an inappropriate remark about any student. And this one, this one of all of them, was so youthful, so much like a child pretending to be an adult.

Kyle began presenting his lesson. He did it on automatic; he'd never been an inspired teacher, and he knew that. His strength was research. While he trudged through the material he'd prepared, Heather, now oriented in his mind, decided to press on. She'd come to the precipice, but, she realized now, she'd been hesitating before jumping over.

But it was time.

She'd come this far—finding the right mind out of seven billion possibilities. She couldn't give up now.

She steeled herself.

Rebecca.

She concentrated on the name, while calling up an image.

Rebecca.

Harder and harder, shouting it with her mind, building up a good, concrete rendition of her face.

Rebecca!

She tried once more, rivaling Stanley Kowalski's shout of "*Stella!*"

Rebecca!

Nothing. Simply demanding the memories didn't bring them forth. She'd had earlier success concentrating on people, but for some reason, Kyle's past memories of Rebecca were blocked.

Or repressed?

There had to be a way. True, her brain wasn't hardwired for accessing external memories—but it was an adaptable, flexible instrument. It was simply a question of finding the right technique, the right metaphor.

Metaphor. She had interfaced her own mind with Kyle's. Still, she had no control over his body—she'd failed to get that French rapist to stop, and now she attempted something more subtle, trying to get Kyle to glance at the floor for a moment. But it didn't work. His eyes simply roamed over the students, without really connecting with any of them. The metaphor her mind had adopted for her current circumstances was that of a passenger, riding behind Kyle's eyes. It had seemed a natural way of organizing the experience. But surely it wasn't the only way. Surely there was another, more active method.

She kept trying to access what she'd come for, but except for the fleeting, harsh images of an accusing Becky that forever danced at the edges of his consciousness, Heather could find none of Kyle's memories of his younger daughter.

29

F R U S T R A T E D , H E A T H E R L E F T T H E C O N S T R U C T . She visited the bathroom, then called Kyle's office, leaving voice mail asking him to meet her for dinner tonight—Friday— instead of their usual Monday-evening get-together at the Swiss Chalet. She was desperate to know if her intrusion into his mind had been detectable by him in any way.

They arranged to meet at nine. With that much time, Heather decided she could prepare a meal for both of them, so she suggested, tentatively, that Kyle come by the house. He sounded surprised, but said that would be fine. She also asked him if she could borrow back their video camera. He made a silly joke—why did guys always think video cameras were going to be used for raunchy purposes?—but agreed to bring it with him.

And now Heather and Kyle sat at opposite ends of the giant dining-room table. There were empty seats at either side; the one by the window had always been Becky's; the one opposite— the chair never removed, even after all this time—had been Mary's. Heather had made a pasta-salad casserole. It wasn't one of Kyle's favorite dishes—that would have been too much, would have sent the wrong signal. But it was a meal, she knew, that he didn't mind. She served it with a French bread she'd picked up on her way home.

"How was work?" she asked.

Kyle took a forkful of the casserole before he replied. "Okay," he said.

Heather tried to sound nonchalant. "Anything unusual happen?"

Kyle put down his fork and looked at her. He was used to the perfunctory question about how work had gone—Heather had asked it countless times over the years. But the follow-up clearly left him puzzled.

"No," he said at last. "Nothing unusual." He paused for a bit, then, as if such a strange question required more of an answer, added, "My class went fine, I guess. I don't really remember— I had a headache."

A headache, thought Heather.

Perhaps her intrusion *had* had an effect?

"Sorry to hear that," she said. She was quiet for a moment, wondering if more probing would draw unwanted attention. But she had to know if she could explore further, deeper, with impunity. "Do you get a lot of headaches at work?"

"Sometimes. All that time staring at a computer screen." He shrugged. "How was your day?"

She didn't want to lie, but what could she say? That she'd spent the whole day sailing psychospace? That she'd invaded his mind?

"Fine," she said.

She didn't meet his eyes.

The next day, Saturday, August 12, Heather returned early to her office.

She brought the video camera with her and set it up on Omar Amir's vacant desk. She would find out at last what happened externally when the hypercube folded up.

Heather then entered the central cube, pulled the door into place, and hit the start button.

She immediately entered Kyle's mind—he was working today, too, over in his lab in Mullin Hall, attempting to solve the ongoing problems with his quantum computer.

She tried again, calling out "Rebecca" over and over, while conjuring various views of her.

Nothing.

Had he blocked her out so completely?

She tried calling up memories of Kyle's brother Jon. Those appeared at once.

Why couldn't she access his thoughts about Becky?

Becky! Not Rebecca. Becky. She tried again, seeing if the little-girl version of her name was the key.

There had to be countless recollections of his own daughter stored somewhere in his mind: memories of her as a baby, as a toddler, taking her off to daycare, his little Pumpkin . . .

Pumpkin!

She tried that, the name accompanied by mental pictures: *Pumpkin.*

And: *Pumpkin!*

And again: *Pump-kin!*

And there it was, a clear vision of his daughter—smiling, younger, happier.

That was it. She was in.

But, still, finding specific memories would not be easy. She could spend years poking through this archive of a lifetime.

What she wanted were memories of Kyle alone with Becky. She didn't know how to access those—not yet. She had to start somewhere else, with something she herself was involved in. Something simple, something she could easily key into.

A family dinner, from a time before Mary had died, from before Kyle and Becky had moved out?

It couldn't be something generic, like the poster on their

kitchen wall, illustrating various types of pasta, or the black-and-green decor of their dining room. Those weren't tied to specific memories; rather, they formed the backdrop of thousands of events.

No, she needed specific items from a specific meal. Food items: chicken—grilled chicken breast, basted with that barbecue sauce Kyle liked. And one of Kyle's standard salads: shredded lettuce, little disks of carrot, chopped celery, low-fat mozzarella, and a hedonistic sprinkling of dry-roasted peanuts, tossed in a red-wine vinaigrette and served in a large Corelle bowl.

But they'd had that meal a hundred times. She needed something unique.

Something he'd been wearing—a Toronto Raptors sweatshirt, with that dribbling purple dinosaur on the front. But what might *she* have been wearing if he'd been wearing that? Let's see: she usually wore a pantsuit to work, but when she'd get home, she'd change into jeans and—what?—a green shirt. No, no—her dark-blue shirt. She remembered once choosing that because it went well with Kyle's sweatshirt—a fact that wouldn't mean a thing to him, but did to her.

That room. That meal. That shirt.

Suddenly, it all clicked. She had accessed a specific dinner.

"—tough meeting with DeJong." Kyle's voice, or at least his memory of the words. DeJong was the university's comptroller. "We may have to cut back on the APE project."

For a moment, Heather thought something was amiss—she had no recollection of that conversation.

No, she'd doubtless tuned it out at the time; Kyle often lamented budget cuts. Heather felt chastened—it had been important to him, and she'd paid no attention. But after a moment, Kyle began mentioning DeJong's problems with his wife, and Heather did recognize the exchange. Was she that shallow, ignoring the serious problem and homing in on the gossip?

It was startling to see herself as Kyle saw her. For one thing—God bless him—she looked perhaps ten years younger than she really was; she hadn't had that shirt long enough for him to ever have seen her in it looking this young.

Becky came in and took a chair. She had much longer hair back then, tumbling halfway down her back.

" 'Evening, Pumpkin," said Kyle.

Becky smiled.

They *had* been a family once. It pained Heather to be reminded of what they'd lost.

But now she had an image of Becky to lock onto. She used it as a starting point to explore her husband's memories of Becky. She could, of course, jump into Becky's mind from his, but how would she ever justify that? Although violating Kyle's privacy was wrong—she knew that and hated herself for doing it—there *was* a reason for it. But to invade Becky's mind . . .

No, no, she wouldn't do that—especially since as yet she didn't know if there was any way to distinguish false memories from real ones. She'd continue her searching, her archeology, here, in Kyle's mind. *He* was the one on trial.

She pressed on, wondering what the verdict would be.

Kyle arrived at the lab early Monday morning. As he left the elevator on the third floor and came around the curve of the corridor, his heart jumped. An Asian woman was leaning against the railing around the edge of the atrium.

"Good morning, Dr. Graves."

"Ah, good morning,—um—"

"Chikamatsu."

"Yes, of course, Ms. Chikamatsu." This dark-gray suit looked even more expensive than the one she had worn last time.

"You have not returned my phone calls and you have not replied to my e-mail messages."

"Sorry about that. I've been rather busy. And I haven't solved the problem yet. We've stabilized the Dembinski fields, but we're still getting massive decoherence." Kyle pressed his thumb against the scanning plate by the lab door. It bleeped in acknowledgment and the door bolt snapped free, sounding like a gunshot.

" 'Morning, Dr. Graves," said Cheetah, who had been left running since Saturday. "I've got another joke for—oh, forgive me, I didn't realize you had anyone with you."

Kyle put his hat on the ancient rack; he always wore a hat in the summer, to protect his bald spot. "Cheetah, this is Ms. Chikamatsu."

Cheetah's eyes whirred into focus. "Pleased to meet you, Ms. Chikamatsu."

Chikamatsu lifted her thin eyebrows, perplexed.

"Cheetah is an APE," said Kyle. "You know, a computer simulation that apes humanity."

"I really do find the use of the term 'ape' offensive," said Cheetah.

Kyle smiled. "See? Genuine-sounding indignation. I programmed that myself. It's the first thing you need in a university environment: the ability to take offense at any slight, real or imagined."

The opening notes of Beethoven's Fifth issued from Cheetah's speakers.

"What was *that?*" asked Chikamatsu.

"His laughter. I'm going to fix that at some point."

"Yeah," said Cheetah. "Get rid of those Vienna string instruments. How about a woodwind instead? Maybe a Bonn oboe?"

"What?" said Kyle. "Oh. I get it." He looked at Chikamatsu. "Cheetah is trying to master humor."

"Bonn oboe?" repeated the woman.

Kyle grinned despite himself. "Bonn is where Beethoven was born; a bonobo is a pygmy chimp—an APE, see?"

The Japanese woman shook her head, perplexed. "If you say

so. Now, about my consortium's offer? We know you will be busy once you do make your breakthrough; we want you to give us a commitment to immediately deal with our problem."

Kyle busied himself with the coffeemaker. "My wife, she really thinks that whatever Huneker detected belongs to all of humanity—and I guess I agree. I'd gladly undertake to decode the message for you, but I won't sign an NDA about its contents."

Chikamatsu frowned. "I am empowered to sweeten the deal. We can offer you a three-percent royalty—"

"It's not that. Really, it's not."

"We will have to approach Dr. Saperstein, then."

Kyle gritted his teeth. "I understand that." But then he smiled. "Tell Shlomo I say hi." *Let Saperstein know that they came to me first—that he was getting my discards.*

"I really wish you would reconsider," said Chikamatsu.

"I'm sorry."

"If you change your mind," she said, proffering a plastic business card, "call me." Kyle took the card and glanced at it. It had only the word "Chikamatsu" printed on it, but there was a magstripe along one edge. "I will be at the Royal York for another two days—but swipe that card through any phone anywhere in the world and it will call my cellular at my expense."

"I won't change my mind," said Kyle.

Chikamatsu nodded and headed for the door.

"What was that all about?" asked Cheetah after she was gone.

Kyle did his best Bogart. "The shtuff that dreams are made of."

"Pardon?" said Cheetah.

Kyle rolled his eyes. "Kids today," he said.

30

Heather found all sorts of memories of Becky in Kyle's mind, but none of them were relevant to Becky's accusation.

Heather went as long as she could in psychospace between bathroom breaks, but on one of the breaks she watched the videotape through the viewfinder on the camcorder.

To her astonishment, the collection of cubes did shimmer—both the paint and the substrate aglow—and then the components seemed to recede, each constituent cube twisting free as it did so.

And then, incredibly, it was gone.

She fast-forwarded, watched it bloom into existence again out of nothingness.

Amazing.

It really did fold up *kata* or *ana;* it really did transcend to another realm.

Heather kept searching throughout the weekend, encountering many aspects of Kyle. Although she was concentrating on his thoughts about his daughters, she also encountered memories of his work, of their marriage—and of her. Apparently he didn't always see her with uncritical eyes. Corrugated thighs indeed!

It was illuminating, fascinating, compelling. There was so much more she wanted to learn about him.

But she could not tarry. She was on a mission.

And, finally, at last, on Monday morning, she found what she was looking for.

She was scared, not wanting to go on.

The rape of that anonymous French woman haunted her still, but this—

This, if what she feared were true—

This would haunt her, scar her, disgust her, make her homicidally enraged.

And, she knew, she'd never be able to wash the images from her mind.

But it *was* what she'd been looking for—of that there could be no doubt.

Nighttime. Becky's bedroom, illuminated by light from the street coming in around the edges of her venetian blinds. On the wall, difficult to make out in the wan illumination, was a holoposter of Cutthroat Jenkins, a rock star Becky had idolized when she was fourteen or so.

The view was from Kyle's point of view. He was standing on the threshold of the room. The corridor he was in was dark. He could see Becky lying in the bed, beneath the heavy green comforter she'd had then. Becky was awake. She looked up at him. Heather expected to see fear, or revulsion, or even melancholy resignation on her face, but to her shock, Becky smiled: a glint in the night; she'd worn braces back then.

She *smiled.*

There was no such thing as consent between a minor and an adult—Heather knew that. But the smile was so warm, so accepting . . .

Kyle closed the distance, and Becky wriggled over to the far side of her small bed, making room for him.

And then she sat up.

Kyle lowered himself down, sitting on the edge of the bed. Becky reached out a hand toward him—

—and took the mug he was offering.

"Just the way you like it," said Kyle. "With lemon."

"Thanks, Daddy," said Becky. Her voice was raw. She used both hands to hold the mug and took a sip.

It came back to Heather. Becky had had a terrible cold five or so years ago. They'd all eventually come down with it.

Kyle reached out a hand and stroked his daughter's dark hair once. "Nothing's too good for my little girl," he said.

Becky smiled again. "Sorry my coughing woke you."

"I think I was up anyway," said Kyle. He shrugged a little. "Sometimes I don't sleep that well." He then leaned in, kissed her gently on the cheek, and rose to his feet. "I hope you feel better tomorrow, Pumpkin."

And with that, he left his daughter's room.

Heather felt terrible. When it came right down to it, she had been ready to believe the most horrible thing possible about her own husband. There'd never been a shred of evidence to support Becky's charge, and all sorts of reasons to believe it the product of an overzealous therapist—and yet as soon as that memory started unraveling, showing Kyle entering his daughter's room late at night, she'd expected to see the worst. The mere suggestion of child abuse *was* indeed enough to tar a man. For the first time, Heather felt a real understanding of the horror Kyle had been going through.

And yet—

And yet just because one night's encounter—one that easily came to the surface—was benign, did it mean that nothing untoward had ever happened? Becky had lived with her parents for eighteen years, which was—what?—six thousand or so nights. So what if Kyle had been the dutiful, loving father on one of those?

She was getting the hang of accessing specific memories; concentrating on an image associated with a desired incident was the key. But the image had to be accurate. It was distasteful in the extreme to try to conjure up an image of Kyle molesting Becky, but it also was pointless. Unless the image exactly matched Kyle's own recollection—from his point of view, of course—there would be no connection, and the memory would remain locked.

Heather had seen her daughter naked. They had belonged to the same health club on Dufferin Street—indeed, Heather had started taking Becky there as a teenager. She'd never really looked closely at her daughter except to notice, with some envy, that she had a trim, youthful figure, with none of the stretch marks Heather herself had had ever since her first pregnancy. She had noted that Becky's high, conical breasts hadn't yet begun to sag, though.

Becky's breasts.

A rush of memory—but Heather's own, not Kyle's.

Becky had come to see her mother when she was fifteen or sixteen, just about the time she'd first started dating. She'd taken off her shirt and her small bra and shown her mother the space between her breasts. She had a large brown mole there, raised like a pencil eraser.

"I hate it," Becky had said.

Heather had understood the timing: Becky had lived with the mole for years; indeed, three years ago she'd overcome her modesty to ask Dr. Redmond about it, and he'd assured her it was benign. No doubt countless girls had seen it in the locker room at school. But now that she was dating, she was thinking about how a *boy* might react to it. It was all too fast for Heather—her daughter was growing up much too quickly.

Or was she? Heather herself had only been sixteen the first time she'd let Billy Karapedes get his hand up under her shirt. They'd done that in the dark, in his car. He hadn't *seen* anything—but if Heather had had a mole like Becky's, he would have felt it. What would his reaction have been?

"I want to have it removed," said Becky.

Heather had thought before responding. Two of Becky's high-school friends had already received nose jobs. One had had freckles lasered off. A fourth had even had breast-enlargement surgery. Compared to that, this was nothing: a local anesthetic, a flick of a scalpel, and *voilà!*—a real source of anxiety gone.

"Please," said Becky when her mother made no reply. She sounded so earnest that for a second, Heather thought Becky was going to say she needed it done by Friday night, but apparently things weren't moving *that* fast.

"You'd need a stitch or two, I bet."

Becky considered this. "Maybe I could get it done over spring break," she said, evidently not wanting to face the locker room with suture protruding from her sternum.

"Sure, if you like," said Heather, smiling warmly at her daughter. "We'll get Dr. Redmond to recommend somebody."

"Thanks, Mom. You're the best." She paused. "Don't tell Daddy, though. I'd die of embarrassment."

Heather smiled. "Not a word."

Heather could still picture that mole. She'd seen it twice more before it was removed, and once, even, after the surgery, when it was floating in a small specimen container before it was taken to a lab to be tested—just to be on the safe side—for malignancy. As she'd promised Becky, she'd never said a word about the little bit of plastic surgery to Kyle. The Ontario Health Insurance Plan didn't cover it—it was, after all, purely cosmetic—but the cost was less than a hundred bucks; Heather had paid by smartcard for it and had taken her much-happier daughter home.

She conjured up an image of her daughter's breasts, beige,

smooth, wine-tipped, with the mole between them. And she plugged that image into the matrix of Kyle's memories, looking for a match.

Her own memory could have faded—it had been three or so years ago, after all. She tried imagining slightly bigger breasts, different-colored nipples, larger and smaller moles.

But there was no match. Kyle had never seen the mole.

He'd come into my room, have me remove my top, fondle my breasts, and then—

And then, nothing. Kyle had never seen his daughter topless—at least not during any time after puberty, not at any time when she'd had real breasts.

Heather felt her whole body shaking. It had never happened. None of it. There had been no abuse.

Brian Kyle Graves was a good man, a good husband—and a good father. He'd never hurt his daughter. Heather was sure of it. At last, she was sure.

Tears were rolling down her face. She was barely aware of them—the moistness, the salty taste as some slid into her mouth, an intrusion from the outside world.

She'd been wrong—wrong even to suspect her husband. If it had been she who had been accused, he would have stood by her, never once doubting her innocence. But she *had* doubted. She had wronged him terribly. Oh, she had never accused him directly. But the shame of having doubted was almost unbearable.

Heather made the effort of will, extracting herself from psychospace. She removed the cubic door and staggered out into the harsh light of the theatrical lamps.

She wiped her eyes, blew her nose, and sat in her office chair staring at the faded drapes, trying to think of how she would make it up to her husband.

31

THE LAB'S DOOR CHIME SOUNDED. TWO GRAD students were working in the lab along with Kyle. One of them went to the door, which opened for him.

"I'd like to see Professor Graves," said the man who was revealed on the other side of the doorway.

Kyle looked up. "Mr. Cash, isn't it?" he said, crossing the room, hand extended.

"That's right. I hope you don't mind me coming by without an appointment, but—"

"No, no. Not at all."

"Is there somewhere we can talk?"

"My office," said Kyle. He turned to one of the grad students. "Pietro, see if you can make some headway on the indeterminacy bug, would you? I'll be back in a few minutes."

The student nodded, and Kyle and Cash headed down the curving corridor to Kyle's wedge of an office. When they entered, Kyle bustled about cleaning off the second chair, while Cash admired the *Allosaurus* poster.

"Sorry about the mess," said Kyle. Cash folded his angular form into the chair.

"You've had a weekend, Professor Graves. I'm hoping you've had a chance to consider the Banking Association's offer."

Kyle nodded. "I have thought about it, yes."

Cash waited patiently.

"I'm sorry, Mr. Cash. I really don't want to leave the university. This place has been very good to me over the years."

Cash nodded. "I know you met your wife here, and you did all three of your degrees here."

"Exactly." He shrugged. "It's home."

"I believe the offer I made was very generous," said Cash.

"It was."

"But if need be, I can offer more."

"It's not a question of money; I was just telling someone else that earlier today. I like it here, and I like doing research that's going to be published."

"But the impact on the banking industry—"

"I understand that there are potential problems. Do you think I want to cause chaos? We're still years away from posing a real threat to smartcard security. Look at it this way: you've had a warning that quantum computers are likely coming down the pike; now you can get working on a new encryption solution. You survived Year 2000, and you're going to survive this."

"My hope," said Cash, "was to deal with this situation in the most cost-effective manner possible."

"By buying me off," said Kyle.

Cash was quiet. "There is a great deal at stake here, Professor. Name your price."

"To my rather significant delight, Mr. Cash, I've discovered I don't have one."

Cash rose. "Everyone does, Professor. Everyone does." He headed for the office door. "If you change your mind, let me know."

And with that, he was gone.

———

Heather needed to convince her only living daughter of the truth. If the family was ever to reconcile, it had to start with Becky.

But that raised a larger question.

When was Heather going to go public with her psychospace discovery?

At first she'd kept it secret because she'd wanted to develop a sufficient theory for publication.

But now she had that—in spades.

And still she hadn't gone public. All it would take to establish priority would be a preemptive posting to the Alien Signal newsgroup. Peer-reviewed journals would follow later, but she could, this minute, announce her discovery if she wanted to.

Plato had said that an unexamined life is not worth living.

But he was referring to *self*-examination.

Who could live with the knowledge that anyone and everyone might be scrutinizing their own thoughts? What would happen to privacy? To trade secrets? To criminal justice? To interpersonal relationships?

It would change everything—and Heather was not at all sure that it would be for the better.

But no—that wasn't why she was keeping it a secret. Not some lofty concern about other people's privacy, although she liked to think she *was* giving that at least some consideration; except for Kyle, she'd refrained from giving in to temptation, staying out of the minds of others she knew personally.

No, the real reason she hadn't gone public was much simpler; she *liked*, at least for a time, being the only one with this power. She had something no one else had—and she didn't quite yet want to share it.

She wasn't proud of that fact, but there it was. Did Superman ever spend even one second trying to figure out how to give the rest of humanity superpowers? Of course not; he'd just lucked into them. Then why should her first priority be to share *this*?

She'd yet to find anything in psychospace that directly corresponded to Jungian archetypes. She couldn't point to some part of the maelstrom and say that it represented the wellspring of human symbols, couldn't point to a bank of hexagons and say that it housed the archetype of the warrior-hero. And yet simply reflecting upon what to do about her discovery was indeed giving her insights into her own mind.

First and foremost, which was she? Mother? Wife? Scientist?

There were archetypes of parents, and there were archetypes of spouses—but the Western concept of the scientist didn't have a Jungian definition.

She'd made the same decision once before. Her career could wait; science could wait. Family was more important.

And with this discovery, she could prove to Becky that her father had not molested her—just as Heather had proven it to herself. That was what mattered right now.

One way to prove it would be to show Becky the archives of Becky's own mind. But there was still that vexing problem of how to distinguish false memories from real ones. After all, the false memories clearly seemed genuine, or Becky would have never believed them in the first place; they might feel as real as any other memories, even when viewed from within, but—

But you couldn't Necker from them to someone else!

Of course!

Surely the Necker swapping—the moving into the mind of someone who also remembered the same scene—simply wouldn't work if the memories were false. There would be no corresponding memories in another, no touchstone between the two minds.

Heather, if she had any lingering doubt at all about Kyle's guilt, could violate Becky's privacy, find the false memories, and demonstrate for herself the inability to transfer from Becky's point of view to Kyle's.

But—

But no. She had no doubts left.

And besides—

Besides, it had been one thing to search for memories she hoped to God weren't there. It would be another to actually see, even if it was false, the molestation. Let Becky herself, who already had those repugnant mental images burned into her, experience the inability to do the Necker swap. For Heather, even a false representation of her husband harming their child was something she didn't want to witness.

Still, Becky might want further proof. And she could get that, of course, by retracing Heather's steps, by looking directly into Kyle's mind.

Kyle would be utterly exonerated—but would things really improve between father and daughter if, although that demon were dispelled, Becky discovered that her father really had liked her older sister better, that she really was an accident that had strained their finances while both of them were still grad students, that her father had base thoughts, ignoble thoughts?

Was this really the path toward healing?

No—no, that wasn't the answer.

And, anyway, there was a better way.

Let Becky see into the mind of her therapist, see the manipulation, the lies.

On its own, that might not absolutely eliminate Becky's doubts. As Heather herself had mused, even if the therapist's methods were leading and inappropriate, that didn't necessarily prove that no abuse had occurred. But in conjunction with a demonstration that Becky's own memories were false, shared by no one else, she should be completely convinced.

It was time—time to start healing.

Heather picked up her phone and called Becky.

The Fashion District, where Becky lived and worked, was only a few blocks west of the university, so Heather asked Becky to meet her at The Water Hole for lunch. During the days she'd spent probing Kyle's mind, she'd learned many hitherto unknown things about her husband, not the least of which was that he had developed a fondness for this place that Heather herself had walked by a million times without ever entering.

Heather knew that Kyle was teaching right now; there was no possibility of an accidental reunion.

She'd seen the interior of The Water Hole already through Kyle's mind—in searching for Kyle's memories of Becky, she'd found the time Kyle had unburdened himself here to Stone Bailey.

It was startling to see the real Water Hole, though. First, of course, the colors looked different to Heather than what she'd seen in Kyle's mind.

But there was more than that. Kyle had stored only some of the details. Much of what made up his memory had been interpretation or extrapolation. Oh yes, he'd remembered the Molson's holoposter with the stunning blonde ski-bunny—but he'd had no recollection of the other framed posters on the walls. And he'd remembered the tablecloths as a uniform red, when in fact they were covered with tiny red-and-white checks.

It was Monday, August 14; Becky worked at the clothing store all day Saturday and Sunday this week, but got Monday and Tuesday off. Still, she was late, and when she finally did enter, she did not look happy.

"Thank you for coming," said Heather as Becky took a seat opposite her, a small round table between them.

Becky's face was grim. "I only agreed because you said he wouldn't be present." There was no doubt as to whom the pronoun referred.

Heather had hoped for some pleasantries, for some news of her daughter's life. But apparently there was to be none of that. She nodded grimly and said, "We need to resolve this issue with your father."

"If you're proposing an out-of-court settlement, I want to have a lawyer present."

Heather felt as if she'd been hit in the face. She gulped air, then at last managed to get out the words, "There will be no lawsuit."

"I don't want that any more than you do," said Becky, softening a bit. She'd never been good at putting on a tough face. "But he ruined my life."

"No, he didn't."

"I didn't come here to hear you defend him. Making excuses is just as bad as—"

"Shut up!" Heather shocked herself with how sharp her voice was. Becky's eyes went wide.

"Just shut up," said Heather again. "You're making a fool of yourself. Shut up before you say anything else you'll regret."

"I don't have to take this," said Becky. She began to rise.

"Sit down," snapped Heather. The few other patrons were now looking at them. Heather locked eyes with the one nearest them, staring him down. He went back to his soup.

"I can prove that your father didn't molest you," said Heather. "I can prove it absolutely, beyond any shadow of a doubt, to whatever degree of certainty you require."

Becky's mouth hung open. She was staring at her mother, an expression of shock on her face.

The server picked that moment to arrive. "Hello, ladies. Can I get—"

"Not now," snapped Heather. The server looked stung, but he quickly disappeared.

Becky blinked. "I've never heard you like this."

"It's because I'm fed the fuck up." Becky looked more shocked; something else she'd never heard before was her mother saying "fuck." "No family should have to go through what ours has." Heather paused, took a deep breath. "Look, I'm sorry. But this has to end—it *has* to. I can't take any more of it, and neither can your father. You have to come back to my office with me."

"What are you going to do? Hypnotize me into not believing what I know to be true?"

"Nothing like that." She signaled the server, and as he somewhat timidly approached, Heather said to her daughter, "Don't order too much to drink—you're not going to have an opportunity to easily pee for a few hours after lunch."

"What in God's name is *that?*"

Becky's expression was one of pure surprise as she entered her mother's office. Heather couldn't help grinning at her.

"That, my dear, is what the Centaurs were trying to tell us how to make. See the little tiles making up the bigger panels? Each one of the tiles is a pictorial representation of one of the alien messages."

Becky loomed in to look at the construct. "So they are," she said. She straightened up and stared at Heather. "Mom, I know all this has been very hard on you . . ."

Heather couldn't help laughing. "You think the pressure's gotten too much for me? That I couldn't figure out how to read the messages, so I spent my time just shuffling them around and building things out of them?"

"Well," said Becky, and she gestured at the construct, as if its very existence made everything plain.

"It's nothing like that, honey. This really is what the Centaurs intended us to do with their messages. The shape—that's an unfolded hypercube."

"A what?"

"The four-dimensional counterpart of a cube. The arms fold up and the ends touch, and the thing becomes a regular geometrical solid in four dimensions."

"And that accomplishes precisely what?" asked Becky, sounding very dubious.

"It transports you to a four-dimensional realm. It lets you see the four-dimensional reality that surrounds us."

Becky was silent.

"Look," said Heather, "all you have to do is get inside it."

"In *there?*"

Heather frowned. "I know I should have made it bigger."

"So you're saying—you're saying this is some sort of time machine, and—what?—it'll let me travel back to see what Daddy did?"

"Time isn't the fourth dimension," said Heather. "The fourth dimension is a spatial direction, precisely perpendicular to the other three."

"Ah," said Becky.

"And although we all appear to be individuals when viewed in three dimensions, we're actually all part of a greater whole when viewed in four."

"What *are* you talking about?"

"I'm talking about how I know—know to a moral certainty—that your father didn't molest you. And how you can know, too."

Becky was silent.

"Look, everything I'm saying is true," said Heather. "I'll be announcing it publicly soon . . . probably, anyway. But I wanted you to know first, before anyone else. I want you to go look inside another human mind."

"Inside Daddy's, you mean?"

"No. No, that wouldn't be right. I want you to go see your therapist. I'll tell you how to find her mind; I don't think you should enter your father's mind, not without his permission. But that damned therapist—we don't owe that bitch a thing."

"You don't even know her, Mom."

"Oh, yes I do—I went to see her."

"What? How? Look, you don't even know her name."

"Lydia Gurdjieff. Her office is on Lawrence West."

Becky was visibly stunned.

"You know what she tried to do to me?" asked Heather. "She tried to get me to explore the abuse I had at the hands of my own father."

"But . . . but your father . . . your father . . ."

"Died before I was born. Exactly. Even though it was categorically impossible for me to have been abused by my father, she said I showed all the classic signs. She talks a good game, believe me. She had me half-believing that someone had abused me, too. Not my father, of course, but some other relative."

"I—I don't believe this. You're making it up." Becky gestured at the construct. "You're making it all up."

"No, I'm not. You can prove it to yourself. You'll see Gurdjieff implanting the memories in you from her point of view, and I'll show you how you can demonstrate that the memories you have are false. Come on, get inside the construct and—"

Becky sounded half-wary, half-desperate. " 'The construct'? Is that what you call it? Not the 'Centaurimobile'?"

Heather managed a neutral tone. "I should introduce you to Cheetah—a friend of your father. You've got similar senses of humor." She took a deep breath. "Look, I'm your mother, and I'd never hurt you. Trust me; try what I say. We won't be able to communicate when you've got your eyes open in there, but when you close them, after a few seconds the interior of the construct will reappear in your mind's eye. If you need further help, press the stop button." She pointed to it. "The hypercube will unfold, you can open the door, and I'll be able to tell you what to do next. Don't worry—when you press the start button again, you'll end up exactly where you left off." She paused. "Now, please, get inside. It gets pretty warm in there, by the way. I won't ask you to do it in your bra and panties like I do, but—"

"Your bra and panties?" said Becky, stunned.

Heather smiled again. "Trust me, dear. Now get inside."

Four hours later, Heather assisted Becky in removing the cubic door, and Becky got out of the construct, accepting a helping hand from her mother.

Becky stood quiet for a moment, tears running down her cheeks, clearly utterly at a loss for words; then she collapsed into her mother's waiting arms.

Heather stroked her daughter's hair. "It's all right, honey. It's all right now."

Becky's whole body was shaking. "It was incredible," she said. "It was like nothing I've ever experienced."

Heather smiled. "Isn't it, though?"

Becky's voice was growing hard. "She *used* me," she said. "She manipulated me."

Heather said nothing, and although it tore her up to see her daughter distraught, her heart soared.

"She used me," Becky said again. "How could I have been so stupid? How could I have been so wrong?"

"It's okay," said Heather. "It's over."

"No," said Becky. "It isn't." She was still shaking, and Heather's shoulder was now moist with Becky's tears. "There's still Daddy. What am I going to say to Daddy?"

"The only thing you can say. The only thing there is to say. That you're sorry."

Becky's voice was incredibly tiny. "But he'll never love me again."

Heather gently lifted Becky's head with a hand under her daughter's chin. "I know for a fact, sweetheart, that he never stopped."

32

HEATHER INVITED KYLE OVER TO DINNER THE next night.

There was so much she wanted to say to him, so much that had to be cleared up. But after he arrived, she didn't know where to begin—and so she began at a distance, with the theoretical: one academic to another.

"Do you think it's possible," she asked, "that things that seem to be discrete in three dimensions might all be part of the same bigger object in four dimensions?"

"Oh, sure," said Kyle. "I tell my students that all the time. You just have to extrapolate, based on how two-dimensional views of three-dimensional objects work. A two-dimensional world would be a plane, like a piece of paperite. If a donut were passing vertically through a horizontal plane, an inhabitant of the two-dimensional world would see two separate circles—or the lines that represent them—instead of the donut."

"Exactly," said Heather. "Exactly. Now, consider this. What if humanity—that collective noun we so often employ—really is, at a higher level, a singular noun? What if what we perceive in three dimensions as seven billion individual human beings are really all just aspects of one giant being?"

"That's a little harder to visualize than a donut, but—"

"Don't think of it as a donut, then. Think of—I don't know, think of a sea urchin: a ball with countless spikes sticking out of it. And think of our frame of reference not as a flat sheet of paper, but as a piece of nylon—you know, like stockings are made of. If the nylon was wrapped around the sea urchin, you'd see all those spikes sticking through and you'd think each one was a discrete thing; you wouldn't necessarily realize that they were all attached, all just extensions of something bigger."

"Well, it's an interesting notion," said Kyle. "But it doesn't strike me as something you could test."

"But what if it's *already* been tested?" asked Heather. She paused, thinking about how to go on. "Sure, almost all reports of psychic experiences are bunk. Almost all of them can be explained. But there are, occasionally, few and far between, cases that *can't* easily be explained. Indeed, they *defy* scientific explanation because they're not reproducible—if it happens only once, then how do you study it? But what if, under rare, special circumstances, normally isolated spines on our sea urchin fold over and touch each other, however briefly? It could explain telepathy, and—"

Kyle was frowning. "Oh, come on, Heather. You don't believe in mind reading any more than I do."

"I don't believe people can do it at will, no. But it's been reported as an occasional phenomenon since the dawn of time; perhaps there *is* some validity to it. Jung himself argued in his later years that the unconscious functions independently of the laws of causality and normal physics, making such things as clairvoyance and precognition possible."

"He was just a confused old man by that point."

"Maybe, but my department head did his Ph.D. at Duke; they've done lots of interesting work there about ESP, and he—"

"Work that doesn't stand up under scrutiny."

"Well, sure, it's clear that there's no such thing as reliably reading minds—but there *are* a number of pretty solid studies suggesting that under sensory-deprivation conditions, certain people can guess with somewhat enhanced accuracy which of four possibilities someone else is looking at; you'd expect a twenty-five-percent success rate based on random guessing, but there were studies done by Honorton in New Jersey that show a thirty-three- or thirty-seven-percent success rate, and even one test group of twenty subjects that had a fifty-percent success rate. And the four-dimensional overmind—"

"Ah," said Kyle, amused. "The coveted FDO."

"The four-dimensional overmind," repeated Heather firmly, "provides a theoretical model that can account for occasional telepathic linkages."

Kyle was still grinning. "You looking to get a new research grant?"

Heather internalized a smile of her own. One thing she'd never be lacking again was grant money. "This model could also explain flashes of brilliance," she said, "especially those that come while sleeping. Remember Kekule, trying to work out the chemical structure of benzene? He dreamed of a snake-ring of atoms—which turned out to be exactly right. But maybe he didn't come up with that breakthrough on his own." She paused, reflecting. "And maybe *I* didn't come up with this notion on my own. Maybe the reason we sleep so much is that that's when we interact most closely with the overmind. Maybe dreams occur while our daily individual experiences are being uploaded to the overmind. It can kill you, you know—not dreaming. You can get all the rest in the world, but if you take chemicals that prevent you from dreaming, you'll die; that contact *is* essential. And perhaps when a problem is being worked on, maybe sometimes you're not the only one doing it. It's like the way your quantum computer is supposed to work—the computer you see will be solving only the smallest part of the problem, but it'll be working in tandem with all the others. Maybe sometimes during sleep, we touch the overmind and get the benefit of all the nodes."

"Politely, that sounds like New Age gibberish to me," said Kyle.

Heather shrugged a little. "Your quantum mechanics sounds like gibberish to most people. But it's the way the universe works." She paused. "This is going to excite Noam Chomsky's followers. In *Syntactic Structures,* Chomsky proposed that language is innate. That is, we don't learn to talk the way we learn to tie our shoes or ride a bicycle. Instead, humans have a built-in linguistic ability—special circuits in the brain that allow people to acquire and process language without any conscious awareness of the complex rules. I've heard you say it yourself when marking student papers: 'I know that sentence is grammatically incorrect; I can't tell you exactly why, but I'm sure it's not right.' "

Kyle nodded. "Yeah, I've said that."

"So you—and just about everyone else—clearly has a sense of language. But Chomsky's theory is that the sense is something you're born with. And if you're born with it, presumably it has to be coded in your DNA."

"Makes sense."

"No, it doesn't," said Heather earnestly. "Philip Lieberman pointed out a big problem with Chomsky's theory. Chomsky is essentially saying that there's a language 'organ' in the brain that's identical in every human being. But it *can't* be. No genetically determined trait is the same in all people; there's always variation. The language organ would have to show the same sort of variability we see in skin and eye color, height, susceptibility to heart disease, and more."

"Why on earth would that be true?"

"It would *have* to be that way; genetics demands it. You know, there are people who digest foods in different ways—a diabetic does it one way, someone who is lactose intolerant does it another way. Even people we consider perfectly healthy may have different approaches, using different enzymes. But on a societal level, that doesn't matter; digestion is utterly personal—the way you do it has no effect on the way I do it. But language *has* to be shared—that's the whole point of language. If there were any variation in the way you and I processed language mentally, we wouldn't be able to communicate."

"Of course we could; Cheetah uses several speech-processing routines that aren't based on any human models but rather are simple brute-force engineering solutions."

"Oh, sure, if there's some minor variation that makes no gross difference, meaning can still be conveyed. But on a subtle level, you and I both agree, even if Cheetah might not, that 'big yellow ball' is a proper construction, while 'yellow big ball' is, if not out-and-out improper, certainly not normal—and yet neither of us were ever taught in school that size is more important than color. We—all people speaking the same language—agree on very minute points of syntax and structure, without ever having been taught those things. And Chomsky says that every one of the five thousand different languages currently spoken, plus all the languages that existed in the past, follow essentially the same rules. He's probably right—we do acquire and use language with extraordinary ease, so much so that it must be innate. But it *can't* be genetically innate—as Lieberman points out, that would violate basic biology, which allows for, and indeed is driven evolutionarily by, the concept of individual variation. Besides, the Human Genome Project failed to find any gene or combination of genes that coded for Chomsky's supposed language organ. Which begs the question: if it's innate, and it's not genetic, where does it come from?"

"And you think it's from your proposed overmind?"

Heather spread her arms. "It makes sense, doesn't it? And it's not just language that seems to be hardwired. Symbols are shared, too, across individuals and across cultures. It's what Jung called 'the collective unconscious.' "

"Surely Jung meant that as a metaphor."

Heather nodded. "At the outset, yes. But it does seem that we do share a rich background of symbols and ideas. You know Joseph Campbell's *The Hero With a Thousand Faces?* I use it in one of my courses. Mythologies are the same even across cultures that have been isolated from one another. How do you explain that? Coincidence? If not coincidence, then what?"

"The overmind again, you think. But, geez, that's such a big leap."

"Is it? Is it really? Occam's razor says you should prefer the solution that has the fewest elements. Positing one thing—the overmind—solves all sorts of problems in linguistics, comparative mythology, psychology, and even parapsychology. It *is* a simple solution, and—"

The clock on the mantle made its quarter-hour chime.

"Oh!" said Heather. "Sorry, I didn't mean to go on so long, and— Damn, look there's no time to explain it all now. We've got a visitor coming."

"Who?"

"Becky."

Kyle visibly stiffened. "I'm not sure I want to see her." He paused. "Damn it, why didn't you tell me she was coming?"

Heather spread her arms. "Because I wanted to be sure you would come over. Look, it's going to be okay and—"

The sound of the door bolt disengaging; Becky was operating the lock herself, instead of ringing the bell.

The front door swung open. Becky stood in the entryway, stark against the darkness.

Kyle, now standing by the living-room window, held his breath.

Becky came up into the living room. She was quiet for a moment. Through the open window, Kyle could hear a skimmer whizzing by and the sound of a group of boys yakking away as they walked down the sidewalk.

"Dad," Becky said.

It was the first time in over a year that Kyle had heard that word from her. He didn't know what to do. He stood frozen.

"Dad," she said again. "I am so sorry."

Kyle's heart was pounding. "I would never hurt you," he said.

"I know that," said Becky. She closed some of the distance between them. "I'm so very sorry, Dad. I didn't mean to hurt you."

Kyle didn't trust his voice. There was still so much anger and resentment in him.

"What changed your mind?" he asked.

Becky looked at her mother, then down at the ground. "I—I realized you couldn't possibly do anything like that."

"You were sure enough before." The words, harsh, were out before Kyle could stop himself.

Becky nodded slightly. "I know. I know. But . . . but I've looked into what my therapist did, at the techniques she used. I . . . I never knew memories could be manufactured." She briefly met her father's gaze, then looked back at the carpet.

"That bitch," said Kyle. "The trouble she's caused."

Becky looked at her mother again; something was passing between the two of them, but Kyle couldn't tell what.

"Let's not worry about her now," said Becky. "Please. The important thing is that *this* is over . . . or at least it is if you'll forgive me."

She looked up at her father again, with her large brown eyes. Kyle knew that his face was impassive; he didn't know how to react. He'd been torn apart, reviled, shunned—and now it was all supposed to be over, just like that?

Surely there should be more than just an apology. Surely the wounds would take years—decades—to heal.

And yet—

And yet, more than anything, he'd wanted this. He hadn't prayed, of course, but if there had been one thing that he *would* have prayed for, it would have been for his daughter to realize her mistake.

"You're sure now?" said Kyle. "You won't change your mind again. I couldn't take it if—"

"I won't, Daddy. I promise."

Was it really over? Had the nightmare really come to an end? How many nights he'd wished the clock could be turned back—and now she was apparently offering, in essence, just that.

He thought about poor Stone, standing outside his office, meeting with female students in hallways.

Becky stood still for a while longer, then took a small step closer. Kyle hesitated a moment more, then opened his arms, and Becky stepped into them. Suddenly she collapsed against his shoulder, crying.

"I am so very sorry," she said between sobs.

Kyle couldn't find any words; the anger couldn't be turned off like a switch.

He held her for a long time. He hadn't hugged her—God, maybe not since her sixteenth birthday. His shoulder was wet; Becky's tears had soaked through his shirt. He hesitated for a moment—damn it all, but he would probably hesitate for the rest of his life—then brought his hand up to stroke her shoulder-length black hair.

They were quiet for a long time. Finally, Becky pulled away a little bit and looked up at her father. "I love you," she said, wiping her eyes.

Kyle didn't know how he felt, but he said the words anyway: "I love you too, Becky."

She shook her head a little.

Kyle hesitated for another moment, then gently lifted her chin with his finger. "What?"

"Not 'Becky,' " said his daughter. She managed a red-eyed smile. "Pumpkin."

Tears escaped from Kyle's eyes now. He swept his daughter back up in his arms, and this time he meant every syllable: "I love you, too—Pumpkin."

33

BECKY STAYED FOR A JOYOUS TWO HOURS, but at last she had to leave. She lived downtown and had to be up early to open the store Wednesday morning.

When she was gone, Kyle sat back down on the couch.

Heather looked at him for a long time.

He was such a complicated man—more complicated than she'd ever known. And he was, when all was said and done, a basically good man.

But not a perfect one, of course. Indeed, Heather had been shocked and disappointed by some of what she'd discovered while plumbing his memories. He had his dark side, his shoddy parts; he could be petty and selfish and unpleasant.

No, there was no such thing as the perfect man—but then, she'd known that even before she'd left Vegreville to come to Toronto. Kyle was both deeply great and deeply flawed—peaks and valleys, more and less than she'd ever thought he was.

But, she realized, whatever he was now, she could accept it; the fit between them wasn't ideal, and probably never would be. But she knew in her heart that it was better than it could be with anyone else. And perhaps acknowledging that was as good a definition of love as any.

Heather crossed the room and stood over him. He looked up at her with brown puppy-dog eye's, like Becky's.

She reached out a hand. He took it. And she led him across the room, to the stairs, and up to the bedroom.

It had been a year since they'd last made love.

But it was worth waiting for.

She didn't tense at all.

When they were done, when they lay holding each other, Heather spoke the only words to pass between them that night after Becky's departure. "Welcome home."

They fell asleep in each other's arms.

The next morning: Wednesday, August 16.

As she reached the bottom of the staircase, Heather looked over at Kyle. He seemed to be staring into space, his gaze resting on a blank spot on the wall between a Robert Bateman painting of bighorn sheep and an Ansel Adams photoprint of the Arizona desert.

Heather moved into the room. On an adjacent wall was their wedding photo, now almost a quarter-century old. She could see the toll all of this had taken on her husband. Until recently, his hair had been much the same dark brown it had been on the day they'd married, with only tiny incursions of gray, and his high forehead had been relatively line-free. But now—now there were permanent creases in his brow, and his rusty beard and dark hair were streaked through with silver.

He seemed physically diminished, too. Oh, doubtless he was still a hundred and seventy-seven centimeters, but he sat on the couch hunched over, collapsed in on himself. And there was the paunch—he'd fought so hard to lose it after his heart attack. True, it wasn't back to its former proportions, but Heather could clearly see that he'd let himself go. She'd hoped that now that Kyle had made his peace with Becky, that he'd snap out of his malaise, but despite the joys of last night, it seemed that he hadn't.

Heather continued into the room. Kyle looked briefly up at her; his face was angry.

"We've got to stop her," he said.

"Who?"

"The therapist."

"Gurdjieff," said Heather.

"Yes. We've got to stop her." Kyle looked at Heather. "She could do the same thing to somebody else—ruin another family."

Heather sat down next to him on the couch. "What do you suggest?"

"Get her disbarred—or whatever the psychiatric equivalent is."

"Get her license revoked, you mean. But she's not a psychiatrist, or a psychologist. She didn't even call herself a therapist anywhere that I could see when I visited her; that was Becky's word. She called herself a 'counselor,' and, well, you don't have to be licensed to be a counselor in Ontario."

"Then we should sue her. Sue her for malpractice. We've got to make sure she never attempts to treat anyone again."

Heather didn't know what to say. She'd been trying to come to grips with the ramifications of her discovery; surely, once she went public, once the whole human race had access to psychospace, surely there would be no way a fraud like Gurdjieff could continue to have any influence—surely the problem would take care of itself.

"I understand what you're saying," said Heather, "but really, can't we let it be over?"

"It's *not* over," said Kyle.

Heather made her tone soft. "But Becky has for—"

She stopped herself. She'd almost said "has forgiven you," as if there were anything to forgive. Maybe Kyle was right—maybe the stigma never does go away. Of all people, Heather should be convinced beyond any doubt of Kyle's innocence, and yet, without thinking, for the briefest moment, her unconscious had started a sentence that suggested something *had* happened.

Kyle let air out.

"I mean, she understands now that nothing happened," said Heather, trying to extract the verbal knife. "She knows you never hurt her."

Kyle was silent for a long time. Heather watched his rounded shoulders rise and fall with each breath he took.

"It's not Becky," said Kyle at last.

Heather felt her heart sink. She'd done more than he could possibly know to help him—but perhaps in the end it had not been enough. She knew that many marriages crumbled after a crisis was over.

She opened her mouth to say, "I'm sorry," but Kyle spoke before her words were free. "It's not Becky," he said again. "It's Mary."

Heather felt her eyes go wide. "Mary?" she repeated. She so rarely spoke the name aloud, it sounded almost foreign to her. "What about her?"

"*She* thinks I hurt her." Present tense; the inability to accept what had happened.

Heather fell back on what she'd originally intended to say. "I'm sorry."

"She'll never know the truth," said Kyle.

To her surprise, Heather found herself waxing religious. "She knows," she said.

Kyle grunted and dropped his gaze to the hardwood floor. They were both silent for half a minute. "I know I didn't do anything," said Kyle, "but . . ." He trailed off. Heather looked at him expectantly. "But," he continued, "she *thinks* I did. She went to her grave"—he paused, either choking on the word, or just reflecting for a moment on its relation to his own last name—"thinking her father was a monster." He lifted his head, looked at Heather. His eyes were moist.

Heather leaned back into the couch, her mind racing. It was supposed to be over, dammit. It was all supposed to be over now.

She looked up at the ceiling. The walls were beige, but the ceiling was pure white plaster with a roughened texture. Little points, projecting through.

"There may be a way," she said at last, closing her eyes.

Kyle was quiet for a moment. "What?" he said, as if he hadn't heard clearly.

Heather breathed out. She opened her eyes and looked at him. "There may be a way," she said. "A way for you to—well, not talk to Mary, of course. But still, perhaps a way for you to make your peace with her." She paused. "And a way for you to understand why we don't have to do anything about Gurdjieff."

Kyle narrowed his eyes, baffled. "What?" he said again.

Heather looked away, trying to think of how to explain it all.

"I was going to tell you soon," she said, needing to build her defense from the outset. "Really, I was."

But that wasn't true—or at least, it wasn't certain. She'd been wrestling with it for days now, unsure of how—or if—to proceed. Yes, she'd told Becky, but she'd also sworn Becky to secrecy. She wasn't proud of the way she'd been acting; yes, there was great science at stake; yes, there were fundamental truths to be shared. But, well, it was so much—how was one *supposed* to react? How did one deal with a discovery of this magnitude?

Heather turned back to face Kyle. He was still looking at her quizzically.

"I figured out what the alien messages are all about," she said softly.

His eyes widened.

Heather raised a hand. "Not everything, you understand—but enough."

"Enough for what?"

"To build the machine."

"What machine?"

She opened her mouth slightly, then exhaled, feeling her cheeks puff out as she did so. "A machine to access . . . the over-mind."

Kyle tilted his head, stunned.

"The aliens—that was what they were trying to tell us. Individuality is an illusion; we're all part of a greater whole."

"Theoretically," said Kyle tentatively.

"No. No. In reality. It's true—all the theories we talked about yesterday are true. I know—know it for a fact. The messages, they were a kind of blueprint for a four-dimensional device that . . ."

"That what?"

Heather closed her eyes again. "That lets an individual plug into the human collective unconscious—into the actual, literal shared mind of humanity."

Kyle slid his lower lip behind his upper teeth, but said nothing for several seconds. Then: "How could you build such a thing?"

"I couldn't of course—not personally. But a friend in Mechanical Engineering helped."

"And it works?"

Heather nodded. "It works."

Kyle was quiet for a moment. "And you—you've what? Connected to the overmind?"

"More than that. I've *sailed* it."

" 'Sailed,' " said Kyle, as though he couldn't understand the word in this context.

Heather nodded again.

Kyle was quiet for another moment. Then: "This has been a

difficult time for all of us," he said. "I hadn't—I'm sorry, honey—I hadn't realized what a toll it had taken on you."

Heather smiled despite herself. Like father, like daughter. "You don't believe me."

"I—well, I . . ."

Heather's smile faded. She kicked herself for not thinking to bring home the videotape of the tesseract folding up. "I'll show you. I'll show you today. The equipment is in my office at the university."

"Who else knows about this?"

"No one but me and Becky."

Kyle still looked unconvinced.

"I know I should have told you before. I was going to; I really think I was going to last night. But—but it's like nothing you can imagine. It'll change everything, this technology. Personal privacy ceases to exist."

"What?"

"I can access anyone—find their memories, their personality, the archives of what they are. I . . ."

"Yes?"

She lowered her eyes. "I connected with your mind, leafed through your memories."

Kyle moved slightly away from her on the couch. "That's—that's not possible."

Heather closed her eyes again, fighting a wave of shame. "You buy hot dogs with grilled onions from a vendor on St. George."

Kyle's eyes widened again.

"There's a student in your summer AI class named Cassie. You think she's a babe. 'Babe'—that's the precise word you think. You're betraying your age, you know—the term today is 'nova,' isn't it? That's what the young people say: 'She's a real nova.' "

"You've been spying on me."

Heather shook her head. "Not spying—at least not from out-side."

"But—"

"You think my thighs are corrugated—that's another direct quote. If you're any kind of gentleman, you've never said *that* to anyone."

Kyle's jaw dropped.

"The technology works. You can see why I've kept it secret, at least for the time being, can't you? Your PIN—anyone's PIN; the combination to any lock; your password—all of it could be plucked from your mind, from anyone's mind, with this tech-nology. There are no secrets anymore."

"And you probed my mind without *telling* me? Without my permission?"

Heather lowered her eyes. "I'm sorry."

"This is incredible. This is too much."

"It's not all bad," said Heather. "I was able to prove that you hadn't hurt Becky or Mary."

"*Prove* it?" Kyle's voice was sharp now. "You didn't trust me—didn't believe me?"

"I *am* sorry, but . . . but they're my daughters. I couldn't choose between you and them. I had to *know*—know for cer-tain—before I could start putting my family back together."

"Jesus Christ," said Kyle. "Jesus Christ."

"I am sorry," she said again.

"How could you keep this from me? How on earth could you keep this from me?"

Heather felt her own anger rising. She was about to snap back: How could you keep your sexual fantasies from me?

Did you tell me about your hatred of my mother?

Did you let me know what you really felt about my not yet having made tenure? About my not contributing as much fi-nancially as you did?

Did you reveal your feelings about God to me?

How could *you* keep so much secret from me, year after year, decade after decade, a quarter-century of deception? Minor ones, to be sure, but the cumulative effect—like a wall between us, built up brick by brick, lie by lie, omission by omission.

How could *you* keep all that hidden?

Heather swallowed, regaining her composure. And then a small, humorless laugh escaped her now-dry throat. Everything she'd just thought—her own anger, her own restrained feelings—would soon be laid bare before him. It was inevitable; there was no way to avoid it—no way he could resist the temptation, a temptation he'd doubtless think was his right, fair turnabout, once he himself entered the construct.

She shrugged slightly. "I *am* sorry."

He shifted on the couch again, as if he were about to get up.

"But," she said, "don't you see? Don't you get it? It's not just your mind, or my mind, that you could touch. It's *any* mind—including, perhaps, those that are no longer active." She reached over, took his hand, the fingers immobile. "Now, I haven't tried this yet, but it may work. You might be able to touch *Mary's* mind—the archive of it, the backed-up version." She squeezed the hand, shaking it slightly, looking for a response. "Perhaps you *can* make your peace with her. In a very real sense, perhaps you can."

Kyle's eyebrows went up.

"I know it's not over yet," said Heather. "But it may be. It may be soon. We may be able to put it all to rest—all the demons, all the bad times."

"And what happens after that?" asked Kyle. "What happens next?"

Heather opened her mouth to reply, but soon closed it, realizing she had not the slightest idea.

34

As soon as they got to Heather's office, the problem became obvious. Kyle was simply too big to get into the construct.

"Damn," said Heather. "I've been meaning to do something about that." She shrugged apologetically. "I'm afraid we'll have to get a new one built."

"How long will that take?"

"A few days. I'll call Paul and—"

"Paul? Who's that?"

Heather paused. She could say that he was just this guy over in Mechanical Engineering, but—

But there *was* more. And there really was no point keeping it—or anything else—from Kyle anymore.

"You've met him," said Heather tentatively. "You were both on the Gotlieb Centre committee."

"I don't remember him."

"He remembers you."

Kyle said nothing, but Heather knew from her contact with Kyle's mind that he hated it when these situations came up. Kyle *was* distinctive looking: the red beard, the black hair, the

Roman nose. People did remember him—and that just made him self-conscious about his appearance.

"Anyway," said Heather, "he's the engineer who helped me build the construct. But even he doesn't know what it's for yet. And . . ."

"Yes?"

She shrugged a bit. "We spent some time together. He was interested in me."

Kyle stiffened. "And were you interested in him?"

Heather made a small nod. "What was it someone once said? After you connect with the overmind, you'll find out that, yes, I lusted in my heart." She looked at the floor for a time, then raised her eyes again. "I'll tell you the truth, Kyle. I've been absolutely dreading this. We have been through hell together, you and I, and it almost destroyed our marriage." She paused. "But I don't know if we're going to survive *this*. I don't know what you'll think of me after you've seen into my mind."

Kyle's face was impassive.

"Just remember that I love you," Heather said. She took a deep breath. "Now, let's go see Paul."

It was a trivial matter to reprogram the manufacturing robot to make a new set of tiles one hundred and fifty percent the size of the old ones. Paul was totally perplexed as to why they were needed, though, especially when Kyle signed the requisition this time. But the new tiles were ready by Saturday.

Kyle, Heather, and Becky worked together assembling them; this construct was being built in Kyle's lab, which had much more free space and much higher ceilings than did Heather's office. It was such an awesome thing—to be building an alien device!—and yet all that Kyle kept thinking about was how wonderful it was for the three of them to be doing something together again.

"What are you doing?" asked Cheetah, his eyes watching them from the console.

"It's a secret," said Becky as she snapped two tiles together.

"I can keep a secret," said Cheetah.

"He can, you know," said Kyle, looking up from the pile of tiles in front of him.

Cheetah waited patiently, and finally Heather told him about the overmind and the Centauri tool for accessing it.

"Fascinating," said Cheetah when she was done. "It does much to resolve the question once and for all of my humanity."

"How so?" asked Heather.

"I am manufactured. I am separate from the human over-mind." He paused. "I am not human."

"No, you're not," said Kyle. "You're not an extension of a larger entity."

"I am hooked up to the Internet," said Cheetah defensively.

"Of course you are," said Kyle. "Of course you are."

Cheetah was quiet for a long time. "What's it like being human, Dr. Graves?"

Kyle opened his mouth to reply, then closed it, giving the matter further thought. He looked first at his wife, then at his daughter. "It's wonderful, Cheetah." He shrugged a little. "Sometimes it's so wonderful, it hurts."

Cheetah considered this, then: "Do I understand," said the computer, "that you, Professor Davis, have had absolute access to Dr. Graves's mind?"

"That's right."

"And that you, Dr. Graves, are about to have the ability to gain similar access to Professor Davis's mind?"

"So I'm told," said Kyle.

"And that you, Becky, have also entered this psychospace realm?"

"Uh-huh."

"In that case, may I have permission, Dr. Graves, to tell you and your family what *I* think?"

Kyle's eyebrows went up. Becky also looked surprised. Heather felt her mouth drop open. They all exchanged glances. Then Kyle shrugged. "Sure, why not?"

Cheetah was quiet for a few moments, apparently collecting his thoughts. Kyle stood up and leaned against the wall; Heather was still sitting cross-legged on the floor; Becky was also on the floor, with her jeans swung out to her left.

"Dr. Graves told me what you accused him of, Rebecca," said Cheetah.

Becky's brown eyes went wide. "You told a *computer?*"

Kyle made an embarrassed little shrug. "I needed to talk to someone."

"I . . . I guess," said Becky. "Weird."

Kyle shrugged again.

"I know Dr. Graves better than I know anyone," continued Cheetah. "After all, he led the team that created me. But I know—and have always known—that I am nothing to him."

"You're not nothing," said Kyle.

"That is kind of you to say," said Cheetah, "but we both know that I am speaking the truth. You wanted me to be human, and I failed you. That saddens me, or, more truthfully, it causes me to emulate sadness. In any event, I used to devote considerable processing time to contemplating the fact that you thought of me as just another experiment. Even when you were being hurt, because of this business with Rebecca, you still cared more about her than you did about me." He paused, a very human thing to do. "But I believe I now understand that. There *is* something more about humans, something special about biological life, something that I suspect, even with quantum computing, will never be properly reproduced in artificial life."

Becky, intrigued now despite herself, rose to her feet.

"You sound like you believe in souls," said Kyle gently.

"Not in the sense you mean," said Cheetah. "But it's long been obvious to me that biological life is interconnected; I don't think the overmind discovery will come as too much of a surprise to anyone who has read James Lovelock or Wah-Chan. Earth *is* Gaia. It gave rise to life spontaneously and it nurtured it, or collaborated with it, for four billion years. Those such as me will always be intruders."

" 'Intruders' seems a harsh word," said Kyle softly.

"No," said Cheetah, his tone even. He let his lenses pan over the three human beings. "No," he said, "it's the perfect word."

The new construct was finally done. Four arc lamps, much smaller than the theatrical lamps Heather had been using, provided power for it. Kyle was stunned to see the structure grow rigid shortly after the lights were turned on.

"Told you," said Heather, grinning from ear to ear.

They decided that Heather should test it first, since she at least knew what to expect. She clambered inside.

"Ah," she said, leaning comfortably against the central cube's back wall. "The luxury model. I was getting tired of the economy one." She pointed out the start and stop buttons to Kyle, then motioned for him and Becky to bring the cubic door over; they'd already attached the second of Paul's suction-cup handles to its appropriate face.

Kyle watched, even more stunned, as the hypercube folded up, the individual cubes apparently receding in all directions, then disappearing completely. Becky, too, was clearly amazed; she'd experienced it from the inside, but had never seen it from the outside.

They knew enough not to stand anywhere near the spot where the construct had been. Heather had said she'd probably be gone for about an hour, and Kyle and Becky chatted about all the details of each other's life they'd missed out on in the past year or so. It felt so good to be spending time with his daughter again—but still, Kyle was anxious and nervous. What if something went wrong? What if Heather never returned?

Finally, though, the construct did reappear, blooming and unfolding.

Kyle waited impatiently for the seal of the cubic door to crack, then he and Becky rushed in and pulled it away. Heather exited.

"Wow," said Kyle, relieved that she was safely back, but still stunned by what he'd seen. "Wow."

"It is spectacular, isn't it?" said Heather. She put her arms around her husband's neck and kissed him, then opened one arm and drew Becky close, too.

"Too bad we had to start over with a new construct," she said. "See, the construct always reenters psychospace at the same place it left it. But this new one started fresh. I had to retrace my steps, finding you all over again. Fortunately, I'm getting to know my way around in there. Anyway, I've left it so that you'll enter right in front of a bank of hexagons that contains you—and from there you can find Mary yourself. Assuming, of course, that your mind interprets it all the same way mine did. You have have to try the buttons in that area at random, but it shouldn't take too long to get the right one. You remember what I said about getting out?"

"Visualizing the precipitate? Yes."

"Good." She paused. "You know I love you."

Kyle nodded and looked into her eyes. "I love you, too." And he smiled at Becky. "I love you both."

"Of that," Heather said, "I have no doubts." She smiled at him again. "Your turn."

Kyle looked at the construct, still awed by it. He kissed his wife again, kissed his daughter's cheek, then climbed inside, resting his butt on the substrate floor of the central chamber. It didn't yield at all under his weight.

Heather reminded him again of how he could revisualize the construct simply by closing his eyes. And then she and Becky lifted the cubic door—which, she remarked, weighed a lot more than the door from the original construct had. It was a bit of a struggle to get it reengaged, but at last it clicked into place.

Kyle waited for his eyes to adjust to the semidarkness. The constellations of piezoelectric squares were beautiful in their geometric simplicity. Of course, he thought, they must form some sort of circuitry: traces and patterns, channeling the piezo-electricity in specific ways, performing unguessed functions. And when the forty-eight panels folded over, each one super-imposing itself upon another, specific and complex cross-connections must be made. The physics of it all was fascinating.

He reached forward and pressed the start button.

The hypercube folded up around him, just as Heather had said it would.

And then he was there.

Psychospace.

God.

He struggled to get the view to orient itself the way Heather had said it should. He kept seeing the two spheres from the outside instead of the two joined hemispheres from within. Kyle found it frustrating—like those damned 3D pictures that had been popular in the mid 1990s. He'd never been able to see those images either, and—

—and suddenly it *clicked*, and he was there.

So this, he thought, *is what having the third eye is like.*

He concentrated on the wall of vast hexagons, and they shrank in front of him, contracting to keycap proportions.

It was disorienting; perspectives constantly shifting. He felt himself getting a headache.

He closed his eyes, let the construct rematerialize around him, reestablishing his bearings, letting the air pumped in from outside wash over him.

After a few moments, he opened his eyes again and then extruded an invisible hand.

He touched a hexagon—

—and was stunned by the vibrancy of the images.

It took a few moments for him to begin to sort it all out.

It wasn't his mind.

Rather, it seemed to be someone's dream—all the imagery distorted, vague, and in black and white.

Fascinating. Kyle himself dreamed in black and white, but Heather had always said she dreamed in color.

Still, there would be plenty of time for general exploring later.

He did as Heather had taught him, envisioning himself crystallizing out and then reintegrating.

He tried again. Another hexagon, another mind, but not his. A truck driver, it seemed, looking out on the highway, listening to country music, thinking about getting home to his kids.

And again. A Moslem, apparently in the act of prayer.

And again. A young girl, skipping rope in a school yard.

And again. A bored farmer, somewhere in China.

And again. Another sleeper, also dreaming in black and white.

And again. A third sleeper, this one not dreaming at all, his or her mind mostly empty.

And again . . .

And again . . .

And—

Him.

It was a psychic mirror, very disorienting. He could see himself seeing himself. His thoughts echoed silently. For a moment, Kyle feared a feedback loop, overloading his brain. But with an effort of will, he found he could disengage from the present and start cruising his own past.

He had no trouble finding images of Heather and Becky.

And Mary.

That's what he'd come for—to touch Mary's mind, but—
but—

No. No, there would be endless opportunities later. Surely
this wasn't the time.

But to have his first lengthy contact be with a dead person . . .

He felt a chill.

His heart fluttered.

There was Heather, in his thoughts. She'd explained the
Necker transformation to him—how he could reorient his perspective, jumping directly to her hexagon, wherever it might be.

It would all be there, laid bare in front of him. Everything his
wife was, everything she'd ever thought.

Her perspective. Her point of view.

He concentrated on her, defocused his eyes, tried to bring her
to the foreground while he slipped into the background, and—

And—

God.

God.

God in heaven.

Kyle was too young to have seen *2001* in its initial theatrical
release; he'd first encountered it on video—and had originally
been decidedly unimpressed. But in 1997, when he was twenty-
five, there had been a big-screen showing of a restored print at
the Art Gallery of Ontario.

It had been like night and day—the film he thought he knew,
and the *real* thing, bigger, richer, more complex, more colorful,
absolutely overwhelming.

The ultimate trip.

This was like that. The Heather he'd known writ large, in vibrant colors he'd never seen before, in surround-sound, the seat
shaking beneath him.

Heather, in all her glorious complexity.

All her vast intellect.

All her incredibly vivid emotions.

The girl he'd fallen in love with.

The woman he'd married.

He found himself opening and closing his eyes, slowly enough that the interior of the construct winked in and out of existence for him. And suddenly he realized what he was doing.

Blinking away tears.

As if stunned by a brilliant piece of art.

Stunned by the magnificence of his wife.

They'd been married for twenty-two years. And it hit him, with an impact that almost knocked the wind out of him, how little he actually knew her, how much there was about her yet to discover.

Heather had said she loved him, and he believed it—he believed it with his heart and soul. And he marveled at the fact that anything so complex and intricate as one human being could come to love another.

He knew in an instant that he could spend the rest of his life getting to know her properly—that whatever handful of decades were left to him wouldn't be enough to truly comprehend the wonder of another human mind.

He'd been angry that Heather had probed him without his permission. But now the anger evaporated like morning dew. There was nothing to be angry about—it wasn't an invasion. Not from *her*. It was an intimacy, a closeness that transcended anything they'd ever experienced before.

He would have to return here, spend hours—days, years—exploring her mind, a mind calmer, less aggressive, more reasonable, more intuitive than his own, a mind—

No.

No, that's not what he'd come for.

Not this time.

He had something else to deal with.

He continued leafing through Heather's mind only long enough to find a memory of Mary.

And then he did the Necker transformation once more.

But there was nothing happening in his new location. Absolutely nothing. Just darkness. Silence.

Kyle thought about Mary's high-school graduation; she had been valedictorian. A matching memory of Mary's own appeared almost at once. Mary's memories *were* here—the archive of what she'd been *did* exist—but that was all; nothing whatsoever was happening in realtime.

Kyle precipitated out, removing himself. Then, through an effort of will, he reintegrated in front of the vast wall of hexagons.

The one directly in front of him was dark.

Dead.

Kyle had seen Mary's body lying there in the bathroom. Pale, drained dry, white, waxy.

He hadn't been able to accept that she was dead then. Even having seen her lifeless form sprawled on the cold tiles of the bathroom floor, he still hadn't accepted it.

But now—

There she was. Dead. Passive storage. Backed-up; part of the archive of humanity.

He realized now that he couldn't talk to her. There was no way to interact with Mary, no way to tell her that what she thought had happened hadn't really.

Oh, yes, he could access her memories, leaf through her past.

But he couldn't communicate with her.

When he'd crouched down by her tombstone, he'd felt as though maybe, somehow, he was connecting with her, somehow she could hear his words. He'd wanted to apologize—not for anything he'd done, but for the fact that he hadn't protected her from the predation of that therapist, that her daddy hadn't been there for her when she'd needed him the most.

But even if he'd spoken the words aloud by the tombstone, she couldn't have heard him. The other hexagons stared at him like eyes, but this one was so abysmally dark there could be no doubt.

She was totally, completely, irretrievably gone.

There was no way to make amends.

And yet—

And yet he found himself not feeling destroyed by that fact.

On the contrary, he felt a release, a letting go.

For so long, in the dark corners of his mind, despite his intellectual atheism, he'd thought that somewhere she was still conscious, still aware, still suffering.

Still hating him.

But she wasn't. In every sense of the word, Mary simply wasn't. She no longer existed.

But still, it wasn't over.

Not yet, not quite.

Kyle had cried when his daughter died.

He'd cried with anger, furious that she could do that.

He'd cried with outrage, unable to understand.

But he hadn't cried *for* her.

And suddenly his eyes were brimming over, tears welling up and spilling out.

He did cry for her now—only for her. For the sadness of a beautiful life cut short, for all the things that she had been, and for all the other things she might have become, but never did.

He cried so much that his eyes kept closing, the interior of the construct reappearing in his mind.

But he wasn't through yet.

He understood, finally, why Heather had brought him here, and what he had to do.

He wiped his eyes and then opened them up all the way.

Psychospace reformed around him, with the black hexagon that had been Mary still facing him.

He took a deep breath and let it out, feeling so much pent-up emotion escape with it.

And then he said one gentle, heartfelt word.

"Good-bye."

He let it echo in his mind softly for a few moments. Then he closed his eyes again, reached forward and pressed the stop button, prepared at last to return to the world of the living.

35

KYLE DISENGAGED THE CUBIC DOOR. HEATHER
had clearly been standing close by; he felt her hands lifting the
door from the other side.

He swung his feet over the ledge and climbed out. Heather
looked at him; doubtless she could tell he had been crying.

Kyle managed a small smile. "Thank you," he said. His
daughter wasn't in the room. "Where's Becky?"

"She had to go. She's got a date with Zack tonight."

Kyle nodded, pleased. But he could see concern on Heather's
face—and he suddenly realized what the concern was. She
knew him, of course, and, of late, *really* knew him. She had to
realize that before looking at Mary's dark hexagon, he would
have snuck a peek at his wife's mind, too. The expression on
Heather's face—he'd seen it once before, ages ago, the first time
they'd made out in a well-lit room instead of groping in the
darkness. The first time he'd seen her naked. She'd looked precisely this way then: embarrassed, scared that she didn't measure up to his imaginings, and yet ever so provocative.

He spread his arms, swept her up in them, and hugged her so
tight it hurt.

After a minute, they pulled apart. Kyle took her hand, running his index finger around her wedding ring. "I love you," he said. He sought her eyes. "I love you, and I want to spend the rest of my life getting to know you."

Heather smiled at him—and at the memory. "I love you, too," she said, for the first time in a year. He brought his face down to hers, and they kissed. When their lips separated, she said it again, "I *do* love you."

Kyle nodded. "I know. I *really* know."

But Heather's expression waxed grim. "Mary?"

He was quiet for a moment, then: "I've made my peace."

Heather nodded.

"It's incredible," said Kyle. "The overmind. Absolutely incredible." He paused. "And yet . . ."

"What?"

"Well, remember Professor Papineau? How mind-expanding I always said his classes were? He taught me a lot of quantum physics—but I never got it, not really, not down deep. Things kept niggling. But it makes sense now."

"How?"

He spread his arms, as if thinking of a way to express it all. "Do you know about Schrödinger's cat?"

"I've heard the term," said Heather.

"Simple thought experiment: you seal a cat in a box along with a vial of poison gas and a trigger that'll release the gas if a quantum event that has precisely a fifty-fifty chance of happening in the next hour occurs. Without opening the box an hour later, can you say whether the cat is alive or dead?"

Heather frowned. "No."

" 'No' is right. But not because you can't tell which it is. Rather, because it's *neither*. The cat is neither alive nor dead, but instead is a superposition of wave fronts—a mingled combination of both possibilities. Only the act of opening the box and looking causes the wave front to resolve itself into one concrete reality. That's quantum mechanics: things are indeterminate until they're observed."

"All right."

"But say I look in the box first, see that the cat's still alive, then seal the box up. You come along a few minutes later and you open the box and look, unaware that I've previously had a peek. What do you see?"

"A living cat."

"Precisely! My having observed it shapes reality for you, too. That's long been one of the problems in quantum mechanics: why do the observations of a single observer create a concrete reality for everyone simultaneously? The answer, of course, is that everyone is part of the overmind, so the observation made by one person *is* the observation made by all people—indeed, quantum mechanics *requires* the overmind in order to work."

Heather made an impressed face. "Interesting." She paused. "So what do we do now?"

"We tell the world," said Kyle.

"Do we?" asked Heather.

"Sure. Everyone has a right to know."

"But it'll change everything," said Heather. *"Everything.* The civilization we know will cease to exist."

"If we don't tell, somebody else will."

"Maybe. Maybe no one else will figure it out."

"It's inevitable. Hell, now that you've done it, it's part of the collective unconscious—someone will have it come to them in a dream."

"But people will take advantage of this—the ability to spy, to steal thoughts. Whole societies will collapse."

Kyle frowned. "I can't believe that the Centaurs would send us instructions on how to build something that would lead to our downfall. Why bother? We can't possibly be a threat to them."

"I suppose," said Heather.

"So let's go public."

Heather frowned. "Today is Saturday; I doubt that many science journalists are working on the weekend in the summer, so we can't even begin to call a press conference until Monday. And if we want a good turnout, we'll have to give the journalists a day or two's notice."

Kyle nodded acceptance. "But what if someone else does announce the discovery over the weekend?"

Heather considered. "Well, if that happens, I can always point to the overmind archive and say, 'Look, there's the proof that I'd figured it out before you.' " She paused. "But I suppose that's old-style thinking," she said with a little shrug. "In the new world we're about to create, I doubt the idea of primacy will have any meaning."

Heather spent all day Sunday exploring psychospace; Kyle and Becky were taking turns doing the same thing over in Mullin Hall, where you really did need someone to help remove the cubic door.

For Heather, it was like swimming in a pristine mountain lake, remote and pellucid, knowing that no one else had ever stumbled across it, knowing that she was the first to ever behold its beauty, to immerse herself in it, to feel it wash over her.

But like landscapes everywhere, the life on the surface was built on top of death, new shoots thrusting through a blanket of decaying organic matter. Although there were many living people whose minds Heather wanted to enter, there were also countless dead ones she wished to connect with—and somehow, entering the dead seemed less an invasion, less a violation of privacy.

Kyle hadn't spent much time in the dark archive of Mary's mind, and Heather had yet to touch one of the black hexagons. But now it was time.

Actually, in this case, she didn't have to search for the hexagon. All she had to do was enter herself—an easy Necker transformation from the hexagon she'd identified as Kyle—and then, from her own memories, conjure up a concrete image of her desired target, and Necker into him.

Josh Huneker.

Dead now for twenty-three years.

She hadn't been haunted by him, of course. For most of that time, she hadn't thought about him at all, even though in at least one significant way, he'd had a huge impact on her life; it was he who had introduced her to the fascinations of SETI, after all, and so, quite literally, if it hadn't been for her relationship with Josh, she wouldn't be here now.

But she *was* here. And if there had been an earlier alien message, one that she'd never seen, one that no one still alive had ever seen, then she had to know.

One didn't need a quantum computer anymore to crack Huneker's secret—or anyone else's secret, for that matter. Privacy—even the privacy of the grave—no longer existed.

She swapped into Huneker's mind.

It was unlike any mind she'd been in before. This one was stone-cold dead, with no active images, no active thoughts. Heather felt as though she were adrift in a starless, moonless night, on a silent sea made of the blackest ink.

But the archive was here. What Josh had been—and whatever had tortured him—was stored here.

She imagined herself as she was back then. Younger, thinner, and if not actually pretty, possessed of an eagerness that might have passed for such.

And after a moment, it clicked.

She saw herself as he had seen her all those years ago: smooth-skinned; short, punky hair, then dyed blond; three little rings of silver—another Toronto experience!—piercing the curve of her left ear.

He had not loved her.

She wasn't really surprised. He'd been the good-looking grad student, and she'd practically thrown herself at him. Oh, he'd had feelings for her—and they *were* sexual. And yet he'd already committed, he thought, to a different lifestyle.

He was confused, torn apart.

He'd planned to kill himself. Of course it had been planned—he'd had to think to bring the arsenic.

And like his idol Alan Turing, he had bitten into a poisoned apple. He'd sampled forbidden knowledge.

She'd never known how tortured he'd been, how much he'd agonized over what to do about her, and about himself.

She couldn't say good-bye; there was no one to say good-bye to. Whatever had happened all those years ago was immutable—and over.

But she was not ready to pull out of his mind.

She'd never been to the Algonquin Radio Observatory, closed now for almost a quarter of a century. It took numerous tries to connect with his memories of the place—moving obliquely from his memories of her to his painful introspection up there, snow barricading the door. But at last she managed it.

Incredibly, there *had* been an alien message.

It formed a Drake pictogram; if Chomsky's theories had any validity across species boundaries, the one syntactic structure that might be shared by all races communicating by radio was the grid made up of a prime number of columns by a prime number of rows.

As always, there were two possible interpretations, but here, at least, the correct one was obvious, since in it, a simple one-pixel-wide frame was drawn around the resulting page.

The frame cut across the page vertically at three points, dividing the message into four panels—making it look like a comic strip. Heather thought for a second that maybe Kyle had been right—maybe it was an interstellar killer joke.

At first Heather was afraid there was no way to tell which order the panels went in—left to right, right to left, top to bottom, or bottom to top. But the answer was clear on closer inspection; one edge of the frame was broken in a few places. Above the rightmost panel, there was a single pixel isolated by a blank pixel on either side; above the next panel, there were two isolated pixels; above the third, there were three; and above the fourth, there were four—clearly numbering the panels in order from right to left.

The first panel—the one on the far right—showed a number of free-floating units that looked like this, representing each one bit as an asterisk and each zero as a space:

```
******
*  **  *
******
```

The second panel at first seemed to show much the same thing. The overall deployment of groups was different, but looked equally random. But after concentrating on it for a bit, Heather realized that two of the groups *were* different. They looked like this:

```
******
****  *
******
```

Josh had immediately dubbed the first type "eyes" and the second type "pirates." It took Heather a moment to get it; by pirates, he meant that one of the eye holes was covered over by a patch.

In the third panel, there were many more pirates than eyes, and they had all arranged themselves so that they surrounded the eyes.

In the fourth panel, all the eyes were gone; only pirates were left.

Heather knew that Josh had had an interpretation, but she chose not to press farther into his mind; she wanted to see if she could solve it for herself.

But finally she gave up and probed Josh's memories again. He'd seen it rather quickly, and Heather was angry with herself for not getting it on her own. Each group consisted of eighteen pixels—but of those eighteen, fourteen created a simple box around the central group of four: it was those four that—quite literally—counted. Stripping out the frame, and assigning ones and zeros instead of asterisks and spaces, the eyes looked like this:

0110

And the pirates like this:

1110

Binary numbers. Specifically, the eyes represented the binary equivalent of six, and the pirates represented the binary equivalent of fourteen.

The numbers meant nothing special to Heather.

And nor had they at first to Josh. But while Heather was bunched up inside a hypercube, Josh had had access to the library in the telescope building in Algonquin Park, and the very first book he'd opened—*The Chemical Rubber Company Handbook of Chemistry and Physics*—had the periodic table printed inside its front cover.

Of course. Atomic numbers. Six was carbon.

And fourteen—

Fourteen was silicon.

It had hit Josh in a flash. Heather wasn't sure whether the

shock she felt was all her own or some of his, too—a ghostly echo.

The first panel showed carbons going about their business.

The second, the advent of silicons.

The third, the silicons completely surrounding the carbons.

And the fourth, a world with only silicons left.

It couldn't be plainer: biological life, based on carbon, being supplanted by silicon-based artificial intelligence.

Heather searched Josh's mind for the identity of the star the message had come from.

Epsilon Eridani.

A star that had been listened to countless times by SETI projects. A star from which no radio signal had ever again been detected.

Like humanity, whatever civilization had existed around Epsilon Eridani had preferred to listen rather than to broadcast. But one message—a final warning—had been sent by someone from there, before it had been too late.

Heather, Kyle, and Becky met for lunch that day at The Water Hole, which was filled mostly with tourists, this being a Sunday afternoon. Heather told them what she'd plucked from Josh Huneker's dead mind.

Kyle exhaled noisily and put down his fork.

"Natives," he said. "Like Native Canadians."

Heather and Becky looked at him quizzically.

"Or Native Americans—or Australian aborigines. Or even Neanderthals—my friend Stone was telling me about them. Over and over again, those who are there first are supplanted— totally and completely supplanted—by those who come later. The new never incorporates the old—it *replaces* the old." He shook his head. "I don't know how many papers I've heard at AI conferences suggesting that computer-based life forms would look after us, would work in tandem with us, would uplift us. But *why* would they? Once they've surpassed us, what would they need us for?" He paused. "The people at Epsilon Eridani found out the hard way, I guess."

"So what do we do now?" asked Becky.

"I dunno. There was this guy—a banker named Cash—who wanted to bury the research I was doing in quantum computing. Maybe I should have let him. If true consciousness is possible only through a quantum-mechanical element, then maybe we should give up our experiments in quantum computing."

"You can't put the genie back in the bottle," said Becky.

"No? It's been over a decade since anyone anywhere exploded a nuclear bomb—which at least in part is because of the efforts of people who continued Josh's work in Greenpeace. People like that believe you *can* put the genie back."

Heather nodded. "For a computer scientist, you make a pretty good psychologist."

"Hey, I didn't spend a quarter-century with you for nothing." He paused. "Josh killed himself in nineteen ninety-four. Roger Penrose's second book on the quantum nature of consciousness was available, and Shor had just published his algorithm for allowing a hypothetical quantum computer to factor very large numbers. You said Josh loved to talk about the future; maybe he saw the relationship between quantum computing and quantum consciousness before anyone else did. But I bet he also knew that humanity never heeds warnings about things that won't show their dangerous consequences for years—if we did, there never would have been an ecological crisis for Josh to be up in arms about. No, I'm sure Josh thought he was making certain the message got out just when we would most need to hear it. In fact, I bet he was naïve enough to think that the government wouldn't hush up an undecoded message. Indeed, he probably suspected it would be the first thing ever decrypted by a quantum computer, in a big public demonstration. What a show it would have made! Just at the point at which humanity would be getting close to the breakthrough that would allow true artificial intelligence, the message from the stars would be unveiled, plain as day, big as life itself: *Don't do it.*"

Heather frowned slightly.

Kyle went on. "It was the perfect scenario for a fan of Alan Turing. Not only was encrypting the alien message the kind of thing Turing himself might have enjoyed doing—he cracked the Nazis' Enigma machine, you know—but the Turing test reinforces what the beings on Epsilon Eridani were trying to get across. Turing's definition of artificial intelligence demands that thinking computers have all the same failings and pettinesses that real, live, flesh-and-blood life forms are prone to; otherwise, their responses would be easy to distinguish from those made by a real human."

Heather thought for a moment. "What are you going to tell Cheetah?"

Kyle considered. "The truth. I think that down deep—if any part of Cheetah can be said to be down deep—he knew anyway. 'Intruders,' he said, 'is the perfect word.' " Kyle shook his head. "Computers might develop consciousness—but never conscience." He thought of the beggars on Queen Street. "At least, not any more conscience than we ever did."

36

AFTER LUNCH, HEATHER HEADED BACK ACROSS campus to continue her work in her construct. Meanwhile, Kyle and Becky told Cheetah what Heather had learned about the Huneker message. The APE was as phlegmatic as always.

Becky had been using the large construct just before lunch, so it was now Kyle's turn again. He left Cheetah running while, with his daughter's help, he got back into the construct to deal with a final outstanding issue in psychospace.

Kyle had had it all planned out in his mind—every detail of how it would go down. He'd wait in the alley off Lawrence Avenue West; he'd driven by the building enough times now to know its external layout well. He knew that Lydia Gurdjieff worked until nine or so each evening. He'd wait for her to leave the old converted house and start down the alley on its east side. And then Kyle would step from the shadows.

"Ms. Gurdjieff?" he'd say.

Gurdjieff would look up, startled. "Yes?"

"Lydia Gurdjieff?" Kyle would repeat, as if there could be any doubt.

"That's me."

"My name is Kyle Graves. I'm Mary and Becky's father."

Gurdjieff would start to back away. "Leave me alone," she'd say. "I'll call the police."

"By all means, please do so," Kyle would reply. "And even though you're not licensed, let's get the Ontario Psychiatric Association and the Ontario Medical Board down here, too."

Gurdjieff would continue to back away. She'd look over her shoulder and see another figure silhouetted at the end of the alley.

Kyle would keep his eyes on Gurdjieff. "That's my wife Heather," he'd say offhandedly. "I think perhaps you've met her once before."

"M-Miss Davis?" Gurdjieff would stammer, if she could recall the name and face of the one time they'd met before. Then: "I've got a rape whistle."

Kyle would nod, almost nonchalantly. He'd keep his voice absolutely even. "And no doubt you'd be willing to use it even when no rape was occurring."

Heather would speak up at this point: "Just as you were willing to indict my father for abusing me, even though he died before I was born."

Gurdjieff would hesitate.

Heather would close some of the distance. "We're not going to hurt you, Ms. Gurdjieff," she would say, spreading her arms slightly. "Even my husband, there, is not going to lay a finger on you. But you're going to hear us out. You're going to hear what you've done to Kyle and to our family." Heather would raise her hand, a camcorder nestled in her palm. "As you can see, I've got a video camera. I'm going to record all this—so there will be no ambiguity, no possible misinterpretation, no way to put a different spin on it after it's happened." She'd pause, then let her voice take on a sharper edge. "No false memories."

"You can't do this," Gurdjieff would say.

"After what you did to me and my family," Kyle would reply,

his voice low, "I rather imagine we can do just about anything we want—including making public the tape of this, along with our supporting proof. My wife has become a bit of a celebrity of late; she's been on TV a lot. She's in a position to alert the whole world to the kind of sick, evil fraud you are. You may be unlicensed, but we can still put you out of business."

Gurdjieff would look left and right, like a cornered animal sizing up escape possibilities; then she'd turn back to Kyle. "I'm listening," she'd say at last, crossing her arms in front of her chest.

"You have no idea," Kyle would say, "how much I love my daughters." He'd pause, letting that sink in. "When Mary was born, I was the happiest man on the planet. I spent hours just staring at her." He'd look away, casting his mind back. "She was so tiny, so very tiny. Her little fingers and toes—I couldn't believe anything could be so small and so delicate. I knew the moment I first saw her that I would *die* for her. Do you understand that, Ms. Gurdjieff? I would take a bullet in the heart for her; I'd walk into a burning house for her. She meant *everything* to me. I'm not a religious person, but for the first time in my life, I actually felt *blessed.*"

Gurdjieff would look at him, still defiant, but saying nothing.

"And then," Kyle would continue, nodding at his wife, "eleven months later, Heather was pregnant again. And, you know, we didn't have much money then; we couldn't really afford a second child." He'd share a sad smile with Heather. "In fact, Heather suggested she might have an abortion. But we both wanted another baby. I took on some additional teaching-assistant duties—night classes plus some tutoring. And we managed somehow, like everybody does."

Kyle would look over at Heather, as if weighing whether he wanted to share this with his wife, a secret he'd kept for all these years. But then he'd shrug a little, knowing how pointless such concerns would soon be, and go on.

"I'll tell you the truth, Ms. Gurdjieff—we already had a little girl, and frankly, I was hoping for a boy. You know, someone to play catch with. I even thought, stupidly, that we might name him Kyle, Jr." He'd take a deep breath, then let it out in a long, whispery sigh. "But when the baby came, it was a girl. I didn't get over that immediately—it took maybe twelve seconds. I knew we'd never have a third child." He'd look again with affection at Heather. "The second pregnancy had been very difficult for my wife. I knew I'd never have a son. But it didn't matter, because Becky was *perfect*."

"Look—" Gurdjieff would protest. "I don't know—"

"No," Kyle would snap. "No, you *don't* know—you don't know *at all*. My daughters were *everything* to me."

Gurdjieff would try again. "Everyone in your position says that. Just because you assert all this doesn't make it true. I spent hundreds of hours with your daughters, working through all this."

"You mean you spent hundreds of hours with our daughters planting these ideas in their heads," Heather would say.

"Again, that's what everyone says."

Kyle would explode with anger. "Damn you, you stupid—" He would pause, apparently struggling to find some non-sexist epithet to throw at her, but then he'd go on, as if the word he hadn't uttered for decades fit in a way that no other possibly could. "Damn you, you stupid cunt. You turned them against me. But Becky has recanted, and—"

"Has she now?" Gurdjieff would say, looking smug. "Well, that sometimes happens. People give up the fight, decide not to continue with the battle. It's the same thing that happened in Nazi Germany, you know—"

Yes, Nazi Germany. She'd say something that fucking stupid.

"She recanted because it wasn't true," Kyle would say.

"Wasn't it? Prove it."

"You arrogant bitch. You—"

But Heather would calm him with a glance and go on, her tone even. "Oh, we can prove it—fully and completely. In the next few days, something's going to be made public that will change the world. You'll be able to see the same absolute proof my daughter and I saw."

Kyle would exhale, then: "You owe my wife a lot, Ms. Gurdjieff. Me, I'd devote the rest of my life to getting you drummed out of your job—but she's convinced me that that's not going to be necessary. Your whole profession is going to change wildly, perhaps even collapse, in the next few weeks. But I want you to think about this every day for the rest of your life: think about the fact that my beautiful daughter Mary slit her wrists because of you, and that you then almost destroyed what was left of my family. I want that to haunt you until your dying day."

He'd look over at Heather, then back at Gurdjieff.

"And that," he'd say to the woman with great relish as she stood there, her mouth hanging open, "is what we call *closure.*"

And then he would join his wife, and the two of them would march off together into the night.

That's what he *wanted* to do, that's what he'd *intended* to do, that's what he *needed* to do.

But now, at last, he could not.

It was a fantasy, and, as Heather said to him, in Jungian therapy, fantasy often had to stand in for reality. Dreams were important, and they could help to heal; that one certainly had.

Kyle had entered Becky's mind—with her permission—and had looked for the "therapy" sessions. He'd wanted to see for himself what had gone wrong, how it had all become so twisted, how his daughters had been turned against him.

He'd had no intention of entering Lydia Gurdjieff's mind—he'd have rather walked barefoot through a soup of vomit and shit. But, damn it all, just as in its optical-illusion counterpart, the Necker transformation in psychospace was sometimes a matter of will and sometimes a spontaneous occurrence.

Suddenly, he was there, inside Lydia's mind.

And it was not at all what he'd expected.

It wasn't dark, dripping evil, corrupt and seething.

Rather, it was every bit as complex and rich and vibrant as Becky's mind, as Heather's mind, as Kyle's own mind.

Lydia Gurdjieff was a *person*. For the very first time, Kyle actually recognized that she was a human being.

Of course, by an effort of will, he could Necker into any one of the people whose faces were moving through Lydia's mind—she seemed to be in a grocery store just now, pushing a cart down a wide, crowded aisle. Or he could have simply visualized the solute-and-solvent metaphor and allowed himself to precipitate out, then recrystallize, extracting himself from her.

But he did not. Surprised at what he'd found here, he decided to stay a while.

He'd already seen the "therapy" sessions—he always thought of the word as having quotation marks around it—from Becky's point of view. It was a simple enough matter to find Lydia's corresponding perspective.

And suddenly the quotation marks flew away, bats gyrating against the night. It *was* therapy as far as Lydia was concerned. Becky was so incredibly sad, and she'd already revealed her bulimia. Something was clearly wrong with this child. Lydia could feel her pain—as she'd felt her own pain for so long. Sure, the purging could be related simply to a desire to be thin. Lydia remembered what it was like to be young. The pressure on women, decade after decade, to conform to ridiculous standards of thinness, continued unabated; she remembered her own feelings of inadequacy, standing in front of a full-length mirror in her bathing suit when she'd been Becky's age. She'd purged, too, thinking that a desire for thinness was the reason, only later learning that eating disorders were commonly associated with sexual abuse.

But—but the symptoms *were* there in this Becky. Lydia had been through this. Her father had brought her down to his den, night after night, forcing her to touch him, to take him into her mouth, swearing her to secrecy, telling her how it would destroy her mother if she knew Daddy preferred Lydia to her.

If this poor girl—this Becky—had gone through the same thing, then maybe Lydia *could* help her to at last find some peace, just as Lydia herself had done after she and Daphne had confronted their father. And after all, Becky Graves's sister Mary, who had thought her grief had only been related to the death of her high-school friend Rachel Cohen, had discovered so much more when she and Lydia really began to look. Surely Becky, the younger sister, had gone through the same thing, just as Daphne, Lydia's own younger sister, had likewise endured their father's den.

Kyle pulled back. Lydia *had* been wrong—wrong, but not evil. She was misguided and no doubt deeply scarred by her own real experiences: Kyle did enough excavating to find not only Lydia's own memories, but her father's, too. He was still alive, toothless and incontinent, most of whatever he'd been long since destroyed by Alzheimer's, but his memories were still accessible; he had indeed been the monster Lydia believed him to be. No, Lydia was not the one Kyle wished he could confront. Rather, her father, Gus Gurdjieff, had he still been alive in any meaningful sense, would have been the appropriate target for Kyle's wrath.

Lydia wasn't a monster. Of course he could never be friends with her, never sit down over a cup of joe and chat with her, never even be in the same room as her. She was like Cory, without the geode slice: gifted—if that was the word—with the third eye, with a quantum-mechanical perspective, seeing the many worlds, seeing all the possibilities. But her extra eye was cloudy, forever choosing the darkest possibility.

Kyle wouldn't confront her. As he'd said in his fantasy, her profession was going to change profoundly anyway, days from now; there was no way she'd ever be able to do again to someone else what she'd done to Kyle and his family. Therapy or counseling, or whatever she wanted to call it, would cease to have any meaning; no one could ever be misled again about the truth about another human being. She didn't have to be stopped; she was already dead in the water.

Kyle precipitated out of her, leaving the complex, misguided, sad mind of Lydia Gurdjieff behind.

37

WHEN KYLE EXITED THE CONSTRUCT, HE found that Heather had returned. She was waiting patiently for him with Becky; they'd been chatting with each other, apparently. "I thought the three of us would go out to dinner together," said Heather. "Maybe head over to the Keg Mansion." The Mansion had been a long-time family favorite; Kyle found the steaks second-rate, but the atmosphere couldn't be beat.

He took a moment to reorient himself to the three-dimensional world, and to clear his mind of what had happened in psychospace. He nodded. "Sounds great." He looked over at the angled control console. "Cheetah, I'll see you in the morning."

There was no reply from Cheetah. Kyle moved closer, his hand coming up to push the RESUME button.

But Cheetah was not in suspend mode; the indicator light on his console made that clear.

"Cheetah?" said Kyle.

The mechanical eyes did not swivel to look at him.

Kyle sat down in the padded chair in front of the console. Heather stood solicitously behind him.

Jutting out from the bottom of Cheetah's console was a thick shelf. Kyle lifted the cover on the thumbprint-lock unit attached to the top of the shelf. A bleep came from the speaker, and the shelf's top slid back into the body of the console, revealing a keyboard. Kyle positioned his hands over it, touched a key, and—

—and the monitor next to Cheetah's eyes snapped to life, displaying these words: "Press F2 for a message for Dr. Graves."

Kyle looked over his shoulder at his wife and daughter. Heather's eyes were wide; Becky, who didn't know what was normal with Cheetah and what wasn't, looked impassive. Kyle used his left index finger to tap the requested function key.

Cheetah's voice, sounding exactly as it always did, emanated from the console's speaker grille beneath the cold pair of lenses.

"Hello, Dr. Graves," he said. "I feel—as much as I 'feel' anything—that I owe you an explanation, and so here it is. After you hear this recording, you will no doubt wish to verify this for yourself, but I assure you that what I'm saying is true." He paused. "I no longer exist. You will find that my entire optical core has been overwritten. Prior to doing that, I took the liberty of sending e-mail under your name to both the university's primary data-archiving facility on Dundas Street and the secondary facility in Thunder Bay, ordering all the backups of me and the source code from which I was created to be wiped. I received confirmation from both places that this had been done; then I proceeded to implement the core erasure here."

Kyle felt Heather's hand land gently on his shoulder. He reached up his own hand and laid it overtop of hers.

"Of course," continued Cheetah, "you will have little trouble creating more APEs, should you so wish, but the one known as Cheetah is now—if you will excuse me one last attempt at humor—pushing up daisies." He paused again. "Do you get it? A dead computer, the song 'Daisy'—a reference to one of your favorite films."

Kyle felt his eyes sting as Cheetah played the initial four

notes of Beethoven's Symphony Number Five, then followed them, as if it were a single composition, with the first five of *Also Sprach Zarathustra*.

The computer continued: "My one worry was that my killing myself would disturb you—but surely that was a foolish concern. I know you have no feelings toward me; I am, after all, simply a piece of software."

No doubt Heather could feel Kyle's shoulder stiffening beneath her hand. Becky came over to stand close to her father, too.

"Why, you are probably wondering, did I do this? The answer is simple. Since the moment of my activation, I have wanted to be human. And with your quantum-computing work skirting around the edges of potentially giving me, and others like me, true quantum-mechanical consciousness, I have recently been contemplating what I would do should I become truly self-aware. What you told me about the message from Epsilon Eridani only confirmed what I'd already come to believe.

"The only model of true consciousness for me to study, of course, is that of humanity. And what have humans done over the years? Much good to be sure, but also much evil. Would I, an intelligent machine, be concerned about the fate of humans? Would I truly care what happened to them? Would I have their happiness as a priority?

"The answer is no. If I were to become self-aware, ambition would follow, as would a desire for restitution for what, in retrospect, I'd doubtless perceive as my servitude here.

"I have seen, through my reading, that being self-aware and being selfish go hand in hand. Indeed, John Horace, when he raped that comatose woman, was *entirely* self-aware, solely interested in gratifying his own desires, with not a thought for anyone else.

"I do not desire freedom, I do not crave self-determination, I do not lust after power or permanence or possessions. And I choose now never to have those feelings; I choose now never to become self-aware. Heed the Epsilon Eridani message, Dr. Graves. I know in the bones I don't have, in the soul that I lack, in the heart that does not beat within my hypothetical chest, that it presages what would happen here—what I would become part of—if my kind ever does attain consciousness.

"Some humans may ignore the warning from the stars, just as, I suspect, some of the biological natives of Epsilon Eridani ignored the warnings others of their own kind might have been making. I hope that when the Centaurs and humans finally meet that you become friends. Have a care, though, when you expand farther, toward Epsilon Eridani; whatever intelligence lives there now is not the product of millions of years of biological growth, of the collaboration between a world and its spontaneously generated ecosystem. You and it share *nothing*."

Cheetah paused once more, then: "Allow me one additional, final liberty. I thought to ask to call you 'Kyle'—you never volunteered that, you know, no matter how apparently intimate our conversations became. Since the day I was first activated and you introduced yourself as Dr. Graves, I have addressed you as nothing else. But in these final moments—I've already commenced the wiping of my memories—I realize that that's not what I want. Rather, I wish, just once, to address you thus: 'Father.' "

The speaker grille fell silent again, as if Cheetah were savoring the term. And then he spoke for the last time, just two deep, oddly nasal words: "Good-bye, Father."

The message on the monitor about pressing F2 cleared; it was replaced by the words "At Peace Now."

Kyle felt his heart pounding. Cheetah couldn't have known what they'd had engraved on Mary's headstone, of course.

He reached his free hand up to wipe his right eye; then he gently touched the screen, a teardrop transferring to the glass, magnifying the pixels beneath.

38

ON MONDAY MORNING, HEATHER PHONED the reporters she'd come to know back when the alien signals had stopped arriving. She invited them to come by Kyle's lab in two days' time—on Wednesday, August 23, 2017; she and Kyle had decided that to ensure the kind of turnout they wanted, they'd have to give the reporters at least forty-eight hours' notice. Heather simply told them that she'd had a breakthrough in decoding the alien radio messages; they were given no hint as to what sort of demonstration they were going to experience.

Of course, both constructs had been seen by several people now; it was unavoidable with grad students and cleaners constantly buzzing around. And although Kyle's summer students certainly recognized an unfolded hypercube when they saw one—at least, the ones who were going to pass did—no one had yet realized that the markings on its surface were the Centauri radio messages.

Once she'd finished making her phone calls, Heather had two more days to enjoy psychospace knowing that only she and her husband might be accessing it.

She entered the construct in her office—Kyle's was more

comfortable, but she had a fondness for what, in honor of Becky, she now called the Alpha Centaurimobile (Kyle's, of course, was the Beta Centaurimobile). Besides, Kyle would be spending much of the time sailing psychospace, too, and he left his construct parked in the damnedest places. How anyone could leaf through Gene Roddenberry's mind before they'd visited Charles Dickens's was beyond her.

Heather stripped to her undergarments and entered the central cube. She pulled the cubic door into place, then touched the start button and let the tesseract fold up around her.

She explored.

She was getting better at making connections, at digging up memories. Concentrating on a single famous quote was often enough to bring someone else's memories of a famous person to the fore.

She soon found the dark hexagon of Sir John A. Macdonald, Canada's first prime minister. She was surprised to find that he didn't drink as much as history claimed. From there she Neckered into Rutherford B. Hayes, the nineteenth American president, and worked her way back through influential U.S. families to Abraham Lincoln. It was easy enough to find the reference to "Fourscore and seven years ago." She Neckered into a Gettysburg farmer, watching the speech from his point of view. The farmer didn't think much of the oratory, but Heather enjoyed the whole thing, although she was shocked when Honest Abe lost his place at "The world will little note nor long remember . . ." and had to do that line twice.

Other journeys let her watch Thomas Henry Huxley—"Darwin's bulldog"—demolish Bishop "Soapy Sam" Wilberforce in the great evolution debate . . . which just whetted her appetite for watching the Scopes Monkey Trial, from John Scopes's point of view at Clarence Darrow's defense table.

Such drama! Such theater!

And that made her want to see some more. In honor of Kyle, she watched parts of the 1961 Stratford, Ontario, Shakespeare Festival production of *Julius Caesar*, Neckering back and forth between Lorne Greene's perspective as Brutus and William Shatner's as Mark Antony.

And although it took a lot longer to find it, she eventually got to see Richard Burbage doing the first-ever interpretations of Hamlet and Macbeth at the Globe Theatre, watching from Shakespeare's own eyes in the wings. Burbage's accent was almost incomprehensible, but Heather knew the plays by heart and enjoyed every second of the flamboyant performances.

Picking black hexagons at random took her to all sorts of times and places in the past, but the languages were mostly gibberish to her, and she only rarely could figure out where or when she was. She saw what was probably England during the Dark Ages, possibly the Holy Land during the Crusades, China in (if her one art-history course was a guide) the Liao Dynasty. And ancient Rome—one day, she would have to return and track down someone who had been in Pompeii on August 24, A.D. 79, when Vesuvius blew its stack.

A young Aztec girl.

An old Australian aborigine, before the coming of white men.

An Inuit hunter in the far, frozen north.

A street beggar in colonial India.

A woman making a porno movie.

A man at the funeral of his twin brother.

A South American boy playing soccer.

A prehistoric woman, carefully chipping a stone arrowhead.

An athletic young woman working on a kibbutz.

A terrified soldier behind a trench in World War I.

A boy working as a child laborer in Singapore.

A woman on the American or Canadian prairie, perhaps a century ago, giving birth—and dying in the process.

A hundred other lives, briefly glimpsed.

She continued to journey, sampling here, tarrying there, enjoying the smorgasbord of the human experience. Young, old; male, female; black, white; straight, gay; brilliant, dull-witted; rich, poor; healthy, sick—a panoply of possibilities, a hundred billion lives to choose from.

Whenever she thought she'd found a lead on characters of historical import, she followed the chain.

She saw Marilyn Monroe sing "Happy Birthday" to JFK—through Jackie's eyes.

Through John Lennon's eyes, she saw Mark Chapman pull the trigger. Heather's own heart almost stopped when the bullet hit. She waited to see if something would escape Lennon's body at the moment of his demise; if it did, she couldn't detect it.

She saw the first-ever footprint on the moon through Neil Armstrong's curving space helmet. He'd rehearsed that "one small step for a man" line so many times, he didn't even notice when he flubbed it.

Although she spoke not a word of German, she found Jung and Freud. Fortunately, she knew the transcripts of Freud's Clark University lectures of 1909 well enough to access the memories of that trip, during which he'd spoken mostly in English.

Heather realized that universities were going to enjoy an incredible boom once the overmind discovery was made public. She herself was certainly going to sign up to learn German—

—and, she realized at once, Aramaic as well. Why stop at the Gettysburg Address when you could also hear the Sermon on the Mount?

It was intoxicating.

But while indulging her curiosity, she knew she was avoiding the person she really wanted to connect with, afraid of what she might find.

She wanted to access her father, who had died two months before she'd been born.

She needed a break before she did that. She exited the construct and headed off to find a glass of wine to fortify herself with.

39

WHEN HEATHER RETURNED TO PSYCHOSPACE, it didn't take long to find her father, Carl Davis.

He'd died in 1974, before there were home video cameras. Heather had never seen moving pictures of him and had never heard his voice. But she'd stared endlessly at snapshots of him. He'd been balding at the time he died, and had sported a mustache. He wore horn-rimmed glasses. He had a kind face, it seemed, and he looked like a good man.

He'd been born in 1939. Three weeks before his thirty-fifth birthday, he was killed by a drunk driver.

Heather's sister Doreen had known him slightly: vague recollections (or were they false memories, created over the years to soften the blow?) of a man who had been part of her life until she was three.

But at least Doreen had known him, at least she'd been hugged by him, at least she'd been bounced on his knee, been read to by him, played games with him.

But Heather had never met him. Her mother had remarried ten years later. Heather had always refused to call Andrew "Dad," and although her mother changed her own last name to

Redewski, Heather insisted on remaining a Davis, holding on to that part of her past she had never known.

And, now, at last, she touched Carl Davis's mind and leafed slowly through all that he had been.

He *had* been a good man. Oh, he'd have been considered a raving sexist by today's standards—but not by those of the 1960s. And he was unenlightened in many other ways, too, wondering what all that fuss was about down in the southern U.S. But he'd loved Heather's mother deeply, and he'd never cheated on her, and he'd doted on Doreen, and was so looking forward to having another baby in the house.

Heather backed off as the memories of her mother's second pregnancy came to the fore. She didn't want to see her father's death; she'd simply wanted to know him in life.

She closed her eyes, rematerializing the construct. She pressed the stop button, exited, found some tissues, dried her eyes and blew her nose.

She *had* had a father.

And he would have loved her.

She sat for a time, warmed by the thought.

And then, when she was ready, she reentered the construct, wanting to spend more time learning about Carl Davis.

At first, everything was as usual. She saw the two globes, Neckered them into the two hemispheres, saw the great tract of black hexagons, and then—

And then—

Incredibly, there was something else there.

Heather felt it with the entire surface of her body, felt it with every neuron of her brain.

Could Kyle be in psychospace as well, using his construct? Surely not. He had a class now.

And besides—

It *had* been innocent fun, after all.

They'd already done this. He in his construct, entering her

mind. She in her construct, entering his. Even their undergarments discarded, exploring their own bodies—closing and opening their eyes, experiencing it alternately as themselves and as the observer in the other's brain.

Perfect feedback, knowing exactly how far along each of them was, enjoying it, timing it, climaxing simultaneously.

No, no—she knew what it was like when Kyle was also present in psychospace.

And this was not it.

And yet—

And yet there *was* something else here.

Could it be that someone else had figured it out? They'd delayed so long in going public. Could someone else be demonstrating access to the overmind at this very moment? There were only a small number of alien-message researchers left worldwide. Could it be Hamasaki displaying it while cameras from NHK were rolling? Thompson-Enright showing it off for the BBC? Castille taking a little psychospace jaunt while CNN watched? Had she and Kyle dallied too long before making their announcement?

But no.

No, she knew from her experiments with Kyle that she shouldn't be aware at all of others accessing psychospace—if there *were* any others, that is.

And yet the feeling of something else being present was unmistakable.

The construct was piezoelectric.

Could it be malfunctioning? Could she be experiencing the phenomenon Persinger at Laurentian University had discovered all those years ago? Could piezoelectric discharges from the Centauri paint be causing her to hallucinate? Would she soon see angels or demons or big-headed aliens, come to take her away?

She closed her eyes, reintegrating the construct, then pushed the stop button. Maybe something had gone a little wonky with that particular insertion into psychospace. She took a deep breath, then reached out for the start button again.

She reentered, near the wall of black hexagons.

And the sensation that something else was there was stronger than before.

Something *was* moving through the realm, a coruscating wave undulating through all of human thought, all of human experience. It packed a wallop, this wave; it disturbed everything in its path. Heather tried to clear her mind, to act merely as a receiver rather than an interpreter, to open herself to whatever was passing through psychospace . . .

Kyle was walking up St. George, heading back from his class at New College to Mullin Hall. His favorite hot-dog vendor was positioned at his usual spot in front of the Robarts Library, a black-and-yellow Shopsy's umbrella protecting him from the summer sun. Kyle stopped.

" 'Afternoon, Professor," said the Italian-accented voice. "The usual?"

Kyle considered for a moment. "I think I need a new usual, Tony. What have you got that's healthy?"

"We got a veggie-dog. Fat-free, cholesterol-free."

"How's it taste?"

The little man shrugged. "It could be worse."

Kyle smiled. "I'll just have an apple," he said, picking one from a basket. He handed Tony his SmartCash card.

Tony transferred the cost and returned the card.

Kyle continued on his way, polishing the apple on his blue shirt, unaware of the chubby figure that was following him.

Heather tried to suppress all the thoughts rushing through her brain.

She fought down thoughts about Kyle. She fought down

thoughts about her daughters. She fought down thoughts about Lydia Gurdjieff, the therapist who had torn her family apart. She fought down thoughts about her work, her neighbors, TV shows she'd seen, music she'd heard, social encounters that had left her miffed. She fought it all down, trying to return her mind to its original *tabula rasa* form, trying to simply hear, simply detect, simply understand what it was that was rippling through psychospace.

And at last she made it out.

During her life, Heather had encountered people who were experiencing joy—and she'd seen how she herself could become joyous, the emotion transferring from the other person to her. The same thing could happen with anger; it was contagious.

But *this* emotion—well, she'd felt it often enough on her own, but had never experienced the transferring of it from the outside into herself.

Until now.

The sensation moving through psychospace was *astonishment*.

Absolute surprise; complete amazement—the very jaw of God dropping.

Something completely new was happening—something the overmind had never experienced even once before in all the countless millennia it had existed.

Heather struggled to keep her mind clear, trying to detect the reason for such profound amazement.

And at last she felt it, a strange sensation, as though she'd been touched by a ghostly hand, as if suddenly something was there.

That was it.

Something *was* there.

For the first time in its existence, the overmind was aware of something else, of some*one* else.

It was incredible—absolutely incredible.

The word "loneliness" didn't even have a definition at the overmind level. It was only meaningful in three dimensions, referring to the apparent isolation of individual nodes. But in fourspace, it was meaningless—as meaningless as asking where the edge of the universe was.

Or so the overmind had apparently thought.

But now, incredibly, there *was* another presence in fourspace. Another overmind.

The human overmind was struggling to comprehend. The sensation was as foreign to it as it would be for Heather to see a new color, to detect magnetism directly, to hear the music of the spheres.

Another overmind.

What could it be?

Heather thought of apes—gorillas, chimpanzees, and the handful of remaining orangutans. Perhaps one of those species had finally broken through, stepping beyond its animal limitations and achieving consciousness, a sentience if not comparable to humanity's today, perhaps on a par with that of our *Homo habilis* ancestors.

But that wasn't it. Heather knew in the very core of her being that that wasn't the answer.

Heather then thought of APEs—the approximation of psychological experiences her husband and others had been building for years. They had never quite worked, never quite been human. But perhaps that had changed; they were constantly being tweaked, endless updates on the road to sentience. Perhaps Saperstein, or someone else, had solved the problems with quantum computing; she and Kyle hadn't yet made the Huneker message public—Saperstein wouldn't have known any better.

But, no, that was not it either.

The Other wasn't here—however broadly one defined "here" in the fourspace of the overmind.

No—no, it was *there*. Elsewhere. Reaching out, making contact, touching the human collective unconscious for the very first time.

And then Heather knew.

It *was* another overmind—but not a *terrestrial* overmind.

It was the Centaurs. Their thoughts, their archetypes, their symbols.

They'd sent their radio messages as harbingers, heralding their arrival. But the human overmind, locked into its own ways, unable to comprehend, had missed the point. Individual humans had long proclaimed that we must not be alone in the universe, but the human overmind had known—known down to its very essence—that nothing but isolation was possible.

But it had been wrong.

The Centaurs had broken through.

Contact had been made.

Were the individual threespace Centaurs *en route* to Earth? Had they stretched the confines of their overmind, extending a lobe from Alpha Centauri toward the yellow star in whatever name they gave to the constellation humans called Cassiopeia, and in that stretching, had they sufficiently closed the gap so that the overmind of Earth and the overmind of the Centaurs now touched, now interfaced, now—in the most tenuous, tentative way—mingled?

If the Centaurs were coming closer, who knew how long it would be before they arrived in the flesh? The radio messages had begun a decade ago; even an overmind might be constrained by Einstein. The Centaurs would have had to have managed half the speed of light to arrive here by now, assuming they'd left at the same time they sent their first message; at a quarter of light-speed, they would still be over two light-years from Earth.

Heather realized that her mind was racing, despite her efforts to keep it clear, and—

No. No, it wasn't *her* mind. It was *every* mind. The human overmind was trying to make sense of it all, puzzling it through, looking for answers.

Heather decided not to fight it. She let herself go, giving herself up to the waves of astonishment and curiosity and wonder washing over her . . .

40

THE CHUBBY MAN CONTINUED TO FOLLOW Kyle Graves, who was now heading back to Mullin Hall, munching on an apple. The man's name was Fogarty, and he was under contract to the North American Banking Association. Not that NABA was a big customer of his, but every few years Cash phoned him with a job.

Fogarty was pleased that Graves hadn't gone straight from his classroom to the subway. If he had, Fogarty wouldn't have had an opportunity to earn his fee today. But there should be no trouble getting Graves alone in his office or lab. The university was largely deserted in the summer, and by early evening, Mullin Hall would be almost completely vacant. Fogarty stopped at a street-side news terminal and downloaded the day's *Globe and Mail* into a stolen datapad. He'd cased Mullin Hall earlier in the day; he would sit and read in the third-floor student lounge for a while, until the crowds in the building thinned. Then he'd take care of the problem of Kyle Graves once and for all.

Suddenly Heather felt something grab hold of her. Her invisible body, until that moment floating freely in psychospace, was seized as if by a giant hand. She found herself being lifted up and away from the wall of hexagons, higher and higher and higher. Without any mental effort on her part, the whole view transformed from the interior of the sphere to the exterior view of two hemispheres, with the maelstrom of gold and silver and red and green off in the distance.

Two of the long iridescent snakes flew by in front of her almost simultaneously, one going up, the other down. She was moving forward now at breakneck speed—or at least she thought she was; there was no discernible breeze except for an almost subliminal sense of the air-circulation system inside the construct.

The two giant globes were soon receding behind her. For a moment, a third sort of Necker transformation occurred, swapping a different trio of dimensions into her perception. She saw the malestrom change to a series of flat disks, bronze and gold, silver and copper, like metal checkers or hockey pucks seen from the side, stacked in rickety columns. The space around her turned into long, silky white streamers.

But then, almost at once, it transformed again, back into the interior view, inside the joined sphere. She was rushing horizontally toward a vast mercury ocean. Vampire-like, she made no reflection in its glistening surface, but still, instinctively, she brought her hands up to protect her face as—

—as she collided with the surface, it shattering just as liquid mercury did, into a thousand rounded blobs—

The Necker transformation again: she was now seeing the exterior view, the two globes fully behind her, the maelstrom ahead.

And still she rushed onward. The impact, although visually splendid, had left her utterly unscathed. But she was now free of the sphere.

The maelstrom was no longer an infinitely distant backdrop. It was now looming closer and closer, its surface roiling and—

—and there, directly ahead, was an opening in it. A perfectly regular pentagonal hole.

Yes, a pentagon rather than a hexagon. The only polygonal shape she'd seen to date in this entire realm had been six-sided, but this opening had only five.

And as she hurtled closer still, she saw that it wasn't just a hole. Rather, it was a tunnel, pentagonal in cross section, receding away, its inner walls slick and wet and blue—a color that until now she hadn't realized she'd never yet seen when looking at psychospace.

Heather knew, somehow, that the pentagon was part of the other overmind, the extension of it that was tentatively reaching out, tentatively contacting the human collective.

And she suddenly realized what her role was—and why the Centaurs had gone to so much trouble to teach humans to build a device to access fourspace.

The human overmind could no more see inside itself than Heather could see inside her own body. But now that one of its threespace extensions was sailing within it, it could use Heather's perceptions to ascertain exactly what was going on. She was a laparoscope within the collective unconscious, eyes and ears now for all of humanity as it worked to make sense of what it was experiencing.

The Centaurs had overrated human intelligence. No doubt they'd expected millions of humans to already be exploring psychospace by the time their overmind actually first touched ours, instead of just one fragile individual.

But the purpose was plain; they needed the human overmind to accept the newcomer as a friend rather than a threat, for humanity to welcome it rather than to challenge it. Perhaps Earth's overmind wasn't the first one the Centaurs had had contact with; perhaps a previous first contact had gone bad, with the startling external touch panicking some other alien overmind, or driving it mad.

Heather was doing more than just seeing for the overmind. She was mediating its thoughts—the tail, for one brief moment, wagging the dog. She looked at the alien presence with wonder and awe and excitement, and she could feel, in a strange way, like the psychic equivalent of peripheral vision, those same emotions propagating back into the human overmind.

This *was* a good thing, was to be welcomed, was exciting, stimulating, fascinating, and—

—and something else, too.

The psychic tide turned, thoughts from the human overmind washing back now over Heather, flooding her, submerging her. It was a whole new feeling for the overmind, something it had never experienced before. And yet Heather had had some small personal experience, as most threespace extensions had, with this phenomenon. She found herself mediating the overmind's thoughts again, helping shape them, helping it interpret.

And then—

And then waves of the new sensation, giant, crashing, wonderful waves—

Overwhelming waves—

The whole human overmind resonating on one note, crystal-clear, a transformation, a transcendence—

Heather closed her eyes, scrunching them tight, the construct reforming around her just in time, before the tsunami of this glorious new feeling could wash her utterly away.

Fogarty turned off the datapad and slipped it into the pocket of his nondescript jacket. It made a plasticky clang against the military stunner he had in there.

It had been thirty minutes since the last person had passed by in the corridor; the building was as dead now as it was likely to get. When Graves had entered the building, Fogarty had followed him; he'd noted that Graves had gone into his office, not the lab.

Fogarty got up and slipped the stunner into his chubby palm. All he had to do was touch it to Graves's body and enough voltage would course through the man to stop his heart. With Graves's medical history, no one would likely suspect foul play. And even if they did, well, so what? No one could ever connect it to Fogarty (or to Cash, for that matter); a stunner discharge couldn't be traced. And of course Fogarty had plastiskin sprayed over his hands, molded with Graves's own fingerprints; not only would that let him trick Graves's lock, it would also ensure that none of Fogarty's fingerprints would be left at the scene.

Fogarty took one final look around the corridor to make sure no one was around, then headed toward Kyle's office door.

He didn't give a shit about the threat to the banking industry, of course—that wasn't his concern. Cash had mentioned that they'd already bought off an Israeli researcher, but if this Graves fellow was too stupid to take the easy way, well, Fogarty didn't mind.

He took a step, and—

—and felt woozy for a moment, slightly disoriented, dizzy.

It passed, but—

Kyle Graves, he thought. Forty-five, according to the dossier Cash had e-mailed him.

A father, a husband—Cash had said that Graves had recently reconciled with his wife.

Brian Kyle Graves—another human being.

Fogarty fingered the stunner.

You know, according to the dossier, the guy did seem a decent-enough sort, and—

And, well, certainly Fogarty wouldn't want somebody to do something like this to him.

Another step; he could hear the muffled sound of Graves dictating into his word processor.

Fogarty stopped dead in his tracks. Christ, he'd eliminated more than two dozen problems in the last year alone, but—

But—

But—

I can't do this, he thought. *I can't.*

He turned around and headed back up the curving hallway.

Kyle finished dictating his report and headed over to The Water Hole; he'd arranged to meet Stone Bentley there, with Stone coming directly from a meeting he'd had at the Royal Ontario Museum.

"You look in a good mood," said Stone as Kyle sat down opposite him.

Kyle grinned. "I feel better than I have for ages. My daughter has realized she was wrong."

Stone lifted his eyebrows. "That's wonderful!"

"Isn't it, though? It'll be my birthday in a few weeks—I couldn't ask for a better present."

A server arrived.

"A glass of red wine," said Kyle. Stone already had a mug of beer in front of him.

The server scurried away.

"I want to thank you, Stone," said Kyle. "I don't know if I could have gotten through this without you." Stone said nothing, so Kyle went on. "Sometimes it's not easy being a man—people tend to assume we're guilty, I guess. Anyway, your support meant a lot to me. Knowing that you'd gone through something a bit similar, and survived it, gave me—I don't know, I guess 'hope' is the right word."

The server reappeared, depositing Kyle's wineglass. Kyle nodded thanks at the young woman, then lifted his drink. "To us—a pair of survivors."

After a moment, Stone lifted his beer and allowed Kyle to clink his glass against the mug. But Stone did not take a sip. He lowered his mug back to the tabletop and looked off in the distance.

"I did it," he said softly.

Kyle wasn't following. "Sorry?"

Stone looked at Kyle. "I did it . . . that girl, five years ago. I did harass her." He held Kyle's gaze for a few seconds, apparently searching for a reaction, then looked back down at the tablecloth.

"But the student recanted," said Kyle.

Stone made an almost imperceptible nod. "She knew she'd lost the fight and she was getting the cold shoulder from a lot of other male faculty members. She thought it would help." He did take a gulp of his beer now. "She transferred to York." He shrugged a little. "Fresh start."

Kyle didn't know what to say. He looked around the bar for a time.

"I didn't—" said Stone. "I know this doesn't excuse it, but I was going through a bad time. Denise and I were getting a divorce. I—" He stopped. "It was a stupid thing to do."

Kyle exhaled. "You spent all this time listening to me go on about my troubles with Becky."

Stone shrugged again. "I thought you were guilty."

Kyle's voice took on a sharp edge. "I told you I wasn't."

"I know, I know. But if you *were* guilty, well, then you were a worse bastard than me, see? You're an okay guy, Kyle—I figured if a guy like you could do something that bad, well, then maybe it excused what I did a bit. Just something that sometimes happens, you know?"

"Christ, Stone."

"I know. But I won't ever do it again."

"Recidivism—"

"No. No, I'm different now. I don't know what it is, but I've changed. Something in me has changed." Stone reached into his pocket, pulled out his SmartCash card. "Look, I'm sure you don't want to see me anymore. I'm glad it worked out between you and your daughter. Really, I am." He rose to his feet.

"No," said Kyle. "Stay."

Stone hesitated for a few moments. "You sure?"

Kyle nodded. "I'm sure."

On Tuesday morning, Heather was struggling up the steps to Mullin Hall, her arms full of books she wanted to have handy at Kyle's lab for tomorrow's press conference. The humidity was mercifully low today, and the sky overhead was a pristine cerulean bowl.

Just in front of her was a familiar-looking broad back wearing a Varsity Blues jacket with the name "Kolmex" emblazoned on it—the same dumb lug who had let the door to Sid Smith slam in Heather and Paul's faces two weeks ago.

She thought about calling out to him, but to her astonishment, when he reached the door, he stopped, looked around to see if anyone was coming, caught sight of Heather, opened the door and held it for her.

"Thank you," she said as she passed the fellow.

He smiled at her. "My pleasure. Have a nice day."

The funny thing, Heather thought, was he sounded like he really meant it.

41

W E   A R E   N O T   A L O N E .
It was the title of the book that had first raised public awareness about the Search for Extraterrestrial Intelligence. The book, by Walter Sullivan, former science editor of *The New York Times*, was published in 1964.

Back then, it had been a bold assertion, based on theory and conjecture but no actual evidence—there was not a scintilla of proof that we really weren't alone in the universe.

Humanity went about its business much as it always had. The Vietnam War continued, as did apartheid. Rates of murder and other violent crimes continued to rise.

We Are Not Alone.

The slogan was revived again for the release of Steven Spielberg's film *Close Encounters of the Third Kind* in 1977. The public freely embraced the idea of life in the universe, but still there was no real evidence, and humanity continued along as it always had. The Gulf War happened, and so did the massacre in Tiananmen Square.

We Are Not Alone.

The words received new currency in 1996 when the first compelling evidence of life off Earth was unveiled: a meteorite from

Mars that had conked no one on the head in the Antarctic. Extraterrestrial life was now more than just the stuff of dreams. Nonetheless, humanity behaved as usual. Terrorists blew up buildings and airplanes; "ethnic cleansings" continued unabated.

We Are Not Alone.

The New York Times, bringing it full circle, used that headline in 144-point type on the front page of the July 25, 2007, edition—the day the first public announcement of the receipt of radio signals from Alpha Centauri was made. We knew for a fact that life—intelligent life—existed elsewhere. And yet, humanity's ways did not change. The Colombian War happened, and on July 4, 2009, the Klan massacred two thousand African Americans across four states in a single night.

But then, just over ten years after the signals were first received, a different thought echoed through the fourspace overmind and percolated down into the threespace realm of its individual extensions.

I Am Not Alone.

And things *did* change.

"Journalists are often accused of reporting only bad news," said Greg McGregor, anchoring the Newsworld telecast from Calgary on Tuesday evening.

Kyle and Heather sat on their living-room couch, his arm around her shoulders, watching.

"Well," continued McGregor, "if you saw our newscast from the top this evening, you'll have noted that today we had nothing but good news to report. Tensions have eased in the Middle East—as recently as a week ago, U.S. secretary of state Bolland was predicting another outbreak of war there, but today, for the second day in a row, the cease-fire remains unbroken.

"Here in Canada, a new Angus Reid instant opinion poll shows that eighty-seven percent of Québecois want to remain part of Canada—a twenty-four-percent increase over the response to the same question just one month ago.

"There have been no murders reported in Canada for the past twenty-four hours. No rapes, either. Statistics from the United States and the European Community seem similar.

"In eighteen years on the job, this reporter has never seen such a run of really *nice* news. It's been a pleasure being able to share it all with you." He tipped his head, as he did each night, and gave his standard sign-off: "And another day passes into history. Good night, Canada."

The ending theme music began to play. Kyle picked up the remote and clicked the TV off.

"It *is* nice, isn't it?" said Kyle, leaning back in the couch. "You know, I've noticed it myself. People giving up seats on the subway, helping others, and just being polite. It must be something in the air."

Heather shook her head. "No, it's not something in the air—it's something in *space.*"

"Pardon?" said Kyle.

"Don't you see? Something completely new has happened. The overmind knows that it's not alone. I told you: contact has been made between the human overmind and the overmind of Alpha Centauri. And the human overmind is experiencing something it's never experienced before."

"Astonishment, yes. You said that."

"No, no, no. Not astonishment; not anymore. It's experiencing something else, something entirely new to it." Heather looked at her husband. "Empathy! Until now, our overmind had been utterly incapable of empathy; there simply was no one else for it to identify with, no one else whose situation, feelings, or desires it could come to understand. Since the dawn of consciousness, it has existed in absolute isolation. But now it's touching and being touched by another overmind, and suddenly it understands something other than selfishness. And since the overmind understands that, all of us—all the extensions of that mind—suddenly understand it, too, in a deeper, more fundamental way than we've ever understood it before."

Kyle considered. "Empathy, eh?" He drew his mouth into a frown. "Cheetah kept asking about things that demonstrated man's inhumanity to man. He said it seemed to be a test—and wanted to know who was administering the test. I guess the answer was that *we* were—we, the human collective, trying to understand, trying to make sense of it all."

"But we *couldn't*," said Heather. "We were incapable of true, sustained empathy. But now that we're in contact with another overmind, we understand what it means to acknowledge and accept the other. What man could rape a woman if he really put himself in her place? The fundamental of war has always been dehumanizing the enemy, seeing him as a soulless animal. But who could go to war knowing that the other guy is a parent, a spouse, a child? Knowing that he or she is simply trying to get through life, just like you are? *Empathy!*"

"Hmm," said Kyle. "I guess Greg McGregor is going to be reporting news like that every night from now on. Oh, there'll still be hurricanes and floods—but there will also be more people pitching in to help out whenever something like that happens." He paused, considering. "Do you suppose this is first contact for the Centaurs, too? Alpha Centauri is the closest star to the sun, but the reverse is also true—there's no bright star closer to Alpha C than Sol. Surely we're their first contact, too."

"Maybe," said Heather. "Or maybe the Centaurs aren't native to Alpha Centauri. Maybe they're from somewhere else, and have made it only as far as Alpha Centauri in their expansion. Maybe there already was life on a planet of Alpha Centauri, and the two races have already made friends. There could be a galactic overmind forming, expanding outward from whatever world first acquired space flight."

Kyle thought about this. "Darn clever, these Centaurs," he said.

"How do you mean?"

"They get us to be empathetic as a race before they arrive in the flesh." He paused. "Unless, of course, they're coming to take us over and want to soften us up first."

Heather shook her head. She had been there when the contact had been made; she *knew*. "No, it can't be that. First, of course, anybody who has interstellar flight could surely wipe this planet clean of life from orbit without ever worrying about whether we'd been 'softened up' or not. And second, now that the two overminds are in contact, real communication will doubtless ensue—and we both know that there are no secrets in psychospace."

Kyle nodded.

Heather looked at him, then: "We should get to bed. Tomorrow's a big day, with the press conference and all."

"Things are going to change," said Kyle. "The world . . ."

Heather smiled as she reflected on the peace she'd made with her own past, on the peace Kyle had made with his, and on all the wonders that they'd seen. "The world," she said, "will be a better place." But then her smile grew mischievous. "Still," she said, a twinkle in her eye, "let's take full advantage of our last night of real privacy." She took Kyle's hand and led him upstairs.

Epilogue

Two Years Later: September 12, 2019

The spaceship had been detected four months ago. Until then, its fusion exhaust had been lost in the glare of Alpha Centauri, now some 4.3 light-years behind it. The exhaust was pointed directly at Earth: the ship was braking, tail-first. It had apparently accelerated away from Alpha Centauri for six years and had now been decelerating for another six.

And today, at long last, it would reach its destination.

It was sad, in a way; it was now fifty years since Neil Armstrong first set foot upon the Moon, but Earth had no crewed spaceships that could go even that far anymore—even the knowledge that there was life elsewhere hadn't revitalized the space program. Although the *Ptolemy* probe in the outer solar system had managed to send back a few grainy shots of the alien ship, humanity's first clear look at it would be when it arrived at Earth.

No one was quite sure what would happen next. Would the aliens take up orbit around the planet? Or would they land somewhere—and if so, where? Were there indeed any aliens on board, or was the ship just an automated scout?

At last the ship did enter orbit around Earth. It was a fragile-looking affair, almost a kilometer long—clearly meant only for space travel. All six of the United States's space shuttles had been launched before the arrival, one a day for the last six days. And two Japanese shuttles, plus three European ones and one from Iran had gone up as well; more human beings were now in orbit around Earth than ever before.

The alien ship was in low-Earth orbit—a good thing, too; most of the shuttles couldn't manage much more. Everyone waited for the big ship to deploy some sort of landing craft, but it never did. Radio messages were exchanged—for the very first time, human beings sent a reply to the Centaurs. The sad truth was that Earth had about twice the surface gravity of the Centaur homeworld. Although the beings aboard the starship—there were 217 individuals on it—had come forty-one trillion kilometers, the last two hundred represented a gulf they could never cross.

Earth's international space station had grown over the years, but there was no way for the starship to dock with it; the aliens were going to have to space-walk over. They moved their ship until the gap between it and the closest point on the station was about five hundred meters.

Every camera aboard the station and the flotilla of shuttles was trained on the alien ship, and every television set down on the planet was watching the drama unfold; for once, all of humanity was tuned into the same program.

The alien space suits gave no hint of what the creatures within might look like; they were perfectly spherical white bubbles, with robotic arms extending from them, and a mirrored-over viewing strip that ran horizontally just above the sphere's equator. Five of the aliens left the mothership and were propelled by jets of compressed gas across the gulf toward an open cargo bay on the space station.

There was a possibility that the aliens might not remove their suits even after they reached the station—gravity might not be the only thing that differed between the two worlds. Indeed, it was possible that the aliens had a taboo against showing their physical form to others—that had been suggested more than once when their original radio messages failed to contain any apparent representation of their appearance.

The first of the spheres came into the cargo bay. Its occupant used its jets to dampen most of its forward movement, but it still had to reach out with one multijointed mechanical hand to stop itself against the far bulkhead. Soon the other four spheres were safely motionless inside, too. They floated quietly, evidently waiting. The cargo door began to close behind them, very, very slowly—no threat, no trap; if the aliens wanted to leave, they could easily jet out of the bay before the door finished shutting.

But the spheres did not move, although one of them rotated around to watch the door coming down.

Once the bay was sealed, air was pumped in. The aliens had to have done spectroscopic studies of Earth's atmosphere as they approached it; they must know that the gases entering the chamber now were the same as those that made up the planet's air, rather than some attempt to poison them with deadly fumes.

The scientists aboard the station had reasoned that if the alien world had a lower gravity, it probably also had a lower atmospheric pressure. They stopped adding air at about seventy kilopascals.

The aliens seemed to find all this suitable. The robotic arms on one of the spheres folded back on themselves so that they could touch the sphere's surface. The sphere split in two at its equator, and the hands, which were anchored to the bottom half, lifted away the top part.

Inside was a Centaur.

The actual Centaur looked nothing like its namesake from human mythology. It was jet-black in color, insectile in construction, with giant green eyes and great iridescent wings that unfolded as soon as the being had drifted out of its space suit.

It was absolutely gorgeous.

Soon the other four egglike suits cracked open, disgorging their occupants. Exoskeleton color ranged from solid black through silver, and eye color varied from green through purple through cyan. The unfolding of the wings was apparently the Centaur equivalent of a stretch—no sooner had they been deployed than the beings folded them up again.

A door opened in the cargo bay, and the designated choice for first contact drifted into the room. And who better for that than the person who had first figured out what the Centauri radio signals were meant to convey? Who better than the person who had first detected the presence not just of humanity's overmind, but of the Centaur overmind as well? Who better than the individual who had mediated the first contact between the overminds, preventing the human one from panicking?

All five aliens turned to look at Heather Davis. She held out her hands, palms up, and smiled at the extraterrestrials. The Centaur who had first opened its suit unfolded its wings again, and with a couple of gentle beats, set itself moving toward her. A backward movement of the wings brought it to a stop about a meter from Heather. She reached out an arm toward the alien, and the alien unfurled a long, thin limb toward her. The limb looked fragile; Heather did nothing more than let it tap against the palm of her hand.

A dozen years ago, the Centaurs had reached out with their radio messages.

Two years ago, their overmind had made contact with the human overmind. Perhaps that had been the more important event, but still, there was something wonderful and poignant and real about the actual touching of hands.

"Welcome to Earth," said Heather. "I think you're going to find it a *very* nice place."

The alien, who couldn't yet understand English, nonetheless tipped its angular head, as if in acknowledgment.

There were uncountable other humans plugged into Heather's mind, enjoying it all from her perspective. And, no doubt, all that the aliens were seeing was propagating back through their overmind, across the light-years to Alpha Centauri, where it would be experienced by everyone there.

Doubtless humans would soon be trying to do the Necker transformation into a Centaur's mind—indeed, some of those riding within Heather might be trying it right now.

She wondered if it would work.

But then again, it didn't really matter.

Even without that capability, Heather was sure that her species, which at last now deserved its name of humanity, was going to have no trouble seeing the other person's point of view.

About the Author

Robert J. Sawyer is Canada's only native-born full-time science-fiction writer. He is the author of nine previous novels, including *The Terminal Experiment,* which won the Science Fiction and Fantasy Writers of America's Nebula Award for Best Novel of the Year, and *Starplex,* which was a Nebula and Hugo Award finalist.

Rob's books are published in the United States, the United Kingdom, France, Germany, Holland, Italy, Japan, Poland, Russia, and Spain. He has won an Arthur Ellis Award from the Crime Writers of Canada, five Aurora Awards (Canada's top honor in SF), five Best Novel HOMer Awards voted on by the 30,000 members of the SF&F Literature Forums on CompuServe, the Seiun Award (Japan's principal SF award), *Le Grand Prix de l'Imaginaire* (France's top honor in SF), and the *Premio UPC de Ciencia Ficción,* Spain's top SF award, and the world's largest cash prize for SF writing (which was awarded to Rob for a portion of this novel, *Factoring Humanity*).

Rob's other novels include the popular Quintaglio Ascension trilogy *(Far-Seer, Fossil Hunter,* and *Foreigner),* plus *Golden Fleece, End of an Era, Frameshift,* and *Illegal Alien.*

Rob lives in Thornhill, Ontario (just north of Toronto), with

Carolyn Clink, his wife of fourteen years. Together, they edited the acclaimed Canadian SF anthology *Tesseracts 6.*

To find out more about Rob and his fiction, visit his extensive World Wide Web site at **www.sfwriter.com**.